The Sacred Skulls Series

BOOK 3

Kito

Destiny Calling

Gregory JL Thomas

A catalogue record for this book is available from the National Library of Australia

AMT Publishing
gjlthomas@outlook.com

Contents

Character List

The Palace

Emperor Hannu Koe
Desora, son of Hannu Koe
Asset Chun
Captain Chenghou
Grand Master, Daiwa

Tarim Caves

Wa Maki, raised Yaan
Sen Ya San, raised Yaan
Tammirie, Maki's daughter
Jeng, daughter of Tammirie
Prince Yaan, Hasuca's son
Hao, former Emperor's Guard

Kadra Village

Sankun, sage
Kale, village elder
Luhou, Kale's daughter
Manchu, elder
Kai, Manchu's son
Ringcha, Kale's sister
Janing, Kale's daughter

City of Samos

Princess Tanica, Hasuca's daughter
Mercanti, Tanica's protector

Devil's Pass

Balzac, owner
Sharia, Balzac's wife
Lucia/Alexa, Balzac's daughter
Jabali/Patch, former vessel owner
Admasin, former Manager to Patch
Yuna, wife of Admasin

ZIMBALI

King Mabutu, Queen Trina
Mensa, Mabutu & Trina's son
Chizoba/Kito, Mabutu & Rani's son
Baako, Mabutu & Trina's son
Chief Kobus, Village of the Keepers
Shay, Chizoba's friend
Princess Rani, Ezra's deceased daughter,
former Queen to Mabutu

ORION

Pharoah Ezra
Queen Sofira
Prince Aitan

MAGNAR

Tzu Hsi, Barbarian King
Porteous, barbarian warrior
Nose-Ring, barbarian warrior

AUDUN

Sheik Kohji

Additional

Norinko, former Asset
Sezou, Norinko's son
Hois, (deceased) Norinko's father
Bandji, witch

Ikua, Bandji's assistant
Mischa, (deceased) Norinko's sister, mother of Tzu Hsi
Hao, former Emperor's guard
Tanica, Hasuca's daughter
Yaan, Hasuca's son
Mercanti, Tanica's friend
Majito, woman with red scarf
Kalgan, Admasin's son
Katanning, Kalgan's mate
Grand Master Xiang, deceased

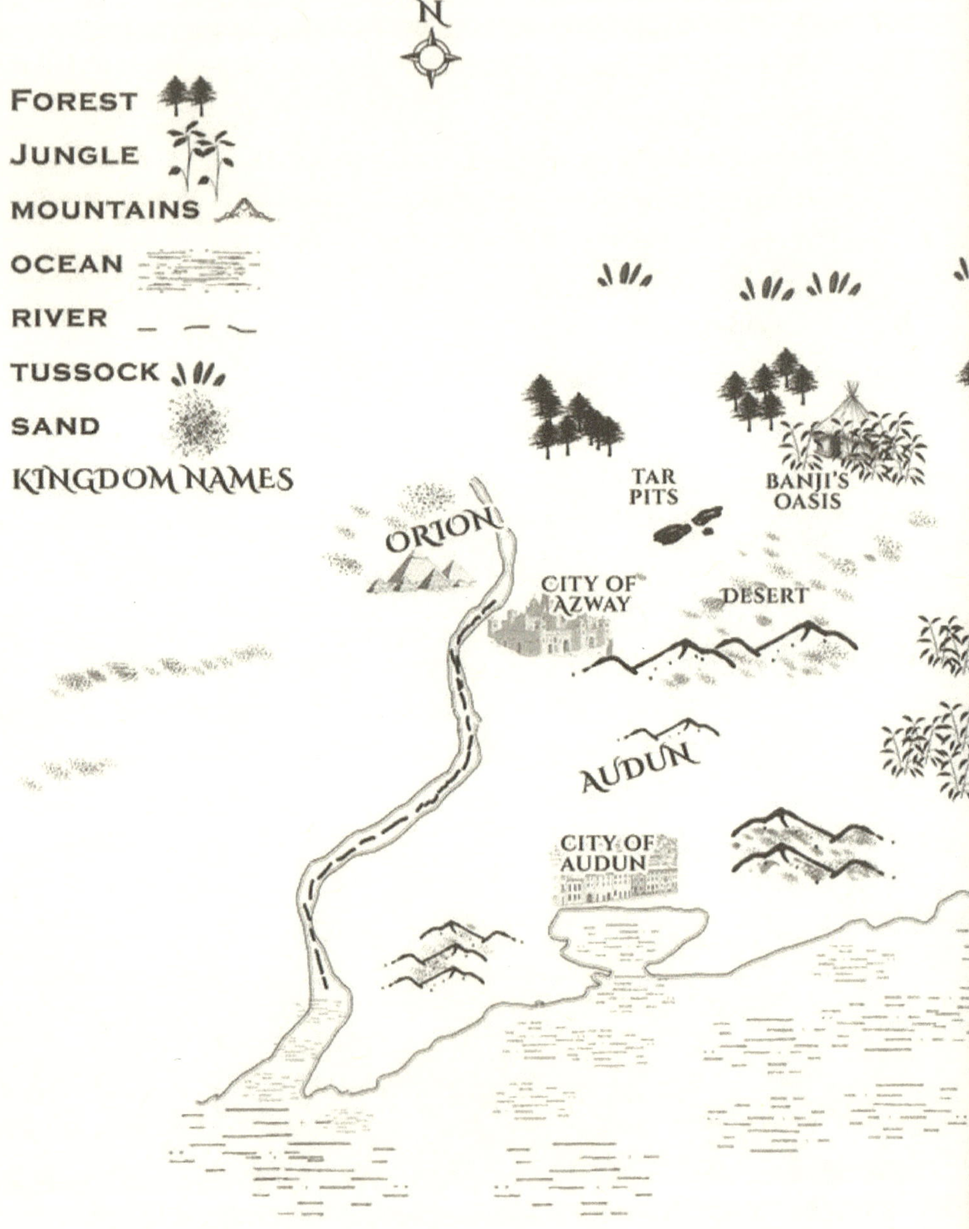

N
FOREST
JUNGLE
MOUNTAINS
OCEAN
RIVER
TUSSOCK
SAND
KINGDOM NAMES
ORION
TAR PITS
BANJI'S OASIS
CITY OF AZWAY
DESERT
AUDUN
CITY OF AUDUN

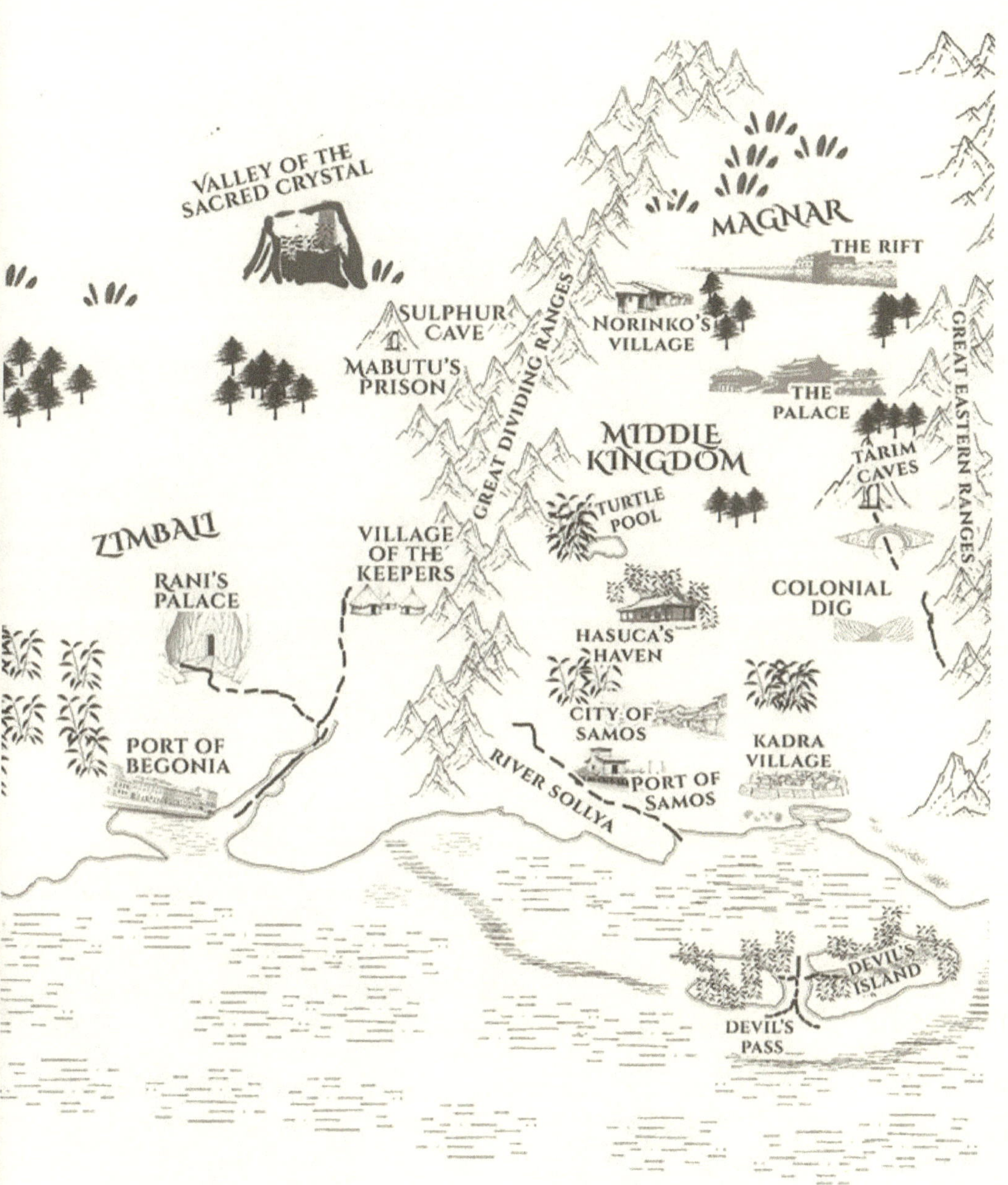

VALLEY OF THE SACRED CRYSTAL
MAGNAR
THE RIFT
SULPHUR CAVE
NORINKO'S VILLAGE
MABUTU'S PRISON
GREAT DIVIDING RANGES
THE PALACE
GREAT EASTERN RANGES
MIDDLE KINGDOM
TARIM CAVES
ZIMBALI
TURTLE POOL
COLONIAL DIG
VILLAGE OF THE KEEPERS
RANI'S PALACE
HASUCA'S HAVEN
CITY OF SAMOS
KADRA VILLAGE
PORT OF BEGONIA
RIVER SOLLYA
PORT OF SAMOS
DEVIL'S ISLAND
DEVIL'S PASS

Prelude

At the Port of Begonia in Zimbali, Emperor Hannu Koe smoothed down his exquisite attire as if he had slain King Mensa's men himself. His goal of achieving control over all the lands was so close he could almost taste it on the warm air. He had rid himself of his Brother, Hasuca. Half a legion had been sent on horseback after the cave-dwelling Yaan, who would now be strung up and slaughtered like his deceitful father. Then, in a turn of events that even he hadn't foreseen, Kito had sworn his allegiance to him and the throne. Even Koe had been impressed as Kito had forsaken his own people who hung mercilessly from the burning ropes. Soon, he would take over Zimbali, but Mensa's ties to Orion and Pharoah Ezra were invaluable to see his plans come to fruition.

Mensa's men lay strewn about at the bottom of the stairs, motionless. Kito stood with his hands up his opposing sleeves, his face unseen in the shadow of his hood.

Mensa scrutinised the strange-looking man cloaked in grey. The steps creaked as they bore the weight of him descending them. "Who did this, and how many must I kill for it?" Mensa demanded.

Kito raised his head ever so slightly but kept his eyes shaded. "The answer to your question is me and only me. However, you are not capable of killing me. My name is Kito, and I work for the Emperor. So, Mensa, we'll be travelling together to the land of Orion to meet with Pharaoh Ezra." He motioned down to the wharf. "Shall we?"

1 The Keystone

Silence hung heavy over the entire wharf. No one would dare instruct Mensa if they wanted to see another dawn. His black face darkened further as he questioned Emperor Koe, who stood, smirking slightly, at the top of the stairs. "He can't be serious?"

"Actually, Mensa, he is. Look at him, he breathes easily and shows no sign of effort, yet all your *best* men lie, well, shall we say, incapacitated." With a casual air, he descended the stairs as he spoke. "Don't feel bad, my friend. I have tried to kill him on at least three occasions. He's quite right when he says you can't kill him. He's a bit of an enigma, really."

Muttering disturbed the quiet of the gathering crowd, but Mensa saw neither a lending hand nor a friend to support him.

The Emperor urged him on. "Shall we then? Time is wasting, and we have far to go and much to discuss, King Mensa."

The Emperor's newly commissioned vessel, *Ocean Conqueror*, towered over them as they approached. Mensa refrained from showing his amazement at its size as he looked it over. If he wasn't looking at it with his own eyes, he wouldn't believe any vessel could be built bigger than old man Tarrant's *Shiraz*. A large pole loomed from the centre with multitudes of ropes running down. *This makes no sense at all. It looks so messy.* Two cabins were set apart to the rear of the vessel, and in the large gap between them was a table comfortably shaded by the cloth overhead. Beyond that was the biggest rudder platform he'd ever seen. He pursed his lips. The platform supported the most ludicrous rudder's pole imaginable, with no less than six men standing there to steer it.

Mensa couldn't contain himself any further. "I can't be seen on this, this ... Just what is *this*?"

The Emperor crossed the plank to board and turned back, looking expectant. "Time is passing. Mensa, if you will."

Mensa glanced over his shoulder.

Kito stood expressionless behind him. He motioned him on. "You're his guest, Mensa, after you please."

Once on board, the crewmen cast off the ropes to depart the wharf. Emperor Koe sat comfortably at his fruit-laden table. He offered Mensa the seat opposite before instructing for wine with meat, cheese and bread to be brought. It was a fine serving by anyone's standard. Head down and cloaked in grey, Kito silently positioned himself behind Mensa's chair.

Mensa flicked a hand towards the oarsmen on the top deck, forward of the cabins. "They won't last long up here in the sun, not once we're out on the ocean."

The Emperor ignored the comment, though his tone was less ambiguous. "Mensa, I have my doubts about your loyalty to my throne. How do you think we can overcome my concerns?"

Mensa's normally confident manner scattered like his slain men. Unsettled by the morning's events, he carefully gathered his thoughts. *Maybe it had been a larger group that had bettered my men and this strange Kito is a ploy?* He narrowed his eyes and glared at the Emperor coldly.

The smirk washed from the Emperor's face. "Kito, I do believe our vessel guest hasn't been quite won over just yet." He leaned forward. "Mensa, I wish to make an ally of you, but make no mistake, I *will* rule Zimbali, with or without you." He hid his disdain at the big white teeth shining from his dark face as Mensa smiled confidently.

Arrogant fool, mused Koe.

"Emperor," Mensa spoke with calm control, "I do think we could make a force to be reckoned with. It is true that I have excellent ties with the Pharaoh, and this would make the two of us a bigger force than the Middle Kingdom alone. Though I realise you can see this already."

"This is true, Mensa, so I must ask once more, what can you offer me to settle my underlying feeling that at any time you could turn the table on me?"

"You ask me to be an ally, Koe, and I am." Mensa relaxed back in his chair.

"Emperor."

Mensa was perplexed. "What?"

"When in your office, I told you to call me *Emperor* and nothing else. Also, you said that you would see me dead for that threat. To be honest, Mensa, I think had it not been for Kito, you would have."

The white teeth disappeared behind Mensa's tightly closed lips, then he forced a smile. "Now, now, Emperor, I do make rash comments from time to time, but really, you couldn't truly think I'd do such a thing. After all, it has taken many years of planning to be in the position we are today. I have no intention of throwing it all away now. It would be incomprehensible."

The Emperor had Mensa just where he wanted him. His words cast off his tongue as he reeled Mensa in. "Yes, I can see how ruining our plan would be for you, Mensa. After all the family blood you have on your hands, it would be a great shame to see someone like Queen Trina suddenly return." His voice trailed off to almost a whisper. "What did you do with your father, Mensa?"

"My father?"

"Yes, your father Mabutu."

Mensa waved his big hand about, trying to look in control once more. "Yes, I do know my own father's name, thank you."

"And he is where?"

"Buried. High up in the mountains." He grinned at the memory of it, his teeth now seeming to have a smile of their own. "We collapsed a cave on the old boy."

"Really?"

"Yes ..." Mensa shrugged. "... though I do suppose I could've just poisoned him in his own palace while dining with his family,

Emperor.”

The Emperor burst out laughing. “Well done, Mensa. Well done.” He clapped his hands several times, then leaned forward, letting his merriment fade. “And what of your brother Baako?”

“Baako, Emperor?” Mensa gulped his wine. The Emperor tried not to let the disappointment of the wasted wine show on his face as he waited. Mensa put down his empty goblet. “He is earning his right to live, as he should, Emperor.”

“As I remember, he was bigger than you, Mensa, so I do hope you have him on a short, strong leash. I don’t like surprises. I prefer strong planning and stronger execution of that planning. We are clear, aren’t we?”

Mensa’s mind worked overtime, and he found himself wishing he had actually *seen* more of his family’s blood spilled. Tarrant had better have Baako on a very strong leash, especially if the Emperor did have his mother. But he had faith – old man Tarrant was no fool, and he was ruthless. No, he’d made the right decision. Tarrant was the best option for keeping Baako out of the picture.

“The leash is unbreakable, Emperor. It’s an invisible leash that binds a son to his mother.” He shrugged again. “Well, some sons. Baako would never threaten his mother’s safety.” He met the Emperor’s eyes once more. “Well, Emperor, if you do have our mother, what more of a guarantee could you wish for?”

The first of the sails was hoisted up. It flapped gently before snapping tightly into full flight. Mensa jumped from his seat. “What in the blazing heavens is that?”

The Emperor was not about to let on that he’d not yet seen the vessel in sail either. It had returned from delivering a vast fleet of Imperial Guard to Zimbali whilst he was still upriver, and since boarding, they had rowed thus far.

Captivated, Mensa watched as the men put away their oars and gathered and tethered the ropes to deploy the sails. The vessel surged through the water. *First he overruns my men, and now this! What else is Koe keeping to himself?’*

The Emperor remained calm and collected, though inside his excitement was palpable. The silk strained under the pressure. *This new vessel is going to go even better than I realised.* His men worked away, seemingly happy with the way it was going. They had sailed the vessel from Middle Kingdom to Zimbali with its load of armed Imperial Guard after all.

Mensa noticed Koe was preoccupied, seeming more inclined to watch the silk overhead than oversee his men. *Ha! The Emperor has not watched this before himself or at least, not much.* He glanced around. At some point, Kito had moved away somewhere. He eased slowly towards the table. Still looking upwards at the silk, he put his hand on the table as if to stabilise himself. He flicked a look at the Emperor for just a split second. On the table, just inches from his hand, lay the meat knife. In less than a heartbeat, the knife was gone. Mensa eased back just as the Emperor turned to him.

"Have you ever seen such a thing, Mensa? I know you haven't."

Mensa barely managed to feign a smile as the Emperor chuckled at his expense. The urge to use the knife burned within him, but Koe was not leading a large, powerful nation by chance. He decided he could wait. At that moment, Kito appeared from around the corner and stopped beside the Emperor. He stood square to Mensa with such intensity that Mensa drew back. He didn't know why this strange man unsettled him, but it gave Kito more power over him for it. And they both knew it.

The Emperor sat once more. "Kito, I see you have also come to speak on this new vessel of ours. Quite something, isn't it?"

"I must congratulate you, sire, on a most remarkable achievement by Middle Kingdom. I imagine it won't be long now before we won't need oarsmen at all."

Kito still faced Mensa as he spoke. "I see they have overseen your need for a meat knife. I shall fetch you one immediately."

The Emperor looked over the table briefly, then waved a dismissive hand. "Quite so, Kito."

Mensa's eyes followed the strange one as he turned and descended the stairs. *It's like the man floats.* He shuddered a little. Was he beginning to know what it was like to feel unnerved?

The Emperor moved on without notice. "I do believe that boy is the most observant I have ever met. Now, where were we? Oh yes …" He lifted his silver goblet of wine. "… you think me having your mother is enough security for me? I think not, Mensa."

Mensa lifted his refilled goblet. "Why ever not, Emperor?"

"Because, my dear man, you wanted her dead anyway."

"Emperor, if I had wanted her dead, I would have gutted her myself, minding not to let her entrails spill over my own two feet."

The Emperor frowned, faking disgust. "Must you be so graphic, Mensa?" He sipped a little more wine. "So why did you keep her alive then? I don't think it was because you were worried about your good footwear."

In an involuntary move, Mensa shuffled his bare feet on the polished decking. "I felt it wise not to burn all my bridges at once. The death of Mabutu was necessary, as was the death of his youngest son, who was just a plain waste of space. But Trina and Baako may still have their use yet."

"Except now I have Trina in my possession."

His overconfident face was almost enough to raise Mensa from his seat. He adjusted his feet for balance. The meat knife would blaze a cold trail of death through his throat in an instant.

"Your meat knife, sire."

Mensa physically flinched at Kito's smooth words. He'd been so lost in his own thoughts that he'd not even noticed his return. He could only hope the Emperor hadn't noticed his reaction, but he was too preoccupied with his goblet to even look up.

"And about time too, young man. I hope you spoke firmly to the staff." Just then a woman arrived with a new decanter of wine. She was quick to fill the Emperor's goblet first. He reached out and grabbed the woman by the inside of her upper thigh, pulling her over to him. A nervous squeal broke her trembling lips, but she didn't dare spill a drop. "My cabin is on the right, and you will be in there waiting for me tonight. So, aren't you the lucky one then?"

Fearfully, the woman placed the decanter and gave a deep bow and a forced smile, before departing in haste. The Emperor swiped up his refilled goblet. "So really, Mensa, why *did* you keep poor old Trina alive?"

Mensa was hoping for a woman to be offered to him, too. Clearly, that wasn't to happen tonight. "Because she was the most popular queen of all time, a 'People's Queen' if you like."

"I thought that was the next in line, Queen Rani?"

Kito's skin prickled.

"Maybe. But I had Baako where I wanted him and Trina also locked in place," he scoffed. "So why spoil a good setup?" He shrugged as he waved his hand. "Only now you have Trina, so you see, Emperor, like I said, you don't need anything else from me. You have my loyalty."

The Emperor lifted his goblet as if to toast Mensa. "No, my *ally*, I have your mother, and I will crumble your world with her safe return into your own lands. As you said, she was the most popular queen of all time, and she knows the truth of your rise to power, and I dare say, she would love to tell her story." He watched Mensa squirm uncomfortably. He couldn't resist just one more jab. "Tell me, Mensa … what did you do with Queen Rani?"

Kito clenched his forearms tightly as he placed his hands up opposing sleeves. He tucked his chin to his chest, bracing so not to move.

"She, too, was quite popular," Mensa said with a slither of a smile. "A friend of mine disposed of her."

"Really, are you sure she's dead, though?"

Self-assured, Mensa scoffed. "She was stabbed with her own knife and thrown into the river. She washed into the Mother Mountain. There's no return from that."

The Emperor raised his eyebrows. "I see. And what did this friend of yours get in return?"

"I gave him a small vessel. He's doing well for himself and still serves me. Assets on the water are valuable in this changing world, Emperor."

The Emperor's smile as he sat under his new sails was so sly, it made Mensa recoil.

***

That night, after the woman in the Emperor's cabin was done with and had departed in tears, Mensa slowly slid out of bed. The knife had explicitly been placed – stuck behind a timber in the door frame, so in easy reach from inside or out. He ran his finger along the blade in the flickering candlelight and slipped it up his sleeve out of sight.

Quietly, he eased the door open. The shade-cloth was low enough to obscure him from the men at the rear steering the vessel.

As happy for the woman as he was for the wine, the Emperor snored loudly. Mensa moved carefully from his door, keeping his back close to his cabin. He took a single step towards the Emperor's cabin, then froze. Slowly, he craned his head left, straining his eyes to look through the dark at the form directly behind the galley. His skin turned cold and clammy. He couldn't see any movement, yet the feeling of being watched overwhelmed him. His instinct told him to return to his room, but he'd never known how to retreat. His shoulders knotted as he urged himself to move.

Against his better judgment, he turned towards the shadows. Still nothing moved. Despite his bulk, his footsteps were easily taken without sound on the solid deck designed to take cargo. Footstep by painful footstep, he eased towards the rear of the galley, then stopped abruptly as the sail gently flapped overhead. With just the lightest glimmer from the new moon cast back from the galley, he blinked to try and clear his eyes as they strained at the shadow inside the shadows. He wiped the cold sweat from his brow as his skin crawled. Suddenly, his heart surged as the grey form of Kito rose up and stepped into the moonlight.

"Out to stretch your legs, Mensa?"

Mensa, his heart racing and full of fear he had never known, lunged forward, the glint of his blade barely seen in the moonlight. Kito took his weight as they crashed down onto the deck. The two tumbled back and forth, rolling into the galley then back around to the side, knocking into oars and sending them scuttling across the deck. Mensa flipped Kito onto his back and straddled him, raining punches into him. His left hand searched feverishly for the blade.

"WHAT IN THE HEAVENS IS THIS?" It was the Emperor.

Mensa leapt back, and Kito rolled smoothly to his feet.

The Emperor stood in just his long pants, holding his black, slightly curved sword. Gold arm bracelets glistened in the poor light.

Kito quickly bowed. "I do beg your pardon, Emperor. I do believe your guest, King Mensa, was just out to relieve himself when I incorrectly mistook him for a guard up to no good. I ask your forgiveness in the matter." He remained with his head dipped.

Why did he just lie to Koe? Mensa frowned.

Furious, the Emperor marched forward, wielding his black blade so it whistled in the night air. Mensa stepped back as the Emperor moved to Kito's side, his neck for the taking. Kito remained motionless. The Emperor breathed hard through gritted teeth, his entire night crew now looking on. He turned to one of the men. "Is this so, man?" he hissed.

The shocked man shook his head, not wishing to swap places with the grey man. "I couldn't see from my post, Emperor. It could well be just as Kito says."

For the longest time, no one moved then, with a small whipping sound, the blade was gone and shortly after, so was the Emperor.

His door slammed.

Kito rose smoothly and faced the man the Emperor had spoken to. "I believe I am in your debt." He put his left fist into his right palm and touched his head, then looked to them all. "And if you want us to be on course in the morning, I suggest you return to your posts." The men disappeared in a flurry. Mensa watched the faceless hood as it turned to him. "Mensa, I assume I will never see you near the starboard cabin in the future."

Mensa scowled. "I had you this time, and I will get you another, grey man. I will watch your blood go back to the soil like the desert drinks the summer rain. This is my oath to you."

The one in grey stopped but didn't turn. Mensa saw the hood nod, then a cool voice came back. "Be careful what you promise, Mensa. Nothing in the eyes of the Gods is missed."

2 Impossible Deal

For many days the *Ocean Conqueror* and its esteemed passengers travelled north up the coast.

As they passed the entrance of the Cove of Audun, Mensa enquired, "We aren't making the stop?"

Koe barely raised his head. "I will inform Kohji of his duties to Middle Kingdom when I feel it's appropriate."

They sailed on for another day before turning into the Mother River. Finally, the three points of the Pyramids of Orion came into view.

The Emperor tapped his hands on the table. "I know you will support me here. You would not wish for me to talk about how their precious Rani died, would you, Mensa?" He laughed sarcastically, looking ahead as the pyramids loomed up large as life. Sounds of song drifted on the air as they eased up to the wharf. He stood and moved to the side of his vessel. "Well, this is more like it."

Lined along the wharf, dancers performed for their arrival, decoratively dressed in their traditional light cotton drapes, coming from behind the neck with a half twist under the breast and tied off behind the back. A tasteful waist wrap tied off on the right hip highlighted their shapely, toned bellies with naval piercings glittering in the sun. Long drapes of material ran out from their clothes and attached to long wooden battens held in their hands as they swept them about to the music. They swayed back and forth in rhythmic movements. The guests watched, spellbound by their graceful moves. The dance went on for some time, increasing in speed, their movements more erotic as it progressed through to the grand finale.

Applause broke out as dancers parted and the Pharaoh Ezra and his wife Sofira stepped through. Ezra swept his arm to acknowledge his dancers, looking as proud as if he'd danced himself.

"Welcome, all. Welcome to Orion."

Disgruntled that his vessel of wings had gone seemingly unnoticed, the Emperor stepped off looking a little outdone. He dipped his head only slightly. "Pharaoh and ally, it is very kind to be made so welcome."

Ezra dipped his head and offered out a hand, but Emperor Koe didn't reciprocate. His smile faltered only a little as he turned to Mensa. "Welcome, King Mensa." They shook hands, wrist to wrist.

"The dancers were most entertaining, Ezra. I thank you for your effort."

Ezra glanced at the Emperor. "Yes, quite so, thank you, Mensa. As always, your manners are respectful."

Oblivious to the comments, the Emperor stood proudly admiring his vessel.

Mensa saw the Sheik of Audun. He'd come forward only after Ezra and his wife had been thanked for the dancers. "Sheik Kohji, this is an unexpected surprise."

Kohji was as black as a man could be, though his smile could warm the coldest climate. He wore, as always, the traditional white, one-piece garment. His head attire seemed to be an endless run of white cloth wrapped around his head culminating in a flat top. Being the tallest there, Mensa had no trouble seeing this.

The Emperor dragged his gaze away from his beloved vessel. "We stopped at the Cove of Audun seeking your company on this trip, but were informed of your absence, Kohji. It is nice to have you here for this important gathering."

Mensa eyed Koe coldly for the blatant lie.

The Emperor returned his exaggerated attention back to his vessel. Noting this, the Pharaoh moved forward to pay the seemingly obligatory homage. "A most unusual-looking vessel, isn't it?"

Just as he spoke, the smooth form of a man dressed in grey alighted. He greeted no one and walked around to stand behind the Emperor. Ezra tried to get a visual on him, but his eyes were obscured beneath his mysterious hood. The man was huge and from what Ezra could tell, young. "And just who might that be, Emperor?"

"*That*, Ezra, is my personal assistant. He goes where I go." The Emperor's face beamed as he pointed to his vessel. "Note the hatches. The cargo can go into the lower hold, keeping the centre of gravity well down when at sea. And there is still room for more cargo top deck if you wish, though there does need to be some room up there for the oarsmen when docking."

Still more interested in the grey form behind the Emperor, Ezra gave little acknowledgement. "You are a guest in my lands, Emperor. You have no need for this assistant to follow you about."

The Emperor slowly turned to face Ezra. "As I said, he is my assistant. He will go where I go or where I tell him to go. Period."

Ezra stiffened at the tone. He moved his thoughts to the vessel once more. "I can see your logic, Emperor Koe, but you must also realise it is a little strange on the eye."

"Yes, but my people say the same about your people, yet you don't see me holding this against you now, do you, Ezra?"

Ezra held his tongue.

Kohji placed an arm on Ezra's shoulder. "What the Emperor is trying to say, my friend, is something so bold that it only looks strange until you get used to it." He turned to the Emperor. "Then we can all see it for what it is."

"Quite so, Kohji.' Ezra smiled. "I see you have your father's flair for pacifying any misinterpretations." He motioned towards the stairs up to the shaded outdoor dining area.

Emperor Koe took the lead almost ahead of Pharaoh Ezra. Mensa followed with the Sheik and the grey man close behind. He flirted openly with some of the dancers and could only wonder what was worn under those garments, if anything at all.

At the large table, Ezra's wife Sofira and their son Aitan were there to greet them. They worked on each side of the table, showing the guests their seats in order. Servants pushed in their chairs as they were seated. The grey man attended to Koe. Once at the end of the table, Sofira cast concern at Aitan's demeanour. Her proud demeanour ran away as she reached out for his arm and whispered to him. "My dear Aitan, you look as if you've seen a ghost, no less." He didn't take his eyes off the grey man. "I believe I have," he whispered back.

Sofira followed his stare. "Yes, I did see him, son. He is particularly large, even for his kind, but you will …"

"No, Mother. It is the grey one I spoke of from the basement. The man who was said to have taken on another's body. The one who dived into the river where the crocodiles were feeding on our guards, and he never resurfaced."

Sofira caught her breath, her hand up to her chest. "Aitan, how sure can you be?" she whispered.

He shook his head. "He has come to me in my *dreams*, Mother."

Sofira moved between him and the grey one, grabbing Aitan by the chin to pull his attention. "You will remove yourself from the table. As soon as it is appropriate, I will excuse myself and find you in the upper room. Go now, please."

She watched as he made his way back to the temple. Her skin began to crawl. She caught her breath as she spun to the source of her unwanted feeling. The grey one was just lowering his head again. Sofira stared at him, willing him to lift his head as she walked around to stand opposite him across the table. He didn't.

The men of nations spoke their politics. Sofira would normally watch closely and pay attention to the body language, seeing who had the hidden agenda, who was playing the conversation and who was genuine. Today, she heard and saw none of it. The grey man consumed all her attention.

When the Emperor was preoccupied talking with Kohji, she bent and whispered into her husband's ear. He nodded. She stood back, checking all their guests were catered for properly as they lounged back under the cotton shades, wafting on the river breeze. Her eyes darted back to the grey man and she shuddered as he lowered his head once more.

Ezra was in conversation with Mensa when the Emperor interrupted.

"Yes, but we have to have a reason behind what we choose to do, otherwise it's just doing something for the sake of it."

Ezra clasped his hands together and placed them firmly on the table. "So, you are in our care right now, yet you tell us you do not trust us, Emperor."

The Emperor adjusted his seat. It was the first time Ezra had seen any emotion in the man since he'd arrived. "I have never said such a thing, Ezra. What's more, I would say it's almost insulting of you to suggest it. Take it back this instant."

"No, I will not. You will, by contrast, explain to us all why you feel you need this man dressed in grey at your beck and call when in our care, as our guest. Do you trust us or not, Emperor Koe?"

The Emperor began to laugh. "Very well, Ezra, but I'm warning you before the fact, so please don't come to me with regret later." He turned his head to the side, and the grey man was there in an instant. "Kito, there is a lower lawn down by the river. It would seem you leave these people feeling a little unsettled, so could you go down there. I will send for you if I require you." He flicked his hand and looked at Ezra. "I don't know where you got this grey man stuff from, his name is Kito and he has now excused himself from our company." Kito had indeed bowed to the Emperor's back and silently moved away.

The men talked on for some time about how they could trade between their relevant countries, extolling the best they had to offer for trade to one another. Mensa had for the most part kept quiet, and it hadn't gone unnoticed by Ezra how the normally bolshy man was now silent.

Ezra turned to the Sheik. "Kohji, could you tell us please, how you see this larger trading going?"

"I feel we've always been able to speak with whom we wished and took only what we needed at the time. Never yet has one nation let down another. I see no reason to change such a balanced, successful operation."

The Emperor rolled his eyes. Ezra wasted no time in encouraging the silent Mensa to speak. "And what of your opinion, Mensa? Where do you stand with this keeping tallies and pre-ordering goods, business?"

Mensa cast a furtive glance at the Emperor's ice-cold expression. Just a hint of a smirk upturned his lips. Staring down at the table rather than maintaining eye contact with Ezra, Mensa coughed, trying to clear the growing lump in his throat. "Well, I think the Emperor has some fine ideas for the growth of our nations."

Ezra's brow crumpled as his mind tried to decipher what games were at play here.

"Ezra, bring down five of your best fighters with their best equipment of choice."

Ezra looked perplexed. "For what purpose, Emperor?"

The Emperor's smug confidence was evident. "Well, clearly you have not been convinced of the power of my nation, so I will show you what we've achieved in the time of my leadership."

"We've already seen your new vessel, Emperor. Admittedly, it's strange but quite impressive."

"Ha. Middle Kingdom has achieved far more than this! The five of your very best men, Ezra."

"As you wish, Emperor." He gave his servant the order.

The leaders sat around the table with minimal talk for some time. They were all struggling with the Emperor's plans. Only he seemed to think he had the best to offer and wanted for nothing.

"One-way trading is not good for your neighbours," explained Kohji.

The Emperor was not to be swayed. He tilted his head sarcastically at Ezra. "How are those men coming along? Time is valuable to me. I hope you would be in more of a hurry to protect your borders, Ezra."

Ezra sighed, struggling to contain his frustrations. "I love and trust my neighbours, though sadly I am discovering the arrogance of some further away. I'm beginning to think we don't have as much in common as I once thought we did, Emperor."

The Emperor's expression dropped dramatically. Menacingly, he leaned forward, just as the clattering of five armoured men came into view. He leaned back in his chair.

"Ah, it's about time too. Ezra, Kito will be sat in the lower garden with his head down. I have no idea where that boy came from or how he does what he does, but do me a favour, have your men surround and kill him for me. If you succeed, then I will be forced to buy everything you have to offer."

Ezra, by far the eldest at the table, was not to be drawn in easily. "And should they fail, Emperor?"

The Emperor scoffed. "Look at your men with their bulging muscles. They have more fighting tools than half my lands. Kito carries nothing more than a hunting knife."

Mensa's face dropped in alarm. "Does he always carry the knife, Emperor?"

The Emperor waved a dismissive hand. "Somewhere under those clothes, yes, always. Well, come on then, Ezra, the day is shortening."

Ezra sighed, shaking a troubled head. "Very well then, but I don't understand why you brought him here for this. What's more, and just for the record, Emperor, I don't like this violence and murder on my lawn. This will not happen again."

Like an excited boy, the Emperor rubbed his hands together. "Yes, yes, very well. Oh, I do like a good show. Shall we?" Kohji's chair rattled on the cobbles as he stood, and the Emperor briskly put a finger up to his lips. "Ssh, half a battle can be won with surprise alone."

The pit of Ezra's stomach churned. Reluctantly, he waved his men forward. Without speaking, the guards separated and spread out to the top of the banks looking down over the lower garden.

Sure enough, Kito was seated with his head down and his back turned. It was poor battle form, but the Emperor was quite specific. *'Attack with surprise.'* Sofira, having said nothing the entire time, now held a shaking hand over her mouth. She hated this violence the Emperor seemed to be feeding on. The Pharaoh nodded, and the first crossbow bolt was released along with several spears, thrown in the same instant.

As the first shot was fired, inexplicably Kito rose and spun around, catching the bolt. Still spinning, he released it back to the bowman. Kito dodged each spear with ease and extraordinary speed. He caught the last spear and broke it over his knee as the four men charged with swords raised. Sofira covered her face on Ezra's shoulder.

The silent audience, bar the smug Emperor, looked on in disbelief.

"Can someone explain to me what is going on!"

Upon hearing all the commotion, Aitan had come running. As he approached, he saw one man well known to him, lying on his back. A single crossbow bolt protruded from his helmet. From the top of the bank, he looked down over the river garden to where two men lay lifeless. Crocodiles fought over the other two. Amid this, with his hood still up, Kito stood motionless in his blood-stained clothes.

The Emperor clapped. "Excellent! Just excellent! Damn that boy never ceases to surprise me. I thought this may have been his limit, but no! Not our Kito! Splendid indeed!"

Aitan glared at the Emperor. "I don't know where you're leading your people, Emperor, but here we believe the Gods …"

The Emperor lunged forward with such vigour, everyone flinched. "I AM THE ONLY GOD YOU NEED CONCERN YOURSELF WITH!" Spit broke through his shaking jowls as he screamed, his angry, shaking finger pointed directly at Aitan.

Aitan stood firm, raising his chin. "You are neither my Emperor nor my God. Do not forget this, Emperor Koe." He turned to his trembling mother and escorted her away.

The Emperor pulled his pocket cloth from his clothing and wiped the spit off his chin. "Such an emotional boy, Ezra. I do hope you work on his etiquette. I'm not sure I like his manner."

"I'm not sure I like yours, Emperor." Ezra waved his finger at Kito. "And you will keep THAT murderous *thing* out of my lands! Are we completely clear?"

The Emperor positioned himself directly in front of Ezra. "Don't you forget we made a pact and, correct me if I am wrong but my side won." Ezra shook with rage as Emperor Koe turned to Mensa and Kohji. "I'm not feeling the warmth I deserve here. I will return to my new vessel and I expect both of you there in moments. Do not make me regret my generosity in letting you say your goodbyes." He ignored Ezra as he turned about and made his way back to his vessel, whistling a tune as he went.

Without a footstep being heard, Kito had left the lower garden and stood a few paces away from them, his hood down over his eyes.

Mensa stepped towards Ezra. "I do so hope you can accept my apologies for today's misfortune. I want you to know I didn't know about his intentions. I will be back, Ezra."

Kohji looked at the faceless grey man with disdain. "Ezra, you have my condolences also for your loss today." Still holding Ezra's arm, he looked towards Kito. "I don't like this either. I don't even understand it, Ezra. I feel our lands are adopting the poisons of another. It's not healthy for our people." They gave another shake and Kohji broke away with Kito following soundlessly behind.

As the men walked off towards the vessel, there was the faintest whistle. Ezra looked up to the higher ground behind him. It was Aitan with more than a hundred archers lined across the mound. Kito grabbed Kohji's arm, turning him about so Kohji could see all the archers. Remorse drained over his face as he spoke to Ezra. "I say goodbye now, my old friend. No regrets."

Ezra shook his head. "No, Kohji, there are other ways. We will see you again."

Kito didn't wait for another word and continued onward towards the vessel, followed slowly by Kohji, occasionally warily looking back to the archers.

With his archers, Aitan waited until everyone was on the Emperor's strange vessel. His veins bulged and his muscles shook as contempt pulsed through him. The one in grey bent down on one knee and bowed, staying in that position as the vessel made its way past. Aitan's eyes narrowed at the grey form, then he spat on the baking sand and turned away.

In the cool of the palace once more, Aitan went over everything that had taken place as he made his way to his father's office. Two armoured guards opened the large double doors as he approached. "Did either of you guards see the one in grey fight?"

One spoke. "We were on the terraces. We saw everything from our standpoint."

"When it was finished and all five men were dead, what was your first impression?"

"I was astounded. His speed was incomprehensible and when he was finished he still had his hood up. It just didn't seem natural in my opinion, sire."

Aitan nodded and turned to the other man. "And you?"

"I knew three of the men and their families. It was a strange death, not worthy of them."

"Though you know you are serving here to protect the temple."

"I will never shirk my duties to protect my Pharaoh, his family and this temple, sire. I have grown from just a boy and this is all I have wanted to do. I am proud in my duty, but that was not an attack. We were not going to war, sire. It was a small, unorganised battle of wits in a garden. Not the way I would have wanted to serve my temple. That's all."

Aitan lowered his tone. "The families will, of course, be looked after. As the protectors of the temple, this is what they were asked to do."

As the doors closed behind him, Aitan marched past Sofira to address his father. "What in the Gods' names was that?"

Ezra was gazing out to the Mother River from the large, open wall. Long white cotton curtains gently wafted in the desert breeze. He frowned. Aitan could have a stubborn streak. Of course, he got this from his mother. Without looking, he instructed his staff. "Refill our water goblets and leave us, please." The maids were quick to do as he asked.

Sofira patted Aitan's back. "My dear son, you know Father will do nothing less than what is right for the people."

Aitan pointed out of the window. "For the people? Go tell the five families who are not getting their loved ones back tonight, it was for the people. *They* are the people!"

"Mind your temper with your mother, boy, and mind your tongue while you are at it. If you want to be our next negotiator, you need not get so emotional. A cool head will rule supreme."

Sofira stepped forward. "You know your father is right."

Aitan paced about, flapping his arms in anger. "I did not see it working so well this morning! And what was the pact the Emperor spoke of?"

Ezra drew back a full breath through his nostrils and grimaced. "Yes, I'm afraid we had a small wager on the fight. He will call a favour when he needs it. In the interim, he is not obligated to take any of our trades."

Aitan's eyes bulged. "What, none!?"

Ezra put his hands behind his back. "Yes, this is so, Aitan."

Aitan dropped his voice. "Then why are we trading with him at all?"

"Because he has amassed an army the size of ours, tenfold." Ezra looked at Aitan intently. "He is just waiting for one of us to defy him."

"My father, I will defy him tomorrow if you will let me."

Ezra scoffed. "I fear you are not getting this picture, my son."

"You have that right. Five men are unnecessarily dead. No trading rights and a 'yes, sire' policy with a nation not even close to our borders. Have I missed something, Father?"

"Yes. The most important thing, Aitan. He wants war, and he *has* the backing of our neighbours. They didn't leave by vessel together so they could sit about saying how wonderful and how much respect they have for the people of our lands. Greed, son … greed is what killed the failed generation, and it is now respawning from Middle Kingdom."

"So, we take the fight to them first! We win over Kohji and move right into Zimbali together. "You saw what Kohji was prepared to do. He was prepared to die just to see this grey man dead. He will back us, but we must go to him convinced, committed in …"

"NO! Damn it. Son, have you not learnt anything I have shown you over the years? Koe wants war! He already has an army of his own *in Zimbali!* He is waiting for the opportunity to unleash his power over Kohji and then us." Struggling to hold his pain, Ezra turned away from Aitan, whose intense gaze searched the floor.

"So, who is looking after the Wall in Middle Kingdom?"

Ezra sighed. "I have given that some thought, but the bottom line is, we have no way of helping the Northerners without first going through Middle Kingdom. The point is, Koe is searching for something more. I don't know what, and neither does Kohji. By moving so many of his guards to Zimbali, he is using stand-over tactics with Mensa. Kohji is concerned he will then use Mensa to stand over him too. That's why Kohji came to me this morning.

We don't know why Koe is moving like he is. It is not about trading and keeping tallies, he is searching for something else. We just can't see what."

Sofira spoke in barely a whisper. "Ezra, we do still have their Queen in the basement. We could use her as a shield against Mensa."

"Err …"

Ezra and Sofira looked at Aitan, puzzled. Ezra spoke carefully. "Son, if there is something you would like to add, now would be as good a time as any."

Aitan had now lost his impetuous demeanour. "I asked Mother this morning to speak with me because of the one in grey. He would be the one who killed one of our men and then dived in with the crocodiles."

Ezra tilted his head. "Are you sure, Aitan? That man didn't resurface and was never seen again."

Aitan nodded with a pained expression. "Sadly, Mother asked the same question, but yes, absolutely, it is the same man, wearing the same garments with the same hood." He paused. "Have either of you ever seen his eyes?"

Ezra and Sofira looked at each other inquisitively. Sofira bluntly answered. "No."

"Just what are you suggesting, son?"

Aitan shrugged. "Nothing. It was a legitimate question, but think on this, you both heard the testimonies of everyone who saw what he did in the basement. I would sooner count the grains of sand in our expansive lands than explain how he did that. Then he returns here as the Emperor's *assistant* and kills five of our best, while empty-handed. Father, the one with the bolt protruding from his eye socket?"

"The grey man caught the bolt and threw it back."

"Caught the … is that even possible?"

"If you had asked me this morning, I would have laughed at the idea. I suppose like what he did in the basement, Aitan, but I saw it with my own eyes."

Aitan stood just inside the wafting curtains. "This is not right; he is not right. Has Koe summoned the devil? Does evil now walk the earth?"

"What have you done with Trina, Aitan?" Sofira asked.

"When the grey man, Kito, came into the basement, he was looking for her, and he told me if I didn't move her upstairs and treat her well, he would return and kill me." Sofira gasped. Aitan continued. "I have moved her upstairs."

Ezra clenched his teeth. "I should have gutted the woman when she got here."

"Father, we both know she didn't ask for what has happened …"

Ezra's nostrils flared and he shouted with such intensity Sofira moved out of the way. "I WILL GUT THAT ENTIRE NATION!"

Aitan turned square to his father. "I understand Trina is the only tangible thing you can focus your pain on, but she was gone long before Rani married Mabutu. And Father, do not forget Rani was also my *sister*. No, there is an opportunity here we need to exploit." He took a deep breath and sighed it out. "Besides, I do have another problem if you do that."

"Son, what is it?"

"The grey man, Kito, comes to me in my dreams. He has told me if anything happens to Trina, he will hold *me* accountable."

Ezra drew back. With a taut face, Sofira's voice trembled. "Aitan, you have not told us this before."

"I didn't want to worry you." Aitan tried to appease his mother. "If Trina is alright, then so am I. But if this man can do all of what we have seen, does he have *no* limit?"

3 Vessel of Wings

The *Ocean Conqueror* surged ahead, carried by the prevailing winds caught in the large expanses of silk. As Kito lowered a bucket through the hatch to get fresh water, memories of his days on the *Shiraz* came to him, as did the broad, beaming face of Baako. He almost smiled as he undressed. He had today's sins to wash away.

He was almost done when he heard Mensa coming down the stairs.

"Just a quiet moment for yourself, Kito?"

Kito remained with his back turned, keen to avoid revealing his arm bracelet or his eyes. "I need to keep my clothes clean, Mensa. They are all I have to my name."

"You have many scars for a young man." Mensa studied the welt-covered forms that tracked Kito's back. "You have lived a full life and must be proud."

"Should I be proud of today's effort then, Mensa?"

"You only did what was instructed of you. I thought it was clever of the Emperor to use you like that. He made great gains for it." He chuckled for a moment. "I also thought you did well under the circumstances."

"Circumstances?"

"Well, yes. You were sat with your back turned when the first bolt was shot." He paused. "It was all just a setup, wasn't it? How could you know what they were about to do?"

Kito scoffed. "Half the river heard them rattling out from the Palace; the rest was obvious. I know in that you would agree."

Mensa lowered his voice. "Why do you work for the Emperor? He's not of your kind."

Kito barely wrung out his tunic before hastily pulling it over his head. Flipping the hood up, he turned from the bucket. "So, tell me, Mensa, what *is* my kind?"

"We are clearly not kin, Kito, so I don't really know, though I would've thought I'm far more beneficial to you than he is." Mensa put a hand on Kito's shoulder as if they were friends.

Kito stood with his trousers in hand, then turned, breaking away from Mensa's hold. "That would be desertion in the Emperor's eyes. Have you not seen his dark side?"

Mensa raised his eyebrows with a wry grin. "Has he a light side?"

Kito flapped his trousers several times before stepping into them. Holding up his tunic, he fastened the waistband and turned square to Mensa. "You need to be more careful with your opinions, Mensa. Discretion is *life* in this game of egos."

"I don't fear you, Kito."

Kito straightened his tunic. "It's not me you need to concern yourself with." He flicked his chin towards the rear of the vessel. Mensa spun on his heel to see Kohji standing at the bottom of the stairs.

Mensa didn't miss a beat. "Ah, my friend, Kohji. You have finished your talks with the Emperor then?"

"Clearly, King Mensa, yes." He let his eyes linger over Mensa just long enough to cause Mensa to wonder how much he'd heard then he looked at Kito. "Kito, that was something I have never seen before."

Kito picked up the bloodied bucket and threw the contents through the hatch. "I don't suppose a man of your stature does his own washing, does he?"

Kohji let out a small laugh. "This is true, but you also know your washing is not what I was referring to. Who trained you to move like that?"

"The way I move is the way I move. The training of what is the right way to move was taught to me by a very wise man from far away. He is dead now, killed by his own brother."

Mensa jibed him. "Ah, so you admit the brother was better than your own teacher, Kito? I, too, was the strongest of my brothers, and I'm also the last left."

Kito closed his eyes briefly and exhaled softly through open lips. "Where is the Emperor now?"

His reaction to Mensa's words didn't go unnoticed by Kohji. "He said he had business to tend to and went downstairs. He asked not to be disturbed."

"He may be meditating. If you would excuse me, gentlemen, I need to do the same." Kito fell into a deep bow and waited for them both to leave.

Once alone, Kito headed to the rear of the galley on the top deck. With a simple leap, he was on the roof. He looked back at the billowing silks to check on his privacy. The guilt of a shameful day ate at his soul. Lowering himself down cross-legged, he breathed deeply, then meditated on the Emperor downstairs. The flicker of dim candlelight came to his visions with the sensation of the Emperor's naked body sweating profusely, long legs wrapped around his waist.

Abruptly, Kito pulled himself back. Resisting the urge to identify the mystery woman, a preoccupied Emperor gave Kito the opportunity to leave his mortal self. However, if the sweat on the Emperor was anything to go by, he didn't have much time.

His head slumped as he slipped clear of his body. The white, silk sails pulled tight and high like the vessel was flying over the ocean. It had a kind of natural beauty. No slaves, no whips, just a graceful, silent flight. His spirit flew around it as the gentle breeze pulled it through the ocean's swells.

With no time to waste, he moved on fast. He trained his thoughts back to the time and the place he wanted to get to and the kaleidoscope of colour engulfed him, drawing him in. It still unnerved him, but he seemed to be getting more control, mastering the skill of transporting through space and time. Though he knew it came with grave danger.

He was almost at his destination time when he heard the faintest call. He slowed. It came once more. He turned to a dim light and eased towards it. The colours had dissipated now and he found himself surrounded by a fog. He felt no danger as he continued forward. The voice called out once more.

Master Hasuca? Kito stopped and listened. A chimp made a cooing sound. *Master Hasuca.*

We have told you before, Kito, there are no Masters on this side. It has been a long time without a visit, my friend.

Kito looked dejected, like the naughty boy caught once more.

You need to let it go, son.'

Hasuca?

The guilt, Kito. It poisons your soul. It was not your fault.

Do we have to do this now, Hasuca? I have many problems so I can't get out often to seek your wisdom.

It doesn't seem to be holding you back, son. Even I was impressed with you this morning. You have many talking of you on this side. You are growing from strength to strength.

Kito shook his head. *I killed five men who did not deserve to die. This is not impressive, Hasuca.* The chimp cooed in a low tone. *Why are you hanging with a chimp? I would've thought you had many friends on the other side, including Master Xiang.*

You lecture me on friends, when you don't recognise your own?

Perturbed, Kito searched his mind, rolling back the years. *From my dreams as a child?*

Hasuca's eyebrows raised with the wisp of a smile. *Only they are not dreams, son, but your own childhood memories.*

Kito drew back. *I lived that?*

Precisely. That was your father that picked you up. Your villagers danced, chanting your name. The scars of the tiger on your back are real, are they not?

I have many scars on my back, Hasuca.

True. And there is a story for each of them. I tried to contact you about your efforts in Samos, with the fire and the slaves …

Kito's temper and pent-up guilt erupted. *I should have been with you! You could still be here!*

The chimp jumped up and screamed at Kito as it waved its fists about. Hasuca spoke firmly. *Stop this nonsense, Kito. Now sit.* The chimp rested at Hasuca's side, still with one hand on his shoulder.

Kito sat where he was and stared at them both. *Why is this chimp with you if I killed it?*

Hasuca let out a tut. *You carry too much guilt for things you have no control over. You can't control all the world around you. Do you not think I felt bad when I finally realised why my father fell ill and died, Kito? I was right there at the table with him, yet I couldn't save him. Do you think this makes me responsible for his death?*

Kito conceded.

Why do you think the chimp hangs with me?

Kito pulled back his hood. *I think it can see how I wanted to be a good tribesman but also loved the wild kingdom around me and so struggled with my duties. I think he loved what I did with the tiger also.*

Ah, there it is, honest, astute and absolutely right. Who poisoned the chimp in the first place?

A tribesman.

Almost.

Not me.

Exactly. Now why can you not be so objective and forgiving with yourself? Here, think on this, son, I sought you out. I know you can find all seven of the Sacred Skulls. I couldn't have done it. Even now, I don't know where they are. Some things are held for the Gods only. But I did seek you out in the beginning because you have the right spirit and drive to find them. It's a delicate thing in life and you have it. Finding you was my entire purpose. I was born a prince and yet my reason in life had nothing to do with the palace. Ever patient, he looked expectantly as Kito absorbed his words.

Eventually, Kito mouthed his thoughts. *But if you left the cab …*

Hasuca's hand went up cutting short Kito's comment. *Son, never has a father been so proud of one of his own, but you must think on this. You must know you are the One. Accept it, embrace it – and live up to it.'*

What if I don't wish to be this One you speak of?

Just as I would never have chosen to leave the palace, Kito. Just as you told your good friend, Jabali, he would not have chosen to have his home, his vessel and his body burned. It just is, and we must learn to get the best out of our lives. I can promise you one thing, Kito, our lives are relative to us and they are never easy. Not for Jabali, not for myself, not for Kohji and not for you either. He hesitated for a moment. *You do realise Kohji was offering Ezra his own death without remorse this morning?*

Yes, most admirable, I thought.

He wanted you dead even if it meant his own death, the ultimate gift for what is right, isn't it, son?' Kito sat silent. *Kito, you know who Jabali is, don't you?*

No, I'm not sure I do.

He is the one they call Patch, from Samos.

Kito drew back wide-eyed. *Patch, the architect and builder of Tarrant's Shiraz?*

The one and the same.

His mind raced. *He could be pivotal if I am to stop Koe and his misled Guard getting to Zimbali.*

Hasuca leant back; he could reveal nothing more. *I believe the Emperor is almost spent. You should be going back.*

Kito reluctantly stood. Hasuca was right; he was running out of time to return before the Emperor was done. *I thank you for our conversation. Please forgive my weaknesses. I still learn, I'm still young.* As he turned away, Hasuca called.

Kito, if anyone else gets the Crystal Skulls before the Chosen One, they will acquire as much power over the earth as the Gods have.

The Master's last words rang in his head as he descended back down to his slumped mortal form. He slipped into his body, blinked a few times and stretched his back. He felt better than he had in a long time, like his soul had been cleansed, though those last words still echoed in his mind.

He felt the familiar blocking returning as he slipped down from the galley roof. *I bet Hasuca knows what that's about too.* He scoffed as he walked back around the port side to the table where Kohji and Mensa seemed to be enjoying each other's company.

Mensa looked up. "Why, Kito, I thought you were going to meditate?"

Kito thought on how the Emperor was almost spent when he left. He realised little or no time had passed. "I'm afraid I couldn't get into the right frame of mind. Do you ever have that problem, Mensa?"

Mensa batted his hand through the air as he laughed through a wide, open mouth. "I don't waste my time with such romantic nonsense, boy." His irritating sniggering continued as Kito turned away and headed downstairs.

Below was completely different to that of the *Shiraz*. Plenty of light and air flowed through the open hatches. There was no stench of sweat from the toil of rowing. Instead, men were sleeping in hammocks.

Kito couldn't see the Emperor. He couldn't feel him either. His irritation grew.

He moved along and climbed the stairs to the galley. The two women working on the next meal stopped what they were doing, surprised to see his large form in the doorway.

"I am Kito and was wondering if I may fetch some water for the table, please."

One answered warily. "Is the Emperor back?"

"No, not quite, though I feel we should be ready. Is he in his room then?"

The other woman answered. "No, Master, he goes down the stairs." She cautioned, "Please don't go down there, Master Kito. His instructions were very clear. He will kill anyone who tries."

Kito was sorry for the fear they lived in. *It may be a free country but they don't have a free spirit. One day ...*

The woman placed a jug of lemon water and three drinking vessels on a tray. She was tiny before his huge frame. "I am no Master. Please never call me this again." Though he spoke softly and calmly, it was all she could do to muster up a feeble smile and a nod.

The other woman stepped forward and whispered. "Is it true, Kito? I mean, what you did this morning?"

"I defended myself, yes."

She took another step forward and spoke even quieter. "Though only a Master could achieve such a thing."

"On the contrary, a true Master would never have found himself in that position in the first place. Pharaoh Ezra was right to call me a *murderous thing.*" He took the tray from the young lady and turned away.

She watched him move off through the lower deck then closed the door. "What do you think?" The other woman was holding onto the bench. "I don't know about you, but he captivates me somehow. I know it seems wrong ..." She tilted her head looking doubtful. "It is wrong, and I'm sure it shouldn't be possible, but he just excites me."

"I know what you mean. He is just gorgeous – and scary – but totally gorgeous."

"He glows like the sun."

They giggled, with hands over their mouths.

***

"Refreshments, gentlemen." Kito placed the tray, his hood up as always.

Mensa tried to recollect, in all their conversations had he ever actually seen Kito's face? Even when he was washing his clothes today, Kito had evaded him. "Kito, do you always serve the tables? It's woman's work after all."

"I am neither King, Sheik nor Emperor, so I'm just serving my fellow man. Is this a problem for you, Mensa?"

White teeth showed with Mensa's arrogance. "I was never the one with the problem, Kito. So, nothing has changed."

Kito was purposeful to pour the first silver goblet and hand it to him. Mensa was just as particular to neither reach for it, nor thank him for it. Kohji silently dipped his head. The third goblet was filled and placed before the spare seat.

"Ah, there you all are." The Emperor looked at the silver goblet of lemon water. "A little late in the day for that, isn't it?" He swiped it up and drank it down. As he settled into his chair, Kito refilled the goblet.

"I shall go to the galley and see if I can find something more suited to your pallet, Koe."

Kohji watched carefully, though the Emperor didn't turn a hair at Kito's familiarity. Kito put the decanter down and left.

The Emperor smacked the goblet to the table and sighed. "Well, Kohji, what did you think of Kito's win today? He really is quite something, isn't he?"

Kohji was obligated to agree. "Yes, of course; never have I seen the likes, Emperor. Though if I may ask, just how much do you pay the young man?"

The Emperor roared with laughter. "Pay him? Kohji, I don't pay him anything."

Mensa was not convinced. "What? Nothing at all?"

"Well, no, I didn't employ him. The Emperor smirked self-servingly. "He *asked* to serve me." His gaze drifted off. Looking pensive, thoughtful even, Koe rose without word, leaving Mensa and Kohji staring at the empty chair, completely lost for words.

Some moments later, Koe returned with a leather wrap. It hit the table with a clang. He put his sheathed sword down next to it and filled his goblet.

Mensa looked concerned. "Are you alright, Emperor? You seem quite thirsty. That's your third already."

For a moment the Emperor looked a little flustered. "I'm fine, Mensa. It's just lemon water after all. I'd be more concerned with your own well-being, if I were you."

All the while, Kohji closely observed the interaction between the two, trying to decipher what games were at play.

Kito returned with a new decanter and placed it carefully on the table. He noticed the leather wrap. "May I say, Koe, I find it extraordinary to have come up this very coast just a few days ago and now we return the opposite way on the same winds. I feel we are making remarkable pace."

The Emperor's face lit up. "As always, Kito your observations are true and right. Sometimes I think you could teach my own Desora a few lessons."

Kito flinched inwardly. He was confused by his own reaction to the mention of Desora. He knew he needed to research it further. "Very generous of you to say so, Koe. I'm sorry he couldn't make this important journey with us. He will hold the key role eventually."

"Yes, quite so. In time, I think the two of you will be great allies for me. He's doing very well for the people of our land, but could learn more from you. All in good time." He emptied his goblet and leaned forward to use the new decanter, taking up the leather wrap as he did.

"Now, Kito, I know you don't carry anything more than that silly hunting knife." Slowly, he pulled the leather tie and rolled out the wrap as carefully as if he were handling a newborn infant. "This was forged by one of the best Grand Masters our lands have ever bred."

The King and the Sheik sat forward, wide-eyed as twin, short swords were revealed. Both nestled in one sheath, the curve of the impeccably balanced swords came together at the tips to almost touch each other. The emblems of Middle Kingdom were emblazoned on both the sheath and the swords' hilts.

The Emperor pushed a ruby stud on the butt of the sheath and slid out one of them. Forged from the Royal black steel, the blade gave not even a glint in the sunlight as the Emperor rotated it in his hand. He took his silk scarf from around his neck and tossed it into the air. With a swift swipe of the sword, the scarf floated to the ground in two pieces. He sheathed the sword and put it back on the wrap. "You would like to try them, Kito?" The words slithered off his tongue as he stroked the soft leather tantalisingly.

The urge to touch them swelled in Kito. He took a step forward, feeling the rush of blood pumping through his veins. With trembling hands, he was drawn to them with a force almost beyond his control. The swords called to him as Queen Rani's crown that he wore on his left bicep pulsed back. Shocked by his own reaction, he could barely contain his excitement. He *had* to pull the blades. They were screaming his destiny!

With his thumbs on the rubies, the swords slid from their sheaths. Kito held them up in unison, captivated at the tremendous beauty of the steel. He stepped back and swiped them about as if he had practised with them since he was a child, like deadly extensions of his own being. He was physically shaken as he remembered Hasuca training him with twin, hardwood swords. The same short swords with leather handles, the same Royal emblems on the hilt.

The Emperor laughed as the swords whistled through the air, the human eye struggling to keep up. Suddenly, Kito froze. Mensa leapt back as Kito marched to the table and threw them down with a clang. Kohji moved back nervously as one of the swords rolled about on the table as if it had a life of its own. To Kito, they did.

"I can't hold these blades, Koe."

The Emperor looked at the blades on the table as he stood. "What's wrong, Kito? Did the blades not pulse? Did they not feel right in your hands?" He sneered. "Yes, they did, didn't they? And they looked right in your hands, Kito. I saw the way you held them with just your index finger and thumb, nimble yet unbelievably strong. I understand your fear, but believe me, after we have trained with them, you will be unable to separate from them." The Emperor smoothly stepped around Kito.

"Train, Koe?"

Koe dropped his voice as he leaned in close behind Kito, his words menacing yet seductive. "That's right. We will train every morning and as many nights as I can give you. We will begin this afternoon at sunset, son."

Kohji had been unable to take his eyes off the swords until the Emperor uttered that one word, 'Son.' Now he couldn't take his eyes off Kito.

***

Mensa reached down from the roof of his cabin. "Well, come on, Kohji, I won't miss this even for you, my friend."

Kohji made the extra stretch to clasp Mensa's powerful arm as he easily pulled him up onto the cabin roof. It reminded him of Mensa's father, Mabutu. Kohji still missed his old friend.

The two men positioned themselves in the centre of Mensa's cabin for their best vantage.

The Emperor stood, bare-chested, opposite Kito who was, as always, fully dressed, hood up. The two observers glanced at one another. Koe waved his sword, warming his lean, toned muscles. Kito, by contrast, was so still it was hard to believe he was a living thing. The twin swords were strapped to his broad back, the tips of the swords together at the shoulders, the handles downwards to each side.

The Emperor's agility was impressive as he taunted Kito, whipping his long sword within a hair's length of Kito's body. He goaded Kito to engage. Kito didn't move a muscle, remaining motionless.

"Damn you, boy. You will engage or so help me …"

A door opened on the side of the galley, and the two maids came out. Koe darted forward before either had a chance to move. With

38

a fistful of hair, he dragged one of the poor women forward in front of Kito, slamming his elbow into her belly. Air whooshed out of her lungs, fear lost to shock and pain. She collapsed down on all fours, starving for breath as the Emperor put his sword to the back of her head. He drew back his cutting edge with deadly intent.

In a flash of grey and the clash of steel, Koe was driven back from the woman.

The two men locked in battle. One of the bystanders rushed in and scooped up the breathless woman and ran to her sobbing friend. Both were ushered into the galley and the door bolted closed.

They moved around the top deck in a speed no onlooker could comprehend. The black swords were hardly visible, their clashing rang the constant tune of combat.

The battle raged into the evening without pause. The Emperor's body dripped in sweat, though neither showed signs of letting up, until suddenly the vessel's bell rang three times. Instantly, Kito stepped back, returning the swords to their strappings behind his back. He bowed in reverence and held it.

The Emperor was drenched, though well composed. He threw his head back and howled like a wolf into the night, flexing the muscles as he did so. For a moment, his golden arm bracelets seemed to glow. "But damn, son, never have I fought anyone like you. Not even my own brother could move like that! That was the most fun I've had for too long." Kito was unmoving as the Emperor sheathed his sword. "Way too long." In a rare show of emotion, he slapped Kito affectionately on the back. He raised his hands in satisfied accomplishment to the onlookers who politely applauded his endeavours.

A towel and a bucket of fresh water were brought out. The Emperor swiped the towel from the servant's hand, rubbed himself down, then dropped it at the servant's feet. After mopping his brow, Kito gently handed it back to the waiting man.

Kohji whispered in Mensa's ear. "What have I missed here? Who is this Kito?"

Mensa kept his eyes on the Emperor and Kito. "I don't know. Never had I heard of him until Koe arrived at my office with this strange man for this journey."

"But Koe calls him *'Son,'* Mensa."

"Kito offered to serve the Emperor some time ago and the Emperor appears to, well, almost *like* the man." Kohji frowned as Mensa continued. "But I did get the better of Kito in a wrestle on this very vessel. He is fast, I will give him that, but he doesn't know wharf fighting, *real* fighting. His background is all in the training."

Kohji looked at Mensa. He wouldn't have believed anyone could beat this bulk of a man, Kito, but he also couldn't doubt Mensa.

"Of what land does Kito derive from?"

Mensa shrugged. "Who really cares, Kohji?"

"It's just, well, I've heard him speak three different languages. I had the best in training for my role to my land, as did you, but his tone is perfect."

Mensa looked blankly at Kohji. "As I said, who cares?"

Kohji's efforts to voice his concerns were wasted on the man he was talking to. He turned to see the grey man outside the galley where the women were ushered away. On the calm night air, Kohji could just hear Kito saying, "The Emperor has his juices flowing, and I think these two women are the only women on this vessel. If they stay out of sight, they may be lucky, for tonight."

Kohji beckoned Mensa. "Shall we return to our table then, my friend?"

"Indeed, Kohji. This has given me a thirst."

"That it has, Mensa. That it has."

The two climbed down from the roof and sat at the table. The Emperor was absent, yet no sound came from his cabin. When Kito appeared, Kohji studied him for any signs of exhaustion. The Emperor had struggled to contain his obvious fatigue when he left but Kito's demeanour was as smooth as silk.

"May I fetch you some water or another bottle of wine? I'm sure there will be fruit stored in the lower deck if you wish to refresh your pallets."

Kohji had seen many fights, some to the death. Never once did he think the Emperor had Kito so much as on the back foot, yet here he was now serving the table in the Emperor's absence.

Mensa slid the empty decanter over the table. "Some wine, I feel, boy."

Kito left with the decanter and returned a short time later with it full of wine. He wiped clean the three silver goblets from the table and lit the torch in the centre. "I do hope this is to your liking." He bowed deeply again and left.

The candlelight just captured a deep frown on Kohji's forehead. Mensa paid no attention as he poured two drinks.

Kito's soft steps startled the servants as he entered the galley. Inside, the man was still pacifying the women. Kito spoke gently. "I have come to ask your forgiveness for the events tonight. Also, as the Emperor wishes to do this every morning and maybe in the evening also, I will ask that neither of you enter the top deck near this time." Kito addressed the man, drawing back his hood as he did. "I thank you for your quick reflex to rescue her, it was most brave."

The man muttered quietly as Kito turned to leave, though anger shrouded his voice. "You both would have killed her ..."

"No, that was not to happen. You are most brave just the same." The door closed behind him with a click.

With a panther's leap, Kito mounted the roof of the galley. Once more, he checked if anyone could see him. He derided his own stupidity, the cloth was still a good curtain. He relaxed as he sat and breathed deeply, sensing the Emperor was busy and the block was down. He thought on this for a moment. *Two women in the galley. There is a third, and she gives me a bad vibration.* Her power was too strong for him. It was all he could do to keep his distance and play the advantage when she was preoccupied.

He sighed as he eased out of his body, rolling his shoulders as his spirit expanded and flexed to its rightful form. He couldn't help but circle the vessel as it cut a smooth and silent path through the ocean. The moonlight reflected over the light, choppy water. He could see the two men sitting talking in the gentle glow of its light. To the back, six men were holding the rudder. He thought about how a normal vessel only needed one person and how Jabali's design was so far advanced, even from this vessel. He burst into laughter, then quickly covered his mouth with his hand. Too late. All six men jumped from their post and fell to the deck. They grabbed at one another.

"What was that?"

"Did you hear that?"

"Oh, the Gods are happy, maybe. It was a laugh, wasn't it?"

"I have no idea."

Kohji was already on his feet. "Of course it was a laugh."

Mensa marched to the rudder deck. "What's all the commotion up there?"

One of the men shouted down. "King Mensa, did you hear the laugh?"

Mensa waved his arm angrily. "The whole vessel heard you laugh. Now hush your noise and get back to your post, or the Emperor will be hearing of your insubordination."

The men returned immediately to the rudder, mouths sealed.

A little confused by the occurrence, Kito continued his flight. The six men had reacted as if it were thunder on their skulls. Twisting and turning as he rose swiftly up into the light cloud, he stopped to admire some of the Gods' most precious work. The night sky with its breathtaking clarity, and the stars too numerous to count. His mind went back to the Emperor just to check. He could see him at it again. With whom he couldn't know. The Emperor grunted on.

The block still down, Kito had some time yet. He sped off through the streaks of colour, taking him to the past. Then he saw the one he was searching for. He slowed, intensely focused. Back in time.

The one he sought was Shay. She was at the Village of the Keepers. He was surprised at his emotional response to her presence, alive and well, talking with Kobus. He wanted to go down and be a part of the conversation but this wasn't an option, not yet. And besides, Shay wouldn't be happy with him and his apparent betrayal. He watched her body language as she spoke in anger, frustration and most of all, pain.

"Kobus, he set the fire to burn the ropes. He *wanted* us to die."

Kobus hunted to find an explanation. "I don't usually make mistakes about people, Shay. Is there something we have missed here? Is there nothing else we could have overlooked?"

She wiped her cheeks with the back of her hand.

"Where did he go then?"

She shrugged. "He ran off! I shouted his name but he didn't even look back."

"And the Emperor?"

"He mounted his horse and rode off after Kito. *He* looked back, laughing."

Kobus trod small trails in the dirt as he paced back and forth. They'd been over this already. He would never have thought this of Kito.

At the sudden sound of the bullhorn being blown the village erupted into a flurry of activity. Everyone knew their jobs and hardly anyone spoke. They did exactly what they were meant to do. Kobus hurried off in the direction of the horn blower.

When he reached the riverbank, his men had their spears ready and bows drawn. On the other side was but one man, lightly built with a full, long grey beard and dressed only in a ragged loin cloth. He stood proud and appeared unarmed. Kobus squinted as he tried to see the man more clearly. He held back the man beside him. "I will check this one myself. Cover me."

"No, Kobus, it's too dangerous. It may be a trap. I must go."

Kobus didn't look back. "No, you will do as I say. You are too young for this one."

Everyone watched as Kobus waded steadily across the river. He shook his head in wonder as he walked up the riverbank towards the stranger. The man faced Kobus, who stopped just short of him. Neither spoke. Kobus released his grip on his spear and it fell to the ground. A murmur swept through the nervously waiting tribe . He reached out and took the stranger's hands, kissing them both on the back as he knelt before him. The stranger pulled Kobus to his feet and put his hands on his shoulders. The men spoke quietly for a moment then embraced tightly.

One of the young tribesmen asked Shay. "What are they doing?"

Shay observed the two elders. "I believe they're crying."

The two men released each other and turned towards the village. Some of the older men came forward as they crossed back through the shallow waters and walked up the bank. Kobus held up one hand. "If this leaves this village I will deal with the perpetrator myself." He held out a hand as the man walked forward. "I give you our rightful King, King MABUTU!"

Instantly the tribe fell to their knees. Mabutu smiled and looked over the people knelt before him. One by one, they rose and began to dance and sing. Tears traced Shay's cheeks. Though a shadow of the man he once was, she remembered him well. This *was* him and it brought back all the pain of losing her best friend, Chizoba. She saw no reason to hold back her tears, no one needed to know *why* she cried.

Kobus grabbed Shay by her elbow. "Come, you must stay and dance with us." She giggled as, without any choice, Kobus dragged her off into the village centre. Around the now roaring fire everyone sang at the top of their voices to the beating drums. It was most intoxicating. The smoking pipe only came out on very rare, special occasions and this was to be one of those occasions as it was handed around the adults. The sweet smell of it wafted through the air. Shay had never tried it before but she was now of age. Holding the bowl in both hands she excitedly put the pipe to her mouth and drew the smoke through the red wine. It bubbled, cooling the smoke and giving it a fuller, richer flavour. She liked it, giddily inhaling the smoke as she handed it on. Everyone danced well into the night.

***

It was early in the morning when Shay woke. She put her hands to her head to steady herself as she rose. Though it was very quiet, she was sure she wasn't the only one up so she decided to leave the village from around the back. She'd just arrived outside the village surrounds when she heard a commotion ahead. With caution she eased forward. She was near the river and pulled back a branch to see several men. One was held at spear point, frightened and begging for his life. She gasped and was about to go and find Kobus when she felt the point of a spear on her own back. She froze.

"Turn around, little girl."

She turned ever so slowly, faced a tall young man, and he wasn't smiling.

"What's wrong?"

"You, little girl. You are wrong."

"I was just …"

"Leaving the village without permission and the penalty for this is death, little girl."

She stumbled back a couple of paces. "No, no. I was coming to the river to freshen up, that's all."

"Then why take the back trail?"

"It is early, I didn't wish to wake anyone."

"But many of us are already up. No, I think you're lying."

"My name is Shay and I am well known to both Chief Kobus and King Mabutu."

The tall man chuckled and motioned towards the river. A man was wading out into the river to speak with the one at spear point.

"Would that be your friend there then?"

Shay opened her mouth to call out to Kobus when she saw him pull a knife. The one held at spear point went down on his knees in the river, the water now rushing around his waist. Kobus was talking but the running water was just too great for Shay to hear their exchange of words. The man on his knees nodded back. He held out his hands as if to be offering something. Kobus said something back. The man shook his head, leant forward on all fours and tilted his head down so his hair touched the water. Shay gasped as Kobus rose his knife high and wielded it down into the back of the man's skull. His body fell instantly limp. The water changed to blood-red and began to pull the lifeless body downstream.

Shay's chest heaved with shock as she tried to maintain her composure. As Kobus washed his knife and turned back to the riverbank, the other men grabbed the body. The spear in her back urged her forward through the brush. She trembled as she walked along the bank towards Kobus. Seeing them, Kobus walked over and stood before her. She looked into his eyes. Never had she thought he was capable of such violence.

Kobus looked beyond her to the tall man. "What's the meaning of this?"

"I found her escaping around the rear of the village and so I followed her to this point. She only stopped to watch you doing your duty for the people."

"Shay, you are shaking badly. Are your nerves good?"

Bewildered, her heart pounded. "I just watched you kill a man."

"This is so. I didn't believe he had the village or the people's interests at heart. Once I was convinced this was the case, I gave him his choice of death. He chose. Now, can you convince me your actions this morning were in the best interests of the people? I thought I was quite clear last night. No one is to leave the village.

No one outside of this village is to know of our King's return."

Shay couldn't stop shaking. Her head spun like it was the night before when she retired to bed. "Please, Kobus, I was just coming to take a swim. You know I have come to this very place many times before when in your hospitality."

Kobus raised his chin. "This is true, Shay, but why walk around the back of the village?"

"Because it's early. I didn't wish to disturb anyone. If you must dispatch of me, Kobus, could I at least speak to the King first?"

The man behind her scoffed and pressed the spear against her back.

"Very well, but when I say stop, that's the end. Understood, Shay?" He addressed the man. "You will not hurt her in any way but you must escort Shay everywhere she goes. Are we clear?"

"Yes, Chief Kobus. Understood."

Kobus sighed as he glanced back to the river then headed back to the village. Shay followed in silence. This was not the Kobus she had come to love and respect.

In the village centre, Kobus pointed to a plot of dirt for Shay to sit. The tall man stood behind her without word. Sometime later Kobus came back and sat in his chair. He leant forward and threw another log on the fire, keeping it alive.

"Shay, have you had a chance to rethink your standing on the Batavia incident?"

She dug her bare feet into the dirt. "Yes but my point of view has not changed, Kobus. I saw what I saw. Kito would now expect me dead."

Kobus tutted aloud. From the accounts of Shay's story, Kito would indeed expect her dead. But he'd seen many things in his time and he was sure there was another point of view. Shay was generally calm and quite wise but she was young and it seemed to Kobus she'd had feelings towards the boy and when the young man had returned, the feelings were possibly even stronger. This would not let her see all the angles in the situation for what they were.

He was brought back from his thoughts with movement in the village. King Mabutu was coming his way. He looked much younger with a shave and he wore a simple long, waist wrap. Though his physique was much leaner he was still surprisingly fit. For a man of his age, it was quite remarkable.

Kobus rose to his feet. "Ah, I see you have tidied yourself up just a little, about time too." The two men chuckled. Kobus kissed Mabutu's hands and touched them to his forehead. Mabutu waited then wrangled him into a big hug. Their deep laughter carried over most of the village. It was a laugh that everyone couldn't help but at least smile with.

Mabutu held Kobus at arm's length. "The river feeds the Mother mountain well. Never have you disappointed, Kobus." He spoke to the onlooking villagers. "I, King Mabutu, can see that all you people of the Village of the Keepers have done your duty. I apologise for my absence though I thank you for doing so well. Your King is in your debt." The people stamped their feet and clapped, rejoicing in song once more.

Kobus showed Mabutu to the best seat at the fire. When the singing had died a little, Mabutu once again stood and the people listened eagerly.

"I have much to discuss with your chief. I know you will give us the correct forum to talk in confidence."

They began to sing and dance once more as they returned to their daily routine.

Kobus was smirking.

"Yes, Kobus?"

"I see your chin is not the only thing you have polished this morning."

Mabutu took a hand to his broad jawline, feeling the lack of whiskers. "It's nice to feel so clean and I thank you also for these garments, Kobus."

"Fit for a King shall we say." Their joviality was short-lived. There was much to discuss and Mabutu was known for cutting directly to the point.

They talked about who took over the running of the lands and if the Queen or either of his sons re-appeared? Kobus spoke with regret. "I'm sorry, my King, but the thinking is our Queen Rani is well dead and your son, Mensa, is the only participating Royal."

Mabutu scowled. "Participating?"

"Some time ago a tall young man came into our village. He said he'd run upriver from the coast and went by the name of Kito. He seemed gentle and polite enough, well spoken. We made him welcome."

Mabutu lifted his chin as if ready for the blow. "But?"

Kobus looked his old friend right in the eye as he motioned to Shay. "This young lady came back with Kito sometime later. She claims he is Chizoba."

Mabutu sat back in his large wooden chair with a thud. His mind spun. The definite death of Rani was crushing but the idea that Chizoba was still living made his heart rush a beat. His emotions were both raw and conflicting. He gave himself time to soak up the situation. He sat forward again and spoke to the young woman.

"You may turn to face your King."

Shay slowly shuffled nervously around from the fire. The tall man, now stood behind the two chairs, lifted his spear defensively. She paid him no attention, focused only on Mabutu.

As recognition dawned his face lit up. "Shay!"

He leapt to his feet, reached down and pulling her up. "By the Gods, I bet you have broken some hearts. Look at you!" His smile slipped as he looked at her pain-ridden face. "What troubles you so badly, my dear?" He turned to the man holding the spear with white knuckles. "You will fetch Shay a seat immediately."

The man stood stock still for a moment then sprinted away.

Shay recounted how she had seen Kito in her village, recognising him instantly and had run after him. Kobus explained to Mabutu that they'd come here and Kito had asked lots of questions about Mabutu and the mountains around the village.

Shay spoke of the strange things he did.

Mabutu frowned. "Strange? Define, my dear."

"He asked for a rope but didn't like what we gave him, so the next morning before light he left the village. No one saw him all day. Then that night, we were all out looking for him when we found his clothes on a large rock well above this village. There was no sign of Chizoba then out of nowhere he smashed into one of the searchers. Chizoba sustained bad burns to his stomach."

Mabutu sat back. "And the searcher?"

"He was hit so hard he had several broken bones. He's still healing."

"I think it may be a little harsh to call that strange, Shay."

She slowly shook her head as she leaned in close. "He was covered in ice." Mabutu glanced at Kobus who confirmed it with a nod. "From head to foot, my King. Pure ice."

"In the jungle? Yes, that is strange. What happened next, Shay? Don't rush, just tell it like you remember it."

"We went back to Batavia." She looked at the ground, puzzled. "He said something strange. He said he was trying to meditate on the village."

"Meditate?"

The tall man returned with a large chair and placed it as Kobus indicated and Shay took her seat. "As I said, he is not the same and can do strange things. Mabutu, you know I love Chizoba but he won't even use his real name. He will only answer to Kito."

"It's alright, my dear, this is not your fault. Please continue as you see it."

She gazed down at the dirt. "It was the only time I saw any real emotion from him. He seemed really confused and upset. He kept saying the village was blocked and he couldn't see. Whatever that meant." She shook her head as if trying to shake the image. "He said for me to go back because Batavia was in grave danger. I'm sorry, Mabutu, but I couldn't leave him, I just couldn't."

Mabutu put a hand on her knee. "You are giving me a picture I cannot otherwise receive. Continue."

"We crept in the back way. Once we were amongst the people, we separated." She struggled to contain her emotions. "They had strung men out over the river and crocodiles were everywhere. I went to find Mother and the moment I did some of the guards grabbed us."

"The guards? Whose guards?"

"Emperor Koe. You know him?"

"Indeed, I do. It was such a tragedy that Prince Hasuca died in the palace fire."

"But he didn't. Emperor Koe killed him not so long ago if Chizoba is to be believed."

Mabutu turned to Kobus. "Strangely I never really felt Hasuca was dead. How would Chizoba know he wasn't?"

"From what I can gather, he grew up in Middle Kingdom," explained Kobus.

Shay butted in. "He says he grew up *with* Hasuca."

"What?" Mabutu's white eyeballs widened.

"Apparently, he fled the fire in the palace then some years later, he intercepted Chizoba who was being taken to the palace. They lived in the jungle just out of the city of Samos. Oh, and that has burnt down now, or something."

"What? The city or the palace?" Mabutu clasped his large hands on his knees.

Shay waved her arms about, flustered. "The city. Samos has burned."

"Has the world gone completely mad? Dear me, these are all crazy happenings." He rubbed his forehead. "Please, continue. Batavia ..."

"Once Emperor Koe's Guard had us, we were strung up over the river." Instinctively, she pulled her sleeves down, covering the rope burns on her arms. "The Emperor was on some fancy platform talking to the people. Then in a flash, Chizoba jumped on the platform with the Emperor. I couldn't tell what he was saying because it was in the Emperor's language. Though …"

"Yes, Shay. You can tell me. So long as you speak the truth, you can tell me anything."

She looked up at him meekly. "It was as if the Emperor and he were well known to one another." She gasped. "I'm sorry, Kobus, but I just remembered that."

"It's alright Shay." He turned to the tall man. "You will fetch Shay some water." The man trotted away immediately. "Continue. They talked like friends?"

She thought back. "No, they argued. The Emperor was arrogant and smug. Kito, I mean Chizoba, was calm and defiant though as I said, I couldn't know one word that was said between them. All I could sense was the anger in Chizoba as I could sense the arrogance in the Emperor. Before I knew it, they were fighting. It was like nothing I'd ever seen before, how fast the two men were." She dropped her head. "Suddenly Chizoba disappeared through a trapdoor on the floor and came out at the side of the platform. I could see that one of the little men was dead though I don't know who killed him or why."

The two men sat quietly allowing Shay to gather her memories. The tall man came back with a bladder and placed it at her feet. She took a sip. Eventually she spoke, quietly as if recounting a nightmare.

"I was so scared. The crocodiles were climbing over one another to get at us. I think I called out to him. They both came our way. I was begging him. Koe was laughing but Chizoba just looked mean, his hood up and his head down, his face always just a shadow. I saw this a few times with him. Every time he disappeared he would come back with blood on him, too much blood. They began to argue again then one of the guards came forward and lit the rope holding one of the men. Chizoba walked forward unafraid of all the guards then Koe said something and he stopped." She apologised as she wiped her red eyes and reached for the mug of water again.

"What happened to the man with the burning rope?" Mabutu probed gently.

"When the rope burned through he fell into the river." Struggling with her emotions she watched as the image of it became evident on Mabutu's face. "Mother was delirious. I was trying to calm her but I don't even think she could hear me now. Chizoba and Koe were arguing with more intensity …" She let out a sob and apologised again, gulping as she drank. "Then suddenly, it was like they had made an agreement. Chizoba walked forward, snatched a torch and lit up all our ropes, Mabutu. I am so sorry, my King; you know I love you, you know I love Rani and you know I loved Chizoba for the earth, but he lit *all* our ropes and walked away. He just walked away! I called his name over and over. I even called him Kito. But he didn't even look back!"

Kobus had heard the story a few times now and Shay had never diverted from it yet still he struggled to accept it. He'd known Shay all her life; he knew her family well but he'd also thought of Kito in the best light. A remarkable young man, apparently of Royal blood. The story just didn't ring true to him.

"We've nearly finished now, Shay, and I thank you. I know it's a most sorry and hurtful story for you but, if your rope was burning, how is it *you*, are here?" She nodded, grateful for Mabutu's concern and insight.

"The moment the Emperor and all his immediate Guard were gone, a little guard came running forward with two buckets and began to extinguish the ropes."

"All of them?"

"Yes, all of them."

"Why would a member of Koe's own Guard do this? Do you think Koe told them to do so after he left?"

Shay was already shaking her head. "No. Koe was looking back and laughing as he went."

"Did Chizoba give the order maybe?"

"No, he'd stormed off. Some said as soon as he had enough room, he broke out into a run. He didn't stop." She grimaced. "And he didn't look back."

Mabutu gently took Shay's hands in his own. "We are nearly done here, Shay, but you know as well as I do, there is one piece missing. I want you to close your eyes."

"Please, my King, no, no …"

She flinched as Mabutu shook her hands. "Listen to me, Shay. You have the scene clear in your head now, it is true and right but you have missed something. Something that can sway the people's point of view. Right now, my son looks to have done a truly unforgivable thing. Whether he likes it or not, he is the only other next of kin to the throne."

Again, she shook her head, her legs now quaking. "He says Rani is dead but your first Queen … Queen Trina … is alive."

Mabutu looked sharply at Kobus. Kobus held up his hand. "I have much to explain my King but first …"

Mabutu looked back into Shay's watery eyes. "Trust me with this, Shay. As your King, I will not take long, but as your King you *will* do this now." She took a deep breath and closed her eyes. He spoke softly. "Listen to my words. Look to where I tell you."

She did as he bid. Her eyes flickered beneath her eyelids. "One man has fallen. Chizoba and Koe are arguing harder," she paused, "Then suddenly Chizoba comes forward with a torch." She squirmed in her seat, her skin cold and clammy in Mabutu's large hands.

"What is his body language? Is he pleased, angry, afraid?"

"I don't believe this Kito is afraid of anyone. He is a murderous soul!"

Kobus flinched at the venom in her voice. Mabutu quickly continued in the same tone. "He is unafraid but what else, Shay, read him. Just one word, say it."

"Angry."

"Another word."

She tilted her head as if trying to read something from the sky with eyes closed. "Hurt," she said lamely.

"Good. Very good. Now, the ropes are burning and he has stormed off, you can see the Emperor laughing and leaving. What else do you see?" She turned her head, looking with eyes shut.

"Tell me." Mabutu's voice was so low it was barely audible.

"I see the little man in a guard's uniform coming. He has two buckets."

"How far has he brought the buckets, Shay? This is your village. He couldn't get them from the river, so how far has he carried them?"

"Two, three hundred paces."

Kobus immediately frowned. Mabutu continued with the same tone. "So, he started to carry the buckets at least at the very moment the ropes were lit, would you think?"

Shay almost smiled. "Yes, at the very latest."

"Good girl. Listen to my words. You are safe with your hands in mine. You feel this?" Shay nodded as her King continued. "Now look at the man. What do you see? Could you know him from somewhere else?"

She frowned, disappointment strewn over her face. "I mean no disrespect but they all look the same to me."

He gently rubbed the top of her hands with his thumbs. "Stay with me. How did this man put out the fires? Did he just pour the water over them?"

She thought a moment. "No, he took off his shirt and dunked it in the water. He couldn't have enough water otherwise."

"So, he was the only one to come with water, the only one?"

"Yes, he was alone."

"No one helped with the fires, no one at all?"

"No. He used his wet shirt to rub out all the fires then … then he turned to his people and talked to them in their language." She began to cry again. "I was trying to talk to Mother to calm her. She was so delirious she couldn't hear me."

"You are a good woman, Shay. You were very brave and I know your mother is proud. I know her well. Now think on the little man. He has his shirt off … does he have a birth mark? He is a fighting man … can you see any scars on him?"

Shay sat up drawing a large breath. Her eyes flashed open. "Oh the Gods, I am but a fool! Chief Kobus, I am so sorry I missed this! The little man, he had a massive scar across his back and belly. Chizoba had captured him in the jungle and we kept him for two days. They spoke at length then Chizoba sent him back to his people."

"So you think he recognised you and because …"

"No, no, you don't get it!" The two men looked at one another, puzzled. "I remember now! When Chizoba let him go he told him, *When you see the candle of life dwindling, you will extinguish it or our lands will consume all your people…* or something like that."

Mabutu looked doubtful. "But you said you didn't understand their language?"

"Sometimes I would ask him what they were talking about, sometimes he would tell me," she scoffed. "And other times he would make silly jokes like the cheeky boy we all knew and loved." She looked to the King, her eyes wide as she realised what she'd said. "Oh, I'm sorry. I mean it with the best of heart."

Mabutu smiled and shook her hands; he wouldn't let them go until he felt them warm once more. "I have but one more question, Shay. It's an easy one for you. Why was your mother so upset when the young man fell to the crocodiles?"

Tears welled up once more. "My King, that is the hardest question. The man was my brother. He was her first-born son."

***

Kito drew back from the scene. His body ached with guilt. Could he have saved the brother? Should he have played the Emperor another way? He tumbled and turned his way back to the vessel that was still frozen in time. As he slipped back into his body and wiped tears from his face he gazed up at the stars. They should've been tears of joy because he'd just watched his father return to the Village of the Keepers, though this wasn't the case. His tears were for his dear friend, Shay.

4 Hao's Life Ebbs

Hao was in the thick of the battle when he saw the glint of a knife. He spun, waving his sword as he went. Before him was the prince. "Prince Desora!"

He walked towards him as Desora looked down at Hao's thigh and the butt of a knife protruding from it. Desora's eyes grew wide as Hao drew it out. Their eyes locked for just a moment. Hao didn't see fear though he didn't see conviction either. He smiled at the prince as he stepped forward and Desora turned to run. He threw the knife catching Desora on the back of the helmet, toppling him.

The silver helmet skittled across the floor as Desora tumbled. He rolled and scrambled to his feet, sword in hand. "Do you even know who I am, fool?"

Hao grinned as he walked forward waving his sword about. "Oh yes, my Prince. But do you know who I am?"

Desora stood defiant. "You are one of the fools that deserted the Wall and then interfered with Imperial business in Samos. You fired a shot at me and missed. Now you will die for it!"

"I am the one and the same. And one of us will die ..."

***

Hao slipped into darkness. He smiled at the release of pain. Not pain from his injuries, that was nothing compared to the pain of his soul. The torment of not knowing if it was war or plain murder. Were the screams in his dreams memories of war, or the voice of his conscience from the injustice of his actions? Maybe his victims called for his soul from the other side? Everything could slide away now and he would meet his Makers. They would decide on his actions in this life. His life would be laid out before him in an undeniable way. He would be judged.

He was ready.

As he rose from the palace garden, he could see Tzu standing over his dead body. The Barbarians celebrated in their victory over the palace. He could feel their rejoicing and their sadness, the pain of many lost brothers. He inspected the palace as he drifted over it, looking down on the steep shale roof with multiple chimneys. He could see that none of the concubines had got out, they remained locked in the Den. Passing through the smoke, he drifted over the valley below. Along two ridges he could see Barbarians standing with weapons.

He could see his friends and the people of the palace walking down a valley away from the palace. Hao had spent the last few seasons doing nothing of what he was meant to do and everything of what he thought was right. This was, in his eyes, just the same. Unable to resist, he pulled away from the yearning to rise, and instead, went down to Maki talking with a woman. He had to see for himself. It must be the princess. He looked for another first and as he descended he saw her leading his horse. The only love of his entire life. Tammirie. Numerous people walked with her. Tears carved tracks down their grimy faces as their feet trudged up the dust. Silently, they moved on.

Hao stood to the side of the solemn procession. If only he could reach out to Maki as he came along last, but he couldn't. He looked to the woman beside Maki. It was the maid who had fought beside him. It was the princess! She walked proud and strong, her deep green eyes big and round. He laughed at his own stupidity because now it made perfect sense. Of course this courageous woman was the sister of Yaan, and daughter of the great Hasuca! Pride welled inside him.

Hao moved from the scene below him and ascended towards the light that beckoned him until he could no longer see the procession. The light intensified before him. He'd heard of such a light and went towards it.

A large hand appeared before his face. 'You seem a little hasty towards the passage of light for a young man.'

'It's my destiny. I have given more than my share of bloodletting, now it's my turn.'

'How can you be so sure, Hao?'

Hao frowned. 'Who am I speaking with?'

A man's chuckle came back. 'Always the gentleman, aren't you, Hao. You certainly charmed your way into Tammirie's heart.'

'You still haven't answered my question.'

'We have met once, face to face on the Wall. You would know me as Grand Master Xiang.'

Hao dropped into a deep bow and Xiang's laugh rippled the air. 'Here, I am no Master and there is no need to bow, Hao,' he chuckled some more. 'All are equal here, my friend.'

'I don't bow because of the stature you once held, Xiang. I bow for respect. For you I will always bow.'

Hao heard the laughter of another man and, if he wasn't mistaken, that of a chimp? 'We have company, Xiang?' questioned Hao.

'Not welcome company, no.' There was a glint of mischief in Xiang's eye. 'Just an old, argumentative friend of mine.' The chimp clapped as the laughing man left and Xiang let out a sigh. 'Hao, I have seen men and women grovel and beg to leave the light yet here you are, striding towards it. Were you not happy in your life?'

Hao thought on this for a moment. 'Before I went to the palace I was very happy.'

'So why did you go?'

'You already know these answers, don't you?'

'Trust me, Hao, you must hear your own words.'

'It was simply for the greater good. Even now, I can have no regrets.'

'Really, Hao? None at all?'

'No. Maki said they had the one we went for. I gave my life for that of a princess. I feel it was a good exchange.'

'Though you took the life of another prince.'

'He only wanted to add to the war. He'd never even been to the Wall or knew the background of what it is about. Without a second thought, he would have simply pushed on in the delusional footsteps of his father.'

Xiang's posture changed. 'You don't agree with the Wall?'

'No, I do not. That's why I left with Bolli. You could tell me what it's about, Xiang.'

'No, I could not.'

Hao pursed his lips. 'Are we doing the right thing, holding the Wall?'

'It is not my place to give such answers. The one you need to seek is a man called Norinko.'

'Norinko? The name has a familiar feel to it. Where do I know it from?'

Xiang clasped his hands together across his front. 'I still don't see what your hurry is?'

Hao knew this was the end of that topic. 'As I said, Xiang, I gave my life. Other than my dear Tammirie, I leave behind no one and so have little regret. The one we went for, the princess, she was worth it, wasn't she?'

'Is that the sound of regret, Hao?'

'Please, Xiang, the grey area between game playing and lying can be so thin, I have distaste for both.'

'Very well. I can at this time only say that all lives, even yours Hao, are a gift from the Gods. It is only our ego and perception that differs them. Please do not try so hard to be frivolous with it.' His voice began to fade. 'Every life is equal, as given by the Gods.'

The sound of a small waterfall broke the ensuing silence. Fog cleared and water rippled in the light. Hao was now sitting on a rock in the middle of a large pond. Surrounded by rainforest and birdsong, someone was calling his name, over and over. A beautiful woman stood on the bank. By her side was a huge white wolf with steel blue eyes together with a smaller wolf with emerald eyes.

The woman was calling. "Hao, come on, Hao! I see you there. Open your eyes ..."

***

Hao grimaced in pain as he blinked then managed to focus on the ceiling.

"There you go, young man. Nice to have you back with us though I didn't like your chances a few days ago." The woman's voice carried a thick, heavy accent. He had to concentrate just to understand. "You have good colour now. There is someone very keen to see you. We will be right back."

Before Hao could ask, the woman was gone. He looked about the large room with stone floors, sawn timber walls and ceiling. The sun was high in the sky, shining through the window which reached from a low windowsill all the way up to the ceiling. Throwing back the covers, he eased himself up on one arm and realised he was naked. He looked for his clothes. No clothing, no short sword, no knife. Nothing. He covered himself once more with a sigh.

His head swam as he reached for the decanter, pleased to find it full of water and gulped it down. Remembering Desora and the knife, he peeled back the cover and looked down at his leg. It had been tended to with a poultice and was well bandaged. He sat back. Nothing to do but wait.

Shortly after, Tzu walked into his room. Hao flinched. "Tzu!"

Tzu looked at the woman who had clearly nursed him then back to Hao. "I'm sorry. Am I overdressed for a visit, Hao?"

Hao scoffed. "No. I just didn't ..." He motioned towards his leg.

"Ah, you didn't think that a Barbarian could manage a poultice bandage, then?"

"No, no. I just didn't think you did them for the enemy."

"Ah, well I may be keeping you alive today, so I can kill you tomorrow." Hao looked blankly at Tzu, who burst into laughter. "Oh, relax man, though I do admit I would have taken great joy in killing Desora slowly. You and me? Now that's a different matter."

Hao shrugged. "Why? He was my prince?"

"Yes, but I watched you kill him. Why did you take so long with him?"

"He had trained from an early age and was very fast."

"Yes, all of this I could see in him, but you were better. Why did you wait?"

"My leg was injured, I was nursing it."

"That should have made you dispatch him earlier. Why, Hao, did you wait?" Tzu leant forward over the bed. "You played him, did you not? What was it you said when you drove in the arrow? I couldn't hear you."

Hao looked up at Tzu. "I give you this on behalf of my shoulder man."

"Oh, I see. This would have been the one that wore the hat you now wear?"

It now dawned on Hao that it was missing. "Not anymore."

"It will be back once I feel you are safe."

"Safe?"

"If you take all a man's belongings he loses his comfort zone. It's amazing what a man will do to get them back before he escapes."

"Ah, safe from departure, I see. And when is that day?"

"Not for some time for you, Hao. I feel we have much to discuss."

"And the captain?"

"As I said that day, I don't like a coward. I delivered him my grandfather's death." Hao looked confused. Tzu held up his hand. "Please, don't ask. I don't think Grandfather would have approved either, but I did it for my men as much as anything. Anyhow, it is done." Hao nodded, though still looked confused. "What is it that bothers you now, Hao?"

"How much time do you have, Tzu?"

"It depends on what's on your mind?"

"At the beginning of this war, the night our old Emperor was jumped in the village, starting …" He waved a hand. … "all this, how does a Barbarian recount that story?"

Tzu stepped back slightly, unsure with the question. "Hao, tell me why you took your time with your prince."

"Because he was a coward with no character!"

"Why so long!?" demanded Tzu, his patience waning.

"Because I wanted him to feel real pain, real fear and the real death he was completely unprepared for!" Hao shook as the last of his words echoed through the room.

Tzu had his answer. "Well, I feel you gave him that." He turned his back and walked to the window, peering down to the valley.

"Did you send out a slaughter party?"

"No, Hao. I told you they could leave and I meant them to leave safely." He turned back to Hao. "The maid you fought beside, who was she?"

"I have no idea. Why would you ask about a maid?"

"How many fighting maids were there in the palace?"

"Again, no idea. This is the first time I've ever been to the palace."

"But you served the palace."

"Yes."

Tzu gazed out through the window once more. "It must be a beautiful place in the winter," he mumbled.

"What?"

"We will talk on the other matter another time; until then, rest up and please, Hao, be careful with my hospitality. Now that I've met you, I do believe you were kissed at birth by the Warrior God himself. I will not take any further chances with such a person."

***

In time, Hao's clothes were returned, such as they were. He was strangely pleased to see the hat there also. Hospitality in war was a rare thing, and he only had this one chance. Hao knew not to burn it. For all the stories he'd heard about the Barbarians, this was nothing like it. He began to question his perception of just what a Barbarian was. After a lifetime of learned hatred, this was no easy thing. Though on a crutch, he was walking once more. Thanks to the Barbarians, he was both alive and walking.

They'd taken over the running of the palace. Anyone found to be intoxicated with drink or opium had to answer to Tzu. This seemed to be an undeniable deterrent, as all the opium had been washed away with the wine.

Hao had been invited to dine with Tzu in the Den. Under the huge spans of unsupported roof, they sat together at a long, wooden table carved from a single piece of timber.

"Did everyone leave, Tzu?"

"Hao?"

"The concubines. What have you done with them?"

Tzu popped a grape into his mouth. "You haven't lied to me, have you? We have spoken about liars and cowards, Hao."

"No, Tzu. The little man you saw me speak to once served here. He told me stories of concubines and a fire. The rafters in this room are burned."

Tzu looked up. "Indeed they are, Hao. The concubines are, shall we say, earning their keep. They will not be hurt, Hao, used maybe, but not hurt. I have had them locked away just in case."

Hao pursed his lips. "I see."

"Well, what else was I to do? It was not like I could have them prepare the food, is it?"

Hao looked suspiciously at his food. Tzu slapped a large hand on the huge table, cutlery and plates bouncing about as he revelled in his own joke. Hao did his best to ignore the other Barbarians who looked at him coldly from the rest of the table.

***

The days passed with Hao slowly getting stronger. There was a loud knock on his door. Three heavy-set Barbarians instructed him to meet Tzu on the front lawn. He made his way down into the foyer to the front entry of the grand palace. It had taken him some time to find his way around the huge place. He walked across the cobbled patio and down the stairs onto the grass where Tzu was standing alone, with his back turned.

Hao made no secret of his approach, though he had barely said hello when Tzu spun on his heel. He saw the glint of the knife and swayed back on his good leg as the knife cut a shallow groove through the skin on his throat. He sprang forward, driving his elbow into Tzu's broad jaw. Both men tumbled and were back on their feet.

Tzu grinned as he sheathed his knife. "As I suspected, Hao, you still nurse your leg."

"Tzu, you could have just asked."

Tzu began to laugh. "Oh, I didn't expect this from one of your kind."

Hao tilted his head. "One of my kind?"

Tzu clasped his hands behind his back and began to stroll across the grass. "See it from our point of view, Hao. We, your nation and ours, had lived in peace for countless generations until the day your Emperor was set upon. The immediate assumption was that we were responsible. So, we were pushed from our lands under murderous circumstances and were still starving until this spring. Yet we are called Barbarians."

"Bolli and I talked on this matter on more than one occasion. The whole story as to how the war began never rang true with either of us. When we questioned the elders on the matter, they would stay tight-lipped. This only concerned us further."

"You and this Bolli you speak of were friends from boyhood, Hao?"

"No, we met the night we killed the two."

"And started the stampede."

"I was not going to mention that again, but yes."

Tzu stopped walking. "This is a painful memory to you?"

"Yes."

"Why? You must have been given a hero's welcome back onto the Wall."

Hao scoffed. "No, Tzu. That was the night Bolli and I left the Wall, never to return."

"I still don't understand."

Hao stamped his good foot. "I murdered a lot of men in a war I was not comfortable with, alright!"

"Are we ever comfortable with war, Hao?"

"We must at least believe in what we fight for."

"And you didn't?"

"Still don't. More now than ever."

They continued to walk, and Tzu noticed Hao was now limping, though not badly. "So, if you never knew Bolli before the fateful night, why did you ask him to go on the mission?"

"It was clear that the woman was his mother."

"Oh, I see. And the man?"

Hao averted Tzu's eyes. "Just a human who I didn't think deserved to die that way."

"And if he was a Barbarian?"

"Are Barbarians human, Tzu?"

"Your lot don't seem to think so. We learnt most of our mind-torture games from your kind."

Hao grabbed Tzu by the arm and spun him to face him. "I have no pride in what our people have done for all these years, and I never stayed to participate. Never!" He ignored the knife pushing into his belly, fabric already cut and blood trickling onto its pin-prick sharp point.

"Tell me, Hao, just how many of your people have your outlook in life?"

Hao stepped back, confused. "I couldn't know."

"Nonsense. Did you not tell me that you went to the city of Samos and freed the people of the burning factory?"

"Yes, this is true. Your point?"

Tzu held out his hands, the blood-tipped knife still in one of them. "Well, Hao, that is a long journey from the Wall. Did you not talk with anyone?"

Hao began to feel queasy. "In the name of the Gods, Tzu, I have never claimed to know everything!"

"I know who Master Xiang was, but who is Norinko? I take it he's a relative of yours?"

Hao bent down to pick a spring flower. He smelled it and let the scent linger in his nostrils. "My favourite time of year."

"Hao, are you quite alright?"

Hao opened his eyes. "Well, I live for now, this is something …" He wiped the blood from his neck and looked to his cut belly. "… though I do feel at times, my days are short."

Tzu watched him studiously. He liked this sympathetic warrior.

Hao continued. "In our culture, we say our family name first, so when we meet someone, the first name will tell them our family ties. I have no idea who Norinko is. Where did you hear it?"

Tzu rolled his eyes. "From you, Hao. You were quite noisy when in the deepest sleep."

"Oh." Hao lifted a hand up to his head.

"Hao, are you not feeling well?"

"Just a little off, I'm afraid, Tzu. Please accept my apologies."

Tzu showed him to a nearby tree stump. "Be seated for a moment, you have pushed yourself a little hard this afternoon."

Hao looked up at the Barbarian's face. Tzu seemed to wear a perpetual sly grin. Hao left well enough alone. A large Barbarian came over and handed Tzu a water jacket. Tzu offered it directly to Hao. "The thing about a lot of blood loss is, it takes a lot of water to help replenish the body."

Hao gulped down the water and wiped his mouth. "You just made that up."

"Actually no. We believe a large part of the body is water." Hao looked doubtfully at Tzu. "Even in our coldest winters, Hao, we need to drink water. If we drink too much alcohol, we need a lot of water the next day. When a man bleeds out, he is not just pale, he is wasted of precious fluids."

Hao stood and stretched his back. As he stared at the stump, his face darkened with rage. "Tzu, give me your sword."

"No."

"You have men with loaded bows behind every bush in this garden. Give me your sword!"

Tzu slowly pulled his sword and handed it to him by the blade. As soon as the hilt touched his hand, Hao began slashing wildly at the stump. Tzu stepped back several paces. When he was finished, Hao prodded up four straps and dropped them on the stump that had been someone's impromptu prison.

Hao shook with anger. "Sometimes, I don't like my own people either." He looked at the palace walls that wrapped around them. "Apparently, we are stood in an arena of sorts." Short on breath, he slowly handed Tzu his sword, hilt first, then bent over, resting his hands on his knees. "I need to rest, if you will."

Tzu waved to some of his men who stood not far away. "Show Hao back to his room. I do believe he has smelled too many flowers today."

Hao raised his head. "Oh, and the blood you have drawn would have nothing to do with it, would it, Tzu?"

Tzu laughed again. Hao would not have thought it possible, but he was beginning to like this Barbarian.

Back at his door, Hao turned to the three escorts, their faces as cold as winter's ice and their eyes colder. "Thank you, men, I will be good from here."

The tallest stood in the centre with a pig ring through his nose. "If it were up to me, you would still be dying, not resting, Man of the Hat."

Hao raised his chin. "Well, it's a good thing for me it isn't up to you, isn't it?" He slammed the door, then rested his head against it, listening for their departure.

They never left.

***

A few days later, Hao went out to the garden at the rear of the palace. Tzu was often there, and it didn't take long to find him. "Good morning to you, Tzu." He offered an arm, and Tzu took it.

"Good morning to you, Hao." They shook firmly, then Tzu stepped back and for the first time, dipped his head. Hao returned the respect with a bow.

Hao looked around at the women quietly pruning shrubs and trimming bushes. "You are making great efforts to keep it tidy, Tzu."

They began to walk.

"Did you think we would eat the roses, Hao? Would this be closer to your expectations of the Barbarians?"

Hao scoffed. "No, though that does not remove my surprise at your effort either."

"I love your honesty, Hao. Even in my own people, honesty to this degree is rare. I feel we are more honest than your own culture, making you exceptional."

Hao frowned, hesitant to respond.

"Come, Hao, what's on that mind of yours?"

Hao shook his head, wondering how to enter such a conversation. A man came forward with a decanter of water and handed it to Tzu, who held it out to Hao. He sniffed it briefly then drank. Wiping his mouth, he handed it out to Tzu.

"You can smell poison?"

Hao shook his head. "No, I just made sure it wasn't wine."

"You did not consider the water or wine to be poisoned?"

"Well, of course, it could be poisoned, but after all we have been through, it would be almost insulting for you to poison me now."

Tzu threw his head back and roared with laughter. He slapped Hao on the back as they began to walk again.

"Tzu, it's not an insult that I ask this, but I don't like sitting about. Do you think I could go out for a hunt one day soon?"

Tzu stopped and turned Hao to face him. "Let me see, you are possibly the most daring fighter I have ever seen. You tried to bluff me that you were the Captain of the Guard and you somehow convinced me to let your people go! I'm still not sure if that one is to come back to bite me on the arse. Now you want me to let you ride out with bow and sword in hand. No, I think not."

"I just need to get out and stretch my legs."

"All the way to a neighbouring village. Not going to happen, Hao."

"I'm not interested in neighbouring villages."

There was a subtle change in Tzu's voice and his demeanour. "I'm not interested in you getting weapons or a horse, Hao."

Hao had pushed Tzu as far as he was going to. He had learnt, in battle, sometimes you are just better off retreating in order to survive and try another day with a different approach. They walked in silence for some time. Ahead, Tzu's people were digging up the ground. "More roses, Tzu?"

"It is a wise man that grows his vegetables inside his walls when in the middle of unwelcoming lands."

Hao had never thought of this. Already, there were numerous plots finished. "Just how long do you intend to stay?"

Tzu placed his hands on his hips. "I like you, Hao, I really do, though this morning you are really pushing our relationship. It is only young yet, my friend."

Hao looked deep into the big Barbarian's eyes. "There comes a time in such a relationship that trust must rule supreme, or we are wasting our opportunity, Tzu."

"Opportunity?"

"Yes. Why do you think the Gods have put us here together?"

Tzu drew back. "You think this is all a part of a bigger plan?"

"Isn't it?"

"I have no idea. Is this why you drank the water?"

"I drank the water because sometimes we must trust for the sake of trust itself."

"That's a big gamble with one's life, Hao."

"No. We have minimised that gamble by taking the time and effort to talk to each other with a little respect, so to learn about one another. I'm getting a better idea of how you think, and I feel I would like us to work forward."

"Just where do you think our relationship is going, Hao?"

"I have no idea."

"Where do you want it go?"

"As I have said, Bolli and I left the Wall and the war because we became more and more unsettled about it. There may be many more like us, Tzu." A flash of anger darkened Tzu's ruddy complexion. Hao recoiled slightly, his back foot stiffened in readiness.

"Hao, just what are you suggesting?"

Hao relaxed ever so slightly. "You can fool all the people for some of the time and some of the people for all the time …" His long wavy hair blew in the morning breeze as his head movements emphasised his words, "… bt our Emperor now has less people fooled than ever."

Exasperated, Tzu threw up his hands. "Yes, but what is it you want, Hao?"

"We could help each other to break this ruse."

"Ruse?"

"Yes. It's like a lie, only more complicated."

"A complicated lie." Tzu considered this. "That may be a very accurate word." He took his time thinking it over. "Just how do you think we would do that? We are talking about a war that has raged bitterly for an entire generation." He lifted his chin at Hao, waiting for an answer.

"Actually, Tzu, I'm not exactly sure, though I would very much like you to give it some serious thought. If you intend to rage revenge on villages, working from this palace out, then please dispatch me first. I will not stand by for that. But, if you were to come up with a strategy to turn my people, to undo the dark world our Emperor have bestowed on this land, then I will commit myself to your service."

Tzu stared open-mouthed.

"Tzu, I know I'm not the best communicator, but have I not made sense here?"

"You have made your point of view perfectly clear, Hao." His voice was monotone. "You will excuse me now, I do have other matters to tend."

Hao extended a hand, and they shook. "Then I thank you for the time you have given." He side-stepped to give Tzu his leave.

"Hao?"

"Yes, Tzu."

"You do understand your limits in this compound, don't you? I really wouldn't like you to try anything silly. My men's instructions are quite clear as to where you belong."

Hao glanced around at Tzu's men, always just a few paces away. "Yes, but I thank you for your reminder." He looked at the grandeur of the palace then back at Tzu. "Strangely, I'm more comfortable in a cave. I do hope you don't hold that against me. Enjoy your day, Tzu." He walked towards the steps of the palace, aware of Tzu watching him go.

Tzu leant back to one of his men. "You heard everything. What do you make of him?"

The man spat in the grass, his deep-set eyes barely visible under his heavy brow. His fingers traced the scar that crossed the left side of his face. "I must say, it is hard to see past that ridiculous hat."

Tzu smirked. "I, too, struggle with that one. You know he was not the one wearing it on the night of the stampede?"

"Or so he said." The man spat again.

"You think he's trying to lead me astray?"

"I don't know if he was wearing the hat or not. It would certainly have been wise for him to try and distance himself from that night."

"He could have told me he wasn't there at all. It is just a hat after all."

"True, though he did try to tell you he was the Captain of the Guard." Deep lines creased his brow. "Why do you think he tried to give you that story?"

Tzu slipped his hands behind his back as they walked on. "I have given this as much thought as anything since that day, my Shaman. The only thing I can come up with is, he has an extraordinary desire to protect the people around him. There was nothing else in it for him."

"If this is so, Tzu, then why is he here talking to you about the war?"

"Do you really think he wants to break the war?"

"He did say if you wish to run attacks on neighbouring villages then you would have to despatch of him first because he won't stand by for that.'"

"It could be a bluff, Shaman."

"Indeed, it could, but I pose you this. Why did he wear the hat into battle with us, if he didn't want to be recognised?"

"You think he wanted us to find him?"

The Shaman shrugged. "It's an interesting concept, isn't it?"

Silently, they continued through the garden. The spring scents on his nose, Tzu couldn't help but smile at Hao's earlier comment. 'My favourite time of year.' He snorted.

"Tzu?"

Realising he had done so out loud, Tzu tried to explain. "Never have I had a man who has influenced me so deeply, so quickly. Either he is eluding us with his own plot, or he really wishes to break the war, which is strange for such a canny warrior. Either way, he has my respect."

"Ah, now this is where you need to be doubly careful, Tzu. Never have oversight of what side he came from."

Tzu raised his eyebrows. "Good advice, my Shaman. Very good advice."

5 The Past Unveiled

The overnight frost had broken, revealing a very fresh moose print. In the dense forest, Hao removed the crossbow from his horse. He cocked it and slipped in a bolt. Leaving the horse behind, he began tracing the tracks, his eagerness difficult to contain. He loved these times. The temperature had been freezing overnight, but after the fog lifted, it promised to be a great day.

He kept his focus true, easing across flat ground, eyeing the prints heading up onto a ridge. He carefully stalked them, then stopped abruptly. Standing motionless, his skin prickled. He quickly scanned the forest for the impending threat. Some distance off, he could make out the silhouette of a man sitting on a large rock. He appeared to be facing his way.

Hao thought about his horse; it wasn't tethered, but hadn't followed him either. He eased forward, minding every step taken. The form didn't move. The element of surprise may still be his. Mist drifted between them as he steadily moved through the frozen undergrowth in silence. As the clouds cleared and the sun's rays burned a trail of golden light through the forest, he stopped. The light would shine over the man before it got to him. He eased down behind a sapling to watch.

Silently, he slipped his finger on the feather-light trigger but, just as the sun exposed the figure, the man raised his head and looked directly at him. Hao gasped and leaned back, losing his balance. The crossbow went off with a twang, shattering the bolt on the frozen ground.

A deep laugh echoed through the forest as the man nimbly jumped off the rock and pulled back his hood. "I don't think this is any way to greet your friend, Hao."

Still fumbling on the ground for his broken bolt, Hao craned his neck and squinted into the sunlight. "Kito, by the Gods, is this really you?"

"Well, I hope so or I'm wearing the wrong garments."

Hao dropped the crossbow and ran forward, snatching Kito up in a clumsy hug. "The Gods have given you back to us! Yes, my dear friend. It is really you!"

Kito jokingly wriggled from Hao's grip. "Put me down, you fool boy. I'm not one of your harlots!"

Hao released him and held him at arm's length. Kito raised an eyebrow, seeing Hao's watering eyes.

"Oh, that," explained Hao, "I had an insect fly right into my eyes just a little way back."

"What, both eyes at the same time, Hao?" Kito smirked.

"Yes, that's right. No need to go on about it."

After exchanging heavy slaps to the back, Kito motioned to the rock. The morning was warming and he removed his top garment and laid it down. Hao followed suit. As they sat on their garments, bare-chested, in the morning sun, both men sighed at the same time then laughed.

Kito then looked more serious. "You went back to the palace, Hao. Very brave."

"It was necessary for the better good, Kito. You did the same in Samos. If you know where I was, then you know why I went."

"Yes. But what is it you wish to achieve now?"

"I was not really expecting to be alive to discuss this."

Kito nudged into him. "Yes, Hao, and that seems to be a habit of yours. Yet here you are."

"You wish to know what I think, Kito? Honestly?"

Kito smirked. "Do you know another way?"

It was Hao's turn to nudge Kito. "Very well then. I think I'd like to find out just what started the war, to then find a resolution."

"That's a big plan, my brother. Many men and women have died for that war."

"That doesn't mean it was ever necessary! It just means both sides fought to win."

Kito pondered the comment. "Talk me through that one."

"Two men get into an argument. Right from the onset, there are two ways to argue." He held up his fingers to count. "One, say whatever it takes to win and, just as important, to be seen to win or two, talk it through in order to uncover the truth then both men can find the correct path forward."

Kito leaned back, resting on his elbows. "You think the Emperor has just fought to win?"

"Exactly." Hao wagged his forefinger. "When Tzu Hsi, the grandfather, came to the palace, he gave the Emperor a message. It's not known exactly what the message was because the only other man present at the time, suddenly disappeared and, of course, Tzu died a slow death himself at the hands of the Emperor, but a message was sent back to the Barbarians to say Tzu had succeeded in his delivery."

Kito rolled over to face Hao. "How do you know all this?"

"I don't know if it is true and right, but I have talked considerably with his grandson, also called Tzu Hsi."

"Really, where?"

"He personally led the charge on the palace. And we've had the occasion to talk."

"Just how does that make you feel?" Kito sat upright. "I mean, you are the last of your family because of …"

Hao interrupted him, putting his hand in front of Kito. "Because of a war on a Wall that I'm just not so sure about anymore."

"You like this Tzu, don't you?"

"I want the truth, not a grudge match. Besides, he seems to have a very wise side to him."

"How so?"

"They healed my wounds and have taken on every chore to keep the palace in as fine a shape as ever."

"What do you and Tzu Hsi talk about?"

"Everything from how important water is, to life itself. They believe water is the essence of all life; it holds the balance, the vibration of life."

Kito was immediately intrigued. "The vibration, how so?"

"I don't really understand, Kito. He said water, even water in our bodies, carries the vibration of life, just as the lake carries the ripples of the pebble to the shores."

"What else do the two of you talk about?"

"We talk a lot of the war and how it began, who is responsible."

"You believe his word on these matters?"

"I think he speaks for the sake of truth, yes."

"I hope I can be as fine a man as you one day."

Hao's eyes twinkled with his cheesy grin. "Maybe one day, Kito, but you will never be as handsome."

When Kito's laughter rippled through the forest, Hao looked about nervously.

"Concern yourself not, my friend. There is no one here that can touch us. Not here and now. I was very careful." Hao's forehead knotted again. Kito continued. "Here, I will show you something." Hao followed as Kito hopped off the rear of the rock then scaled up to the top of a larger one a short distance away. He spoke softly. "This is a time before the war. Listen carefully." Hao was about to ask for an explanation when Kito lay flat on his stomach and peered over the edge. Together they gazed down a valley nestling a small village.

***

The setting was beautiful. A small stream babbled over smooth rocks down towards a bigger river with a huge cascading waterfall on the far side of the valley. Tall trees surrounded the valley, holding the steeper slopes together. On the banks of the river, amidst playing children, goats grazed and sheep were contained in a nearby holding pen. Smoke wafted up through the chimneys of small cottages with steep, heavily thatched roofs and merriment floated gently on the cool, valley air.

Two young lovers were holding hands as they walked from the rear of the village and up towards their viewing point. Hao grabbed Kito's arm with a little concern.

"As I said, no one can touch us in the here and now."

Hao trusted Kito implicitly and so relented with a perplexed frown.

The two lovers came right up under their holding place. The girl looked panicked. "I'm pregnant, I tell you."

"How did you do that?"

"What, really?"

The big Barbarian put his hand to his forehead. "Well, I know *how* it happened, but what are we to do now? Neither of our tribes will accept us."

The young girl reminded Hao a little of Tammirie. He moved his thoughts, wondering why he was watching this, then he saw a third person coming up the hill. There was an obvious likeness now he was close. He defiantly stared at the Barbarian, standing with his hands on his hips and his chin raised to defy the fact that he had barely reached adulthood.

"I think it's time you left."

The Barbarian stood a good head and shoulders above him. "Oh, you do, do you? Or what, little brother?"

"Or nothing, Toza. Neither of us wishes to go there, and bloodletting will not stop my father's temper."

"Your sister should have been more careful to not be carrying a child, little brother."

"You have done your part also, my friend." He held up his hand for the Barbarian to stay calm. "Just give us a little space. I will work with Father. He will know what to do for us all."

The Barbarian drew a long breath. "Very well, but don't forget whose seed your sister carries, Norinko. I'll be back to care for them both, so best you sort out your father."

"Just give us a little time …"

Before he could finish, the Barbarian pointed down the hill. "You don't have much of that."

The young man spun on his heels and looked down the hill to see his father, Hois, striding towards them. He swore and turned back to the big Barbarian. "Very well. You will hear from us soon." He reached out his arm with his hand open.

The Barbarian ignored it, spitting to the ground. "I will come back for what is mine." He eyed the young man coldly. "*Soon*, Norinko." Not waiting for an answer, he turned and jogged easily over the stream and into the forest.

The young Norinko held his sister by the shoulders. "You trust me, don't you, Mischa?" Unable to find the words, she mumbled in agreement. He held her firmly. "Good, let me handle this, I'm sure Father will come around."

Hois was younger than expected. His long hair did little to cover his scars. He was a hunter, though his callused hands indicated he also worked the land. He was fit and proud. He marched directly past Norinko and, without warning, slapped Mischa hard, sending her screaming to the ground.

She clutched her stinging face as she lay there, terrified. "Father?"

Norinko rushed between them and struggled to hold his father back. Hois shook his finger wildly at his daughter as Norinko grappled to contain him. "You tramp with them?! Could you not find one of your own kind to lie with?"

Norinko called to Mischa over his shoulder. "Go! Go to Mother, now!"

Livid, Hois pushed Norinko aside and clenched his fist at her. "You are dead to me, you hear! You are dead!" the words spat from his contorted face.

Mischa burst into tears as she gathered up her skirt and darted off down the hill. Norinko grabbed his father's sleeve to prevent him from running after her. Hois swung around and landed a fist to Norinko's face, then the two men launched into a wrestle. Norinko was fast and strong, but with experience and weight Hois bettered the young man, eventually throwing him back. Norinko was quick to retort, but Hois flashed his steel without warning, covering Norinko's face instantly red with blood from a deep cut through the bridge of his nose.

Poised for retaliation, Hois yelled, "And what are you doing protecting her?!"

"I was brought up to protect *all* my family, by you!"

Hois pointed down the hill to the woman disappearing into the village. "*That* is not your family. In the name of the Gods, boy, she is kin no more!" He gritted his teeth as he put his face so close to Norinko's they were almost nose to nose. "At first light, I will take her to the forest, then she will be no more trouble or shame to the village."

Despair pained Norinko's bloodied face. "Father, no, you cannot …"

"I DAMN WELL CAN! And I WILL!"

Norinko's heart beat wildly. If nothing else, he knew his father was true to his word. "No, Father, there is another way, I'm sure there is." His voice trailed off as he now walked in circles, pulling at his hair. "There has to be another way."

Hois stood firm on the spot with his strong arms crossed. "No, there is not. Tomorrow at first light." He turned to walk away.

"Wait! I might have an idea."

"You need to tell me now, or it's too late, boy. What is it?"

"The Emperor. The Emperor is coming our way in just a few days for his summer meeting."

Hois's eyes narrowed. "Yes … and?"

Norinko walked back and forth with his hand up to his chin as if stoking his beard, though he was barely old enough to grow fluff. "If there was an ambush but without any real spilling of blood, and, in this ambush, the Barbarians were heavily implicated, then we would never need to see them again. You understand?"

"Son?"

Norinko paced around with the newfound confidence of his plan. "Do you actually know *who* Mischa lay with?"

Hois grimaced in disgust. "Do you think I care, boy?"

"Oh, but you should. A Barbarian he might be, but your daughter chose very well. He is Toza, son to Tzu Hsi no less."

"What?"

"Mischa is pregnant with Royal blood, Father."

"But Barbarian blood none-the-less. No. He will have to come with more than just Royal blood if he wants to sit at *my* table. He needs to bring a gift fit for the blood *he* is claiming."

Norinko slumped his shoulders and looked to the earth. His head swam. He pinched his nose between his thumb and forefinger to ease the throbbing and help him concentrate.

"What about the Crystal?"

Norinko looked up. "Father?"

"Yes. Tell him if he has the right intentions towards Mischa and his sown wild oats, he will come with the Blue Crystal, or I will hang his pregnant woman's corpse outside his very own village."

Norinko paled. "Father, what are you saying?"

Hois cupped his hand like he already had the Crystal in it. "I'll be giving the Emperor the Blue Crystal on his arrival, or you can say goodbye to your sister."

***

Hao was entranced in the moment when Kito nudged him. They slipped off the rock and made their way back to their tunics. In silence, they sat down facing one another.

Finally, Hao shook his head. "Kito, so this really was our fault, our doing? The Barbarians did nothing and we have drawn blood, starved their women and children and blamed them for over an entire generation."

Kito had wondered how Hao would react. "Hao, you didn't start this war."

Hao leapt up, throwing his arms out wide. "No, but in the eyes of the Gods, Kito, I sure have drawn some blood over it!" He slapped his arms to his sides, his eyes glazing over again.

"And in the eyes of the Gods, you rode right out of there and never returned, Hao. Also, in the eyes of the Gods, you were there to free all those people in Samos. The Gods miss nothing, least of all your heart and honesty in life."

Hao soaked up Kito's words. "What should I do now?"

"You served on the Wall for many seasons. You entered Barbarian lands and stampeded back out." Kito sighed, watching the humble man. "You have done hero's work over and over and still you live. Why?"

Hao blinked, leaning back. "I don't understand. I ask for your guidance, and you talk to me about my history. Why do you fail me when I need you? We are brothers, and I ask you for your help."

It was reminiscent of his own accusations of Hasuca. Inwardly, Kito smiled to himself. "Never will I fail you, my brother. Come, it's time." He rose smoothly to his feet, drawing up his shirt with him.

Reluctantly, Hao reached for his tunic. When Kito had made his mind up, that was the end. He couldn't be swayed. In truth, Hao liked this about him, but there was something else that bothered Hao. "Kito?"

"Yes, Hao."

"There is one more thing I feel you should know. It's about the palace."

Kito paused from flicking up his hood. "Friends can share anything."

Hao straightened his tunic for an over-extended period, building up the nerve to look Kito in the eyes. "At the palace …" Kito stood blank-faced, waiting. "… when we were fighting the Royal Guard, Desora attacked me from behind." Hao blurted, "I'm afraid *he* did not survive."

At first, Hao thought Kito hadn't heard him. He stood like a pillar of rock. Now he understood his reaction to Desora's name being mentioned on Koe's vessel. "How far in Middle Kingdom has this news reached?"

Hao blinked at the question. "I'm not really sure, I mean, I would have thought it could not have gone any further than the caves."

"That's it?"

"I would think so, Kito. Yes."

"That should work then."

Hao frowned. "You think if the Emperor knew …"

"He would immediately return and release a darkness the likes of which Middle Kingdom has never seen."

Hao frowned deeper.

"Hao, they still think you are dead, don't they?"

Hao scoffed. "I would think that would be best anyway."

"Oh. How so?"

"I'm residing amid Barbarians, stuck out like a sore thumb with this hat. They have not forgotten the horse stampede that Bolli and I inadvertently started, killing too many of theirs, so how long do you think I will last there?"

"You could just not wear the hat, Hao, it must almost be like salt in the Barbarians' wounds every time they see it." Kito looked at the hat. "Anyway, you always said you hated it."

Hao ignored Kito's little grin. "When I pulled Bolli into the factory, he made me swear never to remove it. I made a promise, and besides, no point in trying to separate from it now. It is well etched into their minds. Almost in spite of them, and me, I wear it with pride."

"That's because it had the crown in it, but I have that now, remember?" Kito rolled up his sleeve.

Hao looked at the crown wrapped tightly around Kito's upper bicep. The seven diamonds glowed like they had a life of their own. "Still a little feminine, even on that masculine arm of yours."

Kito ran his fingers softly over the jewels. "But it was Mother's, so I love it just the same."

Hao closed his eyes in regret. "I'm sorry, my friend. I just meant …"

Kito slapped Hao on the back. "No need to speak on it. Never have I heard you mean a bad word."

"Yes, but it's still your …"

"No, Hao, you did not *mean* anything bad, that is the point. Now, Hao, it's time I got you back."

6 The Hunt

Hao woke at the sound of two heavy thumps on wood. He jumped to his feet and searched frantically in the dark for his sword, only to remember he now didn't have one. He waited, not even sure if he had in fact heard the noise. *Was that dreaming or not?* He turned about in confusion. One moment he was with Kito, no … he was dreaming of Kito. *That must be it.*

Two more bangs on the door. He grumbled loudly. "It is still dark. Who is it?"

"You will open the door, or I will remove it and come get you!"

He recognised the voice. "Very well. You can wait one moment and be civilised about it. I'll open the door. Just wait."

Lighting a candle, he dressed and splashed water on his face, then, with a deep breath, he opened the door. In the dim light, he could see the man with the nose ring and three other armed men, all well dressed in furs. "What's this about?"

The man with the nose ring grunted. "I have been told to take you on a hunt. Do you wish to go or would you rather lie about for another day?"

Hao hesitated. Just yesterday Tzu had been quite reluctant about this. "I will just grab my stuff." He closed the door behind him, though he had no need to. He just enjoyed doing it. Smiling as he grabbed some more garments, he reopened the door. "Lead the way, my friend."

The man at the front led the way down the hall. He was little for their people, but he walked with strength and pride. Nose Ring walked beside him, and the other two followed behind. He was strangely familiar to Hao somehow. His deep-set eyes and a cut over the left brow were quite distinctive. The other was clearly a fighting man, heavy built to say the least. Hao wondered if their formation was the setting of a trap or just their training. He walked with them, having neither a care nor a fear.

They weaved through the caves of the lower palace until they came to a stable where five horses were being saddled. The other men went to theirs without a second thought. Hao eyed his with a frown. It seemed not much more than a mule. "How can you expect me to keep up with you, let alone hunt with this?"

Nose Ring looked down on him. "You're here and will do as you're told. Get into the saddle and stop whining like a woman."

Hao scoffed and looked at his horse. "Well, little one, I guess you're not happy about this either." As he gently patted it on the nose, it raised its head and neighed. "Quiet, boy. Come on, we have a ride to look forward to."

Two of the men rode out of the stables as Nose Ring glared at Hao. "Stop the nonsense and just mount the thing."

Hao rubbed the horse some more. It turned about and tried to bite him on the leg. Hao was all too ready for that and gave it a quick whack on the nose. Carefully, he walked around it and lifted each hoof. He patted it on the rump, then pulled twice on the saddle before swinging into it. He smirked at Nose Ring's mounting irritation as he and one other man waited for him to leave the stables, then followed him out, mumbling angrily all the way.

They skirted west around the palace and up onto the road. Hao looked back at the Palace just to refine his bearings. The sun was just rising; it would be a good day from here, though it did concern him that he saw no sign of Tzu on this impromptu hunt.

They rode on to the massive gates. The Barbarians talked in their own language, evidently at the expense of Hao, with his feet almost dragging on the ground. He gave a small wave. Eventually, Nose Ring waved his arm angrily, and the gates were opened.

Before long they were out on the plains heading north, Hao happy to be on open ground once more. His dream from last night was now on his mind as they rode on. As always, they had the little man up front, Nose Ring beside him and the other two behind.

Late in the day, they came to a ravine. Despite them being in Palace territory, the lead man seemed to know exactly where to ride down into it. A little uneasy, Hao followed.

They wound down a small track to the banks of a strong river. Trees clung to the steep banks, increasing in size and density as the ravine became steeper and deeper. More than once, the other horses faltered on the unstable track. Hao's mule may have been slower on the plains but it stood him in good stead now. His was truly a mountain horse, and he was beginning to like it.

At one point, Porteous struggled to control his horse as it slipped underfoot. Its rump backed into the horse Nose Ring was riding, causing it to collide with Hao's. As it scurried close to the slopes unable to get a firm grip on the stony ground, Hao swiftly grabbed it by the reins and tugged it back to solid footings. Nose Ring mumbled under his breath as he regained control and rode on.

The trail rounded a bend, and they came out onto a large flat clearing void of any scrub, just a little stunted grass. Disconcertingly, Hao watched the men dismount without so much as a second look.

A cave nestled at the back of the clearing. The shelter from winter's fury was evident. Here, they would have the protection of the tallest trees and an ample water supply from the river. Hao doubted even the rising smoke from a fire would be seen once it had dissipated through the trees. This was a regular stopping point for them. He dismounted and began to pull the saddle off his little horse.

He had no supplies, no knife, nothing, and so occupied himself by tending his horse. Once done, he walked to the bank over the river. It wasn't a large drop from where he was, but it would be a nasty fall just the same. He heard heavy footsteps behind him and considered his options if attacked. *None.* He didn't turn around.

The Barbarian stood to his right. "You ride well for someone who says he has spent all his adult life on the Wall, Hao."

Hao turned to the man, the one who always rode last. "You know my name; may I ask yours?"

The man continued watching the rushing water below. "There's something special about running water, isn't there? I mean, it's almost hypnotic."

Hao looked down. "I think it's primal, like a basic necessity in life. Fire can do the same thing for me."

"I would agree with that." He looked Hao up and down. "Tzu has told me of your acts of courage. You are a formidable fighter. Is this why you didn't even turn as I approached, Hao?"

Hao scoffed. "No, that's not the reason. I ride like I do because my father was a very good rider and, as a child, we would ride together just for the fun of it." He laughed at the memory of silly things they would do to each other.

The Barbarian watched Hao carefully. "You love him very much."

"I did."

"Is something wrong in your relationship now?"

"Well, yes. He died with my brother on the Wall some time ago," Hao said flatly.

The Barbarian frowned. "You have lost only a fraction of the numbers we have."

"I didn't compare numbers. I simply told you what happened to my father, that's all. You still haven't told me your name."

The Barbarian broke into a smile. "Tzu said you liked to play hard."

"People are dying as we speak, and so, I am not playing." He held his stance as the Barbarian raised his chin. Hao nodded and turned back to watch the stream.

The Barbarian said quietly, "Porteous."

"What?" Hao queried.

"My name is Porteous."

Hao extended an arm. "I'm pleased to meet you, Porteous." Eventually, Porteous reciprocated, and they shook. Hao's smile was welcoming and genuine, and Porteous began to understand what Tzu had been saying.

The smell of food wafted over them from a good fire the men had started. Hao was famished. They ate mostly in silence and settled for the night.

Sleep didn't come easily for Hao. More than once, he lifted his head to look at the cave. He could neither see nor hear a thing, yet it beckoned him somehow. Maybe it was simply the fact that it was there and would provide a degree of comfort, yet they were outside subject to the changeable weather. He pulled his hat down over his ears and eventually drifted off to sleep.

Daylight had hardly broken when he woke. He rubbed the sleep from his eyes, stretched his back and eased out of his camp.

"Going somewhere, Hao?" The glint of a steel ring flickered in the firelight.

"Yes. I was going to relieve myself as I believe most people do in the morning."

Nose Ring rose menacingly to his feet. "That would be really handy, wouldn't it, Hao, to just slip out into the dark."

"Yeah, then make the big getaway on my mule."

The little man who'd been the lead rider laughed aloud. Nose Ring glared at him as he waved his blade over the fire like some kind of mystic dance. "Just don't forget you are now in *our* lands, man of the hat."

After breakfast, they rode back to the track they'd taken the day before and continued downriver. It was some time before they came to a wider section of the river that was relatively calm enough to cross. The water was, as expected, freezing but Hao felt invigorated as he leant over and swept some up with his hand. He splashed it over his face and head without a care. He had all day to dry.

They rode up onto the plains above and continued north for much of the day. The lack of conversation and rhythmic rocking in his saddle brought Hao's thoughts back to his dream of Kito. He pondered it over and over, but just couldn't fathom it. It was so real he'd have thought every bit of it was true and right, a memory of just yesterday, yet he had no idea where Kito was. Had Kito somehow shown him the actual pivotal point, sparking a war that had raged over a generation?

His mind whirled with questions. *How could this be? If it can't, then it was just a nonsense dream.* Though Hao could not suppress it. *What if I have been shown the truth? If it was the truth, why was I shown something from a generation ago, and what am I meant to do about it now? If I could give my life to undo it, I would, but life doesn't undo anything from even just the smallest moment ago. If it is termed 'ago,' it can't be changed, not for all the tears that rain from heaven.*

The day was drawing to a close as they arrived at a shallow valley. Again, a stream meandered through the middle, and again they turned upstream. The grassy meadow made for easy riding, broken only as they rode through pockets of small woodlands. The valley narrowed, and they slowed to a walk, finally stopping at a clump of trees. Tall rocky boulders encased a reasonably good shelter under a giant oak.

Hao dismounted next to Porteous. "Where exactly are we going?"

"Hao?"

Hao raised his eyebrows, crinkling his brow. "Please don't play games with me, I find it insulting."

Nose Ring stood from the fire he was preparing and spoke flatly in his own language to Porteous, who glanced briefly at Hao, then walked away. Nose Ring sneered at Hao. "Like I said, these are not your lands anymore. Do as you're told and you may make another sunrise."

"Don't really care one way or another," Hao said before he'd thought it through, but the words were out, and he'd show no fear now. Defiantly, they glared at one another, neither one backing down. It was only when one of the men said something to Nose Ring that he knelt and resumed tending to the fire once more.

With little else to do, as usual, Hao saw to his little horse. This time, it didn't try to bite him as Hao spoke to it in a low, soothing voice and gave it a long groom.

The next morning, they were on the track at first light. Surprisingly, this time they went over the stream and turned west. They continued for several more days.

Colourful blooms of wildflowers swayed under the weight of the working bees that swarmed them, happy to have survived another northern winter. Hao was not about to point them out to his unwanted company, but he still enjoyed them on the quiet. He surveyed his surroundings as they progressed along. Hoof marks and paw prints from the various game in the area pitted the sandy ground.

He craned his head around to Porteous. "It will be hard for me to shoot anything if I have no tools of the trade."

Nose Ring answered over Porteous. "I'll give you what you need when you need it. Until then, shut it."

Hao stiffened at the attitude of the mongrel. Without thought, he spun his horse and cantered directly into Nose Ring's. A short sword was quickly pressed against Hao's neck. Hao rose up in his saddle and leaned into the blade. "You knocked on my door; you offered the hunting trip, yet now we're out here you won't let me hunt!"

"I care not for your opinion."

"Well, I know that. But what are we doing out here?"

Porteous watched the first trickle of blood roll down Hao's neck. "Hao, you've made your point, though I feel you should just be patient."

Hao didn't relent. Nose Ring's desire to run him through was palpable. Hao tilted his head slightly, keeping his throat on the sword, tempting him further and egging him on. Finally, "Very well, but I hate time wasters.”

Nose Ring scowled. “I hate the hat.”

“I don’t care for your opinion,” said Hao in a flat tone.

Only when Porteous spoke in their native tongue did he sheathe his sword and move his horse on with a swift kick.

Silence resumed as they rode on. Numerous animal tracks lined the banks of a small stream. Hao studied them closely as they crossed it, but still they didn’t track them. He stopped midstream and let his horse have a good drink. He ignored the riders on the other side waiting for him.

Nose Ring called at him, “Oy! Man of the hat. Are you standing in the middle of the river hoping to grow some?”

Hao didn’t even look at him. “If I wanted to be as big and ugly as you, I would be up there standing in that stuff your horse is now dropping.”

Nose Ring spun in his saddle as the lead rider roared with laughter and turned his horse to ride away.

The men rode west for the rest of the day until they came to the edge of a forest. The lead rider scuttled his horse in small circles as he studied the ground. Porteous called out something to him, which he answered, but continued to look. Eventually, they rode a little way north and then entered the forest. As they rode through it, Hao began to feel uneasy. He looked back at Porteous, who looked back blank-faced, indicating nothing was astray.

They rode for some time, but Hao couldn’t shake the ill feeling.

Soon enough, they came to a small pond and dismounted. The little rider walked around the pond enthusiastically, holding a short pole with a hemp string and meat tied to its end. He threw the meat into the water and Hao waited patiently as the little man pulled up the line with a jerk. Clamped to the bait was a large, freshwater crayfish. When it was dumped onto the ground, it let go and he cast the line back into the murky water. Hao turned the cray onto its back to immobilise it, just as the little man drew out another. Hao placed it with the first one.

"Well, it's not my idea of a hunt but it's better than nothing at all." In no time at all, they had quite a collection of crayfish.

They took them over to the fire Nose Ring had prepared, and Hao put them on the ground next to him. Not even a grunt. Hao had his own way of cooking crays, and he pondered if their way would be the same.

Nose Ring cut the cray down the middle from head to tail and placed a few leaves over the two halves to help keep in the moisture and to add a little flavour. He put them down on the coals, seemingly finished in their preparation. Hao looked around the surrounding area. "Ha." He pulled up the longest, green leaves of the lemongrass plant and rolled them up tightly. Returning to the campfire, he dropped them into the heating water with a splash. The splash hissed in the fire, and Nose Ring gave Hao a cold look but said nothing.

That night, after they'd eaten their fill, Hao sat back and soaked up his surroundings and the crisp night air. "Thank you for cooking. Very nice." Nose Ring gave him a look that could have fallen the stars. Hao turned to the lead rider. "And I enjoyed your fishing skills." The little man chuckled.

"Hao?

"Yes, Porteous?"

"What was the grass you added?"

"Lemongrass. It's not just for flavour, it's also very good for indigestion and the liver."

"Until I saw you drink it, I wasn't so sure."

Hao smirked. "I couldn't help but notice none of you drank until I'd had my second sip."

"Wisdom with caution sustains life."

Hao held up his mug. "Quite so, Porteous."

"On the first night, I walked up behind you at the clifftop over the river. You didn't turn to face me. Was this not a little unwise?"

"I have lived unarmed with you all for some time now, and if you wanted me dead, you wouldn't need to take me for a walk in the meadows."

"And if you wanted us dead, Hao?"

"Remember that first night when we headed into that very camp, your horse faltered on the shale? My good friend Nose Ring over there," Hao indicated with his head, "his horse also stumbled. Both stumbled into mine. I could've turned to my right with my beautiful little mountain horse and bullied you both over the cliff, pulling his sword off his right hip as he went, then tried my luck with the last two." He took a long slurp of his lemongrass drink.

If they had their doubts before, they didn't now, as they sat stone-faced around the fire. Finally, Porteous responded curtly. "Quite so, Hao."

Nose Ring glared at Hao, who ignored him, which only made him madder.

***

The next morning, everyone was up as dawn broke. A quick meal of leftovers and they were on their way, continuing west. Hao had an uncanny feeling of familiarity of the area though he'd never been to this part of Middle Kingdom.

It was early afternoon when they came to a halt. The little rider dismounted and tied off his horse. Nose Ring rode past Hao, his smirk was also not to Hao's liking. Something was wrong.

"We will dismount but stay here, Hao," instructed Porteous. Hao shuffled about nervously. "What is it, Hao? You've been unsettled this afternoon."

Hao forced a smile. "We've ridden for many days, and I've yet to so much as load a bow."

"I see." Porteous was unconvinced.

Hao watched the other two men walk off with crossbows and a quiver of bolts each, the heavy-set man wandering close behind. He turned about searching his surroundings. There, in a small burst of sunlight shining through the forest, shone a large, white rock. Hao could almost see Kito sitting on it! A chill ran up his spine as he spun around.

"In the name of the Gods, Hao, what is it?" Porteous urged.

Hao held out a hand for silence and listened. Sure enough, the sound of a mighty waterfall rumbled some distance away in the valley below. On the cliff edge, the two men had cocked their bows and each dropped in a bolt. *This is no hunting trip. It is a murderous trip on the village of Norinko!*

He didn't take a moment to assess the situation. In one liquid motion, he snatched Porteous's knife from his hip and broke into a run, not making a sound as he deftly sprinted forward. He dug in the toes of his boots as best he could on the thick layer of rotting leaves. He was still too far away as the two men settled down to take aim but Hao didn't relent. The village would have no idea they were there, and Hao would not have put it past Nose Ring to shoot a child.

Nose Ring changed his posture; he had his first target. Hao didn't hear Porteous call his name, but the heavy-set man did. Casually, he turned about to see Hao sprinting at him. Hao drove the blade up under the chin of the man who wouldn't have known what hit him. He never made a sound as his limp body fell to the forest floor, leaves puffing out as Hao sprinted on.

Nose Ring and the little man just saw their companion fall as they turned their heads. There was barely a moment to take it in before Hao was on them. He threw himself sideways to take them both with a body blow.

The lead rider was too light for the force of Hao's speed and tumbled several times before disappearing over the cliff. Nose Ring, however, was quick to recover and scrambled up onto the flat above. Hao was upon him before he had time to draw his sword. The two men scuffled on the rocky ground. Hao was agile and quick, but Nose Ring was just too heavy for him.

Porteous watched the two men fighting it out. Hao was clearly out of his depth, but Porteous admired the man's valour. He just would not quit. For all the sickening blows he took, Hao came back for more. For every move the Barbarian made, he already had a countermove. Porteous almost found himself hoping for a miracle, though it was doubtful. The legend of the 'man of the hat,' was to end here and now.

It was inevitable that the Barbarian would finally get the better of Hao, and he did. Now pinned down, Hao couldn't move as Nose Ring straddled his full weight on top of him. Punches rained down as Nose Ring's voice drifted further away. Nose Ring wouldn't stop until the skull was completely collapsed. He was known for it. For Hao, it was almost peaceful now. The pain subsided as did Hao's defending arms, the ringing in his ears now gone, slipping away with his own life.

Suddenly, Porteous was knocked from his feet. His eyes widened as he heard the growl of a wolf. He rolled to his side as it ran past him in the direction of Nose Ring. Its powerful jaws gripped Nose Ring by the throat, shaking him violently. Blood-stained, razor-sharp teeth gripped tightly as they tore into him.

The wolf released the dead man and licked its bloody mouth. Watching on, Porteous fumbled in the dirt, searching frantically for his crossbow. The wolf made its track directly for him, its pure white hair now tainted red. Just feet away from him, it stopped and licked its lips again. Porteous was frozen in fear. He stared into the piercing, steel blue eyes of the huge beast, then, without reason, the wolf turned and trotted away.

Porteous scrambled to his feet, still searching for his crossbow. Seeing it under some leaves, he dived to retrieve it and spun back to look for the wolf. It stood on a large rock not too far away. Porteous quickly wiped away the leaves and took aim.

"If you shoot him, I will have to kill you." Hao's voice was as calm as ever.

Porteous kept the bow pointed at the wolf but slowly turned his head towards Hao. His face completely bloodied, he swayed, holding Nose Ring's loaded bow. Though he was the canniest fighter, Porteous wasn't sure he could make the shot count. "And if I don't shoot the animal, Hao?"

"Then we will both go back and tell Tzu the truth of this insane, shameful mess."

A short distance away, the wolf raised its head, drawing out a long, piercing howl. It chilled Porteous to the bone. "Why should I trust you?"

"If I wanted you dead, I would have shot already."

Porteous cautiously lowered his bow, and Hao did the same, taking out the bolt. He threw it at a tree and screamed long and hard. Porteous drew back, confused.

Hao released his rage without reserve. "In the name of the Gods, *WHY!?* Why could we not have just come out and shot a moose?" Spitting his words at Porteous. "This whole trip was but a lic, wasn't it?"

Porteous pulled his bolt from his bow. "I am afraid so, yes."

Hao turned his back and walked over to the cliff top to look down over the village. The village below was completely oblivious to the bloody death and murder that had just taken place above them. He could hear Porteous but didn't really care what he was doing. He could hear the clinking of steel but paid it no attention as he watched the children below playing. Only the occasional child's squeal or laugh rose high enough above the roar of the waterfall on the other side of the valley. He sighed in relief. If this was the last thing he was to do on this earth, in his mind, it was a good thing. Porteous was not going to take shots from here now, not today.

Porteous stopped just short of him. Still, Hao didn't turn. "Well, what is it you're going to do, Porteous?"

"What is it you wish me to do?"

Hao shrugged. "You could begin by telling me their names?"

"What would you care?"

"Do you wish to bury them?"

Porteous also looked down on the village. "Did you have a family of your own? I mean a wife and children?"

Hao shook his head. "Never had the chance, really. The Emperor put us on the Wall at a young age."

"Is this why you're against the throne?"

Hao clenched a fist of frustration. "I'm not against the throne! I'm against anything that is against the people. Any people! Damn I have told Tzu about this!"

"Very well. Go and wash up, Hao. I will deal with these two."

Hao nodded, then walked directly to Nose Ring's body. He knelt beside the big man and put a hand on his chest. "I guess the Gods wanted you more than I. Gods' speed, my foe." He reached down and undid Nose Ring's belt and pulled it out.

"Wait, Hao. What do you think you're doing?"

Hao stood and strapped the belt on. "I came on a hunt and a hunt I will have on our way back. It's a dangerous place, you know, Porteous. There are wolves and things out here." He looked sternly at Porteous, the best he could with a swelling face. "As I said before, if I wanted you dead it would have happened by now. A friend of mine used to say, 'A man has a right to protect himself.'"

Porteous smiled faintly. "He sounds like a wise man. Was he a good friend to you?"

Hao looked over to the large rock. The huge wolf was gone. "Yes, he is the best."

***

They headed away from the village for the rest of the day, then set camp by a stream that still had ice along its banks. Hao's face was swollen black and blue, practically sealing his eyes shut. It was not realistic to ride like this, so they stayed there for Hao's face to heal. He ate very little, just drank and slept by the fire. The white wolf would walk with him in his dreams. He found it comforting. He couldn't make sense of it or of Kito being one and the same, but he didn't question it. All he knew was Kito had found a way to be there for him when it really mattered. It was a strange place for Hao, with the wolf in his dreams. He and the wolf would track an elk or a bear. When they got within range, it would come to them. Some unspoken connection would pass between them, and the animal would go back to doing whatever it was doing, not one drop of blood spilled. He would spend time with the wolf at a pool with big, smooth rocks and a low, wide waterfall on the far side. Tammirie would be there waiting for them. Then he would wake and be back at the campfire with Porteous. Hao would find his way to the stream and take his time washing, the freezing water numbing his face. Porteous just watched and waited.

The trip back to the palace was relaxed, for Hao at least. He did get his moose, and he also rode the bigger horse. He and Porteous talked about their experience on the Wall. It was interesting to hear the other side. It was far more deadly to try and breach the Wall than to defend it, though Hao had already recognised this.

They also talked about the Sacred Skulls, and Porteous told of how it was said that their Blue Skull was gifted to the former Emperor for the joining of the parents of Tzu Hsi. Hao now knew it was not just a dream he'd had of Kito; it really was the beginning of the war. The Barbarians didn't just want their land back; they wanted their Blue Skull.

As they neared the gates to the palace, Porteous leaned across to Hao with his hand out. Hao removed his belt and Porteous tucked it in his saddlebag. Again, Porteous held out his hand. Hao took off his quiver of bolts and his crossbow and handed them over. Porteous beckoned a third time, wiggling the fingers of his stretched-out palm. Hao made an exaggerated huff and pulled the knife from behind his back.

Porteous smirked. "Now, my friend, we can approach the gates and not get shot."

Hao patted down his clothes. "But a man just feels naked without his weapons."

"Trust me, Hao …" Porteous raised one eyebrow. "… we wouldn't be approaching the gates together if you were naked."

"Fair enough."

They entered with little talk. Hao held his head high and ignored the stares, not making eye contact. The mountain horse dragged a sled with Hao's moose on it, making the most annoying grinding noise on the cobbles all the way to the palace. The inconvenience of it tickled Hao.

Once down in the palace caves, the moose drew the attention of the gathering men. They spoke in their native tongue, much to Hao's disappointment. He would have enjoyed discussing his catch, though Porteous, on the other hand, seemed to be doing well talking of it himself. Alienated from the conversation, he tended their horses.

Eventually, Porteous came over. "I have a message for you to go and see Tzu."

Hao stopped grooming. "I'm not sure I could find my way."

"I will be accompanying you." Hao looked at the horses. "I will have one of our men care for them, Hao. Come now." Hao laid down the brush, and Porteous led the way.

When they arrived at the foyer, several guards joined them. As Hao saw it, the guards could only assume that with only the two of them coming through the gate, something had gone horribly wrong.

Tzu was talking with several other men on the lawn. Hao descended the stairs onto the grassy lawn without slowing his pace as he walked towards Tzu. The other men glared at him as they parted ways, making room for him.

Tzu held out his right arm, though his face wasn't welcoming. Hao stepped in close and, with all his might, gave Tzu his best left hook, followed by one quick right jab. Tzu rolled and came up on one knee fast with his hands held out wide. "Hold!"

Hao spat on the ground. There were more sharp points at him than he could care about. "I went in good faith! I trusted you as an honourable man, but you set me up from the start!"

Tzu rubbed his jaw. "That's not a bad left swing you have there, Hao."

"Damn that and damn your friendship!" The sharp points prevented him from moving any closer.

Tzu's voice was low and precise. "You've had your jab, now settle down so we can talk like civilised …"

Hao leaned forward, and the spears clattered as they moved to adjust their position. He pointed his finger angrily at Tzu over the sharp, steel points. "*You* will not lecture *me* on being civilised. I took no pleasure in killing your men, and I will thank you to make up your mind just what it is you want from me! I would sooner meet my Maker than send any more to meet theirs."

"Well, I'm the right man for that." Tzu waved to his men. "Do not let down your guard for one moment. Put him in his room and *do not* let him leave."

As they shoved Hao along, Porteous called. "Hao."

"What?"

"The one you called Nose Ring … his name was Vulin. They were Vulin, Rabin and Mitron."

Hao nodded and walked on, the clatter of uneasy Barbarians surrounding him.

7 Jabali's Dream

The Emperor was sound asleep, and so, taking advantage of the moment, Kito went to the rear of the galley and sprang onto its roof. His energy was near-spent, but there was still much to be done. He had to grab these opportunities when they arose. The block that prevented his abilities was ever present. He lowered his head and took some long, slow breaths.

He shifted his focus to his next destination. The surging vessel slowed as he was drawn to the light that burst behind his closed eyes, drawing him back to the past, the time and place of his intense focus. He could hear the ship's metal pullies clinking softly against the masts. Clink, clink, as they drifted further away and faded. Then silence.

***

River mist rose from the still waters as Kito and his old cabin friend, Jabali, walked along the dark wharf of the city. Only a few torches burned in the moonless night. Jabali was not of this land, and as such was much taller than any there, but Kito's strides were not easy to keep up with. Tonight, however, Jabali neither limped nor had his cane with him.

"Kito, what are we doing in Samos again?"

Kito's expression was wise beyond his young years. "Why is it you worry about so many things, my friend?"

"I'm confused, Kito. I do seem to have forgotten just what it is we're doing here in Samos. Did I not watch you leave Devil's Island already?"

Small ripples sparkled and appeared to dance as they caught the lit torches before fading as the waters lapped the shore. "I feel this is a dream." Kito didn't seem to be paying his concerns any attention. "Is this a dream?" he urged.

"I'm not altogether happy with the Emperor's vessels. I'd like your opinion about their construction," offered Kito in a low voice.

"Oh, yes, right. Hang on, Katanning and Kalgan worked on those. I know they are young men, but their work was always first rate whilst in my keep," Jabali insisted as he looked up at the man in grey with his hood up. He would never admit it but he was glad Kito was there as his friend. A chill ran down his spine anyway as Kito looked at him questioningly.

"What?" whispered Jabali.

"When they were in your keep, you looked over their work and I'm sure Admasin was even more critical. Now they are the ones overlooking everyone's work. Do you really think either of those two men was completely ready for such responsibility, such leadership?"

Jabali stepped back, almost offended. "I'll have you know both of those boys have grown up into fine young men."

Kito rested his big hand on Jabali's shoulder. "And when they worked under your leadership, I'm sure they were, but now?"

"Nonsense. I'll not stand here and listen to one word more." As if he were wafting a fly off his shoulder, he pushed Kito's hand away and marched towards the first of the Emperor's vessels tied at the wharf.

The wharf was reasonably well lit as he strode out with plans rolling over in his mind. At the gangplank, a guard snored from his wooden chair, tipped back against the far side of the vessel. He hesitated.

"No one here can harm you, Jabali, not here, not now, but please try not to knock anything over."

Jabali scrunched his face as Kito waved a hand of invitation to the plank. He snatched up a torch in frustration and walked on.

First, he headed down the stairs and stopped. He looked above and below them, every plank, wedge, nail and screw. He walked directly to the master pole and looked up and down again, then walked around it twice as Kito waited patiently. Without word, he went down to the next level. Again, he scrutinised the workmanship.

He grumbled under his breath, disappointment evident on his face. "Hand me that bar."

Kito found the steel bar Jabali was referring to. "You won't make too much noise, will you?"

Unresponsive, Jabali handed his torch to Kito, not taking his eyes off the planks at his feet. He placed the bar in a narrow gap and leaned his weight onto it. He eased it back and forth until finally the plank popped out with a crack. He repeated the process until there was a big enough gap for him to slip down into the depths of the huge vessel.

"Here …"

Kito saw the small hand come up from the dark. He leant over and placed the torch in it. The flame crackled as Jabali drew it down into the hull. He looked at the base of the master pole. It was cut into the spine of the vessel behind the main rib. "No, no, no …"

The torch reappeared through the gap and Kito took it without word. Jabali climbed out and placed the timbers back, pressing them into place, sombre-faced. At the side of the vessel, he snatched the torch from Kito and leant over to search the exterior planking. He groaned with effort as he stood upright again.

"Jabali, it's almost time I got you home to Devil's Pass. The yard is under the Emperor's employment now."

"What? Oh yes, if you say so, Kito."

The sleeping guard snored on as they crossed the plank onto the wharf. Jabali grabbed Kito's arm.

"Jabali?"

"I must have one more look. I need to look on this other vessel." He pointed eagerly to a second vessel, markedly larger than the other one, moored alongside.

Kito looked up at the night's sky. "We don't have much time, my friend."

"I won't be long, promise."

Jabali shook his head at its twin masts, one forward of the other for the sheer length of it. Kito could faintly see its name, *Ocean Asset*. He let out a scoff.

"What?" Jabali queried.

"It seems Mr Chun has named this vessel after himself."

"I'm not sure how the Emperor will take to that. Still, I don't know if Asset Chun is a very smart man either." He crossed the gangplank, torch in hand and went directly to the stairs with Kito on his heels.

"Jabali, wait."

"I told you already, I won't be long." He hit the bottom step and froze at the guard staring wide-eyed in the direction of his torchlight. The guard slid out his sword, swearing under his breath and waved it seemingly at nothing. Not once did the guard look directly at Jabali as he lamely swatted at thin air.

Jabali swapped the torch to the other hand. The guard leapt the other way, swiping his sword as he went. Again, he didn't seem to see Jabali, although the light must have flashed over his entire body. Bemused, Jabali swapped hands again and circled the guard, keeping a distance. The guard swore as he spun around frantically with his sword. His eyes bulged in his pale face as he began sweating profusely.

From behind, Kito's hand grabbed the guard's tightly clenched fist on his sword, and his other hand came quickly over the guard's nose and mouth. He slumped almost immediately, and Kito eased him to the floor.

Jabali looked almost disappointed. "I was having fun, Kito."

"No, Jabali, that was mean, and before we left you made me a promise to stay quiet and do as I ask."

Jabali smirked. "Oh yeah. Alright, come on then." He looked for the stairs to the bottom of the vessel. Both men stopped in their tracks on the second level. Before them were innumerable hammocks, and under those were just as many sleeping mats. Concern fractured Jabali's face. He pointed to another set of stairs. This level was the same as the last. Endless hammocks and mats. In the supply room below, they gasped at the room stacked high with armour and weapons. This was a warship. There would be hundreds of guards to come on this vessel alone. And there were four other vessels to match.

Jabali grabbed a steel bar from the stack of tools and hurriedly began to pry out the planks around the master pole. He grabbed his torch and slipped below. Kito couldn't remember if he'd ever heard Jabali swear so, but tonight he certainly did. The torch came back up, followed by Jabali. He placed the boards back and pressed them in. He paced about the floor, shaking his head. "None of this is properly secured. Katanning was always complaining that all the screws were a waste of time and effort." He stamped his foot.

Suddenly, a hand came over his nose and mouth. The torch dropped to the floor as Jabali tried to pry the hand off his face, but it was hopeless, and his head began to swim. Dizzy, the light faded and Jabali relaxed as his friend whispered, "It's alright, I have you, my friend. Relax. Sleep."

***

Jabali thrashed about, struggling for breath. He twisted around, entangled in his sheets, then rolled off his bed, landing with a thump on his cabin floor. The first hint of daylight shone through the window. He scratched his head and looked at his feather pillow with his face still imprinted on it. *Just a dream, Patch, you silly man. It was just a dream,* he assured himself.

He fumbled around and got dressed. As he exited his room, he stopped and looked back at the dishevelled sheets on his bed. Towel in one hand and cane in the other, he closed the door and began his walk in the soft, morning light.

At Balzac's wharf, he undressed, folded his clothes neatly in a pile and placed them on the edge of the wharf with his towel and cane. Quietly, he hobbled into the warm water. The fresh water took his weight, and he pushed off gently, doing breaststroke just as his big friend had shown him. Staying close to the wharf, he eased out into deeper water, trying not to think about the fact he couldn't touch the bottom, but fear began overruling his common sense.

He was about to turn back when he heard the surge of water around the wharf poles. Through the splashes, he could see a dorsal fin and began to laugh. "So, is it coincidence that you show up this morning, or did our friend in common send you to settle my nerves?" A dolphin bumped into him gently. He laughed again. "Nice to see you this morning." He grabbed at the dorsal fin and it dragged him away. He was happy with whatever a dolphin did whilst he was holding it; never did they fail him. Sometimes they would take him right out to the very end of the wharf and back, but he never fretted. He always loved it, though today they were taking him a little further out than usual. Jabali still smiled as they made a large arc around the bay.

As always, when it was almost breaking day, he returned to shore and dried off. He thanked his friends for their participation in starting his day in the best possible way. Placing his hat on and swiping up his cane, he turned to the alleyway once more. He thought about his cabin; it was so quiet these days.

For Jabali, it was an arduous walk up onto the ridge, but it was also salvation from the confines of the cabin. Over the inland sea, the turquoise water rippled in the morning sunlight. In the distance, he could see the mainland, Middle Kingdom. He pondered how he had come all that way to this island. In the sea below his standpoint, dark shadows swam so gracefully that it was hard to tell just how fast they moved, or how big they were. They were nothing like the friends that joined him this morning. He shuddered. *Never again will I pass over these seas.*

With a flick of his cane, he turned and headed back down into the jungle. He thought about all the predators that could take his life here. When he was in Balzac's clinker out on the water, he was so afraid he could barely open his eyes, so now he was stuck on this island. He had often wondered how it came to be. He was so different to these people and he hated the water, yet here he was on a group of islands.

Solitude in the cabin was the only future he could see for himself right now, and at times, he almost wished to bump into one of those deep-sea predators. He looked around the jungle-covered island and forced a small smile. *There are worse places to be marooned.*

If he ever was to return to Samos, he was sure he could get work. His reputation alone would secure him work as a designer at any of the bigger yards. But he couldn't bring himself to so much as buy a ticket to cross. Not that he had the money. No, he was on this island for a reason, of that he was sure. But what that was, he could not know. Sometimes, late at night that was what kept him awake – the not knowing.

Jabali descended to the small pond at the end of Balzac's grounds. The fresh water was so clear it was almost surreal. He shuffled around to the pebble beach where the water flowed out. Leaning on his cane, he reached down and put his hand in the water. It was cooler than the ocean. Vessels were less buoyant in fresh water than salt. Men too. He would not be swimming in this water. Under his instruction, and with the help of Balzac's men, he did though have fresh water to drink and to wash in at his cabin. Balzac was also delighted with his instalments. The flushing toilet was more than Balzac had dreamed of. No more bed pans for him, although no one else got such luxury.

8 Plans

On this beautiful evening under the setting sun, Balzac and the visiting family ate on the balcony overlooking the boardwalk and bay. As always, Balzac and Lucia talked business. Sharia was talking to Yuna about her brother. "I am surprised that you haven't heard of Karlec, Yuna. He runs a hostel for single and abused women. Apparently he is well known for his good work."

Yuna was quite confused; she'd lived in the city her entire life. "I'm sorry, Sharia, never have I heard of such a place. Still, after the fires, I expect he will be quite busy now."

Sharia gasped. "Oh yes, I had not thought of that. It would explain why we haven't seen him for so long. He did come out to see us quite often you know."

Admasin sat silently on the side. Lucia had suddenly gone very quiet, hearing her mother's discussion. She needed to change the subject, quickly. She looked at her dear old friend. "Admasin, is everything good with you?"

The quiet group looked at Admasin. "Oh yes, Lucia. The sunsets here I feel are something I will never quite get used to."

"I have lived here since I married Balzac and the sunsets still mesmerise me, Admasin," Sharia agreed.

Lucia continued. "We could bring Kalgan out to work with us if you wish. If he wants, we could bring Katanning over as well. Both would be major assets to the business."

Admasin shook his head. "Oh Lucia, you are sharp. No, I sent a note to him some time ago because he and Katanning had worked closely with the first vessel, but he said they already had work again and wished to stay. I told him I was proud and happy for them both." He spoke the words but couldn't look at Lucia whilst he said them.

The evening passed and the sea breeze brought a little chill in the air. Balzac led them inside for tea and to look over the plans and the re-setting of the master pole. He rolled out the sheets of paper and Admasin looked them over. He had questioned himself over his suspicions of how the stranger living in the rear of Balzac's complex had assisted Balzac with the designs. He looked at the plans before him. This time there was no doubt. It could only be the work of the man that masterminded the biggest invention of their time, the vessel of sails.

His fingers traced over the drawings as he read the plans. The hand work was not as neat but the man was, after all, disfigured. The fact that he still breathed, let alone was walking again, was a credit to him. Admasin's heart swelled with pride. There would be less men needed on board this sailboat and therefore less space taken up for food supplies. Unlike the traditional rowing vessels this would leave more room for paying goods and, for the first time, the goods could go below deck. Balzac as always, took the credit for the improvements from the first vessel. *Tweaking betterments,* as Lucia had come to call them.

"Balzac, I seem to have a problem with the timber left over to date. Would you mind going over some figures with me?" Admasin requested .

Lucia leant back in her chair. There indeed was some timber left over but they both knew exactly where it was surplus. *What is the old boy up to now?*

Balzac, by contrast, seemed almost overjoyed to be asked back out to the vessel manufacturing. "Yes, of course, Admasin, although I am a little busy right now."

"Any time in the next couple of weeks would be good."

Balzac nodded. "That would be quite alright."

Admasin gestured to Sharia. "I would be most delighted if you could also make the journey. The vessel is in the finishing stages now and please believe me when I say, she is quite the sight."

Sharia was a little taken aback with the invite. Balzac never included her. "Well, if you think it would be appropriate, Admasin."

"By then the master pole will be in place, and we will be closing the deck in around it to complete the major construction. I think it would be very appropriate to show you what your daughter has been doing all these years, Sharia." He didn't dare look at Lucia. He sensed it would be a look he may not survive.

Sharia held her hand to her chest, positively glowing with excitement. "Admasin, that would be truly wonderful."

Admasin clapped his hands together. "Well, that is settled then. We will have you both over in the next two weeks."

Yuna whispered in Admasin's ear. He looked up. "Ah, my dear wife, as always the hostess. Could we have you both for lunch, Sunday two weeks from now?"

Balzac looked at Sharia, her eyes sparkling with anticipation. He let out an involuntary grunt. "Well yes, Yuna, most kind. Lunch on Sunday in two weeks it is then."

Now disgruntled about the women being involved in *his* project, he leant forward and swiped up the last piece of cake on the small table.

Sharia didn't even seem to notice. "I know that you would like to get away early in the morning. What time should I organise breakfast for?"

Admasin and Lucia had previously agreed they would leave well before dawn and would skip eating in lieu of the early departure. Admasin dipped his head. "Thank you, Sharia. I thought breakfast just after sunrise in the gazebo would suffice."

Lucia snapped her gaping mouth shut. "I thought we were ..."

"Now Lucia, I know your mother brought you up better than to rush off after being made so welcome."

"Mother had nothing to do with my upbringing and I will thank you not to make any assumptions about my life here, Admasin,"

Lucia retorted.

Startled by her abrupt manner, the group fell silent. Never had Admasin known her to snap a nasty word at anyone, not even the staff. Balzac rose to his feet with the look of the darkest storm, but Admasin hastily rose from his seat. "Sharia, I'm afraid we may have to leave at the earlier time after all. I'd forgotten Lucia and I had agreed that we would be back with the men just after first light. It does take a little time to get there after all."

Without waiting for a reply, he turned to Lucia. "Lucia, may I see you in my room please." Lucia was staring at her father. Admasin lowered his voice. "Lucia, that would be now please. This old man is needing his bed, my dear."

Yuna kissed Sharia on the cheek and bid her leave to Balzac. "Please forgive me, this old girl needs her sleep also."

Balzac finally stopped glaring at Lucia in order to farewell Yuna properly. Admasin held his hand out for Lucia. She didn't address either of her parents as she marched out, leaving Admasin's empty hand hanging in the frosty air.

He awkwardly turned it to Balzac and shook his hand. "I thank you both again for your extended hospitality. So, it is settled. I expect I will see you both in two weeks so we can return the favour. Thank you both again." He tried not to hurry his exit as Yuna gave chase after Lucia.

On his way down the corridor to their room he considered how he would deal with Lucia and her outburst. It was hard not to look at Lucia as their own daughter. They had all worked together for years and mourned their loss together. He was a little embarrassed for her behaviour towards her own parents. By the time he got to the door he was just as annoyed. He might well give her a piece of his mind. *Yes. I just might.*

He swung open the door to see Lucia hugging Yuna and sobbing openly. Yuna shook her head. 'I don't know,' she mouthed over Lucia's shoulder.

Admasin didn't say a word.

The next morning, the three were met in the foyer by Balzac. Balzac and Lucia ignored each other as they set out down the boardwalk to the wharf.

Just as they entered the wharf, they heard a splash and stopped. Admasin took his opportunity. "You two ladies go on whilst I speak with Balzac for a moment."

Lucia needed no encouragement to continue, though Yuna was surprised. "Really, Admasin?"

"Yes, my dear, really."

Admasin waited for the two women to depart, then gently spoke over the still water. "Good morning, Jabali. Balzac and I would like a word, if you wouldn't mind."

There was no answer, but the gentle ripple told them that Jabali was indeed on his way over. He stopped just on the edge of the light reflecting over the water. "Good morning to you both."

"Morning, Jabali." Admasin smiled. "Yuna and I are having Sharia and Balzac over for lunch in two weeks, Sunday. We would all love to have you come over with them."

Unresponsive, Jabali stood waist deep in the water like a sunken stone. Admasin threw his baited words to reel the man in. "Lucia and I are nearing the completion of the vessel you saw some time ago. You seemed to show great interest in the development of it. It's just for the day, and I do owe you my hospitality, if you remember."

The voice in return was unsure. "Yes. I remember, Mr Admasin."

"By the time you come over, the master pole will be in, though we are having trouble with the rudder, you know. I feel it is just too large for the men to push. Anyway, that's not your concern, is it, Jabali? Sunday, two weeks from now then?"

"Yes. I suppose so, Mr Admasin."

"Excellent. Balzac, you will be good to see Jabali is escorted over, as you have done in the past then?"

Balzac was a little lost for words; there was no real way to say no. "Err … well, yes, of course. That is, if Jabali really wants to?"

Admasin was quick to prevent any other option. "Very well, it's settled. Jabali, we will be happy to have you over with Sharia and Balzac." He gave a small bow. "Enjoy your swim."

Jabali's voice quavered as he responded. "Have a good day, Admasin."

The dropping of the 'Mr' was not lost on Admasin. *If this man Jabali isn't Patch, I will swim back to the mainland with Yuna stood on my back.*

Admasin hadn't swum since he was a child.

9 The Rudder

On the Sunday two weeks later, Admasin stirred the coals in the fireplace. The wood crackled and the sparks popped as they flew up the stone chimney. The kettle over the fire had been loaded with herbs the night before and left to fuse overnight. He pulled out two cups on the ready.

A voice came from the bed. "Why are you up so early? All the men are having a sleep this morning. Why are you pushing so hard?"

"You can't stop old habits, my dear."

"No, but at your age, you don't need to start any new ones either. What bothers you, old man?"

Admasin looked over his shoulder. "Mind your tongue, woman, or I will show you some youth you might not be ready for."

Yuna scoffed. "Oh, a lady would be so lucky." Her smile slipped away. "Though you haven't answered my question."

He sighed and peered into the bubbling pot. Taking up a cloth, he swung the kettle from over the fire, poured their morning drinks, added a little fresh water to each cup, then topped up the kettle and put it back. He thought about how to answer Yuna's question honestly. He turned to Yuna, who was watching him closely, and handed her the cup. "Careful, my dear, it's hot."

"Like it is every other morning. Now what bothers you?"

He looked at her with a cheeky grin. "By the Gods, they did try me when they sent me you."

Her eyes twinkled in her old face. "You must have been a fine, fine man in your former life to deserve me in this one."

Admasin slapped his knee and roared with laughter. "I don't know what it is about you, woman, but you sure know how to turn it around on me." He continued to laugh.

"Yes, my dear, but you still haven't told me. What bothers you? Even your sleeps haven't been settled of late."

He sat on the edge of her bed. "As always, you are one step ahead of me, my dear. I have been dreaming of the grey man."

Yuna pulled back. "What, you mean the one called Kito?"

"The very same."

"Why is it you have had him on your mind? He has been gone for some time now."

"I know what you say. I think it is not a question of *on* my mind though, rather more like he has been *coming* to me."

Yuna frowned. "I don't believe I follow, dearest."

"He has been coming to me asking me to be ready soon. He has asked that we be ready for war with the Asset."

Yuna gasped with her hand over her mouth. "Dear Gods, no. Not war – not out here. How can we help with just one vessel and no warriors? This cannot be so; we are too old to fight. Please tell me you are not going to be a part of this nonsense."

Admasin took up the hand of his only woman and looked into her eyes. "My dear wife, I know you have given me everything I have asked of you, but I feel I must do this one last thing."

Tears welled up in her eyes. "No, no, no, Admasin. Why must you go? Why?"

"Because Kito asked me to."

Yuna stopped shaking her head. "What is it he wants with an old man?"

Admasin drew back just a little. "It is not me he wants, it's the one we call Jabali. He says if I go, we will get Jabali to go."

"What is it he wants with the cripple?"

"Careful dear, he is badly burned but I don't think it's fair to call him a cripple."

"True, though he is hardly battle-ready, is he?"

"Point taken."

"Promise you will return to me, my love."

Admasin was already shaking his head. "How is a man to be good for his word if he is to make such a promise?"

She shook his hand with great vigour. "Promise me," she pleaded desperately.

He looked into her eyes as he had a thousand times before, still she could capture him and all he was. After all these years, his admiration for this woman did not waver. "Yuna, I promise I will return to you when this is done." Slowly, he stood, removed his garments and slipped back into bed. "We don't have long," he whispered.

She looked adoringly at the only man she had ever loved. "That's alright, my love, this morning, I won't take long."

***

Later that day and in the shade of the huge trees over the spring, Balzac guided the small vessel alongside the rooted bank. Normally, they would stay out on the sandy beach, but having Sharia on board, Balzac had insisted they take extra men and row against the current of the mighty spring.

A man was quick over the side to tie off the vessel, then to offer a hand to Sharia. Jabali, after being frozen to the spot white-knuckled for so long, took a moment to urge himself to move. Eventually, he reached out to the side and took the man's outstretched hand. Clumsily, he bumped his knee on the side of the vessel as he stepped out. The man cringed at the sound of it, though Jabali never uttered a word. Pleased with the feel of land under his feet, he made his way across the jungle floor, his cane prodding between the tree roots.

He held his cloth mask to see better and gazed up at the sight before him. He smiled at the vessel, *his vessel,* complete with master pole. His skin tingled as he walked slowly along its length. He looked up at the smooth sides. *Just as me and Admasin had planned on the first model.* He couldn't help but reach up to touch it and run his hand along its side. It was the work of the very best of foremen;

only one foreman could achieve this finish. Admasin. He was oblivious to Balzac standing behind him.

"Jabali, are you alright?"

Choked up, Jabali couldn't even try and speak. All Balzac got was a nodding of the broad, brimmed hat.

"Ah, there you are, and I am so pleased you could make it also, Sharia."

Balzac and Sharia turned to see Admasin, full of smiles and pride, coming their way. Balzac stepped forward with his hand out. "Good morning to you, Admasin." They shook hands, then Balzac bowed.

Admasin kissed Sharia on either cheek. "Please, come on up. Lucia and Yuna have made refreshments for us all."

Sharia couldn't see the entirety of the vessel from down on the ground. She'd never seen a vessel out of the water before. She looked at Admasin, who was now with Jabali, whose hat was shaking, refusing something quite firmly. Balzac, oblivious to this, just strolled along looking at the sheer size of the vessel. The biggest vessel he had ever owned by far.

In moments, Admasin passed them again. "We are very pleased with the vessel, but before I can show you over her, we must go upstairs for refreshments."

There were workers idling about, some Sharia knew, but many she didn't recognise. Most said their welcomes or at least bowed and acknowledged her with smiles. Still, as friendly as they were, it was a little overwhelming. She had not been to this island since Lucia was a child. It was not something they usually did, but this time she held Balzac's hand.

"Mind your step, please," said Admasin. "We have yet to have anyone badly hurt. I would hate for either of you to ruin this for us."

Balzac snorted. "For a moment, I thought you were caring for us."

Admasin chuckled. The staircase was wide enough for two, but Sharia remained one step behind Balzac. She gasped in awe at what met her at the top. The huge room had large openings at the front where storm shutters were tied up to the roof. Beyond that, she could see the vessel stretched out before them. She walked forward without Balzac as the vessel loomed out before her until she was out on the porch holding the handrails. They had come up several flights of stairs and were now level with the top deck of the vessel.

Yuna interrupted Sharia, who was now looking down in amazement at the men below. "Welcome to our home, Sharia. It is my pleasure to have you here."

Sharia slowly pulled her eyes from the vessel. "Hello, Yuna." They kissed on both cheeks. She looked at the table already prepared with lemon juice and hot scones with jam. "Oh, Yuna, did you and Lucia do these this morning?"

Yuna scoffed. "No. Lucia has been on the vessel since first light. That girl has something special about her, you must be so proud."

Silence fell over the group as Balzac pulled out a chair for Sharia and sat himself down, neither one responding directly to Yuna's words. "This really is quite adequate, thank you, Yuna," Sharia said simply.

Admasin shot a look of concern to her but she didn't falter. "Please, make yourselves at home. It is nice to have you both in our humble abode."

They made light talk around the table. Sharia asked a lot of questions about feeding so many men and Admasin explained that some men were better at fishing and some at hunting so they did have a good balance. It was evident that Yuna did all the cooking.

Sharia looked to Yuna. "So, where is this daughter of ours?"

Admasin quickly intervened. "When you are in the hull of this vessel, you might be surprised to know that you cannot hear anything from outside."

Sharia stopped cutting another scone for Balzac and looked up. "What, nothing at all?"

Admasin shook his head. "I apologise. Since I haven't gone down to see her, she would have no idea that you are here."

Over on the vessel, they heard talking and footsteps.

"We cannot do anymore until me and Admasin have decided about the rudder. Now, would you go fishing for the day."

Two men were walking with Lucia. One was arguing the point. "I understand what you are saying, I just think we could …"

Lucia stopped the two men in their tracks as she held up a firm hand. "I am not paying you to do something today only to pay you to undo it next week, now would you just go fishing. It is Sunday, you know."

The men stepped back and bowed. "Yes, Miss," they said in unison.

Lucia softened her tone. "Just go and have some fun. We do occasionally allow it, you know."

Brought around to the idea of a day out fishing, the two men smiled as they left.

Sharia was speechless as her daughter walked towards them dressed in leather pants with a short-sleeved shirt, sweat trickling down her chest. Lucia pulled some of her long, wet hair from her face as she reached the gang plank leading from the vessel to their balcony. Her face lit up as she saw Balzac. "You are here already!"

Balzac stood with arms outstretched to his daughter. "Come to Papa."

Lucia waved her hand. "No, you really do not want to hug me right now." Sharia didn't laugh as Balzac grabbed his daughter and kissed her lightly on each cheek. Lucia then stepped around him. "Mother, I wasn't sure you would come today."

"Yes. Yuna has made quite the effort." Without standing, she gave a fake kiss on either cheek.

Lucia stepped back. "Excuse me, it is twice as hot in the hull of the vessel as it is here. I must freshen up."

Sharia turned back to the table. "Yes indeed, dear." She didn't see the look Lucia gave as she turned away and headed to her room.

Admasin coughed lightly and resumed his conversation with Balzac. "Besides the timber calculations, we have a problem with the rudder."

Balzac looked almost panicked. "Yes, I now remember you mentioned it when you last visited, though as I had said, I have been quite busy, you know."

Admasin let him finish, then nodded. "Yes, Balzac. You did say you were busy. I was just talking about the problems we have. It is to be expected. With such a new design, we have new problems." He paused for a moment. "I feel Patch would have an answer. He had said it would be a problem before we even trialled the model. I could not believe it when we proved him right."

"Patch never went on his own trial?"

Admasin watched Balzac very carefully. "Well, no, he was totally afraid of the water."

Yuna watched Admasin as he baited Balzac, though for what she couldn't know. Balzac was now clearly choking on more than his scone. She rose from her seat with the return of Lucia and poured another goblet of lemon juice. "Here, my dear, you must be parched."

Lucia bowed lightly to Yuna as she took it. She downed the goblet, and Yuna refilled it. Lucia looked at Balzac. "Father, is everything good with you? You looked positively pale."

Admasin rose, slapping Balzac on the back gently. "He had a piece of scone go the wrong way; he has choked a little, that's all, my dear."

Balzac drank a little bit of lemon juice, and perplexed, Lucia watched him closely as she drank more of her own, then suggested, "Shall we go and look over the vessel then?"

Sharia remained seated. "No, Lucia. I do feel someone needs to stay and help with the dishes."

Yuna quickly interjected. "No, no Sharia, you simply *must* look over Lucia's work. I have seen it grow from the jungle floor itself. You have always served me, now please, let me serve you." She bowed deeply and held it.

Sharia could push this no further. "Very well, Yuna, but only because you said so."

"Well, so long as that is settled then, Sharia shall we?" Lucia turned and marched out over the gangplank. A little shocked, Yuna glanced at Admasin, who looked to the floor with a subtle nod. He held out his arm for Sharia to follow Lucia, but she hesitated and looked at Balzac. "After you, of course."

Balzac rolled his eyes. "Yes, I know dear, if the plank can take my weight, it will be safe for you, right?" Admasin laughed to lighten the air a little. Even Sharia had trouble keeping a straight face.

Balzac walked towards Lucia with pride written all over his face. She stood waiting for everyone to arrive before she started, pointing up the master pole. "This is the master pole."

Balzac held a hand up to his face. "My Gods, never have I seen such a thing. "Admasin, can you even get it out of the jungle?"

Admasin stood beside him. "As always, Balzac, very astute. Yes, we will have to cut some branches, but we will not lose any of the trees. We want to use this site again, providing the launch goes well."

Balzac laughed boldly. "Of course, providing you can sail this vessel."

Lucia nudged him gently. "Oh, she will sail, Father." She then pointed. Sharia and Balzac turned to see ropes and pulley blocks tied down on the deck. "There are a set on either side to tilt the sail to suit the breeze. This vessel can catch wind from almost right beside her and turn it to push in line with the vessel."

"Dear Gods …" was all Sharia said without realising it.

Admasin walked to a hatch and opened it with a bang. "Take your time, my friends, there are a lot of steps. It will be quite pleasant for a short time. The men have opened all the side hatches for your visit today."

They all headed down the stairs, Lucia coming last. She heard Sharia gasp at the room on the first level. Balzac turned about. "I cannot believe the space in here."

Admasin placed his hands on his hips, inwardly proud of what they'd achieved. "Because we think we will have more power from sails, we have gone wider. Also, of course, we needed no room for the oarsmen, so this will be the cargo room. With the wider vessel and a lower cargo hold, we feel we can load her up a little more."

Balzac raised his eyebrows, looking a little serious. "You are putting a lot of faith in this wind of yours, Admasin."

"Indeed, I am, Balzac. How many times do you hear of seamen saying they came through having no wind? Always a swell and always a chop, albeit sometimes a light one." Balzac gave little in response.

Lucia walked forward to the hatch, and knowingly, Admasin turned to the rear of the vessel, talking as he walked. "The large hole back here is not a design flaw. We simply haven't finished the plans for the rudder." Just as he got to the hole, he looked down to see the black, broad-brimmed hat disappearing around the vessel. "Jabali, is that you there?" Admasin waited patiently.

Finally, he came back. "Good morning to you, Mr Admasin."

"Good morning to you, Jabali and, it's just Admasin, not Mister. Jabali, we will be here a little while yet, but if you like, you can head upstairs and help yourself to some scones and juice from the table."

Jabali bowed, still not looking up directly at Admasin. "Most kind. I just might do so. Thank you, Admasin."

"Not at all, Jabali. Maybe you could still be there when we have finished our tour."

"Maybe … Admasin."

"No rush. We will be some time yet." As Jabali scurried away, Admasin grinned and turned towards the forward hatch. Balzac spoke again about how much room there was. He and Sharia looked up at the open loading hatches.

Admasin stepped into the hatch leading down another level.

"Yes, Balzac, but mind your heads here, these steps are not so generous in size."

When Balzac aligned himself with the stairs, he was suddenly very aware of his own size. It would be a squeeze. Once at the bottom of the stairs, he could see Admasin and Lucia already at the rear of the vessel, talking.

The hole at the rear was the only light into this area. Balzac stopped to look. Right along the bottom centre was the main backbone of the vessel. It looked much bigger now the room was enclosed. The huge curved, wooden beams of the vessel started at the main beam underfoot, swept out wide then curved up through the ceiling one after the other, along the length of the vessel. It was almost like looking inside a whale's skeleton, with the spine down on the sand then the ribs curving out and up. His father had shown him one when he was a child; he'd forgotten about it until he stepped into this hull today.

Lucia faced the trio coming their way. "You will notice the only light is the hole here; again, this is the rudder that has plagued us. This is below the waterline so this is where the long-life goods and water are kept for the crew."

Sharia held up her hands to question. "But it is so hot here, and when you close this up, surely it will be unbearable?"

"As I said, this is below the waterline, so once she is launched it will actually become the coolest." Sharia eyed Lucia coolly. Lucia knew better than to look to her mother right now.

Admasin took up the conversation. "Also, the extra blocks, pulleys and rope would be stored. Although the ceiling is low here, there is still plenty of room."

Lucia turned them back towards the centre of the room. "This, Father, is what you had us do." She motioned at the master pole. "It really is a masterpiece." She laughed at her own joke. "Pardon the pun." They all laughed, except Sharia. Lucia's jaw clenched. Now they all stood in silence.

Admasin had made one small but obvious change. He waited

for Balzac to comment, but he seemed suitably oblivious to it. *Hardly surprising, it's not really his design in the first place.* Admasin said nothing on the matter, turning to the stairs. "I believe Yuna will have served lunch by now, shall we?"

Balzac eagerly patted his stomach. "Well, after all this exercise up and down these stairs, I would think that is a fine idea. Timber quantities after that, though."

Admasin dipped his head. "Superb, Balzac."

They made their way back to the top deck and over the gangplank to sit at the table. Sharia looked into the bowls of water that Yuna had placed. "It has a rag in it."

Lucia didn't mean to scoff. "It's to refresh yourself with." She took up hers and wiped her forehead and the back of her neck.

Balzac picked up his. "What a fine idea."

Soon enough, everyone was refreshed, and Yuna cleared away the bowls and then placed a seafood salad in the centre of the table. Balzac began to chuckle for no apparent reason.

Sharia looked it over. "Yuna, where did you get all of this?"

"I go to the northern end of the island at low tide. In the sands you can find scallops and cockles, over the rocks are mussels and oysters, along with some that I do not even know the name of."

Sharia frowned. "Then how do you know if it is alright to eat? We may be sick." She clutched Balzac's arm. "Balzac, we might get sick."

Before Balzac could reassure Sharia, Lucia spoke. "For the love of the Gods, woman! Yuna knows exactly how to test food. Do you really think she would put any of us at risk?"

Sharia gasped. Balzac sat up to speak to Lucia, but Admasin quickly grabbed him by the sleeve. He looked at Admasin, who just shook his head. Sharia stood up and threw down her lap cloth. Lucia was just as quick to her feet, pointing across the table. "No, you stay there. *I* will leave the blessed table." Not waiting for an answer, she curtly bowed and, before anyone could comment, she marched over the gangplank onto the silent vessel.

Angrier than Lucia had been in a long time, she walked with no destination in mind. She had hoped her mother would be happy and proud. Father seemed to be, but Mother had done nothing but complain the entire morning. Before she knew it, she was down on the second level, looking to the rear where the rudder needed to be. She heard a noise and walked to the edge of the vessel to look down. It was the man they called Jabali, on the ground looking at the rear of the vessel. She could only see his hat, really.

"Hello, Jabali…" was all she got to say.

He looked up at her. His face and eyes were almost completely obscured with the funny mask, though he seemed completely captivated with her. The poor fellow fell backwards over a tree root and swore under his breath. He quickly fumbled around for his cane and scarpered away.

"Strange man," she said quietly. She stopped for a moment, hearing Sharia talking at the table just above her.

"Oh yes, I'm sure it's just because of the fires of Samos that Karlec hasn't been back for so long. I think he is so amazing for the work he does for all those poor women …"

Anger rose in Lucia until finally she snapped. Before she knew it, she was striding across the top deck towards the gangplank, only to hear her mother huff again. "Oh, really. Balzac look at your daughter, she walks and dresses like a man, though she is, after all, doing the work of men."

By this time, Lucia was at the end of the table. She slammed down her fists, making everything bounce. Admasin reached out and silently put his hand on Balzac's arm, holding him in his seat. Balzac looked briefly at Admasin only to see him gently shake his head again. He looked back at Lucia, seething with rage as she took a breath. "I hope you aren't waiting for dear uncle Karlec to return."

Sharia sat up straight in her seat with her elbows on the table, knuckles under her chin. "Why ever not?"

"Because Mother, he died the night of the fires."

Shock flashed over Sharia's face as her elbows slipped off the edge of the table. "What?"

Lucia's voice was low and steady as she looked at Yuna. "The reason why you can't think of the place Karlec owned is because it was the place known as Happy Hour."

Yuna looked down at the table. "Oh dear."

Sharia looked confused. "What is Happy Hour?"

Lucia stared directly into Sharia's face. "He didn't run a house for abused women, he owned and ran a *whore house* and *he* had the reputation for abusing his women. He preyed on the young and the homeless like the predator that he was."

Sharia sat back in her chair, stricken. "No, that's not true, Lucia. He would never do that! Never. Balzac, make her stop this instant."

Admasin shook Balzac's arm again. Lucia was not going to stop now. "Yes, it *is* right! He was nothing but a woman-abusing, cowardly predator! But you don't have to listen to me now, just like you didn't listen to me when I tried to tell you back then. It makes no difference either way now, does it?"

Admasin wasn't going to hold Balzac back now as he rose from his seat. "What do you mean … Sharia didn't listen back then, Lucia?"

Lucia glared at Balzac. "Dear Uncle Karlec used to get you drunk, then come to my room. Did you never think it was strange he was always gone before daybreak the next day, Father?"

Balzac glared at Sharia. "You knew about this?"

Sharia shook her head, waving an arm at Lucia. "Oh, Balzac, you know she was always letting her imagination get away on her."

Balzac shot a finger out at the vessel. "Is this vessel of sails of her imagination also?!" His voice thundered around the room.

Admasin, unable to protect them, was near neither Lucia nor Yuna. Balzac smashed his fist into the table. "Wait until his return and if he cannot hold my eye when I question him, so help me …"

"I told you! He is dead! Long dead," repeated Lucia.

Balzac's eyes narrowed. "How are you so sure, Lucia?"

Lucia glared at Sharia as she responded. "Because I gutted him with his own knife."

Sharia lunged forward. "How dare you come back onto our lands after you have murdered my *brother!*"

Lucia looked at Balzac, head down at the table as he slumped to his seat, silent and solemn. She screamed as she slammed her fists down onto the table. They flinched and watched as lemonade trickled through gaps on the table to the floor. She departed without further word.

She stumbled through the bottom workshop, tears rolling down her face. Again, she was the victim of someone else's unwanted actions. She smashed her way into the jungle, neither looking nor caring which way she was going. Rage overwhelmed her; she did not believe this time either. Before she knew it, she broke out through the jungle onto the beach. She looked about, baffled as to where she was, then she saw something that took all her attention. Down on the edge of the water was the man called Jabali; he was using his cane to etch in the sand. *Now what's the poor fellow doing?* With the back of her hand, she wiped away the tears.

She watched him as she approached. There was something about how the man was working that captivated her. She walked towards him steadily. He was left-handed, his right shoulder was badly slumped, and he dragged his right leg. Everyone talked about his voice, all a little airy, raspy and strange. Now watching him, something nagged at her.

She slowed as she approached. He was working so fast, so intensely, he hadn't even noticed her. She could hear his raspy voice as he mumbled, his cloth mask puffing out as he spoke. Easing around the end of his work, only metres from him, her eyes swelled as she looked to the sand. *The rudder!*

It was remarkable. The top of the rudder had a large wheel laid flat with a chain that went around it, into the rear of the vessel and then around a roller. The chain then came up through the floor to a wheel that steered the vessel, and then back down around another roller and out to the rudder wheel. Just one endless chain to steer with.

She pointed to the picture with the wheel on the top deck. "How many men to turn this wheel?"

Jabali jumped away, almost falling over. He waved his cane about angrily. "Gods, woman. Do you have no manners? I'll bet you never knock at a door either!" He turned, almost falling over again and stumbled clumsily along the sandy beach just as quickly as he could. He never looked back.

With puffy eyes and a heavy heart, Lucia looked to the heavens and whispered, "Just how much is a woman to endure?" She looked back at the sand picture and the rudder. It wasn't trailing or dragging back like normal, modern rudders. She knelt and placed her spread hands over it. This was no ordinary rudder. It was so simple, so easy, it was too good to be true. They could do this and have the vessel ready in no time. She smiled then looked at the man, stumbling along the beach, dressed in long, black garments in the midday sun. *Strange ... but brilliant.* Where he was going in such a hurry, she could only wonder; it was an island after all. Almost in sympathy, she watched him go. *The pain he must carry for all his solitude.*

It was with heavy footsteps that Lucia climbed back up the stairs. She could hear talking, though Balzac had taken Sharia and Jabali and left some time ago. She had waited in the jungle for them to leave. She breathed a deep sigh and opened the door. Admasin and Yuna were sitting at the table holding hands. She walked to face the table and knelt. Placing her hands on the floor, she bowed her head and waited for Admasin, knowing he would speak first.

"This is not your custom, and this is your land. Why do you kneel before us?"

Lucia lifted her head, her face etched in sorrow. "Because today I have shamed us."

"You have not shamed us, my dear. Would you like to join us for some tea?" Yuna offered as she stood.

"No, Yuna. You have served us all day, now I must serve you both."

Yuna glanced at Admasin as she sat back down. He smiled. Lucia gave a cup to Admasin and Yuna before placing one for herself. She sat with a sigh and looked up at them both.

"Uncle Karlec," she lowered her head and stammered, "he interfered with me when I was just young. I told Mother several times, but she never believed me." Yuna placed her hand gently on her arm and squeezed Admasin's with her other. Admasin reached across the table and held Lucia's other hand as she continued. "Not many could outdrink Father, but Karlec could. In my opinion, he was an alcoholic. He was always gone by sunrise. I knew I couldn't tell Father because he would have killed him, and Mother would never have forgiven him for that. The family would have been ruined."

Admasin and Yuna listened despairingly but without a word.

"I never ran away from home – I chased Karlec to the mainland. I was going to find where he worked, but I didn't realise just how big Samos was. I needed work to survive, to buy time to find him. By that time, I had a new life, then I didn't *want* to find him. I just wanted to forget it all." She shook the hands of her surrogate mother and father. "I had a new family."

Yuna patted her hand. "And our lives are the richer for knowing you, my dear." Then it dawned on her. "So, when those men on the fishing vessel …?"

Lucia sighed, closing her eyes to block out the memory.

Yuna gulped. "My dear, as if that wasn't hard enough for you to begin with."

Admasin nodded. "You have been gone all afternoon. I knew there was no point in searching for you."

Lucia gasped suddenly. "Oh my, how could I forget?"

With a bit of a flinch, Yuna and Admasin sat back. "Forget what, exactly?" he questioned.

Lucia rushed across the room to get some paper and returned.

Yuna looked at Admasin as he shrugged. She picked up the kettle and cups and headed for the stove.

Lucia drew as best she could, at great speed, talking Admasin through the idea. "It is just one chain on a full loop. Check the rudder."

Admasin held his chin as he stood beside her. "Everyone knows that a vessel will turn sideways in a wind; a rudder will do the same in the water. No one could hold it, it would turn sideways and jam."

"No, it has at least one-third more trailing than leading, so it will always have weight keeping it in line, but at the same time, it will have less weight to turn because of the leading edge."

Admasin frowned. "A wheel to turn the vessel? Lucia, this has never been done before." She stopped drawing and looked at Admasin with an expectant smile. His forehead softened as he raised his eyebrows. "What?" She pointed to the vessel with its enormous master pole. He scoffed. "Oh yes, point taken, Lucia." She finished drawing in the rollers and stood back, checking her work was like that on the beach.

Admasin smiled. "Where did you get this, my dear?"

Without taking her eyes off the paper, "Have you talked with him much … you know, Balzac's friend?"

"Jabali? Not much really." He eyed her carefully. "What makes you ask that?"

She shrugged. "I don't know really." She looked at Admasin and Yuna. "I'm washed out. Would you mind if I retired for the day?"

Admasin stepped back from the table. "Of course not, Lucia." He adopted a cheerful look. "I feel tomorrow's going to be a big day."

She gave a curt bow and turned to find Yuna right beside her. Taking Lucia in a big hug, Yuna whispered in her ear. "If ever you need a woman to talk to, I will always be there for you. Never have I doubted your word."

"I know; thank you, Mother."

10 The One

Back on the galley roof of the Emperor's vessel, Kito slipped back into his body and, looking up at the stars, wiped tears from his face. The tears could've been because he had just watched his father walk back into the Village of the Keepers, though this was not the case. His tears were for his dear friend, Shay.

He had gleaned a lot on this out-of-body journey. Holding this moment in time static, whilst getting everything else together, was very difficult. His energy was depleted.

He stood up with a small groan and did some stretches, trying to lose the image of Shay and her anger. He could feel the strapping on his back, knowing the swords were now a part of him, just under the extra flap on his back. He scoffed; it was always to be. *Hasuca had this garment made for them.* Other than a hunting knife, Kito had never needed to carry a weapon before. *Why these deadliest of things, now?* His long, tousled hair bounced as he shook his head. *Maybe it will make sense later.*

That night, he slept on the roof of the galley in the lotus position. It was not a sound sleep.

At first light, after finishing his exercises, he slipped off the roof and headed down. Entering the galley, he said his good mornings and, after feeding himself, went to the table at the rear of the vessel where all three men were sitting. Kito bowed. "May I serve any of you some refreshments?"

The Emperor dipped his head to Kito then spoke to the two men. "Would some tea and banana bread with sweet sauce be to your liking?"

Mensa and Kohji both looked at each other. The Emperor usually never asked. "That would be fine, thank you," answered the Sheik.

Without a word, Kito turned and left. The Emperor looked at his companions. "Well, gentlemen, I don't know about the two of you, but I think we are on the edge of something great." He waved his hand behind himself. "This vessel is more to my liking every time I come aboard. We have set an alliance that makes me the power of the earth and, once I squash a few insubordinates, the earth will know it *and* worship me as they should!"

The table was now quieter than it was when left empty overnight.

The Emperor spoke to the Sheik. "When I've dropped you back home …" He tapped the table to emphasise his words, "… you will gather all your fighting men and be sure they are fully armed."

The Sheik sat forward. "Why do we need to be armed? Are we not simply moving into Zimbali?" He was careful not to make eye contact with Mensa.

The Emperor shook his head with the smallest smile. "Because, my colleague, I will need you further down the track. Oh, and just so we are clear, *you* will be leading your men."

"And who is to run my lands?"

"You need not concern me with your trivial matters, Kohji."

Just then, Kito returned with three stacked plates and a centre plate fully loaded with hot banana bread. One of the woman servants followed behind him with fresh water and the sweet sauce.

Mensa watched Kito closely, trying to scrutinise him with his hood up but, as always, he couldn't really see his face. "Kito, why is it you never reveal yourself to anyone?"

"I reveal myself to those I wish."

"Why not to us then? Are you now afraid, since I bettered you?"

"No, I just think you wouldn't cope in the presence of my handsome, good looks." The servant suppressed a giggle, though the Emperor held nothing back and burst into laughter.

Mensa shot to his feet, his chair rattling over the timber deck. His left hand went to the small of his back, but the knife wasn't there. Kito reached down to the table and picked up the bread knife by the dull blade and reached out to Mensa. "Here, would you like this one?"

Even the Sheik chuckled this time. The Emperor, by contrast, went quiet, sensing something more was at play here. He watched Kito closely. Mensa glanced at the Emperor and stood up straight, composing himself. He leant his hands on the table as his low voice warned Kito. "I made you a promise and I will see you to it, and soon I think." The table was now deathly quiet for the second time this morning.

Kito placed the knife with the bread and moved smoothly around the table to fetch the chair. Mensa stepped back so not to have his back to Kito. The chair placed gently for Mensa, Kito moved back to stand behind the Emperor.

Breakfast was now a quiet affair, though it was noted that it didn't take Mensa long to settle; he ate most of the food on the table. *Though to be fair*, thought the Emperor, *he is twice Kohji and I put together.*

After breakfast, the Emperor excused himself and headed below deck. He eased down the last step, key in hand, and stopped silently at the door.

A feminine voice came from inside the locked room. "Enter," was all she said.

Emperor Koe unlocked the door, stepped in and relocked it. As the lock clicked, she spoke quietly. "You have much on your plate, my ally, yet you seem to feed on it; you appear stronger than ever."

Koe turned to face her. As always, the room was dark with only the glowing coals in the brazier, lighting her beautiful face. "Well, yes, we both know this is what I was born for."

"Really, Koe, and what is *this*?"

"Why do you play these games with me? You know you can't win, yet you still persist."

She moved around the brazier, trance-like. "I have no need for games, Koe, you know this, but we both know that you *need* me." Her voice hung on the air like a winter chill. "And we both know I don't need *anything*. But you, Koe, you need the future. You *crave* the future!"

Koe grimaced at her unnaturally long fingers as she waved them in his face.

She enticed him further. "I have had some interesting scenes of late."

"And what might you have for me this time, Banji?" His eyes followed her dance-like movements as she moved around to the other side of the brazier.

"Oh, you are the cool one, aren't you, always in control, but no, not this time, my friend. This is the big one!" She observed his every reaction closely.

His jaw was tight with anticipation as his words hissed. "Well, come on then, witch, you know yourself, I'm a busy man."

She shrieked as she ran around the room. He spun to follow her sudden movements. Her cackling laughter rang out until she stopped abruptly opposite him again. "I have found your Valley of the Stone Temple, Koe. I know where it is."

"What? Where? Is it in Zimbali as I said it was?"

She waved her long finger through the air. "Oh yes, my friend. It is right where you said it was, and I was right about Kito. He *has* been there, but I have now found another way in. Legend has it there are two ways in. Kito used one, but I have found you an easier way, though only *he* can get you in."

The Emperor's mind reeled. "Kito is under my control. Like everything else, the Gods have served me what I need. When can I go in?"

"You only have two Crystal Skulls, Koe. The legend …"

"The legend states that the man who can hold the stare of the Skulls can hold the information within them. *I* am the man to hold those Skulls!" His chest expanded with his own grandeur.

"What about the Sacred Crystal, Koe? You haven't thought about the Sacred Crystal, have you?"

"Of course I have! It will be in the Valley; it *must* be. I will go to the Stone Temple; the Sacred Crystal will be in there. I'll place the Skulls in it and stare into them to retrieve the location of the others. Simple."

Banji waved one of her fingers slowly in front of her face. The Emperor resisted the urge to snap it off and stab her in her own eye with it. He stood motionless, in control of his emotions. *So close. I am so close.*

Her voice screeched in his ears like the winds of the northern winter. "You have everything you need, Koe, though I must recommend you wait until you have all *seven* Skulls."

"Seven Skulls! Nonsense woman. I *must* be the first! I have two, and once I have the wisdom of those two, I will have no problem getting the rest. Besides …" his voice trailed off.

"Yes, Koe?"

"How can there even *be* seven Skulls? There are only five lands. No, I have these; that will suffice."

Banji could hardly hold back her smile. She drew out a small leather pouch, opened the drawstrings and threw the bones into the brazier. The Emperor leant back as the brazier flared up with a hiss. As the flames settled, she could positively feel his anticipation. *He is so perfect, he won't stop now.* "I feel it is my duty to warn you, Koe, only the right man can hold the stare of the Skulls."

"Sha'Doe delivered *me* that gold." He pulled up his sleeves to show his golden bracelets, "Now Kito serves me, so *I* am *that* man. Now where *exactly* is the Stone Temple?"

She waved a casual hand. "As I said, you are right, Koe, it *is* in the Valley."

"So Kito has seen it then?"

"He did enter the Stone Temple, but he never got to see the Sacred Crystal …" She looked almost vacantly for a moment. "He was challenged, and it would seem, he lost and left."

"Really?"

"Yes, it must be so, because I saw it so."

The Emperor sneered. *Clearly he is no threat to me; he can't hold the stare.* "It is only *I* who can do such a feat, and it is *I* who will get the wisdom."

Banji rubbed her belly as she watched him ranting to himself. She smiled as her eyes narrowed. "Koe?"

He stopped abruptly. "What?"

Banji's eyes drifted again. "Where is the Crystal Skull of Zimbali?"

The Emperor frowned. "Who cares?"

"Do you not think it must be right there, somewhere?"

"After I've been to the Stone Temple, I expect I will see where it is. They are all already mine, Banji."

"Koe, I will give where it resides but you must have three Skulls with you. Two, just isn't enough."

The Emperor gritted his teeth as he glared at her. "If you can't give me at least the village where the Skull is kept, I will not be wasting any time over it."

Banji threw more bones into the fire. Her shrills filled the air as the flames leapt so high Koe couldn't help but look up, concerned about the wooden ceiling they should have been lapping. But when he looked up, there was no ceiling, just a black void. The fire leaped as high as it wished. Through the dancing flames, a scene appeared, completely drawing his attention. He knew it immediately. It was Batavia, capital of Zimbali and there was a Temple. Queen Rani's Temple.

His eyes widened. "Of course, but could it be this easy?" he whispered. Suddenly the flames were gone, as was the image. He looked at Banji. Her eyes rolled around in their sockets and she had a grin that he couldn't bear look at. She was away in a world he didn't even want to know about; it was a world only a witch could be a part of and survive. For now, she was gone to this world. He backed out of the room and relocked the door. Once returned to his cabin, he closed the door securely behind him.

***

Mensa looked at the Sheik; it was time for the day's training. "Top of our cabin?"

The Sheik nodded. "Lead the way, my brother."

On the roof of the cabin, they were careful not to hang their legs over the front; it was just too dangerous with the two swordsmen so intently focused on nothing but each other.

Kito was already there warming up, no swords, just stretches and gentle pushing of fresh air with his hands. He moved like some sort of dancer. The Sheik was mesmerised by it. It was different in so many ways, yet at the same time, it was powerfully familiar, but for the life of him, he could never place it.

Finally, the Emperor came through from between the cabins. "Ah, Kito, just the man I was looking for." Kito became motionless, facing the Emperor. The Emperor sighed. "Now, Kito, we're not going to waste any time over this 'I'm not going to fight' nonsense, are we?"

Kito could barely hear the Emperor; his head was already beginning to hum as the blades on his back grew hotter. He could feel the heat of them, as if they would burn their way out of their own sheaths, calling him to engage the Emperor.

"I could just go into the galley and pull one of the servants out, or you could …"

Kito's head was bursting as it thumped like a drumbeat from within his entire being. The swords burned intently as the arm band on his left bicep began to pulse with them. His muscles trembled like he was losing control of his own being, and if that were to happen, he would be capable of killing everyone on board. There was no one to stop him; he *had to* spa with the Emperor; he had to move and he had to burn this energy. He stared at the Emperor's gold bracelets. He could sense them pulsing with his own, twin swords.

The Emperor's eyes narrowed, and with a bent smile, he whispered, "You need to engage." He leapt forward, his sword swinging down at Kito. Kito leaned to one side and, with a clash of steel, his two swords deflected the Emperor's attack.

Once engaged in sparring, it was hypnotic. Even the kitchen servants came out to watch. The irony was that, as much as they all loved to hate the Emperor and his violent ways, when they watched him spar with Kito, the sight was so spectacular that they could only admire the talent of both men together. It was whispered about in the recesses of the night, but no one could really know who was better. Kito was cool and calm, even after the event, but the Emperor was aggressive, unrelenting and fearless throughout. The two men would leap and jump. Just when one was cornered he would swing from a sail or a rope to redefine his position or run on the walls of the cabins or the galley, seemingly defying gravity. More than once, Mensa and Kohji had to roll away from the edge to keep back from the wielding swords just above their heads.

Then, as always, the bell rang three times. The Emperor stood bare-chested and arched his back. He raised his hands to the sky. "Boy, I do love our spars. Every time is different with you and every time I grow to love it more!" He shook his head with excitement and howled to the heavens.

He dunked his head in a bucket offered to him, then threw his head back, making his hair throw droplets of water high into the air, his wet hair slapping onto his back. He then washed his face and body. Once dried off, the Emperor threw the towel at the man holding the bucket and walked away laughing.

Kito stepped forward and took the bucket. "Thank you."

The man bowed as Kito tipped the contents over the side. As he went to walk away, the man asked quietly, "Why is it you don't have your own bucket brought?"

Kito turned his head. "You have thought about it, and yet you have not brought me one. This is your choice."

Kito went downstairs into the hull to the fresh water and took it back up to the lower hold. He undressed and opened a hatch, watching the water ripping past as he washed himself and his clothes in the bucket. He rang them out and hung them to dry as he sat and watched the water some more. He thought of his brother Baako, and that fortuitous meeting. *Mensa's biggest mistake.* Letting Kito and Baako meet was just plain careless. After all, Mensa did know their ties, even if at the time, they did not.

***

The vessel made its way out of the river to the open ocean. Kito and the Emperor sparred every night and most mornings. The servant now left a bucket and towel down by an open hatch for when Kito went back down. Sometimes when Kito sat and watched the water rushing by, he would close his eyes to let the sun, reflecting off the water, warm his face and bare chest.

Today was one of those days. Sat with his feet up on his thighs, he unbuckled the swords, placing them on his tunic. He closed his eyes and began to relax his neck and shoulders, working down to his chest, back, torso, then … *Is that a brazier of hot coals?* His shoulders tensed. Other than the glowing brazier, the room was pitch black. He could see the coal burning, yet he could smell nothing. He could feel the heat from the coals, yet the room was cool. He moved closer to it. The flames seemed to be calling him closer.

Kito's head rang, the crown burning his left bicep, but the flames drew him ever nearer. He looked down at them dancing over the coals like angels of fire. The hair on his neck prickled, and he stopped. He looked about, black outside of black. The fire beckoned further; he reached out with his left hand to touch one of the dancing angels. He could feel no heat; the hair on his neck prickled with anticipation.

He breathed deeply to keep his composure. His hand neared the

142

coals when suddenly another hand lashed down at his. Immediately, Kito snatched the small pale hand with his right hand, and another hand came out of the dark, and he grabbed that with his left. He pulled them towards him,, and into the light came the face of his nightmares. The ringing in his ears increased tenfold. Her laughter was loud, high pitched. "Ha ha ha you silly boy. You can't hurt me, ha ha ha."

Kito plunged her hands into the coals. The ringing increased a further tenfold, but he held her hands deep in the coals.

She shrieked some more. "Ha, you silly boy. I already have what I need and you can't get it." She cackled louder. Her mouth opened wide, and her canines grew long, then holes formed in the front of them. In reflex, he abruptly released her and turned away.

He sprawled out on the timber floor as salt water sloshed through the hatch of the vessel, hissing on his hot skin. The ringing in his ears had almost stopped, but he could hear the echo of her laughter. *Was that a dream or a memory? Can I still hear her laughing?*

***

Later that day, Kito stood over the table as the men talked about their plans to walk from Audun to Zimbali. The Emperor was careful not to use terms like invade or rule. Kito left at regular intervals to avoid appearing to be eavesdropping, though at the end of the day, he knew what the plan was, and it confirmed everything Hao had said.

The Emperor suddenly stood up. "Well, gentlemen, you will excuse me." The men stopped their discussion and looked blankly at the Emperor. He turned to Kito. "You won't mind looking out for our esteemed guests in my absence."

Kito dipped his head and waited for the Emperor to go downstairs. As he raised his head slightly, he could feel the stares of Mensa and Kohji.

11 Norinko

In the palace, Hao was unsure what day it was, or how many days had passed since he'd been put in his room. Standing at the window, he looked down over the valley before him, smiling at the beauty of it all. The new season covered all the trees with big green leaves, and the grass waved in the summer breeze. He could almost hear the bees at work with the wildflowers. It made him think of his only love, Tammirie. He smiled weakly. *She would love this.* His chest pounded at the thought of her. He needed to move his thoughts on and wondered who else had stood at this window and pondered the workings of life before them, this spot where Nobles and the Emperor himself could have stood and looked over the valley.

His mind went back to his dream of Kito sitting on the rock. He now knew it was real, and that was the beginning of the war. This was why the Barbarians took him to that very village, because they also knew. And they knew the Emperor had their Blue Crystal Skull. He shook his head. Dreams of the future and the past were not unheard of, even for peasants like him, but he also knew the dream was about Kito, not himself. Never had he experienced something like that before.

Hao turned at the sound of the door handle. The door was pushed open by a guard holding a knife. The guard looked shocked to see Hao standing there seemingly waiting for him. He let three more guards holding swords in, and they moved to the bottom of the stairs into the room. Tzu entered and calmly walked past his men to stand forward of Hao. He didn't offer a hand of friendship. Neither did Hao.

Hao smiled. "You flatter me, Tzu."

Tzu turned his head to the side as if to look at his own men and back to Hao. "No, I feel not."

Hao shook his head. "Ah, but you do, Tzu. Vulin would have killed me on his own but for the strangest thing."

"The wolf, Hao?"

"Yes, the wolf." He turned his back on Tzu and walked to the window. "Did Vulin have family?"

Tzu walked forward and looked down over the valley, standing not too close to Hao. "What should you care, Hao? You did what you thought was the right thing, and he picked on the wrong man."

Hao chose his words carefully. "Why did you choose to go so far to attack that particular village, Tzu?"

Tzu turned his head. "Hao?"

"Are there no other villages around here you could have picked on? Why *that* village?"

Tzu smiled thinly. "You do know, don't you?"

Hao turned to face Tzu. "Just a short time ago, I learnt that that was the village that started the war. But when will all this stop? Are you to keep sneaking out and shooting people until there are no more to kill? Is this how you would want to be seen running the lands?"

"OUR LANDS!"

Hao eyed the big Barbarian coldly as he stepped away from the window, pointing a finger at Tzu. "The lands are a gift from the Gods for us to enjoy, tend and nurture so our children can enjoy them just as was intended. Nobody *owns* the lands."

"Oh yeah? Then why do all your people live in caves while I march through your very own palace?"

"My people would have come here to take back our Palace, but I told them not to!"

"On a scale of one to ten, what do you think are the chances that your people would have succeeded, Hao? I will tell you. You would have watched raid after raid failing and your people dying before your very eyes!" Tzu snatched his knife out, waving it as he began to march around. Hao marched opposite him, both now yelling. The guards watched blankly at the spectacle before them.

Saliva spat into the air with Hao's words. "We have more people in our army than you have altogether! We would have come in waves that would have worn you down until there was nothing of you left."

Tzu didn't wait for him to finish. "We have the perfect fortress, made by your lot. We could have stayed here for an eternity using your very own weapons!"

"The Gods would not leave this as so. It is just not right!"

"Then what the *hell* have you been doing in the North for so long!?"

Hao froze on the spot, silent for some time. "What is hell?" Tzu frowned, still with his knife pointed. "What?"

"You said 'what the hell.' What is that?"

"You do not have it? That's right, I did forget. Hell is a place you go if the Gods do not want you in their place after you pass over. It is said to be an eternity of torture for all your wrongdoings on earth." Hao scoffed. Tzu's face softened a little. "Yes, Hao?"

Hao shook his head, holding his arms out wide. "Suddenly, I want to stay here with you, Tzu. I had never thought the Gods had somewhere else to send me. I simply had not considered rejection." Tzu wiped his mouth on his sleeve. Hao studied Tzu as he had many times before. "Why have you not killed me yet?"

"The day is early, don't push your luck."

Hao insisted. "No, really, Tzu. Why have you not taken revenge on me? I had lost to Vulin before we engaged because I always knew he wanted me dead more than I wanted to kill him."

"So why did you engage with him?"

"I told you. I would rather you just dispatched me. I can't stand by and watch you take revenge on villagers."

Tzu eyed Hao coldly. "Your lot did it to ours. That is how you got the line back to where it is now."

"Was …"

Tzu didn't smile. "Stay on track, Hao. What your lot did was unforgivable."

Hao nodded, thumping his fist on his chest lightly. "That was then and *them*. What are *we* to do, here and *now*?"

***

The children ran so hard they were all but out of breath. Just up the hill ahead was a small village on the top of a steep knoll, with sharp wooden poles making a wall around all sides but for one gate. The village houses were built with stone walls and steep, thatched roofs to shed the winter snow. Smoke rose gently out of the chimneys, fires not for the cold now in early summer, but for cooking.

Concerned by the screaming children, people came running out, looking to where the breathless children pointed to see the riders coming up the track. The men rushed back inside to grab swords, bows and spears as mothers grabbed the young and ushered them to the back of the village. The armed men congregated at the gate.

The village elder made his way through and looked down the hill at the approaching riders. He had a bad scar through the bridge of his nose. He leant over to the man beside him. "Your eyes are better than mine, Sezou. Who do you see?"

"Five Barbarians on horseback, Norinko."

"Yes, but are they all Barbarians?"

The man leaned forward as if to make a difference. "There is one; he is not the same."

Norinko smiled. "Hmm, quite so. Maybe my eyes are not so bad." He stepped forward and turned to his men. "You will not shoot unless they attack. Is this clear?" A murmur went about the confused men. Norinko looked at Sezou. "You will be the man of the village. I expect you will hold these men to my instruction."

Slightly hesitant, Sezou shook his head. "Father, I don't feel …"

Norinko's eyes narrowed. "You will keep the parcel out of sight, if I wave then send him down, but not before. Are we clear?"

With his jaw clenched, Sezou nodded.

Norinko headed down the track to intercept the riders. He could hear the talk behind him, but he was the leader and knew the history better than anyone. If anyone were to stop the riders from getting too close before revealing their intentions, it could only be him. Deep down, he also thought it was only deserving for it to be him. His conscience had eaten at him in his nightmares for too long.

Norinko reached the bottom of the hill, still well in range of his own men but a good distance from the gates should these men mean harm to the village. He waited. The men on their horses had spread five wide in the meadow and were now at a walk.

Norinko waited. The horses stopped some distance off, and he could see they were talking before one rider came forward and, at the same time, another dismounted and walked. It was obvious angry words were being exchanged. The one on the horse turned and stormed at the other, but the one on the ground was quick to pull the horseman down.

Clearly a military man, thought Norinko.

The two tumbled through the summer grass before the three others dismounted to pull them apart. More angry words passed. Norinko turned to his men at the gate; they were shuffling about uneasily, seemingly just as confused.

Still Norinko waited as the two men simmered down and were eventually released by the others. Slowly, the two began their walk towards him, with a few more angry words exchanged. Norinko resisted the urge to turn and check that his men were alert. He watched as the two came forward. One was clearly not a barbarian; he appeared unarmed and wore a silly hat. Norinko tilted his head. There were bells ringing in his memory, but he couldn't put the pieces together. It would wait.

Finally, the two men stopped just short of Norinko. The Barbarian flicked his chin towards him. "You have come from your village to meet with us and appear to have no weapon. Brave or silly?"

Norinko smiled. "I have come to see your intentions before you get to our gates. I am not as young as I was and don't intend to engage with four men."

"Four?"

Norinko indicated in Hao's direction. "He is clearly not one of your men."

Tzu smirked. "He could still knife you in the back, man."

Norinko shrugged. "Then my job for the village would be done."

"Brave and wise. My name is Tzu, and this is my companion, Hao."

The last bell went off in Norinko's head. The legends, Bolli and Hao. He offered his arm, and Tzu shook it. The Barbarian towered over him, but he showed no weakness as they shook. Tzu stepped back and Hao then bowed. When they stood, Norinko studied him closely. *Why is he riding with Barbarians?*

"I am pleased to meet you, Norinko."

Hao was strong and tall. *A fighting man and polite.* Norinko liked him. "And you too, Hao." He turned back to Tzu. "You will understand if I don't invite you all into my village."

Tzu's eyes narrowed. "You will not welcome us, Norinko?"

"No. We are a small village of hunters, not war mongers. I will welcome Hao into our village; he can deliver your message well enough."

Tzu's expression changed instantly, but Hao quickly interjected. "Norinko, may I speak with you a moment?"

Hao had begun to turn Norinko away when Tzu suddenly grabbed Hao by the shoulder. Hao spun around with a closed fist, just missing Tzu's chin. His foot followed, kicking Tzu to the ground. Hao tumbled back himself. Both men stood back up, facing one another aggressively. Tzu was the only one with a blade.

Norinko knew his men would be ready to release arrows instantly. He leapt between them. "Whoa, both of you! What in the name is wrong with you two? You come here together to meet with me, but before I even know what you want, you fight each other … twice!"

Tzu's eyes darkened in his contorted face. Hao pointed at Tzu. "Be careful with Uncle Norinko, Tzu."

The two men froze, staring at Hao. Tzu stepped aside, keeping his distance from Norinko. "What are you on about now, man?"

Hao stood almost relaxed as he eyed Tzu but spoke to Norinko. "I just don't think it would be very nice not to invite in your nephew, Norinko."

Still holding his blade, Tzu took another step towards Hao. "By the Gods, man, you have told me some tales."

Hao put his hands to his hips. "Norinko, you do remember your good sister, Mischa?"

Tzu lifted his knife, rolling it about in his fingers. "Just what would you know of my mother?"

"I believe this may be a good time to re-join the family ties, don't you?"

Norinko's mind reeled back. *How could this man possibly know and how much does he know?*

Hao smiled knowingly at Norinko, who was slowly turning pale. "Again, Norinko, I think this would …"

Norinko broke from his trance. "Yes, yes, Hao." He turned to Tzu. "Please forgive me … are you Tzu Hsi?"

Tzu stood rigid, looking at the bridge of Norinko's bent nose. "That's a nasty scar you bear."

"One of the few gifts from my father."

"Mother told the story; she said you were very brave."

Guilt-stricken, Norinko couldn't comment.

Hao nudged Tzu. "You could put away your knife, then we could start this introduction once again, Tzu?"

Tentatively and ever so slowly, he slipped his knife away behind his back.

Hao stepped between the two and put each hand on their shoulders. "Norinko, I would like to introduce you to Tzu Hsi, son of Toza and Mischa."

Norinko stared at Tzu, then re-offered his arm. Tzu took a breath, reached out and shook it.

Hao relaxed. "Alright, Tzu, you do understand Norinko has very close ties with the throne?"

Tzu nodded, not looking away from his own bloodline. "I believe Norinko wears the blue and green belts to represent this entire area, and his close ties with the Emperor also give him the black belt. His word is Royal word."

Norinko was surprised at Tzu's knowledge. "You have come far for a reason. I want to hear it, but feel at this point it would be foolhardy to have all your armed men in my village. You are a leader, Tzu, you will understand."

"Very well, but you said it yourself, I am a leader. How could I know I will safely return to my people?"

Norinko stood silent. Finally, with the glimmer of a smile, Norinko turned and waved to his people at the gate. Hao and Tzu inquisitively watched the villagers.

Eventually, one man came walking through the gate and down the track towards them. As he neared, Hao began to laugh. He looked at Norinko. "How is this possible?"

Norinko smiled proudly. "The children spotted him one morning and so we went about rescuing him. It was not easy, but fortunately, he could speak our language."

Tzu smiled with a broad grin as the man drew closer. "Razo, is this really you?" Razo laughed and offered his arm. The two men shook and slapped backs hard. "We prayed for you to the Gods."

Razo laughed. "I'm sure they were grateful for that, my King, but he sent these people for me instead."

Tzu looked at Norinko. "He is in fine shape, I thank you."

"I think we have much to discuss. My offer still stands as it was, Tzu. Under my conditions, you are welcome into my village."

Razo spoke to Tzu in his native tongue, and he stiffened, eyeing Norinko. Moments passed. Hao and Norinko could only wonder what had been said as Tzu began to walk away. He only took a few paces and turned back to Razo, and spoke with him some more. Razo nodded but stayed where he was. Hao and Norinko looked at one another as Tzu went back to his own men, where discussions were had with raised voices and much angry waving of arms.

Hao's hand slowly, subconsciously went to his hip. Nothing, not even a hunting knife. He refolded his arms, tension building. Norinko looked back at his own people at the gate, crossbows were at the shoulder, though pointing at the ground, the front men down on one knee. They were not comfortable either.

Hao leant over to Razo. "I don't want any bloodshed, Razo."

"Hao, you keep saying this, but you sure can draw it."

If it was not for the man's grin, Hao may have taken it wrong. "It has never been my choice to draw blood, Razo. I just won't turn a blind eye either. Let me ask you, would you really have fired on the children?"

Norinko looked at Razo, who didn't meet his gaze.

"I would have done exactly what I was instructed to do, Hao." Hao looked to the ground, frowning with misunderstanding. Razo was still smiling. "I am just here to serve my King, not to question him. Hao, I am not like you."

"Then what am *I* here for?"

"That is for me not to question, or to know."

Norinko watched Hao carefully as he continued staring at the ground. They all glanced up at Tzu as he came forward leading his horse. He walked directly to Norinko. "We crossed a stream a little way back. My men will return there to camp. I will accept your hospitality." Tzu turned to Razo and handed him his belt carrying the sword and knife. "Take this and my horse. Go with the men for the night. Do not return until the sun is well clear of the mountains and don't enter within bow range. I won't have any misunderstandings."

Razo put on the belt and addressed Norinko. "Again, I thank you. Be safe."

Norinko bowed as Razo went to the horse and leapt into the saddle. He looked at Tzu. "You removed all your weapons?"

"Some damn fool once told me, if we are to do this right then we must go forward with nothing more than trust and faith."

Norinko chuckled and slapped Tzu on the shoulder. "I think this will be a good day to mark in our histories. A very good day."

They walked through the gates and into the village. The small dirt streets were lined with onlookers, muttering of the stampede and the Samos fires. Tzu leaned over to Hao. "You are a living hero to these people."

"No. On both counts, that was not me." Hao ignored Tzu and looked about the simple village. The people were well-dressed and clean. This was a way of life Hao could only vaguely remember, from a time before the war and his throne took his village.

Norinko reached the largest hut near the centre of the village and opened the door with a proud smile. A fire burned on a stone hearth in the centre of the warm, dry room. Hao wondered if the fire was ever allowed to go out. This was a meeting place, not just for the elders but for the whole village to gather as one, at least from time to time.

They settled down on mats set out around the fire. It wasn't long before the villagers began to bring in hot food, a generous amount for a little village. For the most part, the talk was of travel, hunting and seemingly, just getting to know each other. Norinko's son, Sezou, was there, as were a few of his friends and the village elders.

Hao listened quietly to the conversations, both of Norinko and Tzu. As they sized each other up, they avoided discussing who had started the war, but rather how they were to end it.

As the day drew on, they became more involved about borders and how to avoid further conflict. No one argued that the Wall was in the right or wrong place. Hao was both surprised and pleased. To have an end to this, they must first let go of the past, but one question wasn't coming up, and it needed to. Hao waited for the appropriate opening. "Tzu, who do you see owning the palace for the future?"

Tzu adjusted his posture. "Why is it you care, Hao?"

"You are right to ask me this. I don't care, but it needs to be decided on now or we risk it becoming a fight later. The line in the dirt must be drawn clearly, or all this will be for nothing."

Norinko watched Tzu intently as he drew breath to answer. "As the leader of my people, it is truly a difficult question. I think we have lost much land to this war, and we can't survive if you think the borders are to stay at the Wall. You do understand this, don't you?"

"Tzu, you must understand, the palace has stood for our people for too many generations to count. But, yes, we can all see the borders are not as they should be. Many of my people have shared concerns with me about this."

"My people starved and froze to death while your people feasted. Your people's concerns for the borders then carry no weight for me now. None!" Tzu snarled.

Hao was eager to placate Tzu's mounting anger. "I understand your bitterness …"

"YOU understand *nothing* of what it's like to watch your young and old die before their time. We did not start this war, Hao, and we certainly didn't ask for it!"

"But you *could* be instrumental in ending it, Tzu." Hao's words were firm and committed.

Norinko could see both men were holding steadfast to their opinions. Calmly, he interjected. "I remember when I used to sneak across the border to hunt moose with my father. His love of hunting was another of his gifts." He faced Tzu, chuckling as his index finger touched his scarred nose. "Hunting was a far more enjoyable gift." The mood lightened a little. "My point is, in those days, the border wasn't that far from this very village. And that is where it needs to be again, back where it was before the Emperor stormed your village and pushed your people further back over the ridge and erected the Wall." Norinko sighed, raising his hands in the air. "Tzu, I don't care for the palace. You have it. I will personally speak with Prince Desora …"

Tzu waved a finger and tutted, cutting him off in mid-sentence. "I believe Hao has something to tell you on this matter, Norinko."

Confused, Norinko turned to Hao expectantly. "Yes, Hao?"

Hao looked like the child with his hand on the food not for him. "Um, yes, thank you for that one, Tzu." He gazed down at the dirt floor, searching for the right words. "It would seem that he, I mean Desora and I, may have locked swords. I'm afraid he didn't survive."

Norinko gasped and glanced at the elders as they looked to him for answers. He closed his mouth, drawing breath. "Hao, am I to believe you have killed your own prince?"

Hao nodded several times as if to reinforce the answer. "Yes, that would be the short version."

Expecting a somewhat different reaction, Hao and Tzu watched in confusion as Norinko's smile broadened before breaking out into a full belly laugh.

"Norinko, what is it you find funny about the death of the prince?" enquired Hao.

"Tell me, Hao, just why did you lock swords with the prince?"

"We were in a fierce battle with Tzu and his men when, out of nowhere, he knifed me in the leg from behind. We exchanged words briefly, and then he charged me. I defended myself." Hao shrugged; "He lost."

"Clearly. Tzu, I assume this happened in the battle for the palace?"

"Yes, in the final moments, Norinko."

"You can confirm this attack on Hao?"

"I was not witness to every detail, but I can say I watched them battle and tended the wound on his leg, yes."

Norinko frowned. "You tended the wound for Hao?"

Tzu smirked. "Yes, it was quite rude of him, really. I was talking with him after the battle when he collapsed. Lack of blood, it would seem."

"Hao, is this so?"

"They did save my life, yes."

Norinko looked back at Tzu. "You have the palace secure then?"

Tzu folded his arms defensively. "Yes."

"And you have retrieved your Sacred Skull … the Blue Skull?"

Tzu's eyes narrowed. He knew the story from his father, Toza, but he wasn't aware it was common knowledge. "Norinko, just what do you know of our Sacred Skull?"

Norinko held out his arms. "I think if it belongs to you, like the North belongs to you, then you should have it back."

Meanwhile, Hao stared intently at the old scar across the bridge of Norinko's nose and thought back to the scene Kito had shown him. "We have all done things we shouldn't have," assured Hao.

Norinko's remorse shadowed his face. "Sadly, I have done no less wrong than any I know. Tzu, I care not for the palace …" He shook two clenched fists emphatically. "… but we must get the Sacred Skull back for you!"

The elders in the room began mumbling opinions. Hao cut in to avoid further friction. "Tzu, we from Magnar Wall know of your father, Toza."

Tzu's brow creased beneath his mass of red hair. "Really, how so?"

"Like your grandfather, he also had a very good reputation among some of our guards."

Tzu tilted his head. "Some, Hao? Please explain this one to me, though be careful."

"In life, there are always the people that hang in large groups laughing and poking fun at those who do not. They will always take the easy and most popular opinion, if for nothing else but to look and feel better about themselves. The rest of us sit outside that opinion, thinking for ourselves. You and I … we are those individuals. Those of us," Hao tapped his own chest gently, "who sit outside, will on rare occasion, speak of your grandfather's bravery against the Emperor. Your father died fighting the masses on the Wall. When he knew he was truly beaten, he took as many as he could over the side. This was a great battle. For this, he is well known on the Wall."

For a moment Tzu was lost in quiet reflection until the silence in the room made him finally notice everyone was looking at him. "Well, Hao, I didn't know you were so up on your history," he said wryly.

Hao cast a sideways glance at Norinko. "I actually know more than I would wish, but yes, there were many of us who saw glimmers of the truth."

Norinko shuffled awkwardly, moving the situation on. "Tzu, you have been at the palace for some time; is there no chance that your Sacred Skull is there?"

Tzu shook his head vigorously. "We have turned it over room by room. We even toppled the throne as it was rumoured to be underneath. Nothing."

Norinko hid his disappointment. "Your Shaman?"

"He said it wasn't there from the day we arrived, and he hasn't wavered from that opinion."

"Some Shamans are better than others."

"I understand what you're suggesting, but Porteous is one of the best we've ever had."

Norinko's shoulders slumped. "Then the Emperor has taken it to Samos."

Tzu reached out just beyond the mat he was sitting on and scooped up some dirt from the floor, and began to pour it from one hand to another. Not having had varying seasons for eons, it was bone dry. Dust wafted about until Tzu had but a small handful remaining. He opened his hand in front of Norinko.

"Look. It isn't even decent dirt. The Gods gave it to us to grow our crops, make our huts and even dam the water if we need to, all for the sole purpose of preserving life. Yet all we do is fight, argue and spill blood over it. I think they must surely be disappointed in us. Right now, I would not like to face any of our Gods ..." He continued to pour the soil from one hand to the other. "... not because I'm afraid but because I would be embarrassed ... embarrassed of Middle Kingdom, embarrassed of my people and embarrassed of my own actions." He dropped the dusty soil back to the ground, brushing his palms against each other. "Yet, I see more blood being spilled before I see peace."

Norinko spoke softly. "Tzu, are my people safe here in this valley?"

Tzu looked at him coldly. "This has always been your land, Norinko."

"With your word on this, I will take my men down into Samos."

Tzu frowned. "For what purpose, Norinko?"

"I care no more for the palace. My love and respect for it was lost with the death of Grand Master Xiang. Keep it for your people, but I must get your Sacred Blue Skull back. Legend has it they are individual and sacred to each tribe of people."

Tzu smiled grimly. "What is *our* Sacred Skull to you?"

Hao butted in. "What he means is, it would be great to have it back where it belongs, back with the people of the North." Tzu looked at Hao. "Tzu, I will be going with him. It would be great to have you and your men with us."

Tzu's ruddy complexion turned crimson. "You want to march with *my* men ... into SAMOS? Have your berries fallen from your bush?"

Norinko resisted the urge to laugh. "I have to say, Hao, I'm with Tzu on this one. If we are seen showing up with Barbarians, it will be another bloodbath."

"That depends."

Tzu raised an eyebrow. "On what, exactly?"

Hao did his best to act like he had it all worked out. "Tzu, your men had an easy taking of Magnar Wall last spring because there weren't enough Royal Guard."

Tzu waved an arm in exasperation. "Yes, because they were all in Samos!"

Sezou cleared his throat. "Word has it there aren't many guards in Samos either."

Tzu turned coldly. "Then just where do you think they are?"

Sezou shrugged. "Gone. All I was told is that they all left on a huge vessel."

Hao was intrigued. "What else can you tell us about the vessel, Sezou?"

"They had supplies just for the journey, but were heavily laden with armour and weapons. No one would say where they were going or how many Royal Guards were on board. Just that the vessel was brand new and was the biggest anyone had ever seen. It only had the flag for Devil's Pass."

Tzu looked immediately alarmed. "What is Devil's Pass?"

Hao frowned. "What is a Devil?"

"What?" Tzu rolled his eyes in frustration and shook his head. "He looks over the Hell we spoke of, not unlike the Gods look over the earth, only for all their goodness, he is evil."

Hao sat back. "I see."

"Tzu, I haven't been into Samos myself, but the one who gave me this information is to be trusted." Sezou stamped his fist in the dirt. "I would stake my own father's life on it."

"I respect that, young man, but where did this friend of yours get *his* information?"

"Tzu, he assured me that he watched the vessel being loaded and departing himself."

"Leaving just how many of the Royal Guard in Samos?"

"I believe it may not be unlike the few left at the Wall last spring."

"I trust in what my son is saying," Norinko assured Tzu.

Tzu ran his fingers through his tangled hair as he soaked up the information. He looked directly into Sezou's eyes. "You are young, what would you like to do?"

Sezou didn't blink. "If I was welcome, I would ride with you and Hao into Samos."

"This will be no picnic, Sezou. It would be naive not to realise that more people are to die before we have resolution."

"But, as Hao is saying, if we don't try united as one, then there will be no resolution at all."

Tzu gazed into the fire, his face unreadable to those around him. They waited patiently. They all had their own thoughts, their own opinions. Eventually, Tzu raised his head to Hao. "You have been to this Samos before? ... you know the way there?"

Hao closed his eyes, shaking his head. "Not from the palace, no."

"Tzu," intervened Norinko, "I can see you are a family man and I know mine for their word. Once given, their word is stone. I will visit the local villages from here to the palace and bring every young man who can give me his word that he will stand beside your men against the Royal Guard. We will meet outside the gates." He held up a finger "We will not ask to enter but await your company, outside."

Tzu's eyes narrowed. "You will wait outside your own palace gates?"

"It is no longer our palace, Tzu."

"Hao, you will also come to stand against your Royal Guard?"

Hao gave Tzu a weary smile. "I was hoping to ride back to the palace with you to prepare, Tzu."

Norinko slapped his hands to his knees. "Well, it is settled then. As one people for one course of action, we leave for Samos."

Hao held his hand up. "Hang on, my friends, there is a little more to this story I may need to fill you in on."

Not knowing what more there could be to be said, Norinko settled.

Hao drew a deep breath, facing Tzu. "Tzu, I'm sorry, my friend, I have one lie to clear up with you. Since you're now not armed, I feel it is the best time to tell you." He chuckled nervously as Tzu stiffened. "Norinko, this may be of some surprise to you also, but now we have cleared up the Desora issue, it's time you both knew who is next to the throne."

Norinko looked perplexed. "But Desora is the only child, is he not, Hao?"

Hao looked briefly at Norinko, though it was Tzu he focused on to deliver the information. "I'm sorry, Tzu, but I did lie about not having any Royals at the palace that day. Actually, Prince Yaan was there in person."

Tzu had the face of thunder, though his voice gave none of it away. "Hao, you lied to protect your prince?"

"Yes."

"So, you pretended to be the Captain of the Guard to protect him, this Yaan?" Hao agreed. Tzu squinted as he shook his finger at Hao in warning. "Hao, just this once I feel I can respect your intentions, but …" He paused. "… if there is anything else?"

Hao shook his head. "No, Tzu. This was the only lie between us."

"You came to the palace for your prince then?"

"Actually, no, Tzu." Hao looked at the ground then back to Tzu. "The prince and I came to the palace to save his sister, Princess Tanica."

A gasp circulated the room. Everyone knew the story of the baby in the bucket, the fire and the missing people. It was always suspected there was one missing Royal baby but *two?* That was never even contemplated.

Norinko gasped at the revelations. "Princess Tanica? Where did she grow up, Hao?"

"The less I say about these two, the safer their brave saviours will be, though if we storm Samos, we must keep both of these individuals safe." He stood up with determination and a look no one would challenge. "Their mother was of a different land, so they are both tall for these lands, and they also both have very distinguishing eyes. The Princess has large, round, green eyes, apparently like those of her mother. The prince, one yellow, one green."

Norinko's mouth dropped open. "Of course!" His voice fell away to almost a whisper, "Like his father and rightful Emperor, Prince Hasuca."

12 Impossible Shot

Behind the city of Samos, high on Yuson Ridge, gathered the mixed army of the Barbarians and Norinko's people. To either side of Tzu and Norinko, many hundreds lined the ridge just out of sight from the city. All on horses, wearing leather and steel armour, helmets and shields, armed with everything from spears to long bows, daggers and swords, they were war-seasoned and eager. The men's muscles pumped with anticipation as the horses breathed through flared nostrils and stamped hooves, ready for the impending charge to seize the city.

Hao's horse shuffled as he swung from the saddle and drew his bow off his shoulders. He pulled an arrow in readiness and moved forward. From this viewpoint, he couldn't yet see the city. His eyes were on nothing but the ridge ahead, though he knew the city of Samos was spread out below him.

He eased out through the long grass, the bad feeling about this plan still with him from the day they'd left Norinko's village. He'd had nightmares and lay awake wrestling with it. *Who is the threat?* It was a cold place he'd found himself in. Both Norinko and Tzu had agreed it was a good plan, though at night, Hao pondered that if Norinko was organised, he could have Samos ready to wipe out the Barbarians, making him a celebrity and hero with the entire Middle Kingdom. The Emperor would make his whole village wealthy beyond their wildest dreams. If that were to happen, Hao could never live with himself. At the same time, Hao was leading the Barbarian army into the hub of Middle Kingdom's economy. This could ruin the entire nation and *he* would then go down in the history books as the man who orchestrated it.

He stopped and lowered himself to one knee. Long grass brushed up against him. He checked his breathing; he had to get his nerves in place or this would be his blunder of too many lives. Something was wrong. He could feel it like he could feel the warm, salty air bristle his face.

Norinko held the reins of Hao's horse as he watched him approach the end of the ridge, then go down on one knee.

Tzu leaned across. "Have you ever known Hao to pray?"

"I don't think he's praying," Norinko scoffed as he turned to Tzu. "Besides, I might suggest you know this complicated man far better than I."

Tzu grunted, still watching Hao.

Hao lifted his head to see a plume of smoke rising just to the west of their position. Standing, he moved carefully forward. His heart beat faster and blood rushed through his veins. This was the moment of truth. Something was about to etch itself in the history books and, one way or another, he was going to be in it.

Now at the end of the ridge, Hao looked down over the city. Markets were bustling at the salt well, but he could hear screaming and commotion. He strained his eyes to make it out. People were rushing away from a new fire to the west. He watched the black smoke billowing out of a small wooden building. Something about the fire irked him but, for a moment ,he couldn't think what it was. Then it dawned on him. *So much smoke but not one flame?*

Suddenly, a horse bolted from the back of the building, dragging what appeared to be a net. It galloped through the cobbled streets, not slowing until it arrived with a gathering of guards at the salt well. The net opened, and a person rolled out, clearly disoriented. The guards grabbed him, dragging him to his feet. The man straightened himself up as his long, blond hair blew in the wind.

A chill went down Hao's spine as he stood up straight. *Yaan!*

Hao focused purely on Yaan as he was strung to a large wheel. He dropped his bow and thundered back to the two men who'd been watching him closely. Norinko and Tzu glanced at each other as Hao stormed towards them.

"Be ready to march the men forward onto the ridge, but not before I say," Hao ordered.

Without further explanation, he went directly to his saddle and pulled out a long, leather pouch. He held it like he was cradling a newborn baby before placing it on the ground to unroll. Inside were five arrows. They were longer than Hao's hunting arrows and clearly made by a true craftsman. The feathers were all in a curve and each barbed point curved in the same arc. Once the arrow was in its target, it could not be drawn out.

Hao checked them over carefully then swiped them up his right fist. He looked at both men. "I trust you both as my brothers. This will either be my best day or my worst. This is your choice." He spun and marched back to his bow. Neither man spoke, nor did they take their eyes off him.

Hao knelt on the ridge with his bow and slowed his breathing as he watched Yaan being beaten. Screams from the crowd pierced the air as the ground suddenly turned black. It appeared to flow almost like water. Hao breathed slower, calming himself as the black mass flowed around Yaan. He recognised Chun, stood back from Yaan, pointing at the wheel, but seeming to pose no immediate threat.

Hao waited.

He watched the wood being piled up around Yaan's wheel and shook his head. *This will not be good.* Without looking, he reached down and picked up one of the arrows. Slowly, he licked all three feathers, placed the arrow on his longbow and stood, intensely focused as a man came forward carrying a torch and a bucket.

Hao's focus narrowed further until he could no longer hear the noise below him. He wasn't thinking about the history books and how his name would be etched into them. For the first time in weeks, his mind was completely clear and at peace. His gaze drifted calmly to the black smoke, the plume thinning and rising in a straight line, then back to the man with the lit torch. He was speaking to Chun.

Hao grunted as he pulled the bowstring right back to draw the barbed point to his white knuckles that clenched the bow. The back of the barbs cut into Hao's fist and droplets of blood trickled down his knuckles. He arched his back, aiming to the sky. The man with the torch stepped forward and stopped.

The arrow released.

Norinko and Tzu heard the arrow snap from Hao's longbow as it cut an air-slicing line, like Hao was aiming for the sun itself. Every man on Yuson Ridge followed its track.

The arrow flew high. First, the curved barb began its slow turn, followed by the almost flat feathers. As it lost its upward drive, the feathers strained to stand in their perfect curve. The wobble of the arrow absorbing the power of Hao's bow eased, and it flew perfect and true. Ever so slowly beginning to rotate, the arrow drew its arc, first towards the sun, then out straight over the flats before it glided towards the river. Over rooftops it flew till it pointed down at its objective, the torch bearer. With the drive in its length, the arrow sped silently down at the man, first at his head, then just a little lower.

The long arrow pierced his leather tunic and the layers of silk under it, driving deep into the man's chest.

Hao had a second arrow in his bow and was ready to let it fly when his target went down on an unnatural angle and burst into a ball of flames. He paused, confused. The man should not have fallen sideways, though it was a good result just the same. He was about to turn his attention to the fat Asset when he saw people go around the back of the wheel and begin to pull away the wood. Behind plumes of tar-blackened smoke bellowing up at the front, a rescue attempt was occurring behind. They were pulling down the wheel. Hao looked back to the fat Asset, now in a carriage, speeding away. *That figures.*

He looked over his shoulder at everyone in their saddles, Tzu eagerly waving the reins of Hao's horse. Hao beckoned them forward. He packed away his four, prized arrows and swung easily into his saddle, looking down the ridge. The horse pranced on the edge as Hao searched. The wheel was still there, but Yaan was gone. Although apparently saved, his whereabouts were now unknown. Tzu and Norinko flanked him on either side.

"You both could have your own objective here and either way I would be doomed. I want Yaan found safe and untouched." Neither man responded as Hao drew his sword and raised it high. "Horn blower, sound your horn!"

A heavy-set man stood up in his saddle and blew the horn. This was immediately followed by more horn blowing, echoing down through every street below.

The city rumbled as the immense stampede of horses, carrying armed warriors from two lands, speaking two languages, charged down Yuson Ridge into the city.

13 Yaan

Yaan's head fell back once more, he began laughing loudly until Chun stopped his ranting and slowly looked at him. Yaan's eyes were unfocused as he laughed uncontrollably. Chun stepped away from him. "Get fuel and fire now! GO!"

The men came only near enough to throw the timbers at the base of the timber stand. They piled it high until Yaan was only seen from the chest up. His wild laughter had stopped, but he still chuckled and looked deliriously happy.

Chun's neck wobbled as he looked around in confusion, his fat cheeks reddening with growing concern. "WHO has the FUEL?"

A man nudged his way through the men carrying a large container of pitch in one hand with a torch in the other. He was proud and arrogant. "I will light your fire, Asset Chun. His witchcraft can't touch me."

"Yes, quite so then. Off you go, my brave, loyal guard. You'll be rewarded for this. Quick, quick, light the fire."

A twisted smile broke across the guard's face as he walked undeterred towards Yaan. He stopped just short of the timbers to savour his moment of glory.

A loud whirring sound cut through the air, drawing everyone's attention. Suddenly, with a loud thock, an arrow pierced down into the arrogant guard. He looked down to see the long arrow and its feathers protruding from his chest. Bewildered, he slowly raised his head towards Yaan. A crossbow bolt came in from behind and hit him in the right leg. He buckled and collapsed to the cobbles, spilling the bucket of fuel. As his right hand hit the ground, the torch licked the pool of fuel, resulting in an instantaneous fireball.

The flames leapt high, engulfing the now screaming man.

The fuel slowly trickled between the cobbles and ran under the timbers. Yaan's mortal future was in the laps of the Gods. He watched as the screaming man thrashed around wildly, coming to rest against the timbers. Black smoke swirled around the crackling wood rising before him. The last he saw of Asset Chun was his fat, smiling face as he boarded his carriage behind the plumes of black smoke.

A drumroll rang out, followed by a rumbling that tremored over the ground. The gathered crowd turned their eyes towards Yuson Ridge above them, to the largest gathering of warriors they'd ever seen. Most were on horseback, and most were Barbarians!

***

Lost in the light that surrounded him, Yaan felt at peace. He was neither cold nor hot. There was no pain, just a feeling of contentment. He pondered how he got there, but was not altogether concerned. A voice beckoned him. It was soft and calm, helping him feel the same way.

As he walked towards the shadow, he could see another silhouette sitting beside the standing figure. He walked closer. "My name is Yaan."

A chuckle came back. "Yes. We know your name, Yaan. Please, come sit with us."

The light cleared as he neared the two forms, only it was not two men but a chimp, and his own father, Hasuca.

Yaan dropped into a deep bow. "I am sorry, Father, I had no idea ..."

Hasuca laughed as the chimp clapped softly several times. "My dear son, there is no bowing here. Please, I asked you to sit with us."

"So, am I dead then?"

Hasuca paused. "You spent some time with your sister. Tell me, what is she like?"

Yaan looked confused. "She is a beautiful woman, Father. I have been told of the true beauty of our mother."

Hasuca's face lit up. "Ah, yes. She was something truly special. Never have our lands seen the likes of her."

"Every day that Tanica walks our lands, we have her beauty with us, Father."

"Yes, I do believe that is so, Yaan. Does she have fight?"

Yaan scoffed, his face bright with surprise. "Do you not see all from here, Father? Does she fight? Damn right she can fight; she fights like a wild woman …" He hesitated a moment, then, "Didn't you have your friend teach her?"

"Yes, that would be Xiang you're referring to."

"Is he not over here also?"

"Yes, Yaan, that's right. Do you not see him?"

Yaan shook his head. "No, but I have yet to get to know my way around, Father."

Hasuca rocked back and erupted in laughter. "Oh, I do so like a good sense of humour." He chuckled a little more before his face turned serious. "What is Kito like, I mean, as a man?"

Yaan thought fondly of his good friend. "He was fun, you know, cheeky. He would never be the funniest man, but he understood humour and indulged when he could." He went quiet for a moment. "Is time relevant here?"

"Relevant?"

"Yes. Do I have to wait for the years to pass to see him once more, or can we just leap to that moment?"

Hasuca held up a hand. "What is your rush? Be patient, son. There are no schedules over here, that's for sure." Yaan dipped his head in disappointment. "You miss him, don't you?"

Yaan nodded. "Hao thought it was ironic that Kito and I were good friends before we knew our connection."

"You have kept with some fine people, Yaan. My father would say it's a reflection of your own character. That was a gallant thing you tried to do, but did you not learn from the first time?"

"Father?"

"The burning factory … last time it was Bolli who lost his life. Two plumes of smoke, and you rushed back in."

Yaan was ill-prepared for his father to heckle him. "A friend was in need and I went to help."

"And now you are dead and good to no one. A prince lost for his land, Yaan."

Yaan struggled with the turn in the conversation. His temper rose, surprising even himself. "Well, at least I didn't run into the jungle and hide!"

"I went to meet with my destiny. You have squandered yours with one reckless, unplanned attack. You were well out of your depth."

Yaan waved his arm angrily as if to swipe away Hasuca's berating. "I didn't attack anyone, they …"

"Threw out a few crumbs, and you ran into the simplest trap. Now you are where they wanted you all along."

Yaan looked at the chimp, its face placid. "I don't know what to say. I had hoped to make you proud. I just wanted to stop the Emperor. I thought he should be stopped."

"And he will be," Hasuca smiled thinly, "But you must be smarter than this. Bravery is of no use without smarts, son."

Yaan warmed with the way he said 'son.' "But this life has been lost now. You are telling me after the fact, which is of little use to the people I have left behind."

Hasuca said nothing but took a deep breath. It was time.

Yaan frowned at the chimp as it made low cooing noises. Not letting go of Hasuca, it leaned forward and placed its hand on Yaan's shoulder. Yaan began to feel light-headed and dizzy. The light returned even brighter than before.

He winced, squinting his eyes. "Well, at least Kito sent us the rats."

"Did he, son? Said whom?"

***

The light was so intense Yaan scrunched his eyes, shutting them tight, then he heard a voice he knew.

"Come on, my friend, open your eyes now."

He was lying flat on his back. He rolled his head from side to side, sighed deeply, and blinked. "Kai," he said, then frowned. "Where are we?"

Kai peered down at him in the now dim light. "Don't concern yourself with this right now, Yaan."

"We're in a bit of a bother, aren't we?"

"You could say that, yes," Kai whispered.

Then the events of the day came flooding back to Yaan. "Oh Gods, I have killed them!"

Kai remained calm. "When you first took me in, I wasn't sure what we were doing, even worse was that you didn't seem to know either. When we got to Hasuca's home and I saw how he had lived, I knew it was something special. *I* was doing something special. As we trained and came into the city from time to time, I saw and heard how the people lived in fear because they didn't know what their own Emperor was doing or would do next. I knew we had to make a change. I am willing to die to change this. Kerrin and Simesie both died for the best of causes and they were happy to give their lives for it. The people saw the Asset at his worst, and no one there agreed with what he did." He spoke in earnest. "They didn't give their lives for you, Yaan. This was not about *you*." Kai rose and moved away.

Yaan let his words seep in. He knew he was right. He tried to focus on the ceiling above, but couldn't. He went to reach up into the darkness and bumped his hand into timber only inches above his face. He scoffed at his own stupidity, trying to see a ceiling when it was just before his face. He was, in fact, under the floorboards. Only a few missing boards above provided access to his makeshift bed.

There was a scurry of footsteps on the timbers above his head. Dust dropped onto his face, and he shut his eyes tight. He felt two people clamber in and settle on either side of him, and a hessian cover was dragged over the three of them.

Kai whispered quietly in his ear and Yaan could hear the concern in his voice. "Don't make a sound. They're searching the entire city for us."

Yaan felt for the person to his right. *Tanica.* He calmed, knowing she was there. Timbers were placed over them and pressed in by foot. He held his breath as he heard a woman answering the door.

"Hello, please come in." The sound of heavy boots reverberated above them as several men entered, walking directly over their heads. *Who's the woman?* Yaan wondered.

A man spoke. "We are inspecting all rooms for fire damage, by orders of the Asset."

Yaan's legs began to cramp as the woman continued. "Oh yes, so good of the Asset. Please feel free to look upstairs."

"We will examine any room we choose," the man said bluntly.

Yaan's mind reeled. *The Asset is not checking for fire damage, he is searching for me!* He listened as the men inspected the entirety of the small cottage. His legs twitched and ached terribly. Kai slipped his leg over Yaan's, trying to pin them still.

The woman spoke again. "This must be awfully hard work for you and your men. Would you like some tea?"

"Really?"

"Well, yes, I could bake some scones if you would like to wait?" She flirted with the man in charge.

"Um, well, yes. This is very intense work, but I must decline. We have much to do."

"Yes, I suppose you do. Have you done much so far?"

"Oh, much. We have covered most of the valley, and there is a team that has come in from the west, also. We will be just about ready to reconvene then we'll go all the way out to the wharf."

"Oh, that's so far and all of that today?"

Yaan's legs shook uncontrollably now. He gritted his teeth at the pain of it.

"Yes, quite so, my lady. We must do it all today."

His men came back down the stairs, and for a moment, there was silence. Yaan held his legs still, grimacing with the pain as Kai placed his hands over Yaan's chest, trying to hold him down.

"Yes, well, best we be on our way then."

"Very well, thank you again for the inspection."

The door closed with a click. Kai pulled the hessian cover back and pushed up the boards covering them. Yaan was lifted out without a word being spoken. The woman from above scurried from the door to Kai's aid. Concern in her voice, she whispered, "It is too soon and too risky yet."

Kai whispered back. "His sugars are low, and he is dehydrated; the salts in his muscles are making him cramp badly."

Without warning, the door opened, and the Captain stepped in. "I was thinking about the scones ..." He froze for just a moment as his eyes swelled at the sight of Yaan. "What ... is *this?!*" He went to draw his sword, but before the hilt had left the sheath, Tanica ran towards him and with one swift move, cracked his neck. He never made a sound as she eased his corpse inside the door. Kai closed the door swiftly and proceeded to drag his body from the front room, out to the back. Tanica jumped back to replace the floorboards and pull over a mat.

Yaan struggled to walk with his legs still cramping. The woman, still unrecognisable to Yaan, helped him to the back room. He leant heavily on her as she pulled his arm across her and supported him with her shoulder. "Too many people are dying for me. You are now in grave danger also."

She kept her head down. "People have been dying in this city for the wrong reasons for a long time, my prince. Just see that you make these losses worth our pain. Now hush yourself."

They reached the back room and turned to the corner behind the door. Easing him down onto a stool, she opened the door so it almost completely concealed him. She brought him a large drinking vessel and left the room.

Yaan was beyond parched but was careful, taking small sips. He lowered his head into his hands and pondered on what she'd just said. His mind ran through what had taken place. *I passed out from the smoke from the fire. Before that … yes, the rats. Before that, Kerrin and Simesie …* He shook his head. *Just as Luhou had said. Before that, I was dragged through the city. It was a trap! A trap set by Okin and Asset Chun.*

Cursing his own stupidity, he now truly understood Hasuca's berating. Through the small space between the door and the wall, he could see a red scarf hanging over a chair. Remembering the markets and her beauty, he scoffed. *But that wasn't her?* Frowning, he looked around the room. *This woman must be quite well to do to be living in a cottage. A far call from the simple huts that most have throughout the city.*

He heard several people scurrying down the alley at the back of the house and pulled the door further to hide, listening to their chatter as they passed by.

"The Barbarians are invading the city," said one of them.

With a thud to the heart, it all came back to him. *The horn was blown after the fire was lit.* He recalled seeing them just before passing out. Hundreds or maybe thousands of horses and armoured Barbarians. With the element of surprise and their positioning above the city, they had it besieged. *The city is doomed!* Yaan racked his brain, but beyond that, he couldn't remember a thing.

Tanica came into the room with the other woman and whispered, "The Barbarians are said to be searching the houses too. We must go now."

Yaan shook his head. "No. I can barely stand, let alone walk. Put me back under the floor and leave. If I have recovered by tonight, I'll make my way out and see you back at the cave." He leveraged himself up against the wall and stepped awkwardly to the table.

Tanica stood square to her brother. "No! Hao died for us, and I can't just leave you here for them!"

"She is right, Yaan," said Kai as he entered the room. "Tanica, you must leave with Mercanti and go immediately to the cave."

Tanica folded her arms firmly in defiance. "No, you can't look after him alone."

"We all know you are the best fighter here, Tanica, but the two of you should never be together, least of all going through the city now," implored Kai.

"No!"

Kai pointed to the door. "You know I'm right, and you're wasting time. Now go!"

Stubborn as always, she turned to Yaan for added support. He just shrugged with a grim smile. "I don't know if it has ever happened before, Tanica, but Kai *is* actually right."

It seemed that on this occasion, Tanica was beaten. "Mercanti, get what you can carry and only what you need." Mercanti dipped her head and hurried for the stairs. Tanica turned back to her brother. "Yaan, I don't feel good about this."

Yaan was still leaning heavily on the table. "I know, and I'm sorry. You were right not wanting me to come into town."

She looked at Yaan's torn, soot-covered clothes and bedraggled hair. She had come so close to losing him for good. Her tone softened. "Never mind that now. Come on, let's get you hidden."

He grimaced at the bruising to his groin and wondered if he would ever walk properly again. But nothing was forever, he told himself; this would pass, too, one way or another.

Kai helped Yaan under the floorboards again, then lay beside him. He gave Tanica a nod as she handed them food and a water bladder before pulling the hessian cover over them. The floorboards were put in place and covered with the mat. She stood back, making sure it was right, one wrinkle and it would draw attention. She thought about the brother she had only just begun to know, and now she had to leave him.

"Yaan?" she whispered to the floor.

"Yes, Tanica."

"I enjoyed our time together. I have learned much." Yaan was so quiet she thought he may not have heard, then he whispered back, "I too have learned much, Tanica. For this I am forever grateful, but I must ask, how did you send the arrow *and* the bolt?"

"The bolt was mine, but the arrow, of that I have no idea ..."

14 Hunters and Farmers

Tzu's men had mixed with Norinko's men for the sake of language and strategy. Every guard and armed man in Samos was given the same treatment and the opportunity to relinquish his weapons, voluntarily or by force if necessary. Uniforms were confiscated, gathered up and burned in small piles on the cobbled streets, and each guard was told to go home to his family. There was minimal opposition. It was as Hao had said it would be. If they could disarm enough men quickly, it would almost be without bloodshed.

Hao and Tzu were working together disarming the men when a strong smell of smoke wafted over them. Tzu pointed with concern. It appeared fires were being ignited through the middle of the city, east to west. There was no contingency plan for this, and all the teams were well spread out, making communication impossible. Without hesitating, Hao turned his horse for the salt well. Several people had to hastily dodge him as he cantered through the streets.

Hao came to a sliding halt and the surrounding peasants backed away. He leapt from his horse and ran towards the well. Quickly, he drew a bucket of water to hand to someone to throw on the fire. Tzu, who had been hot on his heels, snatched it out of his hands and ran forward.

Confusion spread quickly amongst the peasants. *The legend wearing the hat was with a Barbarian?*

Tzu thrust the full bucket at a man and grabbed the empty one. He pointed at the growing fires and shouted, "Damn you, man, run!" He snatched up more empty buckets, and by the time he was back at the well, he had almost more buckets than he could carry.

But it worked. As quickly as he and Hao could drop them and pull them back, people came and took the full ones.

Shoulder to shoulder, Barbarians and peasants all worked together, dropping and filling buckets then passing them down the line to extinguish the fires consuming their homes, again.

Word was now getting around that the fire had been lit by the Royal Guard. Hao pondered this, perplexed. *Surely my own people would not be so fickle as to make such a mistake twice, in the same city and only seasons apart?* It seemed incomprehensible not to have learnt the first time, but the fires burned nonetheless, and for each one they put out, another started.

Tzu tugged on Hao's tunic so hard he almost toppled over. Tzu pointed at the fires. "Is this truly the depth of your people, man?" he called over the ruckus.

Through the smoke, Hao saw the Royal Guard with torches in hand. He clenched his jaw with rage as he pulled his long bow off his shoulder and marched towards the smoke.

Tzu searched out Norinko. "Can I trust you with my men? There is to be no infighting!"

Norinko put his hand on Tzu's shoulder and shouted. "On the life of my dear sister, I will die for this, here today."

The statement resonated with Tzu, and he gave Norinko a firm shake of the wrist, then hurried to catch up with Hao. He ran through the smoke, coughing and spluttering in the mayhem.

It wasn't hard to follow Hao's track of dead and dying guards. If there had been any concern about Hao's intent before, there wasn't now. The death by arrow had ceased with the last arrow and a bloodied bow. It was death by Hao's sword now. As Tzu rounded a corner into an alley, he gasped. Hao was single-handedly fighting all the guards. With impeccable skill and speed, he spun to stave off the guards that surrounded him. Tzu waited for the opportune moment to leap in beside him and, shoulder to shoulder, the two leaders fought the Royal Guard.

A clamour of armour alerted Tzu to more guards coming from behind. They had circled the block of houses to flank them. Without hesitating, Tzu made large strides to confront them. The guards paled at the sight of the hefty Barbarian heading their way. The rumours were true. Barbarians were in the city!

Their hesitation gave Tzu a degree of edge, along with his size, experience and ability to wield his huge sword, but he was, after all, only human and well outnumbered. Hao and Tzu were losing ground with every surge, but fought on undeterred.

This will be our making. This will be our mark in life before we're sent to drink from the Cup of Truth handed to us by our Makers. The irony of it wasn't lost on Hao. *After being brought up to hate the Barbarians and years of fighting and killing them, I'm now back-to-back with their leader, fighting my own Guard, in my capital city!* He didn't have time to wonder what would be in his Cup of Truth when this – his time – was finished.

Suddenly, just as Hao could feel Tzu right behind him, leaving neither with any room to move, the pressure of the guards' advance eased. A bolt whizzed past his head, followed quickly by another. The guards dropped to the ground before him, making way for the biggest, darkest man he'd ever seen. He held nothing but a long, broken, hardwood oar. He strode past Hao without a word and swung his pole around Tzu, smashing down three guards in one fell swoop. Tzu himself was knocked to the side as the huge man stepped through.

Two more bolts flew past.

The big, dark man gritted his teeth as he flung more guards against the wall in the narrow alley. Huge muscles flexed and bulged, yet he moved with surprising grace. Another two bolts whizzed by, and two more guards would not be going home tonight. In no time, there was nothing but a few fleeing guards.

Bewildered, Tzu and Hao could only watch. Hao shrugged in answer to Tzu's silent question. The dark man watched the guards scurrying away. His dirty shirt was badly torn, and his pants were torn off just below the knees. Barefoot, he towered over them as he approached. "What is all this?"

Hao craned his neck. "I feel I have the need to introduce myself as you have just saved my life. I am Hao." He held out a hand. The dark man ignored him as he walked past. His voice was as deep as he was dark. "We don't have time for this chit chat. Your own people burn your own city, little man."

As the big man walked, he dragged his hardwood pole on the cobbles, causing the most unsettling sound. Hao almost had to trot just to keep up with him. It appeared the man knew exactly what he was doing as he walked an arc around the salt well, looking for fire starters. There were no flames now, but the smoke hung thick in the streets, scattered with countless dead men, bolts protruding from them. Hao frowned at Tzu. Neither could see how this battle had unfolded.

Eventually, they doubled back and came out on the western side of the city centre. The wooden wheel of Yaan's intended demise was not far off. Hao had to see it for himself. He was so intent as he approached, he didn't notice Tzu right behind him. He looked at the burnt remains of the torch bearer. Someone had doused the flames but left the contorted corpse. He covered his nose at the stench of it. It brought flashbacks of the night he and Bolli went to assassinate the two caught in Barbarian lands. He shook his head, pushing the memory aside. Picking up a broken spear, he started to prod the corpse.

Tzu frowned. "Just who is he to you?"

Hao shook his head. "No one but he fell strangely before I could release a second arrow. I just want to check on a hunch."

Tzu looked up through the smoke to Yuson Ridge, amazed at the distance. *Never would I have thought such a shot possible.*

The fire had cooked the body, causing muscles to pull it into a strange, distorted shape. The hands had pulled back and the fingers had clenched into an odd, claw-like pose. Similarly, the feet and toes were retracted and the legs had curled in tight under the man's buttocks. Hao pushed his spear in between the thigh and calf muscle on the right leg. He almost gagged at the stench as he struggled to prise them apart. Tzu buried his nose into the crook of his elbow.

"Tzu, grab that spear over there."

"You have to be joking?"

"No, I'm not. Just man up and hold this bastard."

Reluctantly, Tzu did as he was beckoned and put a hand on the contorted excuse of a man. The body slipped around as Hao tried to manoeuvre it.

"Tzu, would you hold it with both hands, man!"

"My nose has been up in the clean mountain air for almost its entire life. I won't expose it to this putrid rot now."

"Well, put your foot on it then!"

Tzu looked at the corpse for a fleeting moment then put one end of the pole on the man's chest and stood on the other. Hao leant in and prised open the leg. One bolt was poking out of the back of the man's knee. With a grotesque squelching sound as if the leg were made of honey, Hao pulled the bolt from the limb. Tzu turned away, breathing heavily through his mouth. "Do you have any limits, Hao?"

Hao shook the bolt at the ground several times, letting the goo slap against the cobbles. "You can talk, but actually, yes."

A few paces away, a pile of clean bones formed a small mound on the ground as if the man had evaporated standing up. The flesh had been picked clean, collapsing the bones to the ground and leaving his head sitting precariously on the top.

Tzu tilted his head. "What do your lot do with your dead?"

Hao almost laughed, shaking his head. "Where is our big friend?"

Tzu looked around, not realising the dark man had slipped away. "I guess the Gods gave him and the Gods took him away." Hao frowned. "What is it now, Hao?" questioned Tzu.

Hao batted his hand. "Ah, nothing. Come on, tell me what you think of this." He headed back towards the alley and stopped at the first body he found. The body was unburnt, with a bolt protruding from his back. He yanked it out and held both bolts up together with a satisfactory grin. "We have two little allies of our own."

"Just because the bolts are similar, it doesn't mean they were together."

Hao tossed the bolts aside. "Yes, though both were fired from rooftops, and they saved both us and Yaan."

"True."

Most fires had now stopped, and only a few peasants gathered around the salt well, dousing any hot embers that remained.

"Come on, Tzu, it will be dark soon, and we need to ensure we don't have any infighting with the confusion."

The two men crossed the destroyed marketplace, mostly in silence. The dark stranger had made an impression on both men. Norinko awaited them at the salt well, frowning.

"What bothers you, my friend?" Tzu queried.

"Some of our group returned saying that the guards still loyal to the Emperor have withdrawn to the harbour."

"What's so bad about that?"

"There are five massive vessels waiting for them. They leave for Zimbali in the morning."

Tzu looked perplexed. Hao quietly explained. "The Emperor has allies there. They will return with many, many more men like the one who saved us – only they will fight *for* the Emperor."

Tzu looked at Norinko. "Until today, I thought we were the only other people. There was talk of other lands, but none of our people had ever been able to cross the Great Ranges or come down past your lands. But Hao, the dark man beat your Guard, so maybe the Emperor is getting the same beating."

Norinko shook his head. "No, I have met the leader of Zimbali, King Mensa. I also knew his father."

Tzu shrugged his shoulders. "And?"

"A King, two Queens and two brothers have all disappeared. Mensa is the only remaining member of his family. He is now King and a stand-over ruler."

Tzu drew back. "Are you telling me this man, Mensa, took the lives of his own family?"

Norinko just nodded.

Tzu paced around slowly, his head bent deep in thought. "Norinko, how many lands are there?"

"I can't really say. The legend of the Sacred Skulls says there are seven, but I don't know how much of it is true." He was contemplating his next words when Tzu asked, "Does this Zimbali have any neighbours?"

"Yes, they are closely tied with Mensa, although …" Norinko turned to Hao. " … the Pharaoh of Orion gave his daughter, Princess Rani, as the second Queen for King Mabutu. Rani was murdered, so I hardly think they would now be allies to Zimbali."

"So, how big is the Pharaoh's army relative to ours?"

Norinko shrugged. "Hard to say, really."

"Because you don't know how many men they have?"

"No, because I no longer know how many loyal guards the Emperor has." He motioned past Tzu to the small fires that had been lit for groups to gather around. The grateful people of Samos were tentatively arriving with food and water vessels. The men sat in mixed groups.

Tzu frowned. "I do hope they're not trying to talk about fighting on the Wall because …"

Norinko cut him off, pointing to one group. One man from his group was holding his hands up to his head, fingers splayed. The other, a Barbarian, shook his head and held his up with fingers closed. Some of the men laughed, and they swapped words. The language barrier had been breached, at least between explaining the deer and the snow moose. Norinko grinned. "These are not fighting men but farmers and hunters serving a ruler's ego and greed."

Tzu folded his arms. "But the worst ego, your Emperor, will come back and when he does, how many allies will he return with?"

"I feel we have made a very small gain today, though the real problem is not even on these shores anymore."

"We need Kito." Both men turned to Hao as he continued. "We must find Kito and try to unite properly before the Emperor returns with his united front. Once here, it will be too late."

Tzu frowned. "Why is this, Hao?"

"Several reasons," Hao sighed as he looked at the ground.

"You got us here, Hao, we're all ears," prompted Norinko.

"If the Emperor is allowed to show up with overwhelming numbers, all of this will evaporate. Most of these people will simply fall in line with his movement. With each day he is not confronted, he gains confidence and momentum in his delusions. And if he gets back here and learns his son is dead …"

A silent look passed between Norinko and Tzu, and Hao let the reality of it sink in before he put forward his biggest plan yet. "We need to get to the Emperor in Zimbali so we can show his allies that the people of Middle Kingdom do not approve."

Norinko's eyes widened. "You think we might be able to break the pack before they return here?"

Hao pointed to the groups of men. "If he arrives here, you can forget farmers and hunters."

Norinko took a deep breath as he looked around. The day was fading and the men needed direction to keep the calm. He turned to the salt well and jumped up onto the edge. "Listen up, men!" The talk simmered down. "We have just arrived and we have much work to do yet. We will have watchmen throughout the city. Nobody, and I mean *nobody*, will consume wine. You must consider yourselves ready for duty at any time. Rest now, you have done well, but this has only been the first day."

Tzu climbed up and stood to Norinko's right. He swung his arm over Norinko's shoulder, and Norinko was quick to reciprocate. Tzu began repeating everything Norinko had said in his own language for his men. Once finished, Norinko continued. "I, alone, will stay here to look out for all of you. Tzu and Hao are going to take this war – this war that is not ours – to Zimbali. This war that is not ours and that should never have been of Middle Kingdom. This is a war that only belongs to the deluded Emperor. We will take this war away from our lands to the Emperor and finish it for all time. We must stand, not just as one land, but as ONE PEOPLE!"

Tzu followed on to his men, then the two shook clenched fists in the air as if they had already won. All the men jumped to their feet, cheering and reciprocating with waving fists in the evening air.

The two men hopped down off the well. Tzu laughed at Norinko. "I'm pleased we only fought you with steel; I don't know if I could match that tongue of yours. That was very astute, pulling the men together like that."

Norinko put his hand on Tzu's shoulder. "The Emperor has taken your Sacred Skull along with our own. I know you will do us proud, Tzu. The survival of all these lands depends on it."

Tzu raised his eyebrows, glancing at Hao. "No pressure then."

15 The Bridge

Tanica stood looking at the floorboards, thinking over Yaan's question. She had no idea where the arrow had come from. Just then, Mercanti returned. She had changed her clothes, opting for black, faded long pants with a tunic, her hair in a cloth hat tied under her chin. She put a small bag on her back. "Shall we?"

Tanica groaned, looking once more at the rug that hid her brother beneath it and wanting to say more to Yaan, but couldn't. She moved through the back room to check the alley. When Mercanti entered the rear room, she looked about the table. "She must have picked it up," she whispered to herself.

Tanica stood in the open door to the alley. "What?"

"The scarf … she took it. Hang on." Mercanti swung open a cupboard door and grabbed a quiver of bolts, slinging them over her shoulder before grabbing a crossbow.

Tanica grimaced. "Do you even know how to load that?"

Mercanti strode with purpose to the door. "If you have one, so can I."

Tanica shook her head and re-checked the alley before easing outside, her long, flowing dark hair hard to pick in the shadows of the afternoon light.

The two women made good progress, passing from one alley to another. From time to time, they came across other people, but they were homemakers and workers and looked more afraid than the two young women. Not a word was spoken. Sometimes Tanica was unsure about which way to go, so Mercanti, now realising the general direction, took the lead.

Suddenly, a bunch of people came running towards them. As they passed, a man said in fright, "It's them. The Barbarians!" He wasted no time waiting for a reply and was gone in a flash. Tanica turned to the nearest door and slammed her shoulder into it. It opened with a knock against the wall inside. She closed it behind them and put her foot to it. In the hush of the darkened room, they held their breath and waited.

After a moment, Tanica took her weight off the door but it was badly timed and after hearing a noise from the outside, the door was kicked in. It flew open, and the door frame was filled with the form of a Barbarian lowering his boot. He looked at the two women, and a smile crossed his gnarly face. There was a 'thock' and his head drew back as he toppled over backwards, but no sooner had he fallen than another Barbarian blocked the door. Tanica was quick with her knife and felled him without a sound. She dragged him forward, dropping him to the floor. She spun to Mercanti who was dropping a fresh bolt in her cocked crossbow. She raised it to her shoulder and nodded to Tanica. The alley was clear. Pulling the first man inside, Mercanti quietly pulled the door shut, and the two women moved on quickly.

With their backs to opposing walls, they eased along to the end of the alley following a path that led to a stream. Mercanti could see her direction was clear, but by the look on Tanica's face, her direction was not. Mercanti eased across the alley to stand beside her. On a stone, arched bridge stood three Barbarians armed with bows. One had a large horn, carried by a rope over his shoulder, hanging at his waist. One blow and the whole city would hear. They backed away from the end of the alley.

Mercanti leaned in close to Tanica. "If we wait until dark, we could slip in and swim."

Tanica shook her head. "They'll be blocking the entire city from escape. If we get on the roof, do you think you could take one of them with your crossbow?"

"I've never taken aim at a human before."

Tanica's mouth dropped open as she waved her hand back down the alley. "What was that then?"

"I had no choice, did I?" pleaded Mercanti.

Tanica squeezed Mercanti's shoulder. "I think there are a lot of people hiding until nightfall to then try for this bridge. Can you make the shot or not?"

Mercanti's mind raced. "I can make the shot."

Tanica didn't waste any time in turning to a creeper on the wall of a two-storeyed house, and Mercanti quickly followed her lead. In moments, they were on the roof and eased themselves up to the ridge top. Just short of the apex, they stopped and loaded their crossbows. Tanica nudged Mercanti and, putting her thumb in her mouth, made out as if she were blowing it. Mercanti nodded. They crawled to the rooftop and slowly lifted their bows. The light was good enough, although for a crossbow, it would be a very long shot.

Together, they took aim and fired. Two men fell, and the third stood dumbfounded for a moment, then dived down. Tanica saw the mistake in their plan. He was now down behind the stone wall of the bridge. He may have no idea where they shot from, but he didn't need to stand to blow the horn either. Tanica dropped her crossbow and went straight over the top of the apex, running down the other side. Mercanti's fingers trembled as she tried to reload her crossbow. She fumbled the cocking arm. *Come on, come on.* Beads of sweat formed on her brow as her hands shook. *Come on, damn you.*

Tanica landed on the grass and rolled to her feet, only one thing on her mind. With long strides, she strained for the bridge, pushing herself. Her entire focus was on the bridge and the horn-blower. If the horn sounded, there was no telling how many people would be dead by daybreak. It would be all her doing. As she came around the corner onto the bridge, she could see the smallest of the three Barbarians rolling the horn blower over.

Try as she might, everything was as if in slow motion. Her strides too short, her breaths too shallow, and she seemed too far away and too late. The horn was now in reach. As he pulled it around to blow, he saw Tanica running at him with a knife. He drew a big breath. Tanica knew she couldn't reach him in time. *At least I will kill him for his effort.*

She watched him blow with all his might, but only a squeak came out. As she ran as hard as she could, his face turned blue as he watched her and the knife getting closer. At the last second, he stood up with a long sword. He stepped back as he raised it confidently over his right shoulder. In her last strides at him, she turned the knife up in her hand.

In that moment of absolute focus, Tanica heard the bolt coming before it whisked past her head and smacked hard into his chest. The sword dropped from his hand, and he stepped back, gazing down at the bolt with a contorted face. He looked blankly at Tanica as he took another step backward and bumped into the bridge wall. He toppled over without so much as a harsh word.

Tanica looked back at the rooftop. She could just make out the silhouette of Mercanti waving. She fell to her knees, completely spent; her only hope was that no one else would approach right now.

Finally catching her breath, she bent over and grabbed the horn. When the big man had fallen on it, he'd squashed the tip. She put her finger inside and popped the tip back out. She shuddered. *If he'd had time ...* Cutting the rope, she tossed the horn over the side.

By now, Mercanti was heading her way. She handed Tanica her crossbow. "Have you pulled the bolts?"

Tanica shook her head. Mercanti bent over to pull the first one, contemplating how best to handle the body. Tanica went to the other body and put her foot on his chest, taking hold of the bolt. "Think of it as a stag or something you used to hunt."

Mercanti tentatively put her foot on the big man's chest and tried hard to think of a wild boar. She pulled hard. The sinew squelched under the puckered skin but she had to have the bolt back. Finally pulled clear, she wiped the bolt on his clothes and whispered something to the dead man.

Tanica pulled her bolt clear, too. "We need to be going now, Mercanti." She glanced around. "Come on, we have a way to go, and soon it will be pitch-black in the jungle."

"The jungle? Where are you taking me?"

"To Hasuca's place."

Mercanti took a quick couple of steps to catch up. "What … the prince?"

Tanica looked bemused. "Yes, actually."

"Oh, my word, I'm going to the prince's place." She almost squealed as she said it.

"Is this something to be excited about? I mean, he *is* the prince that turned his back on his people. If he had the backbone, we wouldn't be in this mess right now."

"Oh no, Tanica. Father said if Prince Hasuca hadn't left the palace, Emperor Koe would have divided the nation and many would have died."

"Nonsense! If he'd stayed, he would have been the rightful Emperor."

"No. Koe wanted it too much. He would have found allies and civil war would have been on the people. Then the Barbarians wouldn't have been kept in check and they …"

"*They* are actually taking the city as we speak, Mercanti."

"But only because Emperor Koe has taken so many of his Guard to Zimbali. That has nothing to do with Hasuca." Mercanti couldn't contain herself. "I can't believe I'm going to his hideout. Father would be beside himself," she whispered excitedly.

The two walked without further word for quite a while until Tanica asked, "Mercanti, how did you learn to shoot so well?"

"Father always wanted a boy, but mother only bore girls. I was the youngest and well, the most boyish too, I suppose," she chuckled to herself, "So, I was the one he took hunting. He would pack my crossbow so no one knew what we were doing, but once out in the jungle he would hand it over to me. He liked the long bow."

"You talk as if he is dead, Mercanti."

Mercanti stopped. "Sadly, I'm the only one left of my family."

Tanica took Mercanti by the arm. "Oh, I'm so sorry. I didn't know." She gave Mercanti a small hug.

Mercanti shrugged her away. "It was a while ago now. Father was the last one to die. It was the fire at the silk factory, you know. He was one of the guards there. I don't know how really, there were so many stories about how it all happened, trampled by a horse or something. All I know is, he's dead and I'm the last of my family."

Tanica reflected on it. The city would be full of such sad stories now. "So, who was the woman with the scarf? We didn't have time to …"

"It's alright, Tanica, the entire afternoon has been somewhat crazy. That was Arshia, my best friend. She must have come downstairs and left just before we did. Her father used to talk a lot with mine. After father died, her family insisted I stay with them. They are very political, that's why I know at least a little about the prince."

By this time, the two women had reached the edge of Yuson Ridge. Tanica turned back to the city. "Hey, Mercanti, look!"

Down below, they could make out large numbers of people scrambling through the darkness and over the small stone bridge. The people would be fine out in the jungle until the city under siege was worked out. Mercanti turned to her new friend. "You are responsible for all those lives, Tanica. You were right."

A chill ran up Tanica's spine. She spun on her heel, blade in hand and lunged forward. No one was there. She looked around nervously. "Damn I hate this!" she yelled at no one. Still, she moved like she was about to strike. The hair on her arms stood up. She could feel him but couldn't see him.

Mercanti had instinctively crouched to the ground. "Tanica? What is it?"

Tanica whisked her blade about several more times, pacing about, then stopped. She looked at the ground, barely breathing. Finally, she sheathed her sword and shook her head. "We need to go back."

"Tanica?"

16 Chun's Retreat

Earlier that day, Asset Chun climbed up into his carriage as Captain Wan held the door. They looked back at Yaan and the fire. Black smoke shimmered with heat, the flames leaping so high the stupid man would already be dead. As the captain climbed up, he heard Chun chuckle.

"I will be the most powerful man in all Middle Kingdom when the Emperor hears of this, and it hasn't cost me a cent." Chun used his cane to bang on the roof. A whip cracked the air, and the carriage charged away. With wheels of steel on the cobbled road, neither man heard the horns blow from Yuson Ridge.

The carriage swayed and bounced its way through Samos. The captain tried not to focus on the wobbling neck of the Asset. "So, tell me, sire, you have dealt with the estranged Yaan and you have five vessels ready to go …"

"Six! And all the biggest ever built. It has never been done before."

Captain Wan dipped his head. "As you say, sire. You've already sent the first one to the Emperor. Have we had word back from the esteemed as to how well it has gone so far?"

"No, but I did see over all the testings myself, and I must say, it was quite impressive. As you were saying …" Chun raised his chin ever so slightly and looked out the window as if disinterested.

"Ah, yes, as I was saying … you have had Yaan disposed of and the vessels and the city under your very command. I would say, sire, you may be inducted into the Royal family when the Emperor returns."

"I hadn't thought of such a thing! It has happened before, I'm sure." He almost drooled with excitement as he patted his sweaty forehead with his pocket cloth.

"Oh, no. I would think you'd be the first ever after such an achievement. You must be their biggest and most successful Asset yet."

"The Fly family certainly did little with the city in all their generations of management." He flicked his cloth in the air. "Could you imagine where we would all be now if Tark was running it?"

"Oh, the heavens no, sire. It would be quite outrageous."

The two men laughed and the Asset's neck wobbled some more as he looked out the window again. "Yes, quite outrageous."

The carriage came to a halt outside Chun's office by the river. The captain quickly put the step down for Asset Chun, but he waved a dismissive hand. "Be a good fellow and mount your horse. You will instruct the men that when the fire has burnt out, I want the bones collected and brought to me." He was already opening the office door as the captain responded with "As you would have it, sire."

Inside, Chun pulled a map from his desk drawer. It was the Greater Middle Kingdom. He looked to the east. *There are plenty of open meadows there. I could clear the rest for breeding meat for the Palace and make a killing.* His exaggerated laugh at his own pun echoed through the office. "Maid!"

She entered and bowed her head, not lifting it until he had given his order.

"I will have some tea and a few pieces of cake, oh and then some wine to follow and not that cheap stuff I bring out when we have visitors – the stuff we save for the Emperor."

The maid gasped. "Are we to expect a visit?"

"Hardly your concern; now just fetch it or I will get someone who will." The maid's face dropped as she scurried away. Chun went back to thinking about his five thousand acres. He paid no attention to the horse that had bolted up to his outside door. So lost in his own reveries, he didn't lift his head until he heard Captain Wan in the front office.

"Get your things and run for your life! There is no time to spare." He had burst into the office without knocking. "Asset Chun, sire, it's the Barbarians!"

"Have they breached the Wall? Heavens forbid!"

The captain shook his head vigorously and pointed in a northerly direction. "Sire, they are in the *city!*"

"What? *This* city?"

More frantic nodding.

"Raise the guards and hold them as best you can."

The captain tried to explain in an almost pleading tone, "Sire, there are maybe thousands of them."

"Are they armed?"

"Yes, and on horseback, sire!"

Chun scrambled his papers together from his desk and stuffed them into a satchel. "Gather all the men in the city. Don't let them pass the salt well. Set alight all the houses south of there."

"Sire?"

Chun didn't look up at the panicked captain. "It's blowing a southerly, so just set it all alight."

"But there will be people hiding in their dwellings to the north!"

"Sometimes you must sacrifice a few in order to save the greater. All my commerce is done on the waterfront. Without that, I do not *have* a city. Now go!"

The captain recoiled with the venom in the Asset's voice. He didn't bow as he turned and left the office.

Asset Chun swiped up his satchel and marched outside his waterfront dwelling. He looked about nervously. With his cane tucked under his arm, he tried to hurry himself along, shuffling as best his stumpy, rounded frame would allow towards the vessel factory and the five remaining vessels ready to go.

"Kalgan! Where is Kalgan?"

A man turned to see the Asset sweating profusely. He leapt up. "Asset Chun, sre." He beamed with pride. "It is most …"

Chun swung his cane and whacked the man hard on the side of his head. "Where is Kalgan?!"

The poor man dropped to the ground with his hands protectively covering his head. Another worker quickly stood over him, pointing. "In his office, sire. Kalgan is in his …"

The Asset strode off without response and burst into the office. "Kalgan, there has been a change in the plan. You will muster all your men and sail out of here immediately!"

Kalgan jumped to his feet. "What? We're not ready, Chun."

Chun's already flushed face reddened further. He slammed his cane down hard on the desk, shattering Kalgan's cup and wafting his papers into the air. He lowered his voice with deliberate menace. "If *I* say we are to leave immediately, then it is your job to say, 'As you wish, sire.' Is that quite clear, Kalgan?"

Kalgan barely hid his contempt as he eyed the Asset coldly. "As *you* wish, *sire*." He frowned. "For how long?"

Chun waved his cane again as if waiting for a reason to swing it once more. "Take all the provisions we have here and be ready to leave when I say." Kalgan could see the stress in the fat Asset's face. Now he was worried.

Kalgan marched down to the workshop floor and stepped up on a box. "Men, drop your tools and gather around now." He held up his hands, and the men quickly hushed in anticipation.

"There is a threat to the Emperor." The men gasped. Kalgan projected an air of seriousness, though inside he struggled not to laugh at their simple minds. "It is our job to take these fine vessels you have all laboured on and set off to help him."

The men mumbled amongst themselves. Kalgan held up his hands once more. "We must leave immediately." Talk erupted. "Quiet or I will personally deal with any offender!" Silence fell and Kalgan continued quietly, "You will load all the provisions we have here and be ready to leave shortly. Time is of the essence: your

Emperor is waiting."

Kalgan looked for his first mate. "Katanning, you will go immediately to the Captain of the Guard and tell him we will be boarding before sunset. He will understand."

Katanning hesitated; there was more to this than Kalgan was letting on, but this was not the time to question, so he would do as Kalgan bade.

Waved on by Kalgan, everyone rushed off to their given tasks to ready the vessels for their premature departure. Kalgan returned to the office and shut the door behind him.

Asset Chun was back in his leather chair. "The Emperor needs our help? What on earth was that?"

Kalgan waved his hands for the Asset to lower his voice. "I learnt a long time ago that to get the best out of your men, you must give them good reason to get the job done. You might have given me nothing to go on, but I gave them a reason."

The Asset listened to the orders being given by Kalgan's foremen as barrels were rolled out. "Fair enough. The Emperor it is then." He looked at the desk for a moment. "Can we really leave in the dark, Kalgan?"

Kalgan shook his head. "Actually, no. How big is the threat?"

The leather chair squeaked as Chun sat forward and prodded his finger into the desk several times. "We are in grave danger just sitting here right now!"

Kalgan raised his eyebrows. "Very well, the city is not safe then." Chun dabbed his forehead off some more as Kalgan paced the length of the office a few times. "We will board the vessels with all the supplies, then head down river into the jungle and out of sight. At first light, we will head for Devil's Sea."

17 Assassin Sisters

On Koe's vessel, Kito felt a powerful urge to seek out his friends. *Koe has lifted the stakes on this trip. His plans are now out in the open and being put into action. I must now develop plans and move them into place. I must strike back when the time is right.*

Seeing the Sheik and King were good for refreshments, and with Koe downstairs, Kito excused himself and went to the galley roof. The warm sun shone down as he took off his top, folded it and sat down on it. With the sail behind him, there was very little breeze where he sat. He looked over the beautiful blue ocean. *I wonder what the Gods think of the mess mankind is making of their world?* Removing the twin swords, he gently laid them out before him and breathed deeply. He felt the need to remove the crown from his left arm. Holding it in both hands, he rubbed his thumb over the centre. It was almost hot, not unlike the twin swords when he began to think of his next spar with Koe.

He felt the block lifting and lowered his head. Thumbing the burning crown, he relaxed deeper. The block weakened, and Kito focused on his purpose, back to Samos. Back to the time of the fires.

He slipped from his body and weaved up over the sails. He looked down and slowed the vessel's route through the waves. Slower until all movement had ceased. He looked up, flexing and stretching his form. Faster, the colours began to spread and meld. The vessel below him was now moving backwards, and with it, Kito moved back in time.

He didn't listen for the chimp's coo or the soft call of a respected elder. His focus was on Samos with the second plume of smoke billowing up. His nostrils flared at the scent of it. He could taste the ash on his tongue, then he saw it, the plume of smoke with no fire. With searching eyes, he slowed and moved down.

***

Having returned to the city, Tanica and Mercanti ran once more from rooftop to rooftop, their light, fit bodies putting little strain on the lightly built houses. This was a better part of the city and most houses were closely built and two storeys high. It had never occurred to Mercanti to travel through the city this way, but it was so much quicker, and she wondered if travelling through the alleys would ever be the same again.

They were now close to the smoke billowing from the houses. Mercanti grimaced in anger. This was not the work of the Barbarians as she had privately prayed for. Below her was quite clearly their own Royal Guard carrying torches. *Again, they are responsible.* She knew the owners of some of these buildings, and now she had no problem loading her crossbow. She looked at Tanica, who, by contrast, was calm and focused, ready to take care of the task at hand.

As Mercanti dropped in her first bolt, her life would never be the same after today. She breathed evenly as they nodded to each other and pointed at their two targets who moved from house to housewith lit torches. Neither man cried out as they simply fell to the ground. The torches rolled onto the cobbled streets, lolling back and forth. With nothing to burn, they dimmed then extinguished.

As quickly as they could, they ran to the next rooftop, reloaded and fired again at anyone carrying a torch to a house. Further on they ran, targets falling at every stop. Mercanti looked to Tanica and whispered. "My bolts are running thin."

Tanica acknowledged her, then suddenly, something caught her attention. She scrunched her face. "What *is* that?" she whispered. It was an odd sound of wood thumping and cracking. They moved around, trying to see where the sound was coming from. All they could make out was the silhouette of a huge man swinging what looked like a length of wood. The Royal Guard was charging at him, but the big man knocked each guard to the ground with barely a grunt.

The silhouette took the guards' attention from lighting the houses. As graceful and powerful as he might have been, sheer numbers of the guard were to overrun him. Tanica smiled. *Not tonight. Tonight, the Gods have their own plan in place and it isn't the plan of the fat Asset!*

From rooftops came bolts. Not thick and fast but true and deadly. As the fighting guards fell and thinned out, the remaining confused guards retreated. For a moment, the silhouette stood still looking at the bodies, then he turned and looked up directly at the two feminine forms on the roof. He gave the smallest gesture of gratitude, then turned and walked along the alley in the direction most of the guards had retreated.

The silhouette wasn't hard to follow as he bounced what appeared to be a broken oar on the cobbles. It made a powerful sound that echoed through the alleys. Tanica was pleased he wasn't looking for her. The silhouette came across several small parties that were setting fires, and he took care of them without the need to fire a bolt.

Mercanti breathed a sigh of relief. "I think we have them all," she muttered.

Silently, they followed the wooden echo through the back streets of the smoking city. As they heard more fighting, Tanica leapt over the alley to another roof but held her hand out for Mercanti to stay on her side. On parallel roofs, they made their way along, looking down onto a street fight. Tanica could see the silhouettes of two men fighting gallantly against the entire Guard. She squinted to verify what she saw. One was definitely a Barbarian. From her viewpoint, she saw some of the guards break away and head down the street and around the corner, their aim to get in behind the two fighters. Mercanti was already dropping a bolt into her crossbow. Tanica did the same as she heard the hardwood thump down, then silence. The huge silhouette was also in the battle.

Mercanti went down on one knee, leaning out over the edge of the roof to get a good shot up the street. Tanica signalled across to her and they both took aim and fired, making their shots count as they didn't have many bolts left. Once fired, they reloaded and waited to see where the strongest point of the Guard was, then weakened it.

Suddenly, the last of the guards turned and ran. Tanica raced across the rooftops to see which way they were heading, leaping across the void from one roof to the next. Mercanti caught up to her, and they looked down at the fleeing Guard. "They're going to the river."

Tanica pursed her lips. "I think they're going to the Asset. He will be at the shed with the Emperor's vessels. My guess is he'll leave on the first tide tomorrow."

"Coward."

"As is his Guard."

Mercanti looked down at the three silhouettes now heading back down the alley. "But who are they?"

Tanica looked at the men. Suddenly, she got that chill again and spun around. Mercanti never saw her draw the blade but she could see it gleam in the light. Quick to move out of the way, she crouched, looking up. "What is this, Tanica? What is upsetting you so?" she asked, down on one knee with the crossbow raised.

Tanica spun a few more times, mumbling incoherently. Eventually, she sheathed her sword. "Come on, we need to retrieve as many bolts as we can."

Back down onto the street, Mercanti grimaced as she retrieved the bolts. It had to be done. They could hear the hardwood pole dragging along the cobbles in the distance.

Tanica motioned with her head. "We can come back a little later for the rest. The less contact we make with people in the city, the safer Yaan will be."

They ran like thieves through the back streets until they returned to the back door of Mercanti's place. It was getting dark now, but a candle flickered on the wooden sill. Slowly, Tanica drew her short sword and stepped forward. Mercanti grabbed her by the arm and shook her head. She placed herself in front of Tanica and mouthed the word, 'Stay.' The flickering candle made Tanica uneasy, but reluctantly, she stayed as Mercanti backed to the far side of the alley. Slipping along the wall, she was able to see through the window with minimal light on her. Yaan was at the table with Kai, their heads down as they talked in low voices. Mercanti slipped farther along the wall to see all the room. It was clear. She waved to Tanica, who then eased forward, though she was unable to shift the unsettling feeling that they had missed something. She checked the alley yet again. No, it was clear.

Mercanti entered the room and hushed the men with a finger over her mouth before greeting them with a warm hug. Tanica, still uneasy, held back to make sure it wasn't a trap. Through the open door, she watched Mercanti remove her coat and hang it up, stoke the fire and place a kettle on it. The evening was indeed cooling off. Tanica sighed as she stepped through the door. Just as she entered the room, a knife crossed her throat and another point pressed into her back.

"Hold still and everything will be alright," rasped the deep voice.

She froze. *How could anyone have been outside with me?*

Yaan and Kai sprang to their feet.

"Ah, easy woman at the stove, turn about so I can see those steady hands of yours," said the low voice. Mercanti turned with her hands up. The man was crouched behind Tanica. In the candlelight, she could see nothing but the blade at Tanica's throat. The man eased Tanica forward towards the table. "Sit."

Tanica reached slowly for a chair, then quickly flung it, sending it flying across the room. She spun around to face her would-be attacker. Sparks flew from the clashing of steel on steel as they sparred in the poor light. For a time, Yaan and Kai were pinned with backs to the wall as Tanica and the stranger springboarded from one wall to another.

Kai suddenly threw himself between them. "Stop! Both of you! Stop this nonsense immediately!"

Yaan limped forward, looking at the man. "Kito? What the blazes do you think you are doing?"

Kito pulled back his hood, grinning at Tanica. "It is my privilege, Tanica. Xiang told me you were the best."

She spat at him with the venom of a snake, but Kito moved like one, and the spitball narrowly missed him. She didn't smile. "That would be Grand Master Xiang to you, and when did he ever grace *your* presence with his company?"

Yaan was shocked at Tanica's tone of voice, but Kito chuckled and bowed deeply. "I'm sorry, Tanica, it was a most inhospitable entry for me, though I do feel with the talent of you two women, it was also the safest way right now."

Kai splayed his arms at the room and all its broken furniture. "*Safest,* Kito? Are you sure?"

"This is my house you have trashed, Mr Kito!" Mercanti said indignantly. "I feel I am the only one here who has not been introduced." She stood beside Tanica with her hands on her hips and did not so much as dip her head.

Kito looked at her. "I would like to offer my apologies for your house and also offer my thanks. Because of the two of you, many peasants have made it out of the city into the jungle. My name, as you now know, is Kito, and I am at your service, Mercanti." He stood to his near full height, the back of his head bent against the ceiling.

Mercanti squinted. "You were the man in the alley, weren't you?"

Kito shook his head. "No. I have only arrived a short time ago."

Mercanti wasn't convinced. "Yes, you move just like him."

Kito shrugged. "I have no reason to be untruthful to you."

Kai straightened the table and uprighted the remaining chairs. "I'd offer you one Kito but …"

Kito held up his large hand. "Thank you, but I need to stand anyway." He turned to Yaan. "May I ask what your plan is now, my friend?"

Yaan shrugged sheepishly, not really having a plan. "Kito, I must ask how you got here? You were last heading for your homelands, yet after all this time, here you are."

Kito smiled. He couldn't realistically give the truth on this matter and keep his integrity. "May I offer some insight as to how the city is?"

Yaan sat at the table and leant forward to speak, but Tanica cut in. "How did you know about the releasing of the peasants?"

Yaan spoke before Kito could. "I could also ask why *you* have come back here, Tanica, but before we waste time going over the past, we need to clear the future."

Mercanti took Tanica's hand in hers and shook it gently. "Your brother is right, Tanica, let him speak."

Tanica sat, glaring at Kito as he spoke to Yaan. "The city is in good hands, and I see no real danger now. The peasants feed the Barbarians, and tomorrow they will be taken to the river and shown how to fish. Never have they seen such a thing, Yaan."

"What about the language barrier?"

"There are a few, including Norinko himself, who can speak reasonably well in both. They seem to respect him. He is known to the older Barbarians. His sister, coupled with one of them, was thrown out of her village by her own father. It was only because of a young Norinko that she got to live at all."

Tanica's eyes narrowed. Yaan wasn't convinced. "You're sure the city is good, Kito? I have your word?"

Kito dipped his head. "There will be some problems regarding three dead Barbarians on the bridge …" He glanced at Tanica. "…

and a few others missing, but they were warned that some would surely be lost. Norinko will get them past that." He ignored the two women who were watching him with doubting eyes. "Sadly, today was also meant to be mixed tribes. Some Barbarians and some Middle Kingdom, so not to have confusion about the Barbarians taking the city alone. But they didn't trust each other and shuffled back to their comfort zones. Tomorrow, the mixed groups will be reaffirmed, so not to have the same misunderstanding over the intention. Your city is good, at least for a time."

"A time, Kito?"

"A long time."

"Fair enough." Yaan was quiet for a moment, contemplating his options, then he looked up at Kito. "You already have a plan for me, don't you, my friend?"

Kito affirmed with a nod as he checked the expectant faces around the room. "I have another problem and need you to come with me."

Yaan sat forward. "Then I will help, Kito. Where?"

"Zimbali."

Yaan's jaw dropped. "Kito. My lands are full of the Barbarians, the palace for the sake of the Gods is …"

"Your lands and your palace will be fine, but I need your help in *my* lands, Yaan."

Yaan held his head in his hands as he shook it. "It is hard to comprehend that I can do much to help *you*, Kito."

"When we were fishing and I fell sick, you saved me. You saved me when the snake came, and you saved me when we were at the factory fire. Yes, I will need you once more, Yaan. All my lands need you."

Tanica's face was blank. "*Your* lands, Kito? Are you a prince to the throne then?" she said somewhat sarcastically.

He looked at Tanica in the candlelight. "I am son to King Mabutu and the last Queen, Queen Rani."

With that revelation, Yaan began to laugh, but Tanica pointed a warning finger at Kito. "I will come to your lands, Kito. When I see you lie to my brother, I will draw your blood, peasant boy."

Kito's ever-so-slight smile never faltered. "I will accept your company to my lands, but know now, I can make no promise about the safety of either of you. The Emperor is there, and he has the alliance of the people of Audun and Orion. Half of my people also follow the man called Mensa."

"*He* is the King of Zimbali," snapped Tanica.

Kito's shoulders stiffened. "He was only the King in the absence of Mabutu. King Mabutu is back."

"No. Mabutu died many years ago when Queen Rani died. Your people have no chance, even the Pharaoh Ezra would love to flatten your lands after the loss of Rani. I'm surprised he hasn't already." Tanica turned to Yaan, taking up his hands. Her eyes glistened for the love of her brother. "Brother, you cannot go. It would be falling on your own sword."

Yaan looked at Kito. "I didn't get the history training of my sister, my friend. I must take some time to think this over."

"I'm sorry, Yaan, there is no time," objected Kito. "The only way I can get you there is by leaving before daybreak."

"What, tonight?"

"I'm afraid so, yes." He stood calmly as Yaan looked him over.

"Kito, you know I see you as my brother, but for the life of me, I can't see how I can be of any real assistance to you in your lands."

"I understand this, Yaan, but I don't know if you understand your own potential, your talent."

"Kito?"

"When you were on the wheel, you called my name."

Yaan's eyes bulged. "You heard me?"

"Yes."

Yaan's head tilted. "But, brother, I needed you, my people needed you. You never came!"

"I did not need to," Kito said softly.

Yaan's memory worked desperately. *I called him, no, yes, then I called the rats. I called the rats?* Yaan looked up as Kito nodded slowly and smiled.

"I must leave now, Yaan. Without you, I can only see the complete loss of my people, but I can't make you come either."

The two men stared at one another for a time. Finally, Yaan scoffed. "Then I must come and save your ass one more time."

"No!" Tanica banged her fists on the table frantically. "Yaan, please do not do this!"

"I know you don't understand, but I must go," Yaan reasoned. "My brother has asked me for my help. I must go."

"What has this Kito ever done for our people? Nothing!"

"No, Tanica, that's not right," interjected Kai. "I was there when the Emperor released the canal waters without informing us. It washed our people into the Yellow River. It was Kito who gave the warning, and I saw him dive into the rushing mud to save an old woman. He was the only man to come out of the flooded river alive, other than the woman that he saved. Neither should ever have lived."

Yaan stood as best he could, reaching across to take his sister by her shoulders. "Tanica, you know more about these lands than me, but I know more about this man than you. I have seen with my own eyes what this man has done for our people, and without question, I am going."

She stamped her foot. "Then I must go also."

"No. We can't be together. Desora is dead, and we are the only ones left, next in line to the throne."

She didn't budge. "Then I must see that you return to take what is rightfully yours."

Kito nudged Yaan gently. "Yaan, we must go. Kai, could you do me a favour? I need you to go and find Norinko in the morning. Tell him that Yaan and Tanica are alive and well. If he questions you about where they are, then you must not lie. Tell him they are both with me. Can you do this?"

Kai frowned. "I have worked hard to learn from Tanica, Kito. Are you sure I can't be of help?"

"It's important that Norinko gets this message about the prince and princess. I know I can trust you. Kai, do not underestimate your value to Norinko. Breathe easy and be true, you will see yourself as I already do."

Kai looked at Yaan briefly, then bowed before Kito, who then turned to Mercanti. "This will be an arduous trip, I feel you will be of great assistance to Tanica."

Tanica pushed herself between Mercanti and Kito, pointing her finger in his face again. "No Kito! No more of our people! She might be a fantastic shooter, but she's only a hunter. She has no training for this!"

Mercanti pulled Tanica's arm down and held her hand. "Kito, if you think I can help stop this evil from returning to these lands, then I will go."

Satisfied his plan was coming together, Kito dipped his head. "You should go next door and tell your friend Majito not to worry for you."

Tanica drew back at the request. *How could he know about her?*

Yaan coughed. "Kito, we do have another problem."

Kito turned around to Yaan. "I know." His white teeth gleamed inside his broad grin as he pointed to Yaan's crotch. "The boys are blue again."

18 The Dark Assistant

Not knowing the city of Samos well, Hao had asked for volunteers to help steal a vessel. If they were to get down the river, he would need oarsmen who knew what they were doing, as he didn't. Just one of the vessels would suffice. They believed Chun had made at least six vessels to date, although one of those had already been sent to the Emperor, delivering an unknown number of soldiers into Zimbali.

Hao was almost disappointed, though not shocked, at how many men were so eager to abandon the Asset. Being local, they knew the way, and Hao and Tzu followed the group of voluntary deserters in good faith. With Tzu hard on Hao's heels, they ran stealthily through the streets. The air was cool, and the dark night carried with it a sense of desperation as they had to seek out a vessel and leave before daybreak.

A young man led the small party silently through the streets to the waterfront. As they neared Chun's yard, they were more cautious. Creeping through stacks of timber, the young man looked over his shoulder at Hao. "There are no lights burning," he whispered.

Drawing his sword, Hao took the lead. "If there are no welcoming fires, we'll invite ourselves." As they drew closer, he paused. The vessel yard was quiet and lifeless – too quiet – and not one vessel was afloat outside. He pressed on. Hearing his men close behind, he didn't look back. *If this is a trap, we're walking right into it*, he thought.

They moved through the yard to the outside of the main building. Tzu moved beside Hao and muttered, "Call me naïve, but

I expected at least some of these vessel things to be out on the water. That is what they do, isn't it?"

Hao sighed, then, moving towards the main building, he edged along the wall towards a window.

"Psst."

Hao glanced back. Tzu was leaning around the side of the stack of sawn timber. He motioned to Hao, who slowly shook his head, ignoring Tzu's broad smile as he gently removed his hat, tucking it into his tunic. He peered through the window, then quickly ducked down.

Tzu immediately scrambled forward to the other side of the window, his nostrils flaring with anticipation. "What did you see?" he mouthed. Hao shook his head. Tzu eased up to look for himself, then dropped back down into a crouch. "Lucky I have come along to look out for you." He crept past the door, keeping below the window, Hao following. He held up a hand for the men to stay put. Too many swords in a small area were dangerous.

Tzu burst in first, Hao close behind, covering his back. There was a commotion of furniture breaking and items being flung. For the men outside, it sounded like an intense fight for a few minutes. Then silence.

A young man turned to one of the Barbarians and shrugged. The Barbarian did the same in return. They watched on as the gentle glow of a candle lit up the window. Tzu appeared at the door and beckoned them over.

Once inside, the men saw nothing but a lot of papers with drawings and writings. Hao looked at a huge mirror on the wall opposite the window they'd looked through, took one glance at Tzu, and the two burst out laughing. The small group of men were mystified.

Suddenly, there was a huge thump from the room next door, followed by the sound of heavy footsteps that stopped on the other side of a door. Hao and Tzu quickly moved along the opposite wall, stopping on either side of the closed door, swords at the ready.

They barely breathed. The handle slowly turned and the door creaked as it was slowly pushed open with a hardwood pole. A bolt whizzed past Tzu's ear and smacked into the opening door. It wobbled from side to side as, in unison, everyone turned to look to the man with an empty crossbow.

He was staring wide-eyed at the door, not moving.

"I hope you didn't shoot that bolt, little man?" The voice was deep and well-spoken.

Hao looked at Tzu with surprise. "Is that our saviour from this afternoon, big man?"

"The one and the same. Am I safe to enter?"

"Yes, there will be no threat to you." Hao greeted him with an outstretched hand and gestured for the men to lower their weapons with the other. "You never gave your name this afternoon. I am Hao, and this would be Tzu, the man I was with earlier today. Please, you have nothing to fear with me and my friends here."

"I'm not afraid, although ..." He looked at the bolt stuck deep into the wooden door.

Hao rolled his eyes. "I'm sorry. One of my men is a little trigger-happy. Afraid of the dark, I think."

The big man's teeth flashed white in the candlelight as his face softened. He bent over to come through the door, then tried to stand to his full height. The men were astonished as he stood almost upright, the back of his head against the roof.

Sheathing his sword, Tzu turned the table and chairs back onto their feet and offered the dark man a seat. He grabbed two more for himself and Hao. The big man chuckled. He quietly picked up the chair and put it against the wall, then sat on the floor.

Hao looked at Tzu. "Fair enough." He turned back to the big man. "I don't know your customs, but twice I've asked your name and I can't consider you a friend until I have it. Here it is considered rude not to address people properly."

The big man chuckled deeply. "Indeed, you are right. Hao, Tzu, my name is Baako. Clearly, I'm from Zimbali."

Tzu offered his arm, and they shook, and so did Hao. "May I ask why you are here, so far from home?"

"I was looking for my mother. She has lived here for many years, but I think she left when the fire at the silk factory broke out. I spent a long time searching the entire city, and now I'm stranded here."

"Well, Baako, we were going to catch a vessel, but it would seem we're too late."

Baako was beaming before Hao had finished. "It may still be your lucky day, Hao. Follow me and see for yourselves." He looked at each of the two men. "… if you trust me."

The big man moved with a quiet grace around the port. But for a few peasants fishing under the cloak of darkness, the waterfront seemed almost deserted. The fishermen watched wide-eyed as the strange group silently passed by.

Once past the wharf, they entered the jungle. They jogged on for a short time until, after rounding a bend, Baako dropped to his knees and crawled through the undergrowth to the edge of the riverbank. He pointed to the five dimly lit vessels, all tied to the bank in a neat line. One vessel was enormous, the name flamboyantly painted across its stern, *Ocean Asset*. Guarding a sleeping army, just a few men were on the top deck.

Their attention was now drawn to the vessel at the rear, *Titan*.

19 Band of Brothers

Later that night, with crossbows loaded, the two women led the way through the dark city. It was unnaturally quiet. Yaan was carried on Kito's back, trying hard not to complain about his aching groin.

Before long, they were at the waterfront, and Kito motioned to head downriver. He whistled, and the women quickly darted down behind the trees; he pulled his hood up and knelt with his head down, still as stone. Tanica looked at the pain written on her brother's face, beads of cold sweat forming on his forehead. He held a finger over his mouth.

Eventually, Kito lifted his head and took a deep breath. "Unload your bows. We'll go to the rear vessel," he whispered. Quickly, he rose, not waiting for the flurry of questions.

As the women eased the tension off their bows, Kito walked past them and along the narrow track through the jungle to the rear vessel, named *Titan*. He knelt again and lowered his head. Tanica's skin prickled as she looked at him, and she reached for her short sword, but Mercanti put her hand over Tanica's and shook her head slowly. They edged up to either side of Kito. Tanica was about to speak when Yaan quickly put his hands on the shoulders of both women. They froze, feeling the tension in his hands.

A hinge creaked, and the silhouette of a man came to the side of the vessel. Water began to trickle into the river. They waited for it to stop, then Kito gave the smallest of whistles. The silhouette stopped then whistled back.

Kito steadied Yaan to his feet, then whispered, "Friend, slide us the plank."

"Kito?"

Yaan was about to call out, but Kito spun around and quickly put his hand over his mouth, muffling the sound as Yaan shouted into Kito's hand. Kito hissed into his ear until he stopped.

A voice came from downriver. "What's the commotion over there?"

Hao was quick with his reply. "I came up to relieve myself only to find my guard asleep. Should I dispatch him?"

There was a painful silence, then finally, "No. If he's of any more trouble, then you should report him to the Emperor's Grand Master upon our arrival."

"Will do. Thank you, sir."

Hao opened a door, then shut it. The squeak of a door on the distant vessel followed. Kito whispered instructions in Yaan's ear. He nodded. Kito slowly released him, then moved forward as Hao lifted the plank to prevent it from sliding against the side of the vessel. Kito reached up and took the other end.

Soon enough, everyone except Kito was safely on the vessel. He lifted and guided the plank back to Hao. Mercanti nudged Tanica as Kito walked back into the jungle. They watched him turn back to them and sprint at speed towards the vessel. In a single vault, Kito landed on the deck. Mercanti clutched Tanica's arm. The grey fabric of his garment was so hard to see in the dark, but to her, for just a moment, the form seemed more panther than man.

Without a word, Hao led everyone downstairs to the first floor of the vessel. As the door was gently pushed closed, Yaan waited for him to turn about, as he had the only torch there.

When Hao turned, Yaan was beside himself. "Father had said the Gods keep some things to themselves, now I truly know what he meant. Hao, can you ever forgive me?"

Hao handed the torch to Kito, then went down on bended knee. "Yaan, my prince, never should I have let you go to the palace. The rest was my choice and mine alone."

Yaan held Hao by both hands. "But I left you for dead. I was told you were dying."

"And he should have, but I feel the Gods didn't want him." The voice from the dark startled Tanica; instinctively, she snatched her knife, but Kito was quicker. His imposing form stood in front of her with the flaming torch burning close to her face. He moved aside slowly as Hao held his hands up. "Easy, my princess, he is with me."

To shed a little light on the new man, Kito held the torch at arm's length, but Tanica didn't lower her dagger at the tall, heavily muscled man. "He's a Barbarian, I can smell him."

"This man saved my life," Hao responded curtly, and, not one to mince his words, added, "and if you don't lift your little girl manner, I'll slap your spoilt ass then feed you to the crocodiles."

Tanica's anger flared, but Yaan held her back. "Tanica, think on it. This is the man who came to save you from the palace and now that man behind him is said to have saved Hao's life, so there is a lot of debt in this room. Cool your temper, my sister."

Silenced by his firm and decisive words, she slowly lowered her knife. Yaan slowly limped to Tzu and offered his arm. "My name is Yaan. If you truly saved Hao, then I am in your debt."

Tzu looked at Yaan's outstretched arm for a moment, then took it and they shook. "My name is Tzu, and your sister is right – I *am* a Barbarian."

"My sister is young. Tzu, you have a second name?"

Tzu's chin rose involuntarily to the question. "I was named after my grandfather, Tzu Hsi."

"Ah, yes. We know of his legend from the Dome. He must have been a remarkable man." Tzu was unsure how to respond. Yaan reached up and placed a friendly hand on Tzu's shoulder. "Just how did you save this foolhardy brother of mine?"

Tzu laughed. "Well, he did have a nasty wound to the leg and had lost a lot of blood, but as I said earlier, the Gods mustn't have wanted him." Everyone in the room chuckled, though Tzu noticed Tanica was not one of them.

Yaan went on to introduce Kito, then Tanica and Mercanti, who, unlike Tanica, did offer her hand to shake.

As big as Tzu was, he was not as big as Kito. Hao had spoken much of him, and Tzu had watched him carefully from the moment he'd entered the room. Some of the stories were so big Tzu had wondered if this Kito was real, though now, there he was in the flesh. It seemed to him that when Kito had almost moved before Tanica, he had somehow he'd pre-empted her move with the knife, but this was not possible.

Hao recommended they move into the lower hold. He led the way down by torchlight to a single, lengthy room fully laden along the walls with supplies. In the centre, two fat candles burned on a long, wooden table.

Kito descended last. As soon as he touched the bottom step, he saw the huge, dark figure at the far end. The other newcomers hadn't even noticed him. Kito doubted his own eyes. *How could this be?* "Baako?" he mumbled.

Baako lifted his chin. "Yes. Have we met?"

The rest of the group looked at Kito in surprise. He pulled back his hood as he walked steadily around the table, the air thick with anticipation.

"Well, yes. It was in a room not unlike this." At the end of the table, Kito knelt on one knee as Baako drew a table candle forward. He looked at his defining attributes – his steel-blue eyes. He drew back with a gasp. "No, by the Gods."

Neither man could completely stand upright but awkwardly, they hunched over to face each other, each holding the other by their heads. Slowly, they knelt to the floor.

Kito held Baako at arm's reach. "I think there is more to our story than you may realise, Baako."

"I saved you from Captain Tarrant. What else could there be?"

"Just why did you choose to risk your life so much for me?"

Baako was silent for a time, and when he finally spoke, his voice was so low that everyone edged closer to hear. "It was like the

Gods had thrown you down the stairs to me. I looked up and saw three angels smiling down on me. When you rolled out onto the floor, you were different in every way. Your hair was straighter than most, your skin was pale, yet you were not sickly, and when you opened your eyes, they were this blue. Not at all common in my people.”

Kito gripped Baako’s shoulders, his steel blue eyes now a liquid aqua. “We are brothers.”

“Yes, we will always be brothers now.”

Kito shook his head. “No, Baako, I ...”

A strange sound came from the corner as Baako blinked back the rebuff. In a flash, Kito had both blades at the throat of a small, well-dressed Royal guard. The man cowered in the corner as he was bound and gagged.

Kito crouched down in front of the man. “So, who is this then?”

Hao stepped in beside Kito. “This gentleman would be the vessel’s captain. He kindly let us on board.”

“Oh.” Kito eased back. “So, Hao, come morning, just how do you see us managing this vessel with its entire army on board?”

Hao shoved his hands in his pockets. “Yes, well. I would say that we hadn’t gotten that far when I suddenly got the urge to relieve myself, finding you lot loitering outside.”

Kito stood up as best he could under the low ceiling. “Fair enough. But now, Hao?”

“If we have him ...”; he thumbed to the vessel captain, “... we have the crew. Maybe.”

Kito stared at the little man for a moment. Despite the room full of strange warriors from different nations all around him, it was clearly Kito he was focused on. He bent over, leaning his hands on his knees and spoke gently. “I’m going to remove your gag, but before I do, I want you to look at all my friends here. I know you have hundreds of your guards upstairs sleeping, but every one of my friends is a trained assassin. One sound out of you and we may all end up dead, but my promise to you is this: if anything were to happen, not one person will get off this vessel alive. It will be your vessel and your name in the history books for the loss of all these lives. Understand me?"

The man glanced around the group and remained subdued. Yaan touched Kito's arm as he went to undo the captain's gag. "Do you think this is right?"

Kito spoke softly over his shoulder. "Tanica, Mercanti, one sound and the two of you are to go directly to the top deck, lock all the hatches, then set the entire vessel on fire. Do not look back. Clear?"

Mercanti stepped forward and sneered at the little man. "I say we leave him down here and just do it anyway."

The little man's eyes swelled just a hint. Kito concealed his smirk and reached forward and slipped down the gag. "What would your name be?"

"Seiji, I am Captain Seiji. It means …"

"Conductor, yes, I know. Your mother must have been wise. What are your orders?"

"I am to follow the other …"

Kito leaned down, face to face and whispered, "The young lady is a bit of a firebug, you know?"

Captain Seiji shot a nervous look at Mercanti, now holding the other fat candle. "There is a camp way up the river from Begonia, taking the right fork they will be on our port side."

Kito backed away just a little. "Yes, I know the one." The group glanced at each other as Kito continued to question Captain Seiji. "How many guards are already there?"

"I have no idea," the captain pleaded. "One of our new vessels took hundreds, and several other vessels, including Captain Tarrant's, have made many journeys. I don't know, I don't know how many."

Kito glanced back. "Baako, the old man is still living?"

"As far as I know."

"When did you last see his vessel?"

"Since the first fires of Samos. If he was contracted around that time, then he could've made many trips by now."

Kito drew a small dagger from behind his back. The jewels gleamed in the candlelight. Yaan and Hao knew it immediately. He turned it in his fingertips a few times. "Captain, you are going to do exactly what I say. In return, I will guarantee your vessel a safe journey to your destination." He leant forward and cut away the captain's bindings and sat back on his haunches to look at his face. "And you are going to keep my friends here safe and well fed throughout this journey. Is that an agreeable deal for you, Captain Seiji?"

The captain rubbed his wrists. "It's better than the first option, Mr Kito, I will give you that. But what makes you think my vessel needs your help?"

"Let's just say," Kito said, pulling the captain to his feet, "if you do as I ask, your vessel will be the only one that *does* make Begonia, and I mean, the *only* one. This will be written in the history books of all nations, Captain."

The captain's eyes involuntarily looked about the room for confirmation of such a notion. Everyone was unmoved, staring at him. Kito gave him a moment to take in the statement. "You will now lead Hao up to the floor above. With the sound only of a mouse, you will find several uniforms, so some of these men can mix with your own. By nightfall two days forth, your vessel will be the only vessel still under sail and then you will know I am true to my word, Captain Seiji."

Captain Seiji blinked unnaturally quickly several times, then turned to Baako. "You say you served with Captain Tarrant. For how long?"

Baako lifted the candle from the table and raised it to his chin, exposing the scaring around his neck. "Long enough to earn these, Captain."

"I'm sorry, Baako."

Baako softened. "Why? You did not do this."

Kito nudged the captain. "Captain, the uniforms?"

Mercanti and Tanica headed for the door with a candle as Hao beckoned the captain to show the way. Captain Seiji looked at Kito, who reiterated with a whisper, "Quiet as a mouse."

It didn't take long before the group returned. Kito was deep in thought, awaiting them. Captain Seiji had brought some food and water back with him and placed it on the table. He turned to leave, but Tanica quickly sidestepped in his way. "Please, it would be rude for you not to sit, eat and drink first." The captain faltered, then meekly sat at the table.

Kito smiled as he watched Tanica sit directly beside him. He took a large goblet of water and drank thirstily. Somewhere forward in the future, the Emperor's vessel hung suspended in time. He had never held time this long, and the effort was beginning to take its toll. He wiped his mouth. "Baako, Mabutu is back at the Village of the Keepers."

Baako gripped the table to steady himself. It took him a moment to regain his composure. "Kito? You have seen Mabutu?"

Kito's face radiated. "Yes, Baako, I have. He is older and thinner but very much alive and well, and still very strong."

Some at the table knew who Mabutu was to Baako. They ate in silence as the two men talked quietly.

Baako frowned as he broke apart some bread. "Does Mensa ...?"

Kito shook his head. "Not that I know of. Chief Kobus is keeping Mabutu close, and no one is allowed to leave his village now."

"Very wise, but the Emperor is headed that way. If they get to team up ..."

"It is worse than that. When Mensa had Rani killed, he made it look like it was truly the fault of Zimbali. The Sheik is in the middle, he really has no choice in the matter." Kito let Baako absorb all the details. After wondering about his father all those years, it must've been unsettling. He leaned across to Hao. "You were leaving Middle Kingdom, for where and why?"

Hao glanced at Yaan. "The idea is to get to the Emperor before he gets too much of a following."

Baako shook his head. "I have been in the city since the fire. He left shortly after with many guards, and more have gone since. I don't know how many."

Tzu stabbed a leg of chicken with his knife. "I'm sorry to inform you that taking Magnar Wall was a walkover; it was barely a skeleton crew. The palace was just as easy." He tore a strip of chicken off the bone with his teeth.

"You have the palace in your control?" asked Baako.

"For now, yes."

"So why are you here, Tzu?"

Tzu stopped chewing and wiped his greasy chin. "The Emperor has something of mine, and I want it back. The rest you can blame on Hao."

With all eyes now on him, Hao smiled feebly, obligated to explain. "The only way I can see to stop the Emperor now is to take the fight to him. He will not be expecting that."

Baako shook his head. "As I said before, the Emperor has been gone for ages. He'll have spent all this time working on the allies."

"Yes, but none of them need to come to aid the Middle Kingdom, so he will have to give them something first."

There was an uneasy silence as everyone thought it through. Yaan nudged Hao. "After what you achieved in the palace, Hao, I will trust you till the end. How do you see this unfolding?"

Hao glanced around the table. "I don't know enough about the politics of your lands, but I question why the Emperor has left his own lands unprotected?"

Kito was the only one with that answer. "He is searching for the Valley of the Stone Temple. It contains the Sacred Crystal."

Everyone at the table shuffled about, shaking heads. Yaan and Tanica spoke in unison. "That is just legend."

"Legend says," continued Kito, "*He who can hold its stare, will inherit all its knowledge,* and therefore its power. Whether it's legend or not, he thinks it's in Zimbali and to him, that's all that matters."

Hao tapped his hands on the table. "Well, hearing things to date, if I were the Emperor, I'd go to the Pharaoh and get him on side using the death of his daughter. Baako, you said the Sheik will just go with the flow because he's caught in the middle?" Baako nodded the confirmation. "So, I would take the Pharaoh's men through Audun and join with the Sheik's men into Zimbali." He lowered his head in thought. "But where have all the Royal Guard gone?"

Kito flicked his head towards Captain Seiji. "He said they're hidden in the jungle. They will be there to ambush anyone from behind who stands on the edge of Zimbali, daring to face the Pharaoh and Sheik."

Tzu let out a low, long whistle. If Hao was right, and no one doubted he was, the Emperor had the perfect plan. Yaan thought about what Tanica had said about 'falling on your own sword.' He looked at Kito, who was watching him, waiting. "Kito, you said you needed me. If you have a plan, now would be as good a time as any to share it."

A hush fell about them as everyone now waited for Kito's response. "Well, think about it, we have the real leaders to Zimbali, Mabutu and Baako. We have the real leader to Middle Kingdom, Yaan, and we have the leader of Magnar, King Tzu."

Tzu leaned forward. "That may be well and good, but none of us has an army, Kito. They have an army each!"

"This is true, Tzu, but if we stop *these* ships carrying men and, just as importantly, their supplies, that will almost completely stop the Emperor, undermining and humiliating him in front of the other leaders. It will unhinge his own plan before it is set into motion. None of them has an army of hardened warriors that believe in what they are doing. Their armies drag their feet, not wanting to die without reason. But most of all, my friends …," and he wagged his finger emphatically, "… they don't have faith. They don't do their work in the eyes of the Gods."

Hao folded his arms and leaned back. "That's a good start, but how are the few of us going to stop all five ships, Kito?"

"I know Captain Seiji will get us there. I have a small but hopeful plan for the rest."

Silence ensued.

Baako put his broad hand on Kito's shoulder. "We are talking about my homeland. I will fight beside you, my brother."

Hao pondered the stories of how Kito dove into the swollen Yellow River to save one that was not his own. He came into Samos and saved many people who were not his own, and now he was asking for help for his *own* people. He leaned across and placed his knife on the table. "I will be proud to stand beside you, Kito, my brother."

Yaan remembered how a blind Kito rushed forward to save an old woman from the anaconda. He was there when the factory was burning and saved his life. He looked at Tanica's pleading eyes as he placed his knife on the table. "Kito, I would be proud to call you my brother." He looked at Tanica. "Will you go back to serve our lands? I hope you can understand what we are doing here. I hope you can forgive me."

Tanica's chin locked tight, defiant in anger and in pain for his decision. Mercanti took off her knife and placed it on the table. "For reasons I don't understand, I am the last one of my family. If the Emperor is allowed to return unopposed, he will wipe out everything that is not as he wants it. Kito, I would like to give everything I can to help, if you would have me."

Tzu nodded. "Mercanti is right — if I don't come and do everything I can, your Emperor will return to wipe my people from history. Kito, I serve you, to serve my people." His knife was placed as he spoke.

Tanica was still staring at Yaan when she pulled her own knife. He held up his hand. "No, Tanica, you must stay to serve the people. They have no one."

She leapt to her feet, pointing her knife at him. "How dare you," she seethed, keeping her voice low. "How dare you put that on *me!* I am just a maid, brought up a maid, treated like a maid. If I choose to go and learn about *who* my brother is before we are both to *die* then that is the choice of *this* maid." She looked at Kito's placid face. "I don't know about this, *band of brothers* nonsense, but Yaan *is* my brother. If you are so insistent in taking him then you will take *this* maid who *isn't* your sibling!" She stood abruptly and drove her knife into the table. The chair toppled as she turned for the stairs.

All eyes were on the knife as it wobbled back and forth, stuck in the table.

20 The Launch

Early morning glimmers of light cast shadows over the new vessel, stroking the new cloth sails. Admasin sat proudly, admiring the results of their hard work.

"You are out early, my dear. Bad dreams again?"

"There is a mug ready for you," he said quietly as he sipped his tea.

Yuna poured hers and sat beside her husband. "You should smile, my love; she is a beautiful vessel."

"Even with that silly master pole?"

"I think I have gotten used to the master pole. It just looks like a part of the vessel now. Is that strange?" she questioned.

"Well, no, it just shows your intelligence. You understand what it's for and have seen it enough to know that is how it is to be."

She grinned cheekily. "You silver-tongued devil, you want a bit, don't you?"

Admasin nearly splurted his mouthful of tea as he laughed.

"What's all this noise so early?" asked Lucia as she entered the room with a yawn.

Yuna turned her head. "The tea is hot, my dear, sorry if we woke you."

Lucia moaned as she stretched. "With this day finally before us, I didn't really expect to sleep."

Getting her hot mug of tea, she walked out next to Yuna. The three sat looking at the vessel, quietly contemplating what this day would bring. Lucia took a slurp of the steaming tea. "I sure will be happy to see her afloat and sailing."

"Time for a break, my girl?" offered Yuna.

"It just seems to have dragged out a little. I want to see a return for this one."

Admasin watched his beloved daughter closely. "A little cabin fever, my dear?"

She put her mug down. "Hmm, something like that, Admasin. I might just look her over one more time."

"Very well, it would save me doing it."

Yuna laughed aloud. "You couple of kidders, you will both look it over ten more times before launch and ten more afterwards." She waved a hand at the vessel as she departed for the kitchen. "I don't want to see either of you until she is afloat on the spring."

Admasin chuckled as he placed his mug on the table. "Oh, you are a hard woman, Yuna."

"Oh, like I could have held either one of you two back. Go on, get out of my sight; the both of you."

Admasin and Lucia giggled like two children as they headed for the gangplank.

Down in the hull, it was a slow job checking over the timbers for cracking, splitting or the failing of the joint glue. Just like last time, the time before that and before that also, she was watertight. The two moved up into the centre deck and checked that over, and then climbed up the stairs to the top deck.

Admasin pulled a rag from his pocket and mopped his brow. "Bit early in the morning for all this, wouldn't you say, Lucia?"

She stretched her arms above her head, yawning. "Though to be fair, you wouldn't have done it any other way."

He stuffed the rag back into his pocket. "True enough. Shall we rally the troops?"

"I think the troops are already on the job."

They turned towards the bow of the vessel. "Really?" Admasin leaned over and called out to the flurry of activity below. "What time is this to be starting work?"

One man called back. "What, from you, Admasin? Now that's cheeky."

The men burst into laughter, continuing their work of checking that ropes were not crossed or tangled and the blocks were tied off properly.

A lot of new wood had been laid out across the path of the vessel. They'd left the old tree stumps in the ground to hold the jungle floor together in the wet season. The men had stripped off the bark and oiled the timber so the vessel would slip over them easily into the water, pulled forward by ropes tied to its rear and put through pullies and pulled back for the men to draw the vessel out.

Admasin called down. "Are we ready, men?"

Several of the men call back enthusiastically. "That we are, sir!"

"Wait!"

Admasin spun around. "What is wrong, Lucia?"

"Just one moment, Admasin, just one."

He shrugged his shoulders as Lucia turned and ran along the vessel to the gangplank at the rear. Yuna watched her coming with concern. "What is it, my dear? What's wrong?"

Lucia quickly walked the plank. "You, Yuna. You as well, come on." She held out a hand.

"No," Yuna shook her head, "I just cook and …"

"… and clean up and look after everyone so they can look after the vessel. The vessel is as much a part of you and the kitchen, as it is us and the workshop. Come on; come with us."

Admasin shouted. "Lucia, what is the problem? Time is passing!"

"Hang on!" She grabbed Yuna's hand encouragingly. "Come on, Yuna! What do you say … want the ride of your life?"

Yuna laughed as she pulled off her apron with the other hand. "Well, that's an offer that no woman in her right mind would turn down." Her stomach fluttered as she tottered over the gangplank. Never had she considered herself a part of the vessel making. They hurried to the bow where Admasin was waiting.

Admasin frowned. "Do you really think it's safe for Yuna here, Lucia?"

"You seem to think it's safe enough for me, so …" Admasin rolled his eyes with a smirk as Lucia leaned over the side. "Alright, men, this is the moment we have all worked for. It will be no mean feat getting her launched, so there are no free rides."

"You're getting one!" called one of the men. Everyone laughed again.

Lucia placed her hands on her hips. "Just for that, you can be the first to the rope." It was no punishment; their excitement was palpable as they took to the ropes and stood ready.

Admasin was the pace setter, and the men worked to his command. Fit men quickly began to sweat in the jungle heat; it trickled down wiry, muscled arms and off the backs of working hands that clenched the thick ropes. The vessel moved slightly, and the gangplank crashed down.

Yuna grabbed Lucia by the arm. "Oh dear, this is quite unsettling." While she couldn't help feeling nervous, her excitement easily surpassed it. Lucia held her steady, though was more intent on what was going on with the logs below. Admasin nodded with a reassuring wink. The vessel slid steadily along the logs and the timbers groaned under the strain. The men were relentless in their drive to keep it moving, their bare feet driving into the dirt to take hold on tree roots. There was no stopping it now.

Suddenly, the vessel tilted downward. Admasin quickly called for the men to run. The ropes had to be kept tight as the vessel began to slide into the spring. Standing at the bow, it seemed they were going to drive straight under the water. Yuna laughed nervously as the vessel accelerated rapidly. The bow cut deeply into the water, sending a wave high above them that rained back down over the entire forward deck. The vessel ploughed through the water, and the bank on the other side of the spring loomed towards them. For a moment, it seemed they were doomed to smash into it, destroying all their work, but the men held hard on the ropes to slow her up, just.

The men dropped one rope and quickly took up tension on the other as planned. The vessel slowly returned to the launch point. Once close enough, Admasin threw a rope from the bow, and she was pulled sideways to the bank. A makeshift wharf was ready to take its first boarders.

***

On Devil's Fork, Balzac walked along the wharf with his guard in tow. All in all, it was a quiet affair these days. With Samos in chaos, nobody wanted to take their vessel there and anyone that had been there, had left. There was no paying cargo coming or going, other than the old man, Tarrant. He was suspiciously quick with payment, tight-lipped and always left immediately. With no idea what his cargo was, Balzac took payment simply for a full vessel leaving Samos. The frown on Balzac's forehead said he understood that if no one changed the status of Samos, business was to stay at an all-time low, and a low business turnover was the last thing he wanted.

This morning, however, there was something else on his mind. The gentle bumping of a cane on timber almost put a smile on his face. "Well, good morning to you, Jabali. What gives me the pleasure of your company out here at the end of the wharf?"

The quiver of a smile went undetected behind the cloth mask. "Good morning, Balzac, and may I ask you, why you've walked to the end of an empty wharf?"

Balzac chuckled. "Well, my friend, maybe it's because I knew you wanted to speak to me and just wanted to get you used to the water. You do live on an island after all."

Jabali leant on his cane. "Knowing how much I dislike the water, Balzac, that's just unkind."

"If you can't get used to the water, how are you to ever leave?"

"You wish for me to go, Balzac?"

Balzac waved his hands. "Heavens no, Jabali. You have become an important part of our operations here. I just don't want you to be a prisoner here, either."

"To some degree, that's why I have walked out here to see you this morning."

"Oh?"

"I feel it's time we went over to see the vessel."

Balzac smiled weakly. *He also knows.* "What, today?"

Jabali looked down at the ground beside Balzac. "I see you have an overnight bag ready, Balzac."

"Do you want to get one?"

The hat shook from side to side, and Jabali solemnly replied, "No, I'm afraid I won't be needing one."

Balzac noted the strange answer.

As always, Jabali sat in the middle of the clinker, clutching his seat until his knuckles showed white. They anchored in the inlet, and everyone disembarked, Jabali first.

Balzac instructed his men. "You can wait in the shade if you wish, I've no idea how long we will be." He was quiet for a short moment. "If we're not here just before sunset, you may return home."

Jabali's eyes narrowed. *He knows.*

The sand squeaked under their feet as they walked up towards the jungle and the vessel workshop.

"Jabali, if I may intrude on your personal life, just why are you so afraid of the water?"

"I think I must have nearly drowned as a child. I don't really remember."

"Yes, I had a friend like that once – nearly drowned fishing with his father; he too was just a child."

"You had a friend like that once? Where is he now?"

"He married his childhood friend and had a family of his own. He worked in Samos and was very happy, but then his father was too old to run the family fishing business and, as oldest son, he was expected to take it over. He never complained. Unfortunately, one day they got caught in a storm and sadly, he widowed his wife."

Jabali grimaced under his mask. No one said anything after that as they walked up the beach into the jungle. The two men walked through the dense vegetation to where the vessel should be standing, but it wasn't there. They looked to the spring and there she was, standing tall with her master pole reaching high into the trees.

Jabali didn't wait for Balzac; he was drawn towards the vessel. As best he could, he clumsily hobbled over the tree roots, watching the vessel now bobbing on the spring as if it were speaking to him. He reached the small, raised wharf and ascended the stairs, too excited to really see any of the people on the top deck. Steadying himself with his cane, he stepped onto it, ignoring the dread of being on the water as he gazed up at the master pole.

Lucia marched directly to Balzac. "What's *he* doing here?"

Balzac raised his eyebrows. "Good morning to you, my dear."

She reached up and kissed her father on the cheek. "Good morning to you, Father. It's a wonderful surprise to have you here. You just missed the launch, you know."

Yuna and Admasin approached, greeting Balzac with large smiles. "How did you know, my friend?" asked Admasin.

"I'm good, thank you, Admasin. Morning, Yuna," he said curtly. "I didn't know, though Jabali was quite insistent on coming this morning."

Admasin looked around. "He's on the vessel?"

"He's here somewhere," responded Balzac.

Lucia huffed. "He went downstairs. I find him quite rude."

"When he comes back up, I will call him over. He's quite reserved, that's all," Balzac reassured.

"That he may be, but he has no right to be helping himself about the vessel."

Snatching up a torch, Lucia stomped off towards the stairs. It wasn't needed much as they'd had all the hatches on the second deck open, allowing in a little light and fresh air. Still, she couldn't see him. *He went further down?* She huffed some more as she descended into the hull of the vessel.

A grunt came from near the master pole. *What is he doing?* As she neared she could see he'd pulled up the flooring and was down the hole. "Are you quite alright there!?"

His head bumped against the timbers in the restricted space. "Agh! Do you mind not sneaking up on people like that!"

Her anger bubbled. "I am not the one who is snooping around a vessel that is not his! Just who do you think you are?" The venom in her voice surprised even her.

He'd removed his hat to look around in his tight confines and he hastily rearranged his hair over his burns before looking up into her eyes. They glistened in her torchlight. Without question of her new name, he knew her to be his Alexa. She was like a hot knife through his heart, but she could never know who he was. *How could she look at my broken body and love me the way she once did? Who would?*

"I'm a guest of Balzac's, thank you. I don't know if he would approve of your manner." He was careful not to let his face be lit up with his own torch. "If you wouldn't mind, I was about to get up. Though I must say …" He looked back down at the base of the master pole. "… I must say, the workmanship here is second to none."

"Who *are* you?" Her voice was gentler this time.

He didn't look up. "I will see you top deck."

Something niggled in the back of her mind but looking down on this cripple wasn't helping her get the answer. Always dressed in black, all she could see was his slumped shoulder and his long hair pulled over his badly burned head and face. There was nothing more to say; she turned back to the stairs. As she ascended, she thought of the pictures in the sand. *That reminds me …*

Once on the top deck, she sought out Admasin. He was still talking with Balzac as she joined them.

"What, today, Balzac?"

"Yes, that's right. Is everything loaded, including the shot and powder?"

"Yes, we did it before we put in the rudder. It was easier dry dock. But you don't go to sea in a vessel without vigorous testing."

"Then that's what we will do, but to sea we will go. Can you be ready by midday?"

He, too, has had the dreams and the visits by the one in grey. Admasin pondered. He took a deep breath. "Very well, Balzac, but I am the captain of this vessel, and if I'm not happy with her performance at any given point, we will return without hesitation. Are we quite clear on this?"

Balzac was nodding before Admasin had finished. "As you say, Admasin. You're the captain."

"Don't you forget it."

Balzac rubbed his hands together vigorously. "We push off at midday." Just then, he saw Jabali returning and moved away to usher him to the bow.

Lucia looked at Admasin. "What was that about?"

Admasin skirted around the question. "Men have struggled with power since they dwelt in caves. Never you mind Balzac and I." He motioned at the bow with his head. "What was Jabali doing downstairs?"

"Checking our work, would you believe?"

Admasin linked her arm and led her to the stern of the vessel. "Come on, we need to check the workings of this new steering wheel."

She moaned. "We've turned it inside out, testing it. It works brilliantly and you know it."

"Yes, but now we are in water, Lucia."

"And it will work just the same there. Are we going overnight? Father has a bag."

"Yes, indeed, he does and just as soon as I'm happy with the steering, we should do the same."

"Where is Yuna?"

Admasin's eyes twinkled with his cheesy grin. "She went to get changed, grumbling something about my fault for getting her wet." He looked at Lucia with the affection of a father. "That was a nice thing you did for her, bringing her on board for the launch."

Lucia smiled for the first time since Jabali had come aboard. "She has worked just as hard as we have."

"Sometimes harder, I think. I will talk to her about us leaving today." He folded his arms. "It's a little unexpected, I feel."

"So why are we doing it?"

Admasin chose his next words carefully. "Well, at the end of the day, I had no reason not to go today," and before she could question further, added, "If you would be so good as to turn the wheel, I would like to go dry dock and watch the motion."

Lucia let out an exaggerated huff. "As we have so many times before."

Admasin cautioned with his finger as he moved away. "When one is taking so many lives out to sea, my dear, there are never too many times."

She groaned her feelings on the subject as she ascended the stairs onto the raised rudder deck, walking to the wheel with a broad smile. As tall as Lucia was, she wasn't taller than the wheel placed in the centre of the rudder deck. If she stood to the side, she had greater visibility over the entire vessel. She tried not to get uptight about Balzac talking with Jabali at the bow. She waited for Admasin to get into place and signal the turns.

"Right, *Queen of the Seas*, turn to the port side."

Lucia couldn't help but giggle as she turned the wheel, feeling right at home somehow. The wheel was heavier than on the dry dock, but they'd expected that, and even with her alone, it was very achievable.

"To the starboard if you will."

She held tight and spun the wheel.

"Good, now back to centre."

"How will I know?"

"I will tell you."

Lucia turned the wheel back. "Yes, but if you're not there to tell me, how will I know?"

Admasin was watching the rudder. "That's a good question. When you are moving, you will know; if you're not moving, then it doesn't matter. Right, stop there."

She walked to the side. "Shall we get our bags then?"

He checked the crew. "Yes, it looks as though the men have finished loading supplies." He looked back at her. "But we'll do one more check for dampness before we push off."

Lucia couldn't help but flash her captivating smile with a wink. "That we will, Captain."

Admasin and Yuna returned to the impromptu raised wharf, holding hands. They stopped, and he whispered something in her ear. Though clearly not pleased, she nodded and did her best to smile back. He followed Lucia across the plank as a man arrived to take their bags.

Balzac greeted them proudly. "It's almost time, Admasin."

Admasin looked him straight in the eyes. "Yes, Balzac, it's nearly time, and when I say this vessel is good to go, we will go. Now, if you would excuse me, I have final checks to tend." Not waiting for an answer, he left for the stairwell, Lucia on his heels.

Carrying a torch each, they went directly to the hull. They worked around the sides together, then came back to the master pole and lifted the boards. Admasin looked pleased. "Not one drop."

"No, but we both know it's early. The vessel hasn't settled and she won't be settled for another week yet. Admasin, it has taken a long time to get here. Why rush the most important part? Why are you letting Balzac push you forward?"

Admasin continued with what he was doing and calmly answered, "Am I?"

"Damn right you are."

A frown cut deeply into his forehead. "Mind your language, young lady. Never any call for bad language, least of all from you."

Her face softened a little. She loved him like her own father, especially when he got all protective of her. "Yes, Admasin, but you haven't answered my question."

He scoffed at her, seeing right through his poor ploy to get her off the subject. "Every man has his reasons for what he does. Some men are happy to be told, some like to make up their own minds, or at least pretend to do so, and I have my reasons for going out to sea today. A man's reasons are a man's business, Lucia." He looked at her solemnly. "Can I ask if you would stay ashore and care for Yuna?"

"Not on your life."

He grinned. "It was worth a try. Well then, let's push off."

21 Ocean Bound

Lucia ascended the stairs to the rudder deck and stood at the wheel. The crew assembled below as Admasin stood on the front of the rudder deck, holding the handrails.

"Alright, people." The crew hushed as he spoke. "Most of you worked with us from the clearing of the first tree. You milled and built the place that has been our home this entire time, and now our vessel floats before it." There was a bit of banter and shoulder slapping between the men below. Admasin didn't need to raise his voice to command the floor. He pointed to one man. "Kye, I seem to recall you were constipated for a week. We all thought your belly was going to pop." The men laughed at the memory of it. "Then you were running away all the time, complaining that you had dysentery."

The men heckled Kye as he stood with his arms folded, grinning with embarrassment. Admasin pointed to another character. "And you, Ushma, you would have to be the keenest, and worst, fisherman I have ever met." Now holding nothing back, the laughter and jeering carried through the jungle. "You went out every morning and came back empty-handed, *every* morning."

Admasin waved an arm to present Yuna standing on the makeshift wharf. "My own wife spent less time out there and fed us all every day."

Now even Jabali chuckled as Admasin rallied his men. He was pleased for his mask as he choked back his emotion. He couldn't stop looking at the one that was now called Lucia, her leathers fitting her every curve beautifully. His heart pounded so hard in his chest that it hurt.

Balzac had a good laugh too as he watched Admasin point to Ushma again. "Ushma."

The smallest man of the whole crew, Ushma had a broken accent of another land. "What you want now?"

"I don't think you have bathed once the whole time we have worked here!"

"What you mean? I wash lots."

A deep voice came from behind. "The heck you did."

Ushma turned to see several men approaching with a heavy rope in their hands. "What heck you do? You get off me, get off me now or I beat up you all." His words had little effect as the men, albeit in good humour, wrapped poor Ushma in the rope.

"Take him to the side!" called Lucia.

Ushma, purple with fear, looked frantically for Admasin. "What you do … why you do to me? I work for you, I work hard."

Admasin spoke calmly. "Yes, and you had to because no one could work with you." He held up his hands. "Hang on." A glimmer of hope flashed over Ushma's face. The men were quiet, anticipation rife. Admasin held his arm high. "I dub this vessel, *Queen of the Seas*." Ushma was being held horizontal with his head already over the side. Admasin lowered his arm swiftly. "Right, chuck him in."

Ushma screamed all the way into the water. The men waited for the signal from Admasin, then hoisted the rope and dragged him back up the side of the vessel. Admasin looked at a big man on the rope. "Feros, how does he smell?"

Feros scrunched his nose, turning his head away from Ushma. "No better, sir."

Ushma squirmed like a wood grub. "You not nice to me. I no like you!"

Admasin lowered his arm again, and Ushma was dropped in the spring once more. As the men watched over the side, Feros pulled him up and dunked him several times more before pulling him up to the edge of the vessel again. Ushma spluttered and coughed up water.

"How is he now, Feros?"

Feros leaned in and sniffed him. "Not there yet, sir." Ushma was still spluttering when he hit the water. Feros dunked him a few times more.

"What say you, Feros?"

A voice came from the back of the crowd. "He must be clean inside and out now." Another called. "Yeah, I say he's clean, don't you, Feros?"

Feros leaned in to smell a choking Ushma once more. He raised a hand with the rope-clad Ushma and shouted, "He is good!"

Once Ushma was cleared of his ropes, he leapt to his feet and stomped on Feros's toes. Feros called out in pain as he bent over to grab at his foot. Ushma jumped up and bit him on the nose. Feros grabbed him and held him high.

"THAT will do, Feros," said Admasin.

"He bit my nose!"

"Well, it shouldn't protrude so far from your face, Feros."

Feros put Ushma down as he grunted and limped away. Bent over with his hands on his knees, Ushma would cough and splutter for some time yet.

Balzac nudged Admasin. "Well, that was fun and all, Admasin, but I need to know this vessel of sails is going to work."

Admasin leaned in towards him. "Before we go to sea, I needed to know I have control of my men and they will stick together."

Balzac folded his arms. "Ha. This was a test?"

"In a sense of the word, yes, I suppose it was."

"And?"

Admasin looked at his men and watched as Ushma stood up and walked to where Feros sat. Several men followed him; the rest were talking and laughing with Feros. Ushma put out his little hand. "I sorry I bite your nose, Feros, me silly."

Feros held still for a moment, then his face softened. "Oh, think nothing of it, Ushma, all is forgotten, my friend." The two men shook hands. As they released, Ushma said, "But Admasin right about one thing, Feros."

"Oh, what's that?"

"Your nose is too large, even on that fat head." Ushma scrambled for his life as Feros tried to get to his feet, but the men, laughing, held him back.

Admasin was satisfied. "I think we have a tight crew, Balzac, and at sea, it's the most important thing."

"What, not the vessel, Admasin?"

"No, I could build a bridge from here to Samos, but if I don't cross it with the right men, all could be lost."

Balzac raised his chin. "I see. Maybe you're right."

Admasin looked around his crew and spotted the man he needed right now. "Ushma." The crew settled down listening to Admasin.

Ushma came forward. "Yes, sir?"

"Where is the tide at this moment?"

Ushma looked briefly at the sun. "It is full now, maybe just receding, sir."

"Then we don't have much time. I'm about to cast off the ropes and head to sea."

The men looked at one another, confused. "It is too early."

"She has not settled," they mumbled.

Admasin was ready for their comments. "If you don't wish to come for the journey, then I will not hold it against you if you were to leave. But you need to leave now." A few shuffled their feet, but not one of them walked off. Admasin threw his hands up in the air, smiling broadly. "Then, let's cast off!"

With a cheer, the men pulled the ropes away and put their oars in place. First, they would need to row her out. Balzac looked about for Jabali. *He won't stay, that's for sure.* Jabali was nowhere to be seen. *He must be long gone now he has looked the vessel over.* He looked at his daughter, proudly at the wheel.

Lucia caught his gaze. She could never be sure what he was thinking but today she didn't much care either way. Today, they were to sail this vessel. The improved sequel to the one lost, along with all her life, to the fires. Now her father was heavily involved in this one, so much was somehow riding on the success of this one trip. Her emotions ran deep. *Why did I react so rudely to the cripple this morning?* She looked around, pleased that he'd left the vessel at some point. Balzac had said he was afraid of the water. *Strange man, afraid of the water, yet living on an island.*

The vessel was pushed out from the wharf. Lucia could feel the spring beginning to move them towards the river. There was hushed anticipation as it moved – there was no stopping now. The inlet had just enough depth, providing they didn't overrun the turn at the bottom of the river. Ushma said the tide was in, and he was never wrong, though it never got him any fish either.

Yuna watched nervously as they moved away, waving them on. Admasin held his hands in a fist at his chest and gave a curt bow in return. Lucia steered the vessel into the centre of the river. There was a loud crack and some branches crashed to the deck. The men quickly checked the master pole as it scraped through the overhanging branches, but they were ready this time, and the branches were quickly thrown overboard. Ready at their oars, the men followed Admasin's instructions.

The vessel picked up pace as they left the jungle. The river sloshed against the side as the men worked on in silence. Balzac stood at the bow watching; the men were just as nervous as he was. Lucia worked hard on the wheel.

Admasin whispered to her. "Why are you favouring the port side of the river?"

"Trust me." Her focus did not leave the river ahead. "Tell the men to be ready to row for their lives."

Admasin turned quickly. "Ready on the oars, wait for my call."

The speed of the vessel was more than anyone could have imagined. The men held their breath as the vessel groaned and creaked. They would crash into the sandbank on the far side of the inlet for sure.

Balzac's eyes widened as the inlet loomed up at him. A quick glance told him Admasin and Lucia were as concerned as he was.

Lucia spoke only for Admasin. "Almost … ready …"

Admasin slowly raised his arm, and the men brought their focus back to him, bracing themselves on their oars.

"NOW!" she urged.

Admasin dropped his arm and began to call. Lucia spun the wheel as the men pulled on the oars with all their might.

The *Queen of the Seas* leant over heavily. Balzac gritted his teeth as he grabbed the side of the vessel. In the distance, he could see Yuna standing on the edge of the jungle with his men, and wished now he was standing with them. Lucia was fearless, her eyes narrow and focused. It bolstered Balzac as it bolstered the working men facing her on the oars. The vessel was now sideways in the river and about to crash into the rapids in the inlet.

Admasin could now understand what she was doing. This was their moment of truth. "PULL! … PULL!" he yelled.

Water washed over the top deck, knocking several men from their feet, unprepared for the violence of it. The vessel rolled over further, and Balzac feared it would not return. Ropes and pulleys rattled against the master pole as the vessel leaned even further.

"PULL! … PULL!"

The men struggled, digging their heels into the hardwood deck, gripping with their toes amidst the sloshing water. Admasin clutched the handrail at the rudder deck, calling his commands with calm control. Soaked to the skin, the men followed his instructions.

As they teetered on the brink of tipping, the vessel began to straighten up and ride smoothly. They had done it and were now heading out along the inlet. Admasin didn't stop his calls, the men holding tight on the oars. Cheering in relief, they rowed on.

Lucia glanced back at Balzac, now drenched to the bone, though if she wasn't wrong, he was laughing and weeping at the same time.

She smiled nervously at Admasin.

"How did you know?" he asked.

She frowned. "Know what?"

"Don't play with me, my dear." He lowered his voice. "Did the grey man come to you in your dreams?"

She motioned towards Balzac's sodden bag beside the master pole. "Father also, I feel."

"What is it we are doing, really?"

"I'm not sure." She shrugged.

Balzac moved through the men working the oars and ascended the stairs. "Well, if anyone had any doubt about your vessel, they won't now."

Balzac's clothes squelched as Admasin slapped him on his shoulder. "Well, Balzac, every man going to sea has to have his initiation – you just got yours."

"A little advanced warning would have been nice," Balzac scoffed. "I thought we were friends, Admasin."

"We are. And that would've taken all the fun out of it," he laughed.

"True enough, I will give you that. Lucia, how did you know how to go about that?"

She hunched her shoulders. "How did you know to show up with *a bag* this morning?"

He smiled sheepishly. "Family trait, it seems."

Lucia pointed ahead. "What is that smoke about?" Two plumes of smoke wafted up into the hot afternoon sky.

Admasin looked at him. "The guns you insisted we had to put on this vessel … they aren't the ones protecting your business?"

Balzac swore. "The smoke is to say someone hasn't stopped in."

Admasin thought for a moment. "You bluffed it? I assumed you had more."

Balzac looked almost angry. "Do you have any idea how hard it is to make just one of those things?"

"None whatsoever. So, why put the only ones you have on this vessel?"

Balzac just grunted and marched off down the stairs, heading for the bow.

Admasin looked up at Balzac's flag flapping at the top of the master pole. "I know the winds aren't favourable, but we'll head for the Devil's Sea. It's protected and safer for the testing."

Lucia rolled her eyes. "We've discussed this for months now, Admasin."

He chuckled, squeezing her arm. "I know, my dear, I know." The vessel rounded a bend towards Devil's Pass, and Admasin's face turned white. "It can't be."

Lucia shook her head. "No, Admasin. I'm sure it isn't."

Fading into the distance was a huge, sail vessel, much taller and wider than theirs.

"Only one way to find out," was all he could say.

Lucia cleared her throat. "All right, men, let's pull in the oars and see what she can do."

The oars were quickly pulled in and tied to the inside ribs. They hadn't seen the other vessel disappearing into the open waters and talked excitedly among themselves as they worked.

On dry land without a sail, they had practised pulling up the rigging. Having been on Patch's trial vessel, Lucia and Admasin were both very critical about ease of use and practicality. The wind had so much power, everything had to be just right. They'd changed the rigging setup more than once. Admasin looked at how well the men had the rigging moving. "Practice does pay."

Lucia put a finger against her full lips. "Don't jinx us now."

The rigging was not even halfway up when it began to flap and then pull tight. The vessel lurched ahead. Lucia couldn't help but raise her head a little with pride. The men talked amongst themselves at the marvel of it all.

"Mind on your jobs, men. You are paid to be here, no free rides. Now PULL!" Admasin instructed. The men focused, pulling the rigging higher up, now with a little more pace. Admasin watched it get to the top. "Tie off, watch the flag." He had talked to the men endlessly about how to watch the flag, giving the true wind direction. Only then could the rigging be set right. Even though Admasin was the captain, he was adamant that they all needed to know how to make the vessel sail. Suggestions were aplenty, and Admasin made the call for any changes he agreed with.

Balzac puffed a little as he climbed the stairs. "You should see the wave out front."

"It's called a bow wave, Father."

He nodded childlike, pointing up. "All this power from *that!* What a brilliant idea. This vessel is well named as *Queen of the Seas*. What an amazing man he must have been to come up with the first sail." He looked at Lucia's pained face. "Oh, my dear, I am sorry."

"It's alright, Father. It has been quite a long time now, and today …" She looked up at the white sail pulled tight. "… I think we have done him proud."

Still on the wheel, she remembered the curtains in their office on that spring day. Clenching her jaw, she sniffed and looked ahead. Something caught her eye. It was the rude cripple coming up the stairs. "I thought that *he* got off?"

Jabali staggered to the side of the vessel and vomited several times. Admasin hushed Lucia. "I have spoken to you once already today about your manners, Lucia."

"Don't talk to me about manners. He's the rudest man I have ever met!"

Admasin thought about some of the seamen who came into the shop. "I doubt that. Besides, don't forget who gave us the rudder and wheel you are using this very moment." He faced Balzac. "And if I'm not mistaken, those were not *your* drawings you showed us for the master pole, Balzac?"

Balzac suddenly looked coy. "Must we always say *master pole*?"

"You would just call it a pole, Balzac?"

Balzac scrunched his face. "No. I would call it a mast, pure and simple." He pointed up again. "That is the sail and so we are, sailing." He was on a roll now. He pointed to several pulleys. "That's a block of pulleys, so a block."

Admasin was quite taken with Balzac's naming. It had never occurred to him to simplify things. "Balzac, I'm thinking that we aren't on a vessel anymore. Surely she is something more. Any ideas?"

Balzac thought for a moment. "I see what you are saying, but nothing obvious is jumping out at me."

"Think on it?"

"Indeed, Admasin."

"And the plans, Balzac?"

Balzac had thought he was in the clear. He stammered. "I, er ..."

Lucia looked to her father with doubt. "Father, did you lie to us?"

Admasin interrupted. "Oh no, Lucia, he never actually said he did them, he just never said who did."

She made subtle adjustments with the wheel. "So, who did?"

Admasin hesitated, but the truth needed to come out. "Is it not obvious? Who did the drawings in the sand?"

She gasped putting her hand over her mouth, looking at the cripple who was holding up his mask, drinking water. She felt the vessel shift in the water and turned the wheel, cursing under her breath.

Admasin folded his arms. "My dear, we've been at sea for just moments, and you're swearing like you grew up on the water. Is there something you wish to share with me?"

She shook her head. Admasin never took his eyes off her. She sighed. "Very well. I was thinking about the rude cripple ..." Admasin raised his eyebrows, staring at her. She relented with a smile. "Alright. *Jabali*. As I turned the wheel, I know now that I'll always relate it to him."

"Is that such a bad thing? The man did give us this extraordinary design, after all."

"Hmm." She turned the vessel into the Pass.

Jabali looked up at the flag, then walked back towards the rudder deck. He called in a raspy voice. "Mind the rigging. Every time we change the direction of the vessel, even just slightly, the rigging will need adjusting."

The men scurried into activity, letting some blocks off and pulling others tight, slightly changing the angle of the sail. Admasin grinned as Lucia moaned some more.

The vessel surged on.

Jabali wobbled about on his cane, talking with the men as Admasin thought back to when Jabali was a child. He, Kalgan, Katanning and all the other children played for countless days with model vessels. *He really did win all the races. His birth people must have been of the ocean, of that I am sure.*

As they neared the end of the Pass and out onto the open ocean, one of the men pointed and shouted. "There! Who's that? They already have one of these!" The men ran forward to the starboard side and looked at the vessel of sails just like theirs.

"Only it's bigger!" shouted another man as he turned back, looking to Admasin, who acknowledged with a grimace.

Admasin did notice one thing. The other vessel wasn't leaning over like this one was. *They don't know how to sail.* Without shouting, he called on the men. "Mind the flag! Mind your duties, men."

Balzac was impressed at Admasin's respectful authority. The men moved, and the vessel leaned over a little more. He grabbed at the handrail before him. "You sure we're not about to fall right over?"

Admasin never took his eyes off the vessel in front. "If my calculations are right, we should be able to take on at least some water on the top side, though once water has come over the sides, everything begins to change quickly."

Balzac frowned as he leaned over the side, looking at the bottom side of the vessel. "Change?"

"The whole equation of a vessel is water displacement."

"Yes, yes. We went over that at Devil's Pass."

"Well, the moment you let some water over the top, then the equation changes, twofold as well."

"As well?"

Admasin was still watching the vessel ahead. "As well as what?"

"You said, the equation changes twofold … as well. What is that?"

Admasin pulled his eyes away from the other vessel. "You have carried a pail of water. Now imagine a thousand of those on top of one side of the vessel when the wind already has us leaning right over." Balzac looked once more as the swells surged past. "It's called freeboard."

"What's freeboard, Admasin?"

"What you just looked at. Take a line across the top of the waves. That distance to the top deck at its lowest point is freeboard."

Balzac looked concerned. "I'm not sure we have enough freeboard, Captain."

"We have enough, Balzac; we have enough." Admasin looked at the huge vessel ahead. He spoke just for the three of them to hear. "We are gaining on them." Lucia agreed.

Balzac scoffed. "Well, this just might bring Balzac's justice to a whole new level." He walked down the stairs and headed to Jabali. "How are you feeling now, Jabali?" Before Jabali could answer Balzac asked. "Where are my men?"

Looking a pale shade of green, Jabali spoke weakly. "I told them to be sure everything was ready."

Balzac never said another word as he turned solemnly to the stairs for the lower deck.

Lucia made a line towards the bigger vessel, still some distance away. "How close do you want to get to it?"

"I just want to see who's on it."

Lucia was careful with her words. "I'm sure Kalgan has nothing to do with it."

"Of course, he …"

A noise boomed, like thunder had exploded right over them. The men ducked, and Lucia swore again. Admasin gave her a frown. A huge plume of blue smoke wafted back over the vessel, sulphur heavy on the nose. He rushed over to the handrail. "Feros, get down there and tell Balzac to stop firing immediately! Go!"

"Yes, sir." Feros was away down the stairs, but not before another blast went off. Everyone flinched but watched with bated breath to see where the shot landed. Just as the shot was fired, *Queen of the Seas* dipped down over a swell. The ball bounced off a swell only halfway to the last of the other vessels, then launched high into the air, whistling as it descended just to the front of the vessel ahead. The vessel began to drop its sails, slowing immediately.

Lucia nodded as Admasin instructed her to turn upwind of it before going to talk with the men. Jabali listened without comment then, together with Admasin, watched as Lucia headed them along the starboard side of the other vessel. As they levelled with it, Jabali looked at the vessel's name. *Titan*.

The men lowered *Queen of the Seas'* sail halfway and eased alongside the other vessel, but not so close that a man could get from one vessel to another. It was only now that Admasin realised just how much bigger than theirs the *Titan* really was. His back stiffened as he saw a familiar figure. "Kito! This is a surprise," he called across.

"Not as much as the surprise it was to be fired upon, Admasin. I thought we had discussed this."

Admasin blushed a little. "Quite so, my friend. I'm afraid others are a little gun happy." They both had a questioning expression as Balzac arrived.

"Kito, I didn't expect to see you here."

Kito didn't wish to elaborate. "Balzac, always a pleasure although …" He raised his hands. " … the peacekeepers?"

Balzac motioned towards the stairs. "Er, yes, Kito. I have spoken to the men responsible for that."

Kito called across to Admasin. "Just ahead but further to sea are three other vessels like this one, plus one bigger."

"BIGGER!" exclaimed Balzac.

Kito ignored him. "Take out as many as you can. None of them mean well. The Emperor wants bloodshed, and most of the Royal Guard don't understand any different. Following orders of the throne is all they know."

Admasin walked along his own vessel as their vessels passed gently by. "We will do our best if you can assure me that it is right and just, Kito."

Kito lowered his hood. "You have my word. Every vessel is laden with warriors going to a land they have no right to be on, to meet an Emperor who intends to take no prisoners. If I could see another way, Admasin, I would be doing it." Kito had now walked to the bow of his vessel and Admasin had ascended the rudder deck of theirs, both speaking their last before the vessels passed each other by.

"Then we shall do our utmost, Kito."

Kito assured him. "The one you look for is out there. Do not concern yourself, he is a remarkable young man and has a hand on his shoulder. Some will be spared. Also, listen to Jabali, he knows the vessels. Remember, it is better to retreat and be there to fight another fight than to stay on to the death. May the love of the Gods go with you." A chill ran up Admasin's spine with the last of Kito's ominous words. "This isn't going to be easy."

The two vessels were parting as Jabali cracked his cane on the side of their vessel. "You ride the *Titan*, Kito. Do not carry too much sail, your master pole will not take it. It is flawed, as is the sail it holds."

Captain Seiji, standing beside Kito, flinched at the information and looked up at Kito, who flashed a pearly white smile and fell into a bow, holding his hands together at his forehead to respect the little vessel on its mission.

Lucia was scowling when Admasin returned to her. "What did he mean ... Jabali knows the vessels?"

"I have no idea, Lucia."

She looked at the masked man. He was standing near the front of the vessel, looking directly at her. Her voice was somewhat spiteful. "I say we save our men and *Queen of the Seas* and just throw him over the side now."

Admasin drew back. He'd never seen such aggressive behaviour from her before. "Lucia?"

She glared at Jabali. "Obviously, he's a traitor. Kito just said so."

"No, Lucia. Kito said Jabali knew the vessels, and we should listen to his opinion."

"How else could he possibly know about their vessels, if he hasn't betrayed us?" she vented.

"Let me ask you one question. If you can give me a convincing answer, then I will have him thrown overboard immediately."

She spun to face Admasin. "Try me."

"How is it he gave us the wheel that you turn on your own, yet the *Titan* had six men on their rudder stick?"

Lucia flinched. "I never noticed. Six? Are you sure?"

"Yes. I saw it, and they were staring at you. We can go back so you can have a look for yourself." Admasin motioned to the *Titan* now well behind them.

She trusted his word and wanted to move on. "Didn't Kito say there were more further out to sea?"

"Indeed, he did, Lucia, and it's an offshore wind. Out to sea we go." Lucia began to swing the wheel. Admasin called to his men. "Man the blocks, full sails now."

As the sails were pulled around, the wind began to take hold, and the vessel surged forward, making it lean over even more.

Lucia quickly adjusted her turn, and the vessel straightened a little.

It moved faster than ever now. Most of the men looked nervous, though Feros and Ushma had both served time as slaves before finding work with Balzac and simply enjoyed the ride. Their howls and hoots gave the other men the confidence that it was perfectly normal. The truth was, they were just happy to be on the top deck and not pulling oars in iron collars.

But the good mood was quickly broken with one call. "There! More vessels over there!"

Lucia swapped sides of the wheel to get a clearer look past the sail. Her eyes widened at the size of them. She shook her head. "Kito lied."

Admasin didn't take his eyes of the multitude of sails. "How's that, Lucia?"

"Well, look! There are five sails, not four."

Balzac stood up straight. "Can we really take them on? With this?"

Jabali spoke behind him. "Yes, Balzac. We are faster, stronger *and* we have the peacekeepers."

"Yes, but we can't fire them in this swell, Jabali."

"I have been thinking about that. Are you prepared to stay with the guns?"

Balzac frowned. "For what purpose, Jabali?"

"Please, come and I will show you." Balzac looked at Admasin as if he needed permission, and Admasin simply stood blank-faced. Jabali spoke quietly. "Balzac, we don't have much time."

Balzac flinched and stepped forward to the stairs. "Yes. Let's do this then, Jabali."

Jabali stopped as he passed Lucia. "Kito cannot lie. You need to think about his every word."

She seethed as he hobbled to the stairs and waited for him to go down into the vessel out of sight. "Admasin, just how does one little vessel take on five bigger vessels?"

Admasin was studying the group of vessels. "Four. That biggest one has two masts." He continued to scrutinise them. "They're not too spread out. Safety in numbers, they're not confident in their ability to sail." The double-masted vessel was in the middle, one vessel up front and two trailing behind the biggest vessel. Lucia had to listen hard as Admasin was barely speaking to anyone. "When I used to go hunting with Father, we once came across some Sika deer. They were walking single file through the forest. I didn't know why, they just were. Father came up with the idea, if we would pick off the ones at the rear first, we could maybe get more than our share." He paused. "I think we should go right through the last two."

"And do what? The guns are of no use in the swell."

Admasin smiled. "We will have faith and sail forth, my dear."

"That's a lot of faith, Admasin."

"Have you ever met Kito?"

"As a matter of fact, I have stopped and spoken to him more than once."

"He is a remarkable man, don't you think?"

"He is just a boy."

Admasin could read people better than that. He saw a memory flash over her face then a hint of anger. "Lucia?"

She knew he was right. "Well, we're sailing at the last two then, aren't we?"

The two vessels to the rear were larger than theirs, easily the same size as the one Kito was on.

Admasin leaned forward as if it would aid his eyesight as he searched. A frown imprinted itself into his forehead. *Where are you, my son?*

22 Baako's Return

Baako looked at the little vessel, *Queen of the Seas* as it sailed ahead. It seemed to be out of its league taking on all the bigger vessels, though to be fair, there was no doubting its seaworthiness. After all, it had seemingly sprung from nowhere and caught up to them.

He sighted Kito, who was talking quietly with the rudder men and Captain Seiji. Clearly, none of the men were comfortable speaking with him. The captain was trying to sound authoritative.

"I just don't see any reason to be leaving the company of the other vessels. We have no threat out here and need to be arriving as a group, or someone will ask why we didn't stay together. I, for one, don't wish to be answering to the Emperor."

Kito answered in a low tone. "I can see what you're saying, but I also know what that little vessel is capable of."

The captain shook his head. "A few wildly shot balls of iron will not deter me. They didn't even find their target."

"At that point, they were not trying to find their target. The question is, if they do, what answer would you have?"

The captain raised his chin as his crew waited expectantly, but before he could blurt out his answer, Baako spoke. "Kito knows those people better than anyone here. As he said the night before we left, if he's right about the little vessel that caught us so easily, you will then be the *only* one to show up for the Emperor."

The captain shuffled uncomfortably. He thought about the little vessel and its iron balls. They made the most frightful noise as they whistled past. He coughed into a clenched fist. "Very well, but remember you're all here uninvited to this vessel. If at any time I feel we're not doing the right thing for the Imperial Throne, I will remove all of you from my vessel. Are we clear?"

Kito dipped his head. "You are most wise, Captain. We should break east immediately and not look back."

The captain signalled to the rudder men, then spoke coldly to Kito. "Be it on your head, strange one. Be it on your life and the lives of your friends."

Baako watched on. Kito could've stood over and dominated the conversation at any time, yet he never once looked like he was going to resort to that. Kito bowed to the captain. "Providing you stay with your wise decision, Captain, everyone here will arrive safe and well." He bowed again and moved away. Baako watched him descend the stairs and didn't notice the captain come forward.

"Hey, black man."

Baako looked at the captain.

"How long have you known him?"

Baako shrugged. "We are brothers."

The captain scoffed. "No, you don't look alike."

"There is more than one type of brother." He motioned to the rudder men. "Are these not your brothers to the throne?"

The captain stiffened as if insulted. "Certainly not. I'm the captain, after all."

Baako smirked as he moved away. "Have a good day, Captain."

Tanica and Mercanti were talking quietly when Baako approached with a broad smile. "Did either of you see where Kito went?"

Mercanti motioned to the stairs. "Yes, Baako, he went below deck."

"Thank you, ladies."

At the bottom of the stairs, he paused to let his eyes adjust. Tzu and Hao were sitting together and, had he not been so keen to speak with Kito, he would've left them alone. "Gentlemen."

Tzu raised his head in surprise. "Surely you can't be addressing Hao or me?" Hao smirked, almost wishing he had the same quick wit and friendly nature.

"I was looking for Kito. He came down this way. Did you see which way he went?"

Hao flicked his hand towards the stairwell. "He never spoke but took those stairs down lower. Everything good, Baako?"

Baako flashed a smile again. "Yes, I just wanted to speak with him about his intentions when we get to Zimbali." Taking a torch, he headed lower.

On the lower deck, a group of men were huddled in a corner playing a game with a paddle and two coins. Hunched over under the low ceiling, Baako approached. They scowled at the sight of him.

"Hello, men. Could you tell me which way Kito went?"

No one spoke, but they glanced at a small set of stairs at the centre of the vessel, not far from the master pole. "Thank you all, very helpful." He moved around the men, keeping his eyes on the stairs.

There was little light down in the cargo hold. Baako used his torch to rummage around. *These are the only stairs down, so he must be here amongst the supplies, somewhere.*

***

Back upstairs, Tzu looked at Hao. "No, we've been through the caves under the palace and through every room. It just isn't there. Besides, if Kito's right in what Koe is doing, the Emperor would certainly have taken it with him now."

Hao frowned. "When I was on the Wall, I always thought it was merely a legend."

Tzu shook his head adamantly. "My father had to give it to Hois for the life of my mother."

"I know this story. Norinko's father?"

Tzu drew back, surprised. "Yes, Hao."

"You were in his village and never beheaded Norinko?"

Tzu held up a hand for Hao to settle. "I thought we agreed, we need to rise above this stuff, Hao, or when will it all end? I mean,

Mother said Norinko was not much more than a boy at the time. Now he seems almost more driven than I to get it back." Tzu thought for a moment. "If you turned the situation around and looked at it from another point of view, he saved my mother, and by doing so, I am here now. Could I not just as quickly kiss the tops of his feet for that?"

"You're a better man than I, Tzu."

Tzu winked. "Yes, though I thought we already knew this."

Hao laughed with Tzu. He could only respect Tzu for his ability to not let his own anger and spite blind the full picture.

Heavy footprints echoed on the boards as Baako came over, clearly concerned.

"Baako, what's wrong?" Hao asked.

Baako stopped just short of them and rubbed his heavily creased forehead. "Did you see Kito come back up after I went down?"

The two men shook their heads. Hao knew Kito better than most. "Kito can step as quietly as any I know, but he couldn't have slipped past Tzu and me without being seen."

Baako looked around the room, shaking his head. "This cannot be."

***

That afternoon, everyone on the top deck saw one plume of black smoke some distance behind, but nothing else. The other vessels had not caught them, just as Kito had said. Captain Seiji had gone deathly quiet. Kito hadn't been seen for some time, and almost everyone was concerned for him. Tanica had not said anything either way.

The days grew long as the *Titan* journeyed on. They finally turned into the port for Begonia and entered the river. Baako made sure he and the others stayed below deck; no one could know they had entered Zimbali. From there, they peered through portholes, seeing everyone looking at their strange vessel. The vessel lowered its sail, and the Royal Guard began to row.

Hao moved up beside Baako and lowered his voice. "They are watching the strange vessel."

Baako shook his head slowly. "Do they? Or do they look on at another vessel of Royal Guards arriving in lands where they don't belong?"

On the incoming tide, the vessel made good distance. They stopped and camped against the riverbank by night. By day, they kept rowing, changing the rowers on a regular basis. Now in his own lands, Baako couldn't help but go ashore each night and make a small fire. There he would smell his jungle. The sounds of all the various creatures of his lands sounded around him, bringing a sense of calm and belonging. In his own jungle, he sat, for the first time in a very long time, a free man.

On the second night, Tzu leaned over the side of the vessel and asked quietly, "Baako, would I be intruding if …?"

Baako looked up from the crackling fire. "Please, my friend, all of you are welcome."

Before long, all the men and two women were around the fire telling stories. Some of the Royal Guard came to the side of the vessel and watched on. Hao decided they were possibly envious since they couldn't join them. These would have been the best of times if it weren't for their purpose of being there. Silently, for Baako, these were to be the worst of times.

One evening, Captain Seiji walked down to the end of the plank behind him. "Baako."

The big man turned smoothly to face him, dipping his head slightly in respect for the man's customs. "Yes, Captain Seiji?"

The captain reached out with a bag. "I took the liberty of putting some provisions in here."

Baako slowly took it. "Captain?"

"If the Emperor got word that I have brought you all here," he looked around the motley-looking gang, "Well, suffice to say, it wouldn't be good for me, nor my entire family."

"I see."

"You know where you are, Baako?"

Baako's white teeth shone in the fading light. "Yes, of course. This is my home."

"Very well."

"Captain."

"Yes, Baako?"

"If you sail right out of here in the morning, no one will know you were ever here. If you stay, these lands will consume you and every man on board."

The captain raised an eyebrow. "Consume, Baako?"

Baako was unmoving as he slowly repeated the word. "Consume."

The captain stood blank-faced. "Oh. I see."

The following morning, Baako and his friends saw the *Titan* off. It was pointless for Baako to tell them to head downriver for their own good. The captain would do as he was ordered by the Asset, nothing else.

Baako kicked dirt over the dwindling fire, stomping it down with his hardened bare feet. He looked to his five companions. "My friends, if you're ready, we have a few days run."

23 Sacred Skull

Kito looked down on the Emperor's vessel, the *Ocean Conqueror*, willing it to slowly move forward, both on the ocean and in real time. Everything was as he had left it; he was back to the same moment as when he'd left.

He moved towards his mortal form, holding Rani's crown, felt the heat burning his hands as he merged back into his body. He stretched his limbs, put the crown on his bicep, dressed, and then slipped quietly down the stairs. Completely washed out, he lay splayed in front of the open hatches and quickly fell into a deep sleep.

***

A few days later, the *Ocean Conqueror* sailed directly into the Port of Audun, where a very disgruntled Sheik disembarked.

Back out on the ocean, the vessel continued to the Port of Begonia. They docked, and before too long, a large crowd had converged to look at the strange vessel with its huge pole in the centre. The Emperor stood with his hands clasped behind his back as goods were quickly unloaded and the crew returned to the vessel. Mensa also disembarked. On the jetty below, he looked decidedly rebuked as the Emperor called down to him.

"Be sure your tribes are ready and waiting. I don't wish to have anyone return to their lands unexpectedly." It was a cool farewell as the vessel set off without so much as a handshake.

Mensa thundered off to his office as the crowd gave way to the seething man, giving him a great deal of space. The laughing Emperor waved a hand as the men rowed hard on the oars, heading upriver, directly for Batavia, deep in Zimbali.

Kito was at the bow as they rowed deeper into the jungle. He wondered what Hao and his friends were thinking with his sudden departure without a word from the *Titan*. *It's not like I can say my goodbyes and hop over the side. No, some things must be done in the cloak of darkness. Besides, they will be fine now I've spoken with Admasin on his little vessel.*

His ability to travel through time had progressed to a tremendous level, moving between time and place, acting only upon what he thought needed to be done when he arrived there. *Am I right? Is this the Gods' will?* he questioned, though he knew no one would answer.

The Emperor snapped Kito back to the present. "You know where we're heading, Kito?"

Kito looked at the jungle ahead. "Yes. Clearly, Batavia has something for you."

"There you will find me the Green Crystal Skull, son." The words slithered off the Emperor's tongue.

Still, Kito didn't meet the Emperor's eye. "Could you not have just asked Mensa? If anyone knows of its whereabouts, he would."

Emperor Koe clasped his hands behind his back. "Except the ignorant fool doesn't believe in the legend, therefore he must have no idea of its actual whereabouts."

"Then, in all of Zimbali, Koe, why Batavia?"

The Emperor raised his chin smugly. "I have very good information. The sort of information that has gotten me thus far." He prodded Kito with his finger. "The Skull is there and *you* will find it."

Kito held his tongue, deciding not to speak on the matter further. He did, however, know that neither of them would be welcome there.

***

The following day, *Ocean Conqueror* pulled into Batavia. Several fishing vessels had to make a quick exit as the Emperor's vessel took up the entire wharf. The Emperor stood unconcerned as the gangplank was slipped down onto the wharf.

Kito walked up beside him. "Koe?"

The Emperor didn't turn. "Yes, Kito?"

"I would recommend I go alone, given our history of the poor man being fed to the crocodiles in front of his sister and mother."

The Emperor raised his eyebrows. "Oh yes, that's right. I had forgotten." He looked about indifferently. "No, we will proceed together."

"But no Royal Guard, Koe?"

"Just you and I, Kito."

The Emperor walked the plank with his hands clasped behind his back. He seemed oblivious as the marketplace hushed to an uncomfortable quiet as they made their way through. Kito was searching for Shay. He couldn't feel her, but there were so many vibrations to sort through. All ugly and all focused on them. Their hatred burned Kito's soul.

As they neared Rani's disused palace, the Emperor let Kito take the lead. He walked in at ground level and stood in silence for some time. The Emperor waited patiently.

Kito let everything slip away, emptying his mind. Empty, except for the screaming Skulls he'd seen and heard at the Stone Temple in the valley. Green eyes glared into his through the darkness behind his closed eyes. The Skull was calling him. He focused on it calling his name again, louder and closer, its eyes burning.

With his eyes shut, he moved to the stairs and began to climb. The swords on his back began to pulse in rhythm with the crown on his arm, the cries getting louder, calling his name, ever closer. He ascended higher. The voice became clearer, now screaming, 'KITO! KITO!' Further, he climbed.

He turned a corner into a room, eyes still shut. The Skull flashed at him, and he swerved to avoid it, knocking the Emperor back to the wall. Kito recovered quickly.

The Emperor staggered back to his feet and dusted himself off. He looked at the vines growing through the vast room of high, stone ceilings. Kito stopped halfway along the room and turned left. Before him were two large, stone thrones. The Emperor grinned but didn't move a muscle. Kito stood still for the longest time. The Skull wasn't calling him anymore. Total silence. In his mind's eye, he searched the main hall where they stood – the hall that belonged to the King and Queen, his father and mother.

He opened his eyes and walked forward to the thrones that faced out over the entire village, past the markets and right out to the wharf with an uninterrupted view. Now standing beside him, the Emperor admired his vessel.

Kito couldn't feel the Skull anymore. He could neither see, nor hear it. He called it several times in his mind. *Nothing.* He flicked up his hood and lowered his head. Silently, he turned and walked towards the back of the hall behind the thrones. As he moved back, the Skull began calling once more. Its power intensified, and as he reached the wall, piercing green eyes flashed, and the Skull screamed at him louder than ever.

He shuddered. *This is it. This is the Sacred Skull of Zimbali!* He put his hand to the solid, rock wall, so well crafted not even a blade of grass could fit in the joints. The stone felt cold to his fingertips as he moved along the wall, feeling for something, anything. Each time he moved away from behind the thrones the screaming stopped. *It is here, somewhere.*

He took a step back and studied the wall. No two blocks of rock were the same shape yet they were perfectly placed and formed to the next. Some of the blocks were so large it seemed impossible that any number of men would be able to lift them. He couldn't imagine how the palace had been erected at all.

Kito turned to see the Emperor making himself comfortable in one of the thrones and looking down at his vessel. He walked around it to face him. "Koe, I can feel the Skull, though it is very well hidden. I will need to explore further."

The Emperor's nostrils flared. "What do you mean, explore further? Is the damn thing here or not!?"

Kito lowered his voice. "Yes, it's here. It's just a matter of revealing it."

The Emperor leaned forward on the throne. "Well then, reveal it, *boy*."

"If you would, Koe, I will safeguard you back to the *Ocean Conqueror* then I would like to return here for as long as it takes to get the Skull."

The Emperor eased himself up from the throne and smoothed down his black silk gown. He put his face close to Kito's. "See that you do, Kito."

They descended the stairwell and walked out through the markets. Kito stopped at the gangplank as the Emperor stepped onto his vessel and spoke only to the guard who awaited him. The plank was withdrawn and Kito bowed until the Emperor had departed from view.

He turned back to the disused palace. Ignoring the angry stares, he looked up at what was once a grand palace. The jungle vines now seemed to be making it theirs. Ever so slowly, one leaf, one vine at a time, the jungle was taking it back.

The temple was quite magnificent, so loved his mother must have been. He stood proudly admiring the engineering masterpiece his people had made for her. He studied the design. It was completely symmetrical, rising evenly on both sides for many floors. He could only just make out the room where the two thrones were. Unusually, they were not at the top.

He headed towards it through the quietening markets and entered the stairwell. This time he climbed up to the floor of the thrones, then went one higher. Although similar in shape, this floor was a little more enclosed along the front, private almost. It dawned on him that the top flights were for dwellings. These would be Royal dwellings. *Possibly not where you would hide a Sacred Skull*

He admired all the detail in the stonework, with the same closed joints, impeccable in their finish. This did, however, bring the same problem; it was impenetrable. He climbed each of the remaining floors and checked around. No two rooms were laid out the same and none gave him so much as a hint as to where the Skull may be.

Now on the top floor, Kito walked out to the edge and looked down. In the fading light, the vessel now glowed with lanterns. He looked over the village and its markets and the jungle spreading down to the river. It was beautiful in every way. *This is home. My home.* He closed his eyes, searching for a memory. Shay had told him this was his home, but for all his trying, he couldn't remember any sort of life here.

It had grown dark, and laughter floated up from the vessel. Under the lights, Kito could see several figures sitting around the rudder, talking and no doubt, drinking. He sat in the lotus position. *Koe isn't at the table!* He lowered his head and gently tested his mind for any blocks. It was clear. He descended quickly to the main hall and sat in one of the thrones, concentrated and pulled free of his mortal self, then drifted down directly to the vessel. As expected, the Emperor was sweating and grunting. Kito pulled away and drifted high up into the evening air, searching the jungle for a night flyer. Fruit bats screeched and fluttered amongst the treetops. He focused his energy on them. In a surprisingly short time, their wings ceased to flap, and they hung there frozen, suspended in space and time. With a broad smile and more than a little pride at his growing abilities, he headed west at a great pace.

Kito slowed as he neared the Great Western Ranges. Lights from the many campfires sparkled below him; they, too, were frozen in time, each curled flame halted in mid-dance. It was the Village of the Keepers. He swept along the river and into the tunnel. He almost scoffed at himself, remembering how he'd dared to enter it on a round raft.

Drawing himself down onto the stairs, he walked boldly into the light. Around the last corner, Rani stood waiting for him. "Hello, Chizoba."

She was so beautiful. Her warm orange gown swept out over the floor. He bowed deeply, then stood. "Hello, Mother. It is again my pleasure to be in your presence."

Her chuckle filled the caves. "Ah, you have your father's tongue, don't you, son." She chuckled again.

"I wouldn't know." Rani's dress turned a slight blue. He smiled. "Though I would like to think so."

Her dress lightened somewhat. "What brings you here, son?"

"You are right to ask. I do have a problem you may be able to help with."

"Yes, go on, Chizoba."

Kito shuffled uncomfortably at the name. "It's about the Sacred Skull of Zimbali."

Rani's dress immediately turned crimson. "Why is it you ask about this, Chizoba?"

"I can feel it in the palace built for you, though I can't find it."

"Because you're not meant to. It carries too much power."

"Too much power for me?"

"For anyone, Chizoba. People don't handle power well. When one gets more than another, they tend to forget about everyone else. Afraid of losing their status, they strive for more, to control and manipulate. It very quickly becomes a self-feeding, closed loop."

"Yes, I have witnessed this, though the Skulls were made for a reason. I don't feel they're of any use locked away either."

"True, but they have the power of the Gods and are very dangerous." Kito looked at the ground and Rani's dress began to turn blue. "You aren't going to stay, are you, Chizoba?"

"There's a lot happening, Mother. I have much work to do."

"Must it all be about you?"

"It *is* about me. How many people have stood at the entrance of this great mountain river and wondered what was down here? But I am the one that is here talking to you. I can move through time, from place to place. Why and how I cannot know, but it gives me the ability to move people into a position so that maybe, just maybe, we can stop this evil. If I don't, someone else will get the Skulls. Mother, I don't want them for myself, I just don't want the wrong person to have them either." He looked at the enormous Sacred Crystal in the next room. Its massive power surged with a light pulse in the crown on his left bicep. Then it occurred to him. "You do know Baako is free and on his way back to Zimbali as we speak?"

Rani gasped. "I always knew he was alive, even after all these years. He is returning to his rightful place."

"Also, I need to tell you … Mabutu is back at the Village of the Keepers."

Rani's dress warmed to orange again. "Yes, Chizoba, I could feel that change, that he was so close. We have been talking, you know?"

Kito flinched. "Talking? How?"

"If he calls me in his sleep, and he does, I can go to him. He says Trina is alive?"

Kito hadn't planned to mention this. "Yes, Mother. I have been to Orion and seen her."

"Is she well?"

Kito lowered his voice. "They keep her prisoner."

Her dress turned crimson. "Why?" Then it turned black with the stark realisation. "It is because of me, isn't it?"

Kito attempted to sound reassuring. "It will not be for long. She will be free soon enough."

Rani studied her son for some time. "Sometimes in life, the most indirect way is the only right way." Kito wouldn't turn away until her dress colour said he could. Eventually, it lightened to orange. She looked at him in earnest. "You will visit me when you can, won't you?"

"One way or another, Mother, I will be back."

Rani did her best to smile, though her dress gave her away. "Please be careful, my son."

"You're not going to give me the Crystal Skull's location, are you?"

"I only ever saw ours once. I liked nothing about it. Whether it was made by the Gods or not, I felt it was too much for one person to consume or control. I never liked the feel of it. I never liked the sight of it, and I have no idea of its whereabouts."

Kito's head tilted. She wouldn't lie to him. "Do you know where it was kept back then?"

Rani smiled faintly, thinking of what he'd said about the wrong person getting it. "I think it was in the throne room. Sometimes I thought I could hear it calling my name."

He dipped his head. "Until next time, Mother," and he turned away.

Rani gasped. Kito didn't walk out of the room; he simply faded and was gone. She could feel the power of her only son growing.

Kito exited the cave over the river. *Oh no.* He panicked at the sight of the fires burning as normal now. He realised he must've lost control of time when near the Sacred Crystal in Rani's cave. He sped directly to Batavia. The block was returning, although he could feel his acceptance back to the present.

Kito rushed to the thrones in the stone palace. Emperor Koe was just getting to the top of the palace stairs. Sword in his hand, he was almost foaming at the mouth. As Koe stepped onto the top floor to check the thrones, bats suddenly flew up around him. He slashed wildly as more bats surrounded him, screeching and flying at speed. He tried to cut them down but they were just out of reach, circling him.

Koe waved his sword about but it was futile. "Banji!"

Kito smiled to himself. *So, this is the woman he is with.* "Koe, this way. Quick!"

The Emperor spun to see Kito holding up a torch in a corridor. He struggled to keep his balance, swiping the bats as he moved towards the torch. As he entered the corridor, the bats disappeared.

Koe fell against a wall, breathing hard. He studied his surroundings. It wasn't a corridor but a tunnel. He looked at Kito, his wild eyes inflamed with anger. "When I am a God King, so help me I will wipe all witchcraft from this damn earth!"

And Banji would be the witch. She is the block!

Finally, Koe stood up straight. "And you …" He poked Kito in the chest several times. "… had better have very good news."

Kito looked at the Emperor's contorted face. "As a matter of fact, Koe, I do. You remember the last time we were in this village?"

"You gave your word to serve … *me*," he snarled.

"This is the way I came into the village. I felt the Skull, here."

"Well then find it and put it into my damn hand, boy."

Kito stepped back and bowed. "I will need some space, Koe. If you would like to return to the vessel, I …"

"You will find it, right here, right now, while I wait!" Saliva dribbled down his chin as he spat out the words.

The crown on Kito's bicep pulsed hot. He turned on his heel and held the glowing torch down the tunnel a short distance. *Nothing.* He turned back. The Emperor couldn't miss Kito's piercing blue eyes in the torchlight, glazed over and unfocused. The crown pulsed again. He moved forward. Still looking at Kito's eyes, the Emperor slowly backed out of the tunnel into the large room, leaving Kito just inside the entrance of the tunnel.

The crown grew hotter on Kito's arm, so hot he had to resist the urge to remove it.

He turned to his left – nothing but solid rock. He turned to his right – the same – but this time the crown stopped pulsing. His senses tingled, drawing him back to the spot. He slowly moved the torch over the wall again, then stopped. There was one small, black recess in the black wall.

The Emperor watched wide-eyed as Kito slowly reached into the recess, further and further. The stone wall seemed to envelop his arm. He braced himself and pulled. There was a distant click in the throne room. He withdrew his arm and went back in.

Now protruding from the back of one of the stone thrones was a flat platform, and on it lay a Crystal Skull. As Kito lifted it, its green eyes flashed at him. This was the Sacred Skull of Zimbali.

The Emperor drooled as he pulled a silk sack from his pocket and slowly reached out and placed it over the Skull. Delicately, he lifted it as Kito withdrew his hands. The Emperor flinched as the stone platform instantly slipped back into its slot, disappearing like it was never there.

Kito sensed he'd had help. He rubbed the cooling crown on his arm and whispered, "Koe, I will extinguish the torch, and we should move quietly back to the *Ocean Conqueror* under the cloak of darkness."

The Emperor couldn't speak for excitement. With a sly grin, he nodded. Kito waved the torch vigorously to extinguish it.

In silence, they slipped out into the night.

24 Queen of the Seas

Admasin, Lucia and the crew watched closely as they drew near the last two of the four big vessels, where hundreds of uniformed men looked back at them, curious and menacing. Their little vessel with its raggedy-looking crew was quite the joke to them.

The *Queen of the Seas* dipped down into a trough and surged back out. Just as it levelled out over the crest, two enormous explosions made everyone flinch.

No one on the bigger vessels moved. For the longest time everyone just looked on, waiting to see what happened next. When it did, the uniformed crew fell about, jeering and laughing. Both gun balls had hit a swell and bounced several times before dipping down with a small splash. The balls hadn't even reached their vessels.

Still, the little vessel surged forward.

Jabali came out from the lower deck and shuffled to the bow. Lucia could just see him under the curtain of the sail. He spoke to the men. "Half the mast! Half the mast!"

Lucia began to shake her head, but Admasin interjected. "No, let him be, we have nothing to lose and everything to learn." She held her tongue and the wheel in line. As the men lowered the sail halfway, Admasin began to laugh.

Lucia looked at him. "What?"

"As I said, my dear, everything to learn. Feel the vessel, feel how she rides under your feet."

Lucia thought on it, though she couldn't take her eyes off Jabali. He looked at her and then pointed his cane towards the rear vessel. They could see its name now: *Voyager*. They were getting so near she could feel the stares of the men leering over her as she stood in her leathers. Then she understood Jabali's instructions. The *Queen of the Seas* was carrying less sail, meaning it no longer dove into each swell, creating a more stable platform to fire from. She saw him walk forward to the bow. He took his time, then began to raise his cane. He held it, paused, then slammed it down hard onto the deck. Almost instantly, both guns roared again. The Royal Guards held out their arms, taunting them as targets, pointing and laughing. But this time, it would be the last thing some would ever do.

The *Voyager* was hit just under the top deck. Splintered timbers and shattered bones ripped from torn flesh rained down over the deck and beyond. The other ball hit right on the waterline with the most deafening, hollow sound. The *Voyager* immediately began to slow as its bow lowered. Every passing swell pumped more water into it. This would be its last voyage.

Jabali waved his cane towards the other vessel, *Avenger*. Lucia turned the wheel. He waved them directly ahead, once more holding his cane high over the deck. Lucia looked nervously at Admasin, and he gave an equally nervous smile back, then watched ahead. As they cruised past the *Voyager*, they couldn't help but look through the broken hole. Bodies floated in the flooded vessel as more water surged in, sloshing them about.

"Mind the flag, men; mind your duties," called Admasin.

They were so close to *Avenger* now that there would be little time to reload the guns. The vessel surged up a swell and just as it crested, it seemed to ride it. Jabali smashed down his cane and the two guns boomed.

Stunned at what had just happened to their sister-ship, the Royal Guard barely moved when the guns were refired. The first ball crashed over the rudder deck, breaking the rudder stick clear off the vessel and instantly killing the men holding it. They were thrown over the side like toys. Again, the second ball ploughed in right on the waterline, breaking the timbers like tinder.

The moment the guns had fired, Lucia quickly swung the wheel. Everyone held on for the imminent collision.

Jabali yelled. "Brace yourselves, men!"

It was fortunate their rudder had slammed to one side because their vessel collided with the rear of the *Avenger*. The crew clung on tightly as it straightened momentarily then slid back onto its side. The *Avenger's* sail fell slack, then snapped tight again. A deep groaning sounded as the creaking timber strained, followed by loud popping sounds. The sail suddenly fell forward, just clearing the top deck.

Leaning heavily on his cane, Jabali hobbled across the deck. His legs were not seaworthy, but his command was that of a captain. "Mind your duties, men. Let off that block so the sail can swing around clear of the big vessel. Nice job."

The men rushed forward, releasing the rigging, their sail turning just in time as the vessels collided with more groaning timber.

Lucia gripped the wheel, white-knuckled with a steely determination. The *Avenger* was already listing badly away from them. Men, with nowhere else to go, poured over the top side of the vessel as it slowly rolled. She looked at Jabali. He was calm and in control, walking between the men, waving his cane as their vessel shook and shuddered. The *Queen of the Seas* had lost its momentum, having momentarily jammed on the larger vessel.

He reassured the men. "The bigger vessel will pull away from us here, just be patient, any moment now."

Just as he spoke, they broke free of the damaged vessel, and the men adjusted the rigging without a word. It didn't take long before they were back on pace. Turning right, they kept their distance from the rolling *Avenger*.

Sailing ahead of them, Admasin pointed to the biggest vessel of them all. Superior to anything he'd ever dreamt of, he couldn't believe they had managed to get it down the river out of Samos. Having no plan, they simply began steering towards it.

Jabali wanted to steer them farther out to sea, but Lucia had been directed by Admasin, and that was good enough for her. They were gaining well now.

Admasin wiped his brow on his soaked sleeve. "They are raising their sails farther now. This may not go our way." He didn't notice Jabali standing up front, insistent that they go out wide.

"We have a smaller, lighter vessel, and we're already at full pace," Lucia assured Admasin. "It will take time to get that beast going. We can catch them."

It was true. They were travelling at speed and making good gains. Admasin called from the rudder deck. "Pull those blocks tight, men. We need all the power we can get. Work them tight, every ounce."

Jabali moved through the men working in earnest and grunting hard. He could smell their efforts as he passed by. He snapped up at Lucia at the wheel above. "What the blazes do you think you're doing?"

She was quick to snap back. "Who *the blazes* do you think you are? This is neither your vessel, nor your fight!"

He pointed his cane at her. "And you are a very rude woman. How many vessels have you captained to be such an expert on battle approach?"

Lucia's jaw dropped and she rushed forward to the handrail, leaving Admasin to quickly grab at the wheel she'd neglected. She pointed down at Jabali. "And how much could you possibly know about the sail vessel you are riding, to be telling *me* which way to go? *YOU* are the one afraid of the blessed water! And as for rude people, I think you might be an expert on rude! You are the rudest man I have ever met ..."

Jabali waved his cane up at her before she could finish. "... *You* will mind your mouth, Alex ..."

Their war of words was interrupted as one of their men screamed out in pain. Arrows rained down on them, whirring overhead before thumping into the wooden deck.

Admasin called out. "Dive for cover! Take cover!"

Everyone darted to the side of the vessel. Admasin shoved Lucia to the cover of the higher sides, spinning the wheel as fast as he could.

The vessel leaned over hard, exposing the deck to the influx of arrows. Jabali tumbled and slid down towards the side on his stomach. An arrow drove deep into his thigh. His head snapped back as he howled, skidding into the side of the vessel with a thud, his hat falling away. He scrambled around searching frantically for it when his eyes locked on Lucia. She was down on her side, looking at him through the top railing. His heart sank at the look of sheer disdain on her face. He gritted his teeth and dragged himself towards his hat flapping about just beside him. Quickly, he grabbed it and shoved it on to conceal his wretched face.

As he straightened the eyelets on his mask, something caught his eye. It was his worst nightmare. *Flames!* He watched open-mouthed as they came over in their smoking arcs. Hundreds of arrows of fire. In a matter of moments, they slammed down all over the rear deck creating billowing plumes of toxic, black smoke. He looked up to see Lucia going to Admasin at the wheel.

He reached out a desperate arm. "Alexa. Gods NO!"

25 Insubordination

Asset Chun stood with his fingers intertwined and resting easily on his belly. His chest made a feeble attempt to match his stomach. "Well, men, *that* is how you squash any threat to the throne. *Queen of the Seas?* Pathetic, I say; just pathetic." He watched as the little vessel limped out to sea, barely visible for the thick smoke.

One of the men beside him asked, "But who are they with the smaller, faster vessel of sails?"

The Asset shrugged, almost concealing his short, fat neck. "Don't really care," he replied before turning to a very quiet captain. "Kalgan, you must be happy to see the little vessel squashed?"

Captain Kalgan tried to mask the sick feeling in his stomach. "Yes, well done, Asset, though should we now turn about and pick up our men?"

The Asset shook his multiple chins. "No, we have neither room nor the time for the extra men. Forward with our *Ocean Asset.* The Emperor awaits."

"Sir, those are our men over there." Almost lost for words, Kalgan pointed back to the *Avenger.* Now without steering, it bobbed like driftwood on the swells, taking on water and sinking. Behind that, the *Voyager* was completely inverted. Like ants clinging to a floating leaf, men covered its hull, waving frantically.

Impervious to their pleas, the Asset simply looked ahead. "As I said, the Emperor awaits."

"No, those are my men, and we are turning about. Now!" Kalgan signalled to the men on the rudder. "Turn now, starboard side." The riggers awaited his instruction. "Turning starboard side, ready the sails, turning starboard side!" The men, pleased not to be leaving their comrades behind, were quick to oblige the captain's orders and the huge vessel did a wide arc to come back alongside the stricken vessels.

Asset Chun's face reddened in fury. "I will be informing the Emperor myself of your insubordinate actions, Captain Kalgan." His cheeks wobbled incessantly as his head shook. "You have set your own death sentence!"

Kalgan ignored his every whine. "Man the nets, port side!" No one even looked at the Asset as they followed Kalgan's instructions. The *Avenger* was floating right-side up, but the main deck was now underwater. "Be sure you get every ounce of drinkable water off that vessel. I don't care that you must dive for it!"

Several shouts came back. "Call heard, Captain!"

Kalgan inspected his own vessel. It was lacking. Seeing what the *Ocean Asset* was doing, the vessel that had been leading the four, the *Pursuit*, had also turned around and was now on the other side of the *Avenger*, picking up men. Kalgan frowned. *There are too many and it's taking too long to get all the supplies, but I have to, we'll need them to complete the journey.*

"They're back! The little vessel is back!" a crewman shouted anxiously.

Far off in the distance, one lone sail moved across the horizon. Kalgan had no choice. "Man the sails! Man the sails!" The sails began to rise as instructed. "Only half mast, half sail!"

The *Ocean Asset* began to pull forward. The men on the stricken vessel looked at him with their arms out, pleading desperately. Kalgan knew if they were to have any way of surviving the little vessel, they had to at least be a moving target. He checked the *Pursuit*. It too was now moving away.

He'd now lost sight of the little vessel. He strained his eyes and moved forward on the deck to get a clearer view. Nothing. He could hear some of the men talking.

"They saw us coming. They're making a run for it!"

"They got out while the going was good."

Kalgan shook his head. He wasn't so sure. The mission ahead was now far from Kalgan's mind. It was nearly dark. *Where is Katanning?* Kalgan hadn't seen him come off the stricken *Voyager.* He'd received the letter of his father's intention to rebuild at Devil's Pass. *That little vessel must surely have been him and Alexa. All those arrows. Many made their targets.* He'd heard cries of pain from the little vessel. *Have I taken my own father's life?*

Heavy boots thudded on the stairs as Kalgan wearily ascended them and walked to the rear of the vessel. He looked back at all the men they were leaving behind. Their desperate pleas faded into the distance as they slowly fell away. He held his arms out wide, lifted his face to the heavens and closed his eyes in quiet prayer. There was nothing more he could do.

***

On the little vessel, Jabali rolled onto his back and looked at the arrow sticking in his thigh. The arrow point had pushed up under the skin. He grimaced as he shuffled about and placed his leg so the butt of the arrow was on the deck. *This has to be done.* With his two hands on his thigh so the arrow point was in the gap between his hands, he braced himself. He raised his hands and slammed them down. The point sliced through his skin and pants as he howled again. The arrow was now clean through his thigh. He tore the cloth mask off his hat. Aligning the arrow point with an eyelet, he tied it off tightly around his thigh. It quickly began to turn red. Grabbing his cane, he staggered upright and leaned on the side of the vessel.

The men had put out the fire. It was mostly just the arrows burning. Only a few had made it to the rear of the vessel, and fire had not had time to take hold.

Admasin scurried over to his side. "You are hit."

Letting his hair fall all over his face, Jabali grimaced. "I have had worse, Admasin." He looked about. "Go back."

Admasin drew back. "What?"

"Turnabout. We will cut faster than them to be in front. We will attack the front, smaller vessel first."

Admasin shook his head. "We are ..."

"In good shape, Admasin. We are better than they are, and we are armed. Turn about."

Admasin looked into Jabali's eyes for a moment. "So be it." It took him some time to convince Lucia to turn around, but when they did, the wind helped them pick up pace quickly.

Jabali looked up the mast and turned to Ushma, their smallest crewman. "I need you to do me a favour?"

"Yes, what you want?" Ushma asked nervously.

"I want to tie you to the rigging then we'll hoist you up to the top."

Silence. Finally Ushma asked, "First you drown me, now why you rig me up?"

"So that you can tell me where you see the other sail."

His face lit up. "Oh, Ushma have best eyes on board. You good, hoist me." It wasn't long before Ushma was at the top of the mast.

The sun was setting, and doubt began to hang over Admasin's crew, though the pace of the vessel driving forward was quite remarkable.

"Sails, three sails I see!" Ushma pointed forward over the starboard side.

Jabali smiled. "Perfect!" He turned to Lucia. "Keep this heading, please." Not waiting for another scold, he turned to the crew. "As soon as we can see them ourselves, you can let our little friend down." The men nodded. "But first, I have one more request, so gather around, men, if you would."

They were losing light, but they did see the other sails. It wasn't hard to track them with their torches burning on deck. Ushma was eased down. They continued to sail almost past the first vessel when Jabali instructed them to turn and sail directly at it. From the bow, he looked back at Lucia and pointed his cane.

She shook her head. The cripple was leaning hard on the handrails, she could see his blood-stained pants and the arrow protruding from the back. Jabali pointed for Lucia to cross just in front of the first vessel, the *Pursuit*. "What in the Gods is he doing?" she muttered to Admasin.

"He's using the *Pursuit* for cover. Staying on the wind side, I think we will pass around the front of it and then get a clean shot down her side at the *Ocean Asset*."

She waved her hands in resignation. "He doesn't want to go home, does he?"

"Well *I* have a promise to keep. Just do as he says, he has got us thus far, my dear."

Jabali raised his cane, tip down and poised. They waited. When the cane slammed down, both cannons rang out together. The cane once again waved a slight directional change and the men were quick on the blocks as the *Pursuit* towered over them. Just to the right of the bow, they could see water pouring into its gaping hull. The bloody water swallowed up the dead men floating around in the deluge as *Queen of the Seas* surged by.

***

Kalgan heard the most horrendous noise. The quiet evening was shattered and it could be only one thing. *The little vessel!* Men on the *Pursuit* just ahead screamed. They had been hit hard. Kalgan marched down the stairs but couldn't see it. Asset Chun was giving orders to the Imperial Guard. Kalgan swore under his breath as he looked up in horror at the flaming arrows shooting up from their bow into the evening sky. *The stupidity of it!* His own men, seeing the archers following instructions, began to panic.

"Stay calm. Mind your post, men; rudder to the starboard. Rudder to the starboard!"

Chun paced the deck, barking his instructions to the Guard as they blindly fired hundreds of flaming arrows. Some collided into each other sending a few indiscriminate arrows in the direction of the *Pursuit* out in front. They hit the vessel's sail and flames quickly engulfed it, turning the night into day.

Kalgan couldn't see the *Queen of the Seas,* but he wasn't going to run into the inferno ahead of them either. The fibres from the *Pursuit* burst up into the warm air as large patches of burning sail blistered down on the panicked men on the top deck. Screaming balls of fire rained blindly into the ocean as it hissed its welcome.

A boom shook the *Ocean Asset* violently. The *Queen of the Seas,* with its iron balls, was near. Kalgan's ears rang and he stumbled forward. He had just one thing on his mind. *The Asset.*

The men scrambled to the rear of the *Ocean Asset.* "We are hit! We are hit!" The ones below poured up from the lower decks, making the vessel too top-heavy and at risk of rolling over with the pull of the sails.

"Go back. Get back downstairs!" Kalgan yelled desperately.

It was futile. No one could even hear him. No one *wanted* to hear him. He pushed forward as best he could, finally breaking his way through the men.

Asset Chun was sitting on the deck, leaning his back against the side of the vessel. Immobilised in fear, he was staring at his knee. Protruding from the top was a long splinter, his white, silk trousers torn and oozing blood. It had come from the lower deck and had driven all the way up through his foot and lower leg, smashing out his kneecap. He was still very much alive, but now pinned to the deck. Kalgan was confident the Asset had given his last orders.

***

As the *Pursuit's* sail went up in flames before them, Jabali shielded his face from the heat, but time was of the essence. As they drew closer, he hobbled forward, ignoring the falling embers. He raised the cane and looked back to Lucia. She was clearly stricken but firm at the wheel. As they rounded the burning *Pursuit,* she nodded to him, steering them directly at the bow of the second vessel, the double-masted *Ocean Asset.*

Jabali was about to raise his cane when he saw Asset Chun. He would recognise him anywhere. With a resolute thud, he slammed his cane down on the deck. The guns rang out. Smoke, thick with the smell of rotten eggs, wafted back over the deck of the *Queen of the Seas.*

One iron ball caught a swell and never resurfaced. The other ball bounced sharply, catching the huge vessel just under the bow with a deafening explosion into the side as the top deck lifted violently.

The *Queen of the Seas* carried on around the side of the burning *Pursuit,* their sail leaning dangerously close. The men on the *Queen of the Seas* looked at their sail, then back to the huge vessel with its two sails. It was leaning away from them, trying to go around the other side of the now fire-engulfed *Pursuit,* using it as a shield from *Queen of the Seas.* But the blazing vessel would rain embers all over the *Ocean Asset.*

It took precious time to reload the cannons and Jabali watched the *Ocean Asset* looming over them as they charged forward. No one spoke. Jabali averted his eyes from the men on the other vessel beside them, burning and jumping to their watery graves. The swells surged up the side of the *Pursuit* like watery hands reaching up to receive them into the deep.

Admasin's crew looked at one another, questioning their own fate here, today, with the enormous *Ocean Asset.* With no deck lights themselves, they watched Jabali ever so slowly lifting his cane up in the light of the burning *Pursuit* as they passed by. He'd been very specific about his instructions, the crew ready on the blocks, eyes on his cane in the burning red-orange firelight.

The huge *Ocean Asset* loomed further over them, turning across their bow. The cane was raised and held high. Their vessel surged up a swell and the cane slammed down onto the deck. The two cannons blasted out and smashed two small holes in the side of the *Ocean Asset*. The cannons reverberated violently, sending tremors throughout the *Queen of the Seas*. Their sail slammed down.

Everyone dove down as splintered timbers whirled over their vessel. Like the very arrows of the enemy, they speared into anything and anyone they struck.

Tears rolled down Lucia's face as she steered directly at the iron-ball holes as Jabali had instructed. The massive timbers groaned and fractured as the vessels collided. *Queen of the Seas* came to an abrupt halt, throwing everyone forward. They were now lodged into the side of the huge *Ocean Asset*.

More timbers cracked and broke. The *Ocean Asset* moved on despite the gaping hole, and the little *Queen of the Seas*, half into its hull, began to twist as the *Ocean Asset* dragged it sideways. Lucia looked up at their mast – it was dangerously close to the side of the *Ocean Asset*. She felt their vessel roll over as more timbers gave way and wondered how much of the breaking timber was of their own vessel. The white-water now washed over their side as the *Ocean Asset* dragged them along.

Suddenly, there was a loud tearing sound as the *Ocean Asset's* huge sail tore up the middle. The front mast groaned deeply as it lurched forward, then stopped. Ever so slowly, it creaked and wavered, finally giving way with a snap at deck level. The big vessel began to roll back towards them.

Lucia breathed relief as their vessel began to shift with the change.

The noise of timber rubbing on timber was deafening. *Queen of the Seas* rocked then with a shudder began to dislodge from the *Ocean Asset*. Like a melon pip being squeezed out, it shot away. With surprise and joy, the men jumped to their feet, peering up at the *Ocean Asset* as it surged by, completely oblivious to the little vessel it had ejected.

Lucia was quick to take control of the wheel. They would not be giving archers another opportunity.

"Ready on the blocks," Admasin calmly stated. The men were quick to his command. The *Ocean Asset* was too close to raise the sails, though they were ready.

Admasin stood on the starboard side, looking up at the *Ocean Asset* as it slipped by, water pouring in through the enormous hole in its bow. With the sail ripped and the other mast broken, it was a vessel without integrity. He searched feverishly but couldn't see the one he searched for. As they neared the end of the *Ocean Asset*, Admasin called to one of the men leaning over the side. "Do you know Kalgan?"

The man glanced away, then looked back. "The captain went downstairs to inspect the damage."

Admasin shook his head. "It is doomed. I am sorry."

"Most of us felt we were doomed when we left port." The man raised his hands to the skies. "What should we do now?"

Admasin wondered if there would be a flurry of arrows raining down on them at this point, but it was as Kito had said to him in his dreams: *They are a people without conviction in their journey.*

"Cut away that broken mast and throw everything that does not support human life overboard."

Admasin's crew was now raising the sails. As the vessels parted company, Admasin held his hands together to his forehead and gave a curt bow. The other man did the same and watched the 'silly little vessel,' raise its sail and leave.

***

On the top deck of *Ocean Asset* came a voice from behind Ip. "What are you doing, Ip?" It was Ip's good friend, Kagu.

"Cut the rigging for the broken mast and drop that torn sail. I'm going to find Kalgan."

"He's downstairs. Ip, I don't know if you want to go there."

Ip stopped to look at Kagu. "Oh, and why is that?"

"Because those last two balls got inside the hull and never came back out."

Ip shrugged. "And?"

"They bounced inside where the men were. There will be a lot of carnage. Some were in their hammocks sleeping, Ip. It was no way for a warrior to die."

Ip solemnly dipped his head; he was going downstairs regardless. At least now he was forewarned.

As he descended the stairs, the men were just beginning to carry up the wounded. Kagu was right: their wounds were ghastly. A lot would not live the night, and there was nothing anyone could do but keep them comfortable until death. When he reached the bottom level, even with the warnings of Kagu, it was shocking. Water was pouring in through a massive hole, swirling the bodies about and turning them in small eddies thick with blood and shattered timbers. He said a quick prayer under his breath and looked for the captain. He was out waist-deep in water trying to find survivors.

"I got another one," called one of the men. Ip saw him pulling a man to the stairs. He went over to help him, then frowned as the man got closer. "Who is this? He's not in uniform." The man was dressed entirely in black.

"All I know is he's alive. Help me with him, would you?"

The two men carried the man to the top deck and laid him out. "He really does have a lot of injuries. Poor man will never be the same."

Ip shook his head. "I know he is bleeding but I think this man has old injuries also." He pointed to the leg with an arrow protruding. "Look, that one is bandaged."

"Come on, there are others that need our help before the whole floor floods."

The two men went back down, passing many others carrying up survivors. They'd only just got back to the bottom when they saw Captain Kalgan.

"That's it, men." Kalgan instructed.

Ip looked at the large hole. The air whistled out through a small gap at the top as the water poured in.

Kalgan shook his head. "I will not lose any more men trying to save the injured."

The men muttered in accord; the captain was right. On the next level, there were already men waiting with timbers. The captain pushed away the stairs, letting them fall below. "Okay, seal it up."

Any possible survivors were now doomed. With it sealed, they would be trapped in the rising waters. Without a word, the men stepped forward and nailed down the boards. Captain Kalgan stayed and watched until the final nail was driven in.

Ip followed him to the top deck. "Captain, I want you to see this one."

"See what?"

Ip headed away. "Over here, please, sir." Other than the stars and a few torches for light, it took Ip a little while to find the man in black. "Ah, this is the one." They both looked down at the wretched man who'd now rolled onto his side, his long scraggly hair over his face. "Who is this one?"

Kalgan frowned. "I have no idea. He was downstairs?" Kalgan thought for a moment. "I wonder if he was on the little vessel."

"Could he have fallen off when they ran into us?"

"I'm thinking so, yes."

"Bit of a blunder that, really."

Kalgan looked perplexed. "Sorry?"

"Running into us like that."

Kalgan shook his head. "No, I think it was their plan."

"But they were lucky to survive."

"Yes, but it has stopped us." Kalgan looked at the man in black. "Can you watch over this man, do what you can to keep him alive. I will talk to him when he is next conscious."

"Yes, sir." Kalgan turned to leave. "Oh, Captain."

"Yes."

"There was an older man on the little vessel. He asked after you."

"Really, what did he want?"

"I don't know. He just asked after you by name, not title."

"Did you give him my title?"

"I did, sir. You were down in the hull at the time. He then told us to drop the sails and throw away everything not needed to support human life."

Kalgan took a deep breath and sighed it out. "That was good advice."

"We thought so, but why would they try to kill us and then try to save us?"

"No, they didn't want to kill us; they were just willing to do anything to stop us."

Ip thought on this. "So, you know who the old man was then?"

"I believe I do." Kalgan looked down at the man in black again, tilting his head with a frown. "Keep me informed of any change, won't you."

"Yes, sir."

Kalgan went to the rear and leant on the rudder pole. He could faintly see the *Voyager* nearby with its master pole stuck up in the evening sky, catching some of the light from the burning *Pursuit*. The overturned *Avenger* would be there somewhere, but he couldn't see it.

The stars cast twinkles on the flat ocean, the stillness masking the catastrophic events that had just occurred. Kalgan quietly prayed it would stay like this overnight so the vessels would not drift apart, though he had no idea what he was going to do in the morning. He pushed the rudder stick right over to one side as if it would somehow take them back to the others.

The captain of his own stricken vessel on its maiden voyage stepped back to the side of it and slumped down onto the floor. Now he had stopped, he realised just how bone-tired he was. He looked up at a shooting star, couldn't even begin to make a wish on that one. So many men had died this day, just one day at sea. He thought about how many might be inside the overturned vessel. He tried to shake the image of the burning men wearing armour who knowingly ran over the side to douse the flames, only to never return to the surface. Then there were the men who died sleeping in their hammocks in this very hull. *Maybe they were the lucky ones. Who knows what fate awaits us now, drifting at sea, sinking.*

A blood-curdling scream pierced the night air. Kalgan shot to his feet, looking out into the darkness behind them. "What was that?" he called into the night.

"Sharks, sir," came a voice from the *Voyager*. "They have been circling us since the first men went overboard. All the bodies are gone. It seems now they swim over the deck taking live ones."

Kalgan looked on, utterly helpless. "I can't see you from here but can you adjust the rigging?"

"Sir?"

"If you raise both lots of rigging just a little then maybe the men could all get into the folds of the sails."

"Sir, the rigging is under water."

"In the name of the Gods, boy! I can't perform a bloody miracle from over here. You must work it out as a team. Every problem has an answer, but just how you achieve it is what separates the men from the boys."

There was no answer. Kalgan scolded himself for snapping at the poor fellow who had simply answered his question. He could hear the murmurs of conversation; he never heard his name, but he could imagine what they were saying.

He slumped back to sit at the side, put his head down in his hands and wept.

26 The Gathering

The Emperor now had the Crystal Skull of Zimbali, and the smile on his face said it all. They had left Batavia and were heading back down the river. They turned hard left at the fork and started upriver towards the Royal Guard's camp.

Kito had put himself on one of the oars. All the other oars had two men, but he was on his own. His oar groaned as much as any. Barefoot and shirtless, he wore the swords strapped to his back. The Emperor would insist on it. The men behind him eyed his scarred back with the swords, but he didn't care. This vessel living was making him soft, and that was dangerous for his future, and his future was looming close. He could feel it.

Kito sensed his brother Baako was in the jungle, though without sitting down and meditating, he couldn't be sure exactly where he was. If he were behind, then it might be hard to hide the Emperor's vessel at their camp. If he were just ahead, then it wouldn't matter. He leaned into his work and tried not to think about it too much. It was not easy, and the blessed block was up.

Kito now knew who the woman was that Koe was rutting with. She was the witch, Banji, and *she* controlled the block. He would have to be very careful not to find himself engaging with her. Other than being a desert dweller, he knew nothing about her, except that she was far stronger than he.

He felt the oar in his hands, listened to his body and pushed it to its limit. Cutting the oar in deep, he pulled with all his might. He had to stay in pace with everyone else, but that didn't mean he couldn't dig deeper, loading his oar more.

Kito was deep in his work when he felt the vibration changing. The fog that clouded his mind began to withdraw. He didn't venture out. At this point, he had no reason to. He turned his head to one side, trying to lose the vision of the Emperor rutting again.

WAIT, he told himself. Eventually, he knelt, placed the oar on the floor and closed his eyes. Slipping out of his body, he twisted and turned as he ascended, looking down to see that everything was still. No one was rowing. The vessel was neither moving upstream, nor going back down. The ripples weren't even breaking away from the bow. He looked around and could see several birds, frozen mid-flight.

Alright, got that, but I must concentrate on both the time and my task. I can't have a repeat of my mistake when I went to Mother in the cave, although I think that might have been because of the Sacred Crystal with Mother.

He crossed the river and began to follow the track he had run not that long ago. He didn't go far before he found them all, midstride, heading to the Village of the Keepers. He looked a little closer and smiled. All the familiar faces were there. They had all made it safe. He made note of Tanica and Mercanti there, with Baako leading the way. *My wild plan may just have a chance.*

He returned to his body, and the vessel surged forward as he took up his oar, resuming his rowing with a little beat in his heart. It was coming together, but whenever the block was here, he couldn't think about his intentions. He instinctively knew Banji would be able to interpret them.

For now, he had nothing more to do other than enjoy the work on the oar. It was not too long before he could feel the long tentacles of the fog envelop his mind. Banji was back.

Kito continued rowing, as the Emperor would get a drink and sit in the shade to enjoy it. He doubted if Koe would notice all the birds, the sound of the primates calling one another, maybe warning of a jungle tiger lurking about. So many sounds of the jungle, and Koe would notice none of it because he had never thought beyond himself, and never would. *That will be his undoing.*

The blades began to pulse hot on his back, and the beat of the drums started to ring in his ears. He resisted looking about to see if anyone else could hear them; he knew it was just in *his* heart, within him only.

Just then Koe walked forward between the cabins. "Kito, what is the meaning of this?"

"Some of your men are suffering dysentery, so I took one oar to help out."

"Nonsense. No son of mine is made to work, least of all on the oars."

"No one made me, Koe. I offered. The captain was quite insistent that I took a place on the rudder, but I argued I could handle an oar on my own thereby taking two places. It was my choice and still is, Koe."

A call came from the front. "Camp ahead, sir. Port side, two hundred paces, sir."

The captain called from the rudder deck. "Call heard. Call further instructions when required."

"Call heard, sir."

Kito flashed a smile. "This would seem to be a fruitless argument, Koe, now we are here, although …"

The Emperor had just turned away, but turned back with one eyebrow raised. "Yes, son?"

"As this is a used route by tribesmen, I might be favouring putting your vessel out of sight."

"And just how do you suggest we achieve that one, Kito?"

"A little further up is a good-sized stream. I think we would fit."

"And just how would you know this?"

Kito let his smile shine wide. "Why, Koe, I believe these are my lands."

The Emperor stepped forward to stand square to Kito as he rowed. "I do not think Mensa would like to hear you talking about *his* lands like that, Kito."

"From what I can gather, Koe, these were never his lands, and he will not have them much longer."

Koe placed his hands firmly on his hips. "Oh, and how do you see him losing his position?"

"The sharp edge of his past will sweep down and cut him from the future. It will be the will of the Gods." The Emperor's face darkened, and Kito continued to row, watching the Emperor. "Can you tell me your plan for him is far from my prophecy, Koe?"

The lifting of the Emperor's chin was an involuntary reaction to Kito's candid comment. He scolded himself for letting Kito catch him out like this. *Always Kito. Only Kito.* With authority, he glared at him. "Yes, and you will have my back at all times, won't you."

"It is my duty to the throne."

"Only a little further upstream?"

"It will snake around right behind the camp."

Keeping his eyes on Kito for a moment, the Emperor slowly turned away.

Kito inwardly chuckled. *A blow to the ego. Nice.*

They just managed to get the *Ocean Conqueror* through behind the camp, just as Kito had said. In fact, it would be easier to see the camp than the vessel now. It seemed that no one had spotted the camp yet, although it was located in an unoccupied part of the jungle.

Everyone was involved in unloading the vessel. There was a lot of talk about this new way of travelling, telling how it was the first of its kind. Kito ignored the tales, following the Emperor through to the main campfire where his chair was still placed. He was happy to sit opposite the Emperor, in the dirt. There would be talk, and facing the Emperor would allow him to see any physical reactions, as seldom and subtle as they were.

There was, however, very little talk over dinner, other than a brief visit from the captain. He may have been invited to sit with them had he not been so obvious about wanting it so much. The

Emperor simply enjoyed saying no and watching the little egotistical man taking it as if a physical blow. For Kito, this meant the Emperor would now talk endlessly to him. He waited.

"So, son, tomorrow we will load supplies and head for the Valley of the Stone Temple."

Kito didn't look up from his dinner. "I thought you needed all the Crystal Skulls first?"

"Ah, but I have some of the Crystals, so it will be easier to find the rest."

"If you can get in the Valley, that is."

The Emperor leant forward menacingly before he spoke. "*You*, Kito, will get me into the Valley."

Kito slowly looked up at the Emperor. "I can get you in if you can fly like the condor or swim like the salmon, otherwise I know no other way in, Koe."

The Emperor leaned in further, resting his hands heavily on his knees. "You will get me to the cave of the rotten eggs. You know the one: it has many fish bones outside. From there, I will show you the way in, and you will take me there, boy. The lives of all your nation and the nations around it depend upon *your* success, here and now. You do understand?"

The Emperor already had enough support to do what he threatened. Worse, he had a clear description of Mabutu's cave. Kito fingered the food of his light meal. "We can leave at first light if you wish," he said as he took another mouthful.

The Emperor leaned back in his chair. "That we will, son. That we will."

The remainder of the evening was quiet and sombre. When the Emperor rose and left without a word, Kito made himself comfortable by the fire. He watched the flames dancing over the hot coals, wondering how he had gotten himself into such a mess. *Am I really going to assist the Emperor in getting to the Valley of the Stone Temple? Have I really gone in there and not felt its presence? How could Hasuca believe I was the one, when I'm now in this situation?*

The swords pulsed gently on his back. Sitting up, he removed them. Watching the smoke gently wafting up through the trees, he wondered about the Emperor and the swords. Even though now he was not touching them, he could still feel them. He could also feel the block. He turned his attention back to the fire. A leaf began twirling down towards him. Not looking up, he brushed it away. Another leaf dropped down. The block now changed. He closed his eyes and concentrated on the leaf. Just as it was in reach, he gently wafted it away. He had to think about the next leaf dropping and nothing else. It was not hard; several leaves were now spiralling their way. He smiled as he batted them away. *Just the leaves, focus on the leaves.*

The block dropped.

He put his hands on his chest and breathed deeply. *I've got to get this right.* The smoke from the fire slowed, then stopped rising. He eased from his body and went to the vessel. Deep in the hull, he could see a brazier and in its red glow, the Emperor's naked flesh held down another. *Banji!* Kito knew this to be the woman the Emperor yelled at when they were in Rani's Stone Palace. He shook his head. *Twice in one afternoon?*

He looked at her face. Her head was turned side-on. She was also frozen, but completely focused directly on him. He could feel her power and backed away immediately. *Is this the edge Koe has over me? Banji is his power.* He went back to the campfire, still frozen from movement. He rose to see the chimps were pulling more leaves to drop at him. *Are they just letting me know they're there, or are they displeased with me? Is all the jungle displeased with one of its children?* He shook the thoughts from his mind. He was about to unleash a crazy man with all the world's powers combined. *Hasuca!*

Kito climbed and climbed, calling his name, pulsing it out as far as he could reach. Finally, as Kito stopped ascending, the pulse returned.

"Kito, what is all the fuss?"

Kito fell into a bow. *"Hasuca, thank you for coming, I feel I'm in too deep and require your assistance."*

"Really, says who?"

Kito halted for a moment. *"Well, clearly I do, Hasuca."*

"And who died and made you the expert on such things?"

"No one. I just feel …"

"Nothing. You feel nothing but fear of failure, and that is overriding your own judgment."

Kito stopped. Anger swelled in him at an alarming rate. He threw out his arms. *"Is that it? I have come to you in a time of need and this is your idea of help?"* Hasuca drew back at Kito's outburst as the young spirit swirled about in small circles. *"The future of all nations …"*

"All nations, Kito?"

"What?"

"Well, how many nations have you seen?"

"Everything. From Orion to Middle Kingdom and the North."

"Oh."

Kito leant in. *"There are more?"*

Hasuca, with the chimp standing by his side, calmly slipped his arms up the opposing sleeves. *"That is not for me to say, except, have you accounted for all seven Crystal Skulls, Kito?"*

Kito drew back a little. *"Well … no."*

"So why all the panic over a run in the jungle tomorrow then?"

Kito's head was a blur of options. He fell into a deep bow and held it. *"Please forgive me, my Master."*

"Oh, don't be so hard on yourself, you have your whole life yet, you are still but a boy."

Kito stood straight to look into Hasuca's eyes. *"Maybe, though I'm not 'the One,' as you said I was."*

Hasuca raised his grey eyebrows. *"Really, Kito. And what 'One,' did I state you were?"*

Before Kito could retort, Hasuca began to fade, leaving nothing behind but his gentle laughter and the chimp's clapping.

Kito could only sigh. *More homework it seems.* He exhaled loudly as he began to descend back to his body. As he descended to the chimps frozen in time, he had a thought. He smiled and put two males in a compromising position then moved all the chimps in one way or another so they were all looking at the two. He took all the leaves they were about to drop and laid them over the two. *What goes around comes around,* he thought with a cheeky smile. Kito moved back and settled down, releasing the hold. The chimps above him began a ruckus of angry screams, leaping around through the jungle canopy.

With a smile, Kito pulled his hood over his head and slept.

***

The next morning, the Emperor was at the fire before sunrise. In a gentle tone that did not go unnoticed, "I assume you are ready to take me to the Valley, son?"

"Indeed I am, Koe. I'm almost looking forward to the journey."

The Emperor smugly slapped his hands together. "That's the spirit, son. I must say, I too am looking forward to this adventure, though I must admit, keeping my mind on each day and its tasks will not be easy with the impending prospects for me."

Kito looked up from his breakfast. "Koe?"

"*Immortality*, son. I will finally fulfil my destiny as a God King, no less. All my life, I have known I was meant for something great, now I'm accruing the Skulls, and what's more, the neighbouring lands are helping. This is their destiny also, and they know it. This is why they're helping me to achieve it. They know *I* am the one."

Kito sat sombre-faced. Immortality with the Skulls had not occurred to him. Until recently, he was content that there were no Skulls. *Could Koe really become immortal? He is full of greed, lust and a lack of respect for anything other than himself. This would be the end of the earth as we know it.*

After breakfast, he walked to the edge of the camp to do his stretches. The Emperor would find him when he was ready.

Kito was deep into his routine when he heard horses galloping his way. The Emperor, leading six men on strong, black horses, cantered through the morning mist towards him. It was quite the spectacle. He came to a stop and turned his horse about to introduce the men who rode with him. They made quite the impression – clearly all Masters, dressed in stained leather and pure, black silk. They had the best in black steel armour and all had the twin, long curved black swords strapped to their waist on the left, all with the Emperor's emblem on the hilt. Kito had seen nothing quite like them, other than the Grand Master, Xiang.

"Kito, I would like to introduce my Master of the Guard for Zimbali, Grand Master Daiwa and his chosen five."

Kito bowed, not just to the Grand Master but to each of the five Masters. "This is my privilege to be in your company." He looked at the Emperor. "Are we expecting trouble, Koe?" The moment Kito said the word 'Koe,' Daiwa's swords swept out of their sheath, and he charged his horse towards him.

The Emperor kicked his horse forward to intervene. "Stop!"

Kito hadn't moved a muscle. Daiwa glared at him. "He dares to disrespect you in my presence. I will behead him!"

"And then we will have no way of knowing how to get to the cave of rotten eggs. No beheading today." The Emperor stared down the Master. Holding his swords upright, the Grand Master backed up his horse, never taking his eyes off Kito.

Satisfied, the Emperor turned to Kito. "Kito, would you kindly lead the way on this auspicious day."

For a moment, Kito stood staring at Daiwa, then turned to the five followers. By and large, they seemed unmoved. He recognised one of them from when the panther had come into the camp; he was one of the witnesses. He remembered him because he was so calm. Kito addressed Daiwa. "We have far to go and it will take many days. Pace yourselves."

The Grand Master Daiwa scoffed as Kito began to trot off down the jungle track, his bare feet barely leaving an imprint over the morning damp as he ran.

There were two tracks, the foot track being the most direct, but the horses had to follow the track used primarily by elephants. This weaved around the dense jungle through the softer, easier parts. Kito was seldom out of sight, sometimes just above their track, sometimes he was on it, but always leading. He would stop to refill his water at streams, but otherwise, he never let off the pace. As the day wore on, the five Masters began to exchange looks and wonder about their sweating horses, struggling in the jungle heat.

Kito ran them all day, every day. By night, the men would sit together around a campfire whispering, but Kito never turned a hair over it. He had heard all the whispers before.

One afternoon, he slowed to a trot, then to a walk. He turned around and held up a hand. The Emperor stopped on the spot. Kito eased down into a thicket. The men waited as the sound of water trickled over rocks.

Finally, Daiwa eased up beside the Emperor and whispered. "I will lead us down into there on foot if you wish, sire."

The Emperor had barely shaken his head when a whistle came from upstream. Kito waved them forward. The Emperor kicked his horse on. "A nice gesture just the same, Grand Master."

The Master's jaw clenched.

They made their way a little further upstream, then crossed over into a meadow. The green grass was welcome for the horses and the fig trees towering overhead gave great shade. Just beyond was a low, wide waterfall tumbling into a large, green pool.

Kito gestured. "I thought this would be the perfect place to camp tonight."

The Emperor looked up at the sky. "A little early to be stopping, Kito."

Daiwa mumbled behind them.

"Indeed it is, Koe, but tomorrow we will begin the climb. A small rest today and the horses will be stronger for it."

To Daiwa's disbelief, the Emperor dismounted and handed the reins to Kito. "Very well then, here we shall camp tonight."

Kito ignored Daiwa's dark face as he walked the Emperor's horse towards him. He stopped before the Grand Master. "I was going to give this horse a wash-down in the stream. I will do yours also if it pleases you, Grand Master."

With no more than a grunt, Daiwa kicked his horse and rode away.

"I will take that to be a no then," Kito said to no one in particular.

After washing the horse, he led it up to the meadow. He let it sniff its own saddle hung over a low branch, then took off the bridle and released it. The men talked in whispers as Kito walked away, leaving the horse untethered.

The Emperor, of course, had made himself comfortable on a half-buried log in the banks of the pool. Kito approached. "Koe, would fish and freshwater crayfish be to your liking this evening?"

The Emperor smiled. "That sounds like a nice change, Kito. Shall I leave it in your capable hands then?"

Kito took off his shirt. "It would be my pleasure, Koe." He removed his swords and trousers, then waded waist-deep into the warm, green water. He listened to his own heartbeat. He had to be completely focused. He slowed his heart further, breathing deeper. He could now feel the vibration of all the creatures in the pond. Slower, deeper. Eyes closed, he eased down into the water. With barely a ripple, he was gone.

Curious about this strange man, all the Masters were now looking at the pond. Daiwa sidled up beside the Emperor. "Sire, what … is he doing?"

The Emperor didn't take his eyes from the pond. "Getting dinner," he said quietly.

Silence hung in the air as the men continued to look on. Kito had been gone for some time, and Daiwa leaned in close again. "You don't really think he will actually get something, with his bare hands?"

"This boy has never ceases to amaze me."

"Never, sire?"

The Emperor didn't look up to Daiwa but whispered, "Watch."

More time passed, and the warriors began to shake their heads. Then, without warning, Kito burst up through the water. Drawing a deep breath, he was holding a huge salmon in one hand, and two crayfish by their spiky horns in the other. They all appeared to be dead.

Daiwa was motionless but the other Masters excitedly ran into the water to take his bounty. The Emperor clapped his hands in satisfaction, then leaned back on his log, speaking quietly to Daiwa. "As I said, never does he disappoint." He eased himself out of his seat as the Masters brought out the catch. "Bravo, son. Now, how do you intend to cook it?"

Kito's eyes glistened as the water dripped down his face. "As the salmon is fresh, I suggest we eat it as is. I will go on to cook the crayfish the way I learnt as a child."

Sarcasm slithered off Daiwa's tongue. "What ... no eel to complete the meal, boy?"

Kito dipped his head. "I can catch one if you wish, Grand Master?"

Daiwa scoffed his disapproval as he turned and stomped away. Two of the Masters came forward. "We can fetch wood and light the fire for you," offered one of the men. Kito recognised him as the one who had witnessed the panther in the camp.

"Masters Bo and Jian, that would be most helpful. Thank you." Kito took the crayfish and headed to the nearest bank of clay.

Later that evening, the men sat in the contentment of their full bellies. The salmon had gone a surprising distance, feeding everyone. Kito pulled back the coals and rolled the large, clay ball into the water where it hissed and spat for a moment. The Masters were hesitant when Kito picked up a large rock and smacked it down on the clay.

Nothing. He smacked it down again, and this time a small crack appeared. With his two large hands, he pried the clay apart. It split open with a pop and to everyone's surprise, revealed a bright red, steaming crayfish. Kito broke off the tail and pulled his knife, cutting the tail down the middle of the underside. He handed this sweetest part of the cray to the Emperor. The head he gave a quick clean in the pond then handed it to Jian. The warriors excitedly talked in low tones as they broke open the legs and sucked out the meat. Kito pulled out the second clay ball and repeated the process.

Once they'd all had their fill, Kito excused himself and picked up the scraps to scatter them downstream. He sat on the bank for some time, gazing up through the treetops at the countless stars. Cooking the crayfish that way was with risk, but he couldn't resist. Almost disappointingly, the Emperor hadn't batted an eyelid. *I wonder if Hasuca would approve of that stunt?* He could still feel the block, so he wouldn't be going to ask him about it now. *How can the witch be so powerful to block me this far from the vessel? Unless she is close behind.* The hair on the back of his neck stood up at the thought. *What fire am I playing with? And if she has such power, what's her game, and her gain?*

At a nearby tree, he flattened out some grass, pulled up his hood and lay down for some sleep. There was still chattering around the campfire. He smiled at the idea of companionship. It was a lonely walk, this life of his.

He drifted off to sleep.

***

The camp was woken suddenly by the screaming of a man. One of the Masters came running from the fire carrying a torch high. "What is it? What's there?" He waved his sword about. The others quickly exited their grass beds.

The Emperor scowled with his own torch in hand. "What is the meaning of this commotion?"

They looked down and, in the torchlight, there were more eels than they could count. Master Daiwa was clambering out of his bed in the middle of them all.

"Where is that Kito? I will personally kill him!"

The Emperor looked at him inquisitively. "Why?" he said in a flat tone.

Daiwa kicked one of the eels. There were dozens oozing over one another, squelching as they writhed around. "Because he must have baited my bed with the scraps!"

A call came from the stream bank. "No, the scraps are over here and there isn't a single eel on them."

Daiwa stamped a foot attempting to remove an eel wrapped around his leg. "Of course not, the eels are all over here! Where is he?"

The Emperor walked calmly over to a nearby tree with his torch. "Daiwa, keep it down would you. I do believe he is sleeping, and in two shakes of an *eel's tail*, I will be doing the same. Now stop this nonsense!"

For the first time, possibly ever, Daiwa, a true Master who had trained from childhood to the Grand Master he now was, struggled with his own emotions. He was left standing in a pool of slime from the slowly departing eels. The only thing that stopped him from completing his visions of his cold, black steel running through Kito's heart was the thought of the repercussions from the Emperor. *What does that boy hold over him?*

***

The next morning, everyone was up at daybreak. The Emperor was one of the first to the fire, where he found Kito sitting and chatting with the night guard.

"Morning, Koe. Slept well, I expect?"

The Emperor frowned as he sat on the log. "As a matter of fact, no, Kito. I was woken in the small hours of the morning. Did you not wake at all?"

Kito shook his head as he lifted a good-sized stick and began to spread the coals. "I must say I slept very well and was up early. Hope you don't mind salmon again, though this time I have cooked it." He was mindful not to look directly at the Emperor as he pulled the clay form of a large salmon out of the fire. This time, even over the block, he sensed Koe felt a little uneasy. *Must be the early morning catching him off guard.* He was careful to crack the clay down the ridge of the salmon, splitting it open nicely. He placed one half in front of the Emperor.

"I have put some herbs in – hope it hasn't spoiled it for you."

"I am sure it will be fine," came the cool response.

Grand Master Daiwa was next to the fire. Kito quickly pulled out a second clay patty. He pushed it about in the cool pebbles until he could just handle it. Ignoring Kito, the Grand Master greeted the Emperor as he sat beside him on the log. Kito worked carefully on the last bit of clay. It broke open, and the other men watched closely to see what it was. He dusted off the broken clay, and there on the bottom half lay a cooked eel. He swiped it up and went directly to the Grand Master and held it out to him. "The clay draws out the slime; it should be most tasty."

For a moment, the air was thick with anticipation, then the Emperor burst out laughing. The Grand Master frowned his disdain as his men also laughed. He looked back at Kito with his head down and the food held out. The Grand Master could almost feel Kito's red, beating heart in his hands. *He wants me to do it.* Daiwa took the food, thanking Kito through gritted teeth.

"Not at all, Grand Master. I was told you caught it yourself last night."

The men sniggered under their breaths.

Kito made a good feast of it, and the Masters also seemed pleased with their morning meal. After washing, he went over to the Emperor's saddle. Without need of encouragement, the horse came over and nudged him. "Well, good morning, my friend." It neighed, nudging him again. Kito chuckled as he sorted out the saddle.

The man who took the morning watch came over. "You have a special way with animals."

"I respect them and they respect me. That is all, Master Kinjo."

"No, Kito. You are a Master of some kind, I can tell. Besides, I love my horse, but if I didn't tie it off at night, by morning, I would be walking. The Emperor's horse came without request and you don't even ride it."

Kito continued to put on the bridle and do up the straps. "Maybe, Kinjo, that is why it likes me."

Kinjo laughed gently. "You are the man that took Naja from the Royal camp last season?"

"What makes you ask that?" Kito took up the reins.

The Master grabbed Kito by his arm. He was quietly shocked at how hard his muscle was. "Naja is a friend of mine who was taken by a crocodile. We all saw it. Two days later, he just walked back into our camp alive and well. He wouldn't say what happened, and we left him be. Then, weeks later, the Emperor went into the city of Batavia and started a bloodbath. They were a quiet people, hunters of the jungle and fishermen. They didn't deserve to be slaughtered that way. The Emperor put some of the people out over the river; crocodiles got one man, but Naja knew exactly what to do: he was ready with buckets of water before the Emperor even left. This saved some lives."

"Many more were lost and many more will be lost."

"Then stop this," Kinjo implored.

Kito continued with the horse preparations. "What makes you think I can?"

"He calls you 'son.' What is that about?"

A low, menacing voice came from behind them. "I see my horse is nearly ready. We need to make up for yesterday's early stop, don't we."

Wide-eyed, Master Kinjo spun on his heel. He could only wonder how much the Emperor had heard. Kito, by contrast, behaved like he didn't care.

"Koe, your horse is ready. It will be a good climb to our next stop, so yes, we do need to make a strong start."

The Emperor eyed Kinjo, who was nervously shuffling his boots. The Emperor's voice was almost pleased now. "Very well, son."

Kito handed the reins over. "How was your salmon? To your liking, I hope?"

"Yes, wonderful Kito. I did enjoy my breakfast thoroughly, although, Kito, I don't know if you made a friend of my Grand Master with his breakfast this morning."

Kito thumbed over his shoulder at all the dead eels in the grass as he grinned. "It seemed a shame to waste them. He did mention them yesterday after all."

With a scoff, the Emperor was in his saddle. He turned to the other men and called through the fig tree meadow. "Well, come on then, the day is wasting."

The men hurried their saddles to the ready. Kito looked up at the Emperor. "I will make a start and warm up. Stay on this side of the stream, and you can't go wrong."

The Emperor flexed his fingers as he slipped his hands into his leather gloves. "I won't go wrong since I will be right behind you."

"Very well then, Koe, it is you and I."

Kito walked at a strong pace for a little while then did some stretches against a tree. Hearing the other horses coming, he looked at the Emperor. "Shall we give them a run for their money?"

The Emperor's face lit up. "Let's do it."

Kito turned and broke into a strong run. Behind him, the Emperor galloped his horse, steering it left to right as the meadow gave way to the jungle. It was as Kito had said, the track turned up onto the winding foothills of the Great Dividing Range.

The horses worked even harder to keep up with Kito. His agile body sprang easily over twisted vines and dense foliage as the riders struggled to keep to the tracks, zig-zagging this way and that. As the day went on, they climbed higher, and the jungle changed subtly. The trees were not quite as tall, and the occasional rocky outcrops had more undergrowth.

Kito ran on.

Right on dusk, they stopped by a stream. Kito breathed steadily with his hands on his hips. The horses, by contrast, had their mouths open, drawing air and sweating profusely. They were keen to stop on the small, flat area to drink and nibble on a little grass. The men gave them a good rub down before returning to their diet of dried fruit and meat. There were eels in the stream, but Kito didn't want to further push the Grand Master into a confrontation, yet.

They did this for several more days, then one morning, Kito waited for everyone to be mounted and ready. He typically never spoke to the group, so they turned to face him and waited in silence.

"As you can see, we have moved into a different climate and so the forest has changed. Can I ask that you have your crossbows out and ready? There will be the opportunity to get some fowl and game up here. Also, the predators have less game to hunt, so …"

The Grand Master sat forward in his saddle. "I will tell the men when to have their weapons ready, and not you. Are we clear, boy?"

"It never hurts to …"

"My men will do as *I* say. Period."

Kito bowed deeply. As he stood, he briefly looked at Master Jian, then turned and jogged away. It didn't go unnoticed that the Emperor had said nothing either way.

Over the following days, they crossed several clear fields, but today, at this one field, Kito stopped. The horses came to a halt behind him. The field was quiet, and the long, lush grass waved in the gentle breeze. Kito cast a look at Master Jian. Chills ran down

Jian's back and he subconsciously reached for his crossbow. The Grand Master turned in his saddle, and Jian's empty hand pulled away. Kito began to cross the field.

A cock pheasant called out and took to the air. Quickly, the Grand Master stood up in his saddle and threw a knife. The pheasant immediately dropped to the earth with a thump. The Grand Master turned and looked at Jian; he dipped his head, dropping out of his saddle without a word.

The Emperor scouted the silent meadow. *It's too quiet.* He scrutinised Kito. He'd watched this young man for a long time, very closely, and he too appeared uneasy. Kito searched in his mind, but Banji still had the block up.

Jian walked out and lifted the pheasant to retrieve the knife. It was a clean kill. He looked at the Grand Master, but in that moment, the Grand Master's face dropped from arrogance to shock and panic. The men suddenly reached for their crossbows. Jian was so focused on them that he never heard the rustling grass behind him. He turned to see what the men were staring at and froze. Bounding towards him and gathering speed was a black panther. Its fur moved with the power of its muscles and its long, white claws gathered traction with every leap towards him. Jian could see its bright yellow eyes intently focused on him. He drew his knife as he lifted the pheasant to block the panther's mouth but it was futile. The panther was at his throat so hard and fast it broke his neck with a crack. Several bolts whisked by as the panther and Jian tumbled in the long grass. In a flash of black fur, the panther was gone, leaving only the lush grass waving over Jian's dead body.

Stunned into silence at how shockingly quick the scene had passed, everyone sat in their saddles looking down in disbelief. Master Kinjo spoke first. "I will bury him."

The Emperor flicked his hand. "No, we don't have the time. He can go back to the earth."

Kito broke through the group, drawing his swords and began to slash at the long grass. The men drew their horses back for fear of being sliced. In moments, there was a large, clear area around Jian's body. Kito put away his swords and collected the grass. He lifted Jian in his strong arms and gently laid him out as if he was sleeping. The Masters dismounted and began to help. Kito stepped back and looked down at him. He lay with his eyes shut in a perfect bed of grass. Only his face could be seen as the Gods shone their light on it.

Daiwa's leather saddle creaked. "I don't know if I approve of the palace's swords being used to cut grass, boy."

Kito held Daiwa's horse's reins. "I serve the Emperor and not you. Master Jian was serving the Palace and was a friend to me. I choose how I serve the Emperor and *his* men."

The two were locked, unmoving.

The Emperor nudged his horse forward. "Kito, could you lead the way?"

Kito slowly released the reins, but his eyes were still focused intently on the Grand Master Daiwa. Suddenly Daiwa's horse reared up, almost throwing him off, but he held tight. His horse twisted and bucked several times, and Daiwa struggled to hold on. He kicked it into a canter and managed to get it into a strong run around the field. The wind whistled in his ears as the horse cantered in a large arc, then directly back to Jian. Daiwa looked down at him. He looked at peace. When he looked up again, everyone had gone. With a final glance at Jian, he cantered to catch up.

***

For several more days, they moved further up into the Range. It was now a solemn trip, though the Emperor seemed mostly oblivious to it all. They pushed on.

The forest now gave way to areas of prolonged rocky outcrops covered in scrub. The tracks in these areas were narrow and steep. Kito pushed himself hard; sometimes his lungs burned, but he could still set a better pace than the horses on these unstable tracks.

On dusk, they came into a grassy area. To their left was a tall, thin waterfall that poured into a small pond below, feeding a babbling brook that ran through a small field.

Kito turned to the Emperor. "This is the best place to camp. Also, I feel we should leave the horses here until our return."

The Emperor looked at Kito pensively without speaking. Everyone had gathered around in silence – it was as if either Kito hadn't spoken or the Emperor hadn't heard. Both were completely unmoving.

Finally, the Emperor ordered, "We will camp here tonight."

Kito dipped his head and walked forward to take his horse. "If you want to send some of the men forward of here, they will get some game."

"Is this so, Kito?"

"Yes, Koe, if you wish."

The Emperor pointed at two of the Masters. "Well, you heard the boy; go on ahead with crossbows ready. I expect you to return with game."

Daiwa's eyes narrowed as Kito spoke to the men. "You will see long-horned, white beasts on four hooves. They only live up here. Be alert as they are skittish. One will feed us well."

Excitedly, the two men drew out their crossbows, cocked and loaded them and eagerly headed onward.

That night, they ate fresh, cooked goat and talked happily for the first time since the loss of Jian.

The next morning, Kito crossed the stream and waited. He bowed deeply before the Emperor. "I see you choose to ride. Please be very careful, the track will at times be narrow and covered in loose rock and scree." He turned and broke out into a gentle run.

Over the next few days, the forest gave way to more rock and scrub. The horses began to lose condition, and Master Kinjo's horse started to limp. He managed to get the stone out but it would do no more than walk now. They loaded all the supplies on it and

Kinjo took Jian's horse and led his own.

The water crossings became less frequent, so they stopped at every one to refill their water bladders whilst the horses drank thirstily. Camping was a rocky affair, with this and the thinning air, the men grew weary but pushed on without complaint.

Dark clouds loomed over the Ranges, and thunder rumbled overhead. Kito watched the ominous black sky. "Koe, we need to find shelter."

The clouds were like those the Emperor had seen coming from the north at the palace. Deep black, with huge green domes underneath as if they were supporting giant eggs. He walked his horse up and stopped beside Kito. "You think it is ice, son?"

"Yes, Koe. A lot."

The Emperor turned back to the men. "You heard Kito; we need to pick up the pace to find shelter. Let's move it!"

Kito had already run ahead. Master Daiwa mumbled under his breath, charging forward with the Emperor.

Quickly, the storm descended upon them, and the horses became skittish as lightning tore across the sky above. The thunder was constant and deafening. It quickly grew so dark it was hard to think that, just a little while ago, they were climbing with the sun beating down. The wind howled; if they didn't find shelter shortly, all manner of grief would be on them.

Around a bend, Kito saw a large stone overhang. As he ran across a rocky clearing, he heard a strange noise. It sounded like the stripping of leaves and breaking branches, followed by large rocks being smashed into a pond. *But there can be no pond?* As he reached the cliff overhang, the first one crashed beside him. It was a huge piece of ice. Giant hail smashed down around them. The Emperor and his men rushed under the cliff. All but the last Master, Kinjo. He was leading the lame horse when a huge hail hit his horse, instantly crushing it to the ground. Kinjo catapulted from the saddle. Neither the horse nor Kinjo moved. The lame horse simply walked onward to the overhang with the hail crashing down everywhere.

Without hesitation, Kito darted out into the dark storm. Water and ice reflected by the lightning flashed the scene intermittently before the men. They watched as Kinjo, clearly confused, rose to his feet. The thunder roared as torrential hail descended upon him. He stumbled and fell over again. This time, as he got up, he was now very close to the top of a cliff. Kito sprinted forward, drawing his sword as he went. Calling Kinjo would be futile.

The Masters stood motionless beneath the overhang, watching helplessly.

Kito slashed the saddle from the dead horse and hefted it over his head. He turned to Kinjo, who had collapsed again precariously close to the clifftop. He grabbed Kinjo and slung him over his shoulder, then threw the saddle over the top of them both, turning back to the overhang. He could see the Emperor crouched down watching, smiling. Master Daiwa stood stone-faced, and the other three Masters stared, open-mouthed, at the scene unfolding before them.

Twice the saddle took the force of plummeting hailstones, and twice Kito staggered but would not go down. As he rushed into the safety of the overhang, he lifted away the saddle. The Masters quickly took hold of Kinjo. Dropping the saddle, Kito went to the back of the overhang. He was breathing hard as he lay down on his back with his arm over his face. His ears were ringing from the deafening force of the storm. He could feel the block stronger than ever. *She was watching this*, he thought. *Did she create this to test me?*

He breathed out a deep sigh and quickly drifted off to sleep.

27 The Best in Men

Alone, Kito ran along a gravel track in the jungle where a stream babbled by on his left. Around a bend, the gravel gave way to stone — not just any stone — it was one singular, solid piece. There were no joins, no cracks. Just perfect. He ran on until the path led him to a wide area doused in thick fog. He held still. Feeling no danger, he walked forward into the cool, damp fog.

Passing through a wall, the fog swirled around him like a huge cylinder. Above, he could just make out a blue dot, the clear sky.

Before him were wide, stone stairs, like the footpath and stairs in the cave where he'd met his mother, Rani. The same faultless stonework. The stairs led up to a huge building, its towers reaching for the Gods themselves. He ascended the stairs; the tall doors before him were open, so he entered.

The room inside seemed even bigger than the building from the outside. He could see no joins, not even in the huge floor that lay out before him. He heard a whisper. Someone, something was whispering his name. The hair on his neck stood up so hard it prickled. He stepped forward. There were no windows, though he could see everything perfectly, no dark recesses, no shadows. The stone roof reached impossible heights. Everything was clean. There were no bugs, bats or birds, and it was deathly silent.

A whisper …

Kito moved forward to what seemed to be the centre of the room and looked back. The doors were not there anymore and yet he'd come in through them. He turned in slow circles counting seven corridors leading from the centre. It was symmetrical in every way.

He heard the whisper and spun to face it. It whispered behind him again, and he spun again. Another whisper. He turned just in time to see a huge Crystal Skull, with blazing red eyes, screaming at him from a corridor, its menacing mouth opening wide as if to engulf him. Another whisper, and he spun back around. This time, it was a Skull with green eyes coming from another corridor, screaming with its mouth gaping open. He neither flinched nor ducked. He reached for his swords, but they weren't there. He looked down, and he was naked. Another whisper. He spun again to see a Skull coming at him with golden eyes blazing and mouth fully open, screaming his name. Repeatedly, the Skulls came at him, screaming and screaming until eventually, he stopped and screamed back.

"STOP!!"

His voice echoed back and forth, shattering the silence. Nothing but his own echo returned.

"What is this?" He could feel the eyes on him, though he could see nothing but stone. "If you have nothing but silly games of an old legend, then I must leave." He stood still, waiting for something to happen. Nothing did. He faced a corridor which was the same as each and every corridor, then walked the length of it. He neared the stone wall at the end, wondering what was going to happen.

Still, he walked on.

The wall before him faded, and he stepped out into the sunlight on the large patio at the top of the stairs. He heard his name whispered, but this time he didn't look back. He was now dressed, and the swords pulsed on his back. He descended the stairs and into the fog.

The dark enveloped him.

***

Kito awoke to the sound of a fire crackling. He rubbed his eyes at the reflection of it on the damp, stone roof of the overhang. The lightning was still flashing some distance away but without thunder, just the steady fall of rain. Getting up, he went to the fire where a Master was sitting guard.

"Hello, Kito. Slept well, I hope?" he asked quietly.

Kito sat cross-legged. "I did indeed. Thank you."

"Hungry?"

"Yes, actually. Famished."

Without word, the Master fetched food and a drinking bladder. Kito thanked him, then realised the food was freshly cooked meat. "Where ..?"

The Master smiled. "The horse was dead before it hit the ground."

Kito looked out to where the horse had lain. Lightning lit up the rainy sky with multiple flashes. The corpse was gone.

"We got rid of it so is didn't attract any mountain cats."

"Good work, and the meat is quite tasty."

"Nothing to waste, at least." The Master nodded his head to the distant lightning through the rain. "That was a moment of grand bravery, Kito."

Kito responded with a mouth full of food. "No. I am well known for my rash stupidity."

The Master replied slowly. "No, Kito. You are well known for being a Master."

"I am no Master," Kito snapped .

The Master was silent as Kito ate. He watched the lightning, not looking at him. "Orton is my cousin, and you remember Quinn, of course. Jong never did get over her death."

Kito stopped chewing. "Is he dead now?"

"Yes. My cousin says he died of a broken heart."

"I am sorry."

"Yes, though I think he is happy with Quinn again."

"What is your name?"

"Please forgive me. I am Master Uttah."

Masters that served the Palace didn't have a first name. Generally, from the moment the training of a Master commenced, the Palace became their only concern. That was their duty in theory, though it wasn't always how it worked in practice. Having travelled for many days together, Kito never doubted Uttah's dedication to his Palace and Emperor.

"It is my pleasure to be in your company, Master Uttah."

"And mine in yours, Kito. May I ask you a question?"

"A question does not offend. I will answer if I have the knowledge."

"It was Orton's favourite story, the one about how they put you in the cage at the Colonial Dig, then one morning they went to work and you were no longer locked away. Even Jong could never offer an explanation. How did you get out?"

Not looking up, Kito shrugged and continued to eat. "People see what they want to see. Sometimes this is exaggerated when they need a miracle. They saw what they wanted and nothing less."

"So, one of them let you out? Orton said this couldn't be so, because Zekec would have whipped them to death for it."

"The worst of times brings out the best in people, Uttah. This is what makes the human race strong."

Uttah leant in close. "We slaughter one another. We slaughter our children, our women and the fathers of other children. You don't see this in the wild, so I ask you this, Kito, which species is the animal?"

Kito slowly looked up. "Why, then, did you become a Master, Uttah?"

"It was not a choice for me, Kito. If I were a woman, I would have been a concubine. Either way, I serve the Palace and have no family."

"You could have been a guard and served the Palace, Uttah. You are the best of the best."

"I decided, if I am to do something, I must do it to the very best of me. You would know about that, Kito."

Kito frowned. "Oh? And what makes you so sure of that one, Uttah?"

"Because, had you asked for a horse, the Emperor would have given you one. Yesterday, you saved Kinjo as we all watched on. Just as you saved Orton's grandmother."

"I failed that one."

"Nonsense! You did something no one else considered. Quinn

simply offered a younger life for the saving. The Gods will shine on her for that, and they should." Uttah looked nervously over his shoulder into the dark cave, then back to Kito. "You knew, didn't you?"

"Knew what, Uttah?"

"You stopped at the edge of the field. You knew about the panther, didn't you?"

"You believe I served up Master Jian as a meal for the panther?"

"I never said that."

"Whether you offered that point of view or not, it is the fallout of your direction of thought, Uttah."

Uttah looked at the lightshow. Through their conversation, it was fading into the distance. "I see your point, Kito. Nevertheless, it is not what I meant."

"I know, Uttah. Just let it be, as it was just to be for Master Jian."

"Because he saw it in the camp, Kito?"

"Orton's grandmother worked for three seasons on the canal. On the last day of work, she was swept away to an unfitting, ungraceful death. Did she see into the panther's eyes? No, it is just the way sometimes. Maybe it's in the plan of the Gods. Maybe it's in our destiny. I have seen many bad things happen to good people."

Sombrely, Uttah lowered his voice. "Are any of us getting off this mountain?"

"Yes, but please, not too many questions. I don't know everything."

"Though you do know much, don't you?"

"I know some, and it is not a blessing, Master Uttah."

They heard the Emperor coming forward to the fire, straightening his silk gowns. "I do miss the comforts of the Palace sometimes, but the experiences you get when in the saddle are second to none. Look at that view."

Kito and Uttah were so caught up in their conversation, they had failed to see the first glimmers of light making the last of the storm appear as if on fire.

"Morning to you, Koe. Slept well, I hope?"

The Emperor sat next to him to watch the sun rise behind the last of the fiery clouds. "Not as well as some. I observed you were out early in the afternoon."

"Quite so, sire, though I did make up for it by being the first up this morning."

"Indeed, you did."

Uttah served some hot tea to the Emperor, and before long, everyone was at the fire asking Kinjo how his head was.

"Mother always said my head was the hardest part to land on."

They laughed together. Friendship and bonding would make them stronger for this journey into the unknown. They had almost lost two on this trip so far, and they weren't even there.

After breakfast, the fire was extinguished and the men mounted their horses. Kito would run no more, as the horses were in poor shape. Having lost Jian's horse the day before, Kinjo led his own with the limited supplies. The track was single-file in places, with occasional trees giving way to mostly rocks and scrub.

They were now well above the winter snowline. The men trudged on, peeking over the side of the mountain tracks from time to time. The cliffs above were just as daunting, their peaks seeming to caress the clouds above.

It was mid-afternoon when they came to a particularly bad section of track. It was futile to instruct the Emperor to leave the horses behind, so Kito could say no more as he passed through, then stopped to watch what the Emperor would do. The Emperor himself looked calm, if not totally unaware. The horse stopped, shaking its head. The Emperor kicked it forward, whipping it on either flank. It stamped a hoof, then moved forward and neighed, trying to get the bit in its teeth.

It only took a few tentative steps then faltered on the scree. The Emperor quickly tried to guide his horse out of danger but its hind quarters slipped around to the cliff. It dug its front hooves in hard but there was nothing solid to gain traction on. Its hind went over and the Emperor was to go with it, but for a Master sprinting in.

The Emperor landed hard on the track and in the same moment, Kito was there, holding the reins of his horse, trying to help it back up. The horse's front hooves slid further as the gravelly track gave way. Its neck pulled out tight with Kito trying to hold it, his shoulders and arms bulging with the strain. The horse tried to get its hind legs up. It was almost getting a grip when the Grand Master's sword whirred down. Kito tumbled backwards and sprang to his feet. The horse was gone.

The Emperor leapt to his feet. "The saddle packs … where are they?"

Uttah stepped forward. "They were thrown to me, sire."

"Where is that man?"

Grand Master Daiwa slid his sword away. "Where is what man, sire?"

The Emperor glanced at Kito holding the cut reins in his right fist. The Emperor looked back at Grand Master Daiwa. "Well, someone pulled me from my saddle, saving my life. I wish to congratulate him."

"I believe it was Master Kinjo, and he is now lost, Koe," responded Kito.

The Emperor stepped forward. "Lost, Kito? Please explain."

Kito stared at the edge. "Kinjo came to save you but, to throw you onto the track, he had to throw himself over the side. He ended up holding the tail of the horse you were riding. Unfortunately, we have lost your horse, and Kinjo with it."

The Emperor looked blank-faced at the cliff edge, then shrugged. "We have the saddle packs, that's the main thing."

Kito turned to Grand Master Daiwa. "If you were not an employee of the Palace, I would whip you to death with these very reins."

The Grand Master flinched and quickly drew his sword. Kito whisked the leather reins about in the thin mountain air, which whistled with his intense focus.

"STOP!" roared the Emperor.

Shaking with anger, Daiwa pointed his sword at Kito. "All things are equal. Man and woman, night and day. And one day …" His jaws clenched. "… I will get my opportunity to sort you, boy."

Kito's voice responded low and steady. "Be careful what you wish for, Grand Master." He stepped back and bowed. Daiwa did not reciprocate.

No one said a word for the afternoon, although the Emperor did break out in a cheerful whistle from time to time. He was the only one still riding, now on Daiwa's horse. The horse faltered several times, but the Masters were always there to put it right on the path again.

As the days passed, the cliffs got higher. The mornings were bitterly cold and damp, but once the sun rose high, they would dry off and soon enough be warm; then, overnight, they would be chilled to the bone again. The wind howled over their small, crackling fires.

More days passed.

Kito knew they were getting close to the cave of the fish bones and sulphur by the topography below. To his left was an ideal overhang to camp under. He turned to the Emperor. "I feel this will do for our next night, Koe."

The Emperor didn't hesitate. "Really? Are you sure this is as far as we could go today, Kito?"

"This is right for tonight. I will walk further alone."

The Emperor sighed. "So be it then. Run ahead and do not return unless you have great news."

"That would be my intention," Kito responded dryly.

Kito enjoyed a gentle run, then broke into a strong pace. With the cliff above and a massive drop to his side, he watched his every step, though run on he did. Sliding to an abrupt halt, he smiled at the scattered bones before him. They were now white and brittle, but this was the place. Years of fish bones cracked under his feet as he approached the boulders. He recognised the setting immediately.

He climbed up them and peered into the cave with a dirt floor and a smell of rotten eggs. He wondered how mentally strong Mabutu must have been to be locked in here alone for so long and keep his mind. *What kind of man would do this to his own father? And what does this have to do with the Valley of the Stone Temple? For the life of me, I can't see the connection.*

After some time, he decided there was nothing more there and began his way back to the overhang where the Masters were making camp. He was enjoying his return run when he came to a standstill. His hair bristled as his eyes searched the sight before him. He'd already passed this way and never noticed it. Yet there it was. Perfectly moulded, rock.

The rock formed a shallow, but perfect, cave. He couldn't blame himself for missing it as it led back behind the way he'd come. Though, how had he missed the perfect footpath?

He walked into the cove. The rock had no joins. It was so smooth he had to reach out and touch it. No dust, cobwebs or sign of birds. He'd seen this rock before, in the dream after the hail. He walked back out onto the path. Just off the perfect rock footpath, he saw large footprints. He could only guess that was the way back to the Village of the Keepers, and the footprints were Mabutu's.

Kito stepped back onto the path towards camp. This had to be what the Emperor was looking for, though he could see no point for it. It led nowhere. His mind so preoccupied on his return journey, before he knew it, he was walking back into camp. The fire crackled, and the smell of cooked meat made him realise just how hungry he was. "Evening, Masters."

Everyone except the Grand Master answered. The Emperor motioned for him to sit opposite him. Kito sat cross-legged and made himself comfortable as Uttah handed him some meat. Kito dipped his head. The Emperor waited patiently for Kito to get settled.

"Well, do we have good news, son?"

Kito ignored Daiwa grunting under his breath. "Indeed, Koe, I do. It was nearer than I thought."

The Emperor slapped his knee. "Ha, I knew it. You found the cave with all the bones."

Kito nodded as he ate. "I found more than that."

The Emperor was almost drooling. "Yes, Kito, do go on."

"I found a cove ..."

Daiwa threw his hands up. "Look about you, boy. We sit in a cove!"

Kito continued to eat, letting the echo drift away. "The rock in this cove was smooth and clean. It was not natural. It was not something of this world."

The Emperor leaned forward. "It was dry and warm?"

"Yes."

"It was neither windy nor loud?"

"Not a sound."

The Emperor sat back and slapped his thigh enthusiastically. "That is it then. Tomorrow we will enter, and life as we know it will never be the same." He gazed at the blank faces. "You will all go down in the history books as the men who witnessed it. You can thank me later."

Letting his food drop to the dirt, the Emperor stood and paced about, hands clasped behind his back, his face glowing with excitement. "I can barely wait. The day the entire world has waited for. I, the chosen one, will rise to lead all!"

Uttah rose to his feet. "With your permission, Grand Master, I will take first watch." No one spoke, so Uttah gave a quick bow and headed out into the dark.

Later that evening, Kito walked out into the descending night. "Uttah, may I sit with you?"

Uttah was sitting on the rock at the edge of the cliff. "Please Kito, be my guest."

Kito sat gazing down over the jungle that was now almost entirely dark. "The lands sleep for another night."

"This is our last night, isn't it, Kito?"

"Uttah?"

"Tomorrow, we will all die. I think even the Emperor might die."

"I hope not, Uttah. That would mean I have failed him."

Uttah turned to Kito. "Does it? Or does it mean you have succeeded in something much larger?"

Kito nodded in understanding. He could hear the Grand Master and the Emperor talking in the camp some distance away. He was careful to speak quietly. "We can only make the choices within our duties to the throne."

"Yes, though I find myself struggling with my duties to my Gods, Kito. You must understand that everything about this journey has not been natural. From the moment we landed in the jungle, things were different. Did any of the other Masters tell you about the black roses, Kito?"

Kito turned his head to Uttah. "Where did you see those?"

Uttah still watched the fading sunset. "Each of us, including our Grand Master, had a black rose dropped into our laps at the Zimbali camp."

"When?"

"Does it matter when the rose was delivered? It was delivered, that is enough."

"It just fell out of the sky?"

"Nature grew them. Monkeys delivered them." Uttah looked deep into Kito's eyes. "Tomorrow, we will die. Other than you, we will all die."

"What makes you believe I am the only one not to die?"

"Everything about you is different, Kito. I mean this in a most beautiful way."

Kito sighed. "Though this is not a blessing, Uttah." He stood and placed a supportive hand on Uttah's shoulder. "Tomorrow will be a trying day, I do not doubt it. When it is your turn, try to rest up. Only the Gods know the future. We are here just to fulfil our journeys as best we can. Remember, Uttah, you are not just the best of the best, I think you are also the best in men, and that is the most important."

28 Father's Apology

Admasin had stood at the rear of *Queen of the Seas* until even the burning *Pursuit* could no longer be seen. The man on the compromised vessel had said Kalgan was its captain. Admasin had to trust Kito when he'd said Kalgan and many others would be fine and cared for.

Balzac arrived top deck. "Admasin, have you seen Jabali?"

"I thought he was with you. Did he come down to you at all?"

"No, Admasin, he certainly did not."

Perplexed, the two men immediately marched to the bow where he'd stood. Shards of timbers were strewn everywhere, even protruding from the outer siding like the bristles of a porcupine, but there was no sign of the man dressed in black. Balzac slowly looked down at the discarded cane.

They solemnly walked to the rear deck where Lucia was at the helm. Tears streamed down her face. Seeing her father holding the cane told her more than she wanted to know.

Darkness had now descended, and everyone agreed they should lower the sails and sleep until dawn. There was nothing and no one to chase them anymore, and little more to do other than return to Devil's Island.

***

Two days later, with the *Queen of the Seas* returned, Balzac walked to the end of his wharf where one of his guards stood. "Is that smoke on the outer ridge?"

The large man agreed. "Yes, sir, a vessel coming in from the ocean. Who do you think it might be?"

"Well, how could I possibly know that? In the name of the Gods, man." Realising he'd snapped a little too abruptly, he added more calmly, "We will just have to be patient, won't we?"

"Yes, sir," came the lame reply.

Balzac paced back and forth. At every turn, he couldn't help but look to see if it was one of those sails. He paced some more and checked again, squinting as, ever so slowly, the vessel came into sight. He spun back to the complex, cupping his hands. "Sails! Sails are coming in!"

It looked a sorry sight. Large holes were ripped through its tattered sails, and the vessel looked beaten, but it limped into the bay right on nightfall. The sails were lowered and replaced with the oars to help it the last few hundred paces into the wharf.

Admasin held Yuna's hand as Lucia and the crew from their little vessel made haste along the wharf. It seemed to take forever as they watched the vessel dock. Never had there been more anticipation on Balzac's wharf.

It was the *Voyager,* badly patched and labouring slowly into land, but, nevertheless, buoyant. Weary men threw down the docking ropes.

"The boarding plank, men, hand over the boarding plank," Balzac ordered. He turned to one of his bodyguards. "Go ahead and get as many water bladders as we have, and bring fruit, bread and cheese to the beach. Go!"

The man headed for the complex, wondering what must have happened to Balzac on *Queen of the Seas* just two days before. Service without secure payment? This was not his boss anymore.

Once secured to the wharf, the men poured off the vessel in droves, some carrying the injured on makeshift stretchers. Balzac welcomed them with slaps on their shoulders, telling them they would be served on the beach forthwith.

When the multitude of men finally finished piling off the vessel, Admasin called out. "Katanning!" Yuna took a full breath at the sight of the young man as he stepped onto the plank.

"Admasin, Yuna!" He trotted down the plank and over to hug them both. He recognised the unasked question in their eyes, turning them back to the vessel at the last man to get off. Kalgan.

Kalgan looked at his questioning parents. Holding his arms wide in explanation, "I had to make sure everyone was safely off, didn't I?" He walked down the plank, offering a greeting to Balzac, but never missed a step, walking directly to his mother and father. Yuna sobbed, clinging to her son as Admasin put his arms around them both.

When Yuna finally let Kalgan go, he stepped back to speak with them properly. He was startled as Admasin took his hands and eased down onto his knees. "How is a son expected to forgive his father for firing upon his mortal soul?"

Kalgan knelt with his father. "Did you know what vessel I was on?"

Admasin shook his head and, with watering eyes, replied, "I was assured you would be alright. I had hoped that meant you were still in Samos building the next vessel."

"Then you did the most amazing thing, the *only* thing you should have done. You did what was right, Father. I am honoured to be your son."

Balzac watched these two remarkable men and thought about his own daughter, now comforting Yuna. She had shown him so much since her return and, only now, was he beginning to understand the amazing company she had kept all those years. Was she a product of her upbringing, or was she influenced by these people she had kept with whilst missing from his life? Right now, he didn't care. Raising his arms, he called their attention. "Everyone, to my office!"

Kalgan pulled his father to his feet, who then pointed at Balzac. "Nonsense! To your cabinet!" Up went the cheer as they made their way along Balzac's wharf to his office.

Through the night, the men told stories of how the day had unfolded. They all had their own way of remembering the events.

Kalgan received a reaction more than he had thought when he mentioned the one called Jabali. Admasin almost fell off his stool. "He is alive then?"

Kalgan couldn't help but glance at Lucia with a solemn look. He held up two hands. "Well, yes, but …" He went on to tell how Jabali pulled everything together. They'd saved the drinking water from most of the vessels, and he'd instructed the repair of the *Avenger* and *Voyager*. They only just boarded everyone in time before a huge storm blew in. He told of how they'd tied the two vessels together, the *Avenger* still being full of water. Realising it was dragging too much on the *Voyager*, Jabali had cut the rope from the bow of the *Avenger*. In the storm, the two vessels were quickly separated. This was the last they saw of the *Avenger* and all its men.

The room fell silent, thinking on the fate of Jabali and all those on board.

"When Jabali came downstairs and told me his plan to ram the *Ocean Asset*, I was totally afraid," admitted Balzac. "Then, when I looked out past the peacekeepers and saw how late he was leaving the last shots …" He shook his head, keeping his emotions in check. "… I just looked up at the underside of the top deck, waiting for that last drop of the cane. I mean, he knew how exposed he was and he waited … he just … waited for that one, last, moment."

Lucia glanced at her father. She'd never heard him speak of another man in quite this regard before. Balzac shook his fist. "He knew we could load faster than that. He had dropped his cane faster before, but he waited."

The room was quiet for a while. Beaten beyond tired, Kalgan and Katanning excused themselves and went to check on their men. By and large, the men were all snoring on the beach. With a smile, they went down to the waters' edge and washed, fully clothed.

At the top of the sandy beach, the two men lay down on the grass. Neither could believe they were both there, and alive. It was a restless night thinking of all the men who were not there with them. Too many good men. They wondered about the *Avenger.* Could it possibly make it under those conditions? Jabali certainly wouldn't. Neither was going to say so in the office, but they'd seen him take the entire wrath of the rope as he cut it. A large portion of it had whipped back at him with intense power, knocking him from sight, and life. Nobody needed to hear about that.

The two men lay on the beach looking at the stars, sleep eventually taking them both.

***

In the early morning, Kalgan was disturbed from his deep slumber.

"Sir, sir, there are fishermen at the wharf!"

Kalgan rolled over in the sand, trying to get himself up. He squinted at the rising sun as he finally rose to his feet. "Who, what fishermen? What in blazes are you on about?" The man pulled on Kalgan's sleeve; he snatched it back. "Unhand me … how dare you!"

The man grabbed Kalgan by both shoulders. "Captain Kalgan, some fishermen have come in and said they'd seen a strange vessel. It's on the inland sea!"

Kalgan looked bewildered for a moment, then like a clap of thunder, it dawned on him. He shook the man urgently. "Where is Katanning?"

"In the office with Balzac, talking with the fishermen."

Kalgan began to sprint towards the wharf. "You get Katanning!"

The man began to make chase in earnest. "Where are you going, Captain?"

"Damn it, Ip, to the *Queen of the Seas!*" Kalgan ran along the wharf, yelling as he went to the crew on his beaten vessel. "Man the oars. Man the oars!"

The vessel was instantly a commotion of activity. The men feverishly sprang up to work despite their torn uniforms, missing footwear and blistered hands. Kalgan waved his arms as he ran towards the other vessel. "No, no, I want *Queen of the Seas.*" Bewildered, his crew disembarked and followed suit. As he boarded, he ordered, "You men, get ready to go immediately!"

One asked defensively, "Where is Admasin?"

"My men are out there somewhere without water or food. My vessel is not worthy of another trip, so I am commandeering this one. If you don't wish to serve me, you may leave, but you leave now!"

A big man at the back spoke in a strong voice. "Your men are our men. I go." Immediately, the men began pulling out oars and casting off ropes.

Katanning only just made the plank as the men pulled it in and the oars pushed off.

Kalgan looked back at the big man. "What's your name?"

"Feros. At your service, sir."

"You were out there two days ago?"

"I was."

"Then you know as well as anyone what this vessel can do. Can you take the helm?" Feros darted a look to the wharf – there was no sign of Lucia. Kalgan lowered his voice. "Feros, we just don't have time." Feros nodded as he marched briskly up the stairs to the wheel.

Katanning approached, his face full of expectation. Kalgan turned to him. "How sure are you?"

"The fishermen were quite descriptive. It *has* to be them."

Kalgan pumped a fist in the air. "If any man could pull this off, Jabali could." He called to the rudder deck. "Around we go, gentle now, keep it steady." He looked at the sky. "I can't believe just how clear it is."

Katanning nodded. "I know, it was like a bad dream, wasn't it?"

"It was more than that." He grimaced at the thought of all the lost men. "It was way more."

The two men stood shoulder to shoulder as *Queen of the Seas* made surprising pace through the bay and turned right towards the inland sea.

"Right, men, let's get the rigging up!"

The sails were hoisted high and snapped tight, and in the glory of the sun, *Queen of the Seas* surged ahead. With an air of excitement, the oars were pulled in and tied away. "Watch the rigging, tie everything off properly, men," Kalgan reminded them calmly.

Once out, the vessel turned west, and every eye searched the horizon.

"Captain, I speak you?" a small man said.

Kalgan didn't take his eyes off the sea. "Can you see the vessel?"

"Help you, me can."

Kalgan and Katanning turned to look at him. Neither recognised the little man. "And who might you be?" asked Kalgan with a hint of confusion.

"My name is Ushma. I am man from this vessel, sorry. But men hoist me up big pole, I see further than anyone."

Kalgan and Katanning glanced at one another. "Alright," said Kalgan, "You want to go up the master pole, Ushma?"

"Last time it work. It work now."

"You know what you need?"

"Yes, sir."

"Then be my guest."

"Thank you, sir." Ushma bobbed his head as he scurried away.

Without further word, Kalgan and Katanning continued searching as best they could.

"Katanning, you are a better navigator than I."

Katanning called to his crew. "Starboard side. Turn starboard side. Ninety degrees now." Little Ushma had indeed been hoisted up the master pole and clung to it as the sail billowed below him. "Ushma! We will be turning about, hang on!"

"Sir. Call heard!"

The sail swung gently, staying with the wind, and the vessel began to turn immediately. The men at the bow continued to search.

As the day drew on, conversation grew thin and hope even thinner. They looked and they searched. As they saw the reef east of Devil's Pass, Kalgan made his next call, and the vessel came around portside.

All afternoon, they sailed in a zig-zag motion through the inland sea. It was hot and dry, and the men's blistered hands were now torn. Sweat trickled through open wounds, but it was without complaint. Now *Queen of the Seas* had an uncanny silence to it. The day was drawing to a close, and so they'd have to navigate back by dark.

Kalgan turned to Katanning. "At a certain point, I am also responsible for *these* men."

Reluctantly, Katanning agreed. "As you say, sir." He was about to make his last call of the day when Ushma cried out.

"There! Three points of the starboard bow!"

Katanning quickly changed his intended call. "You heard him, men, three points starboard! Get on it!"

Kalgan searched expectantly. "Well?"

Katanning squinted. "I can't see a thing."

Another call from Ushma. "Dead ahead! It is them I say!"

The crew squashed forward to the bow, all jostling to see. Pinned against the railing, Katanning called over his shoulder. "Easy, men. If they're there, we will be with them shortly. Let's not start any silly seaman rumours now. Back away. Back away."

As *Queen of the Seas* eased towards the *Avenger*, they gasped at its poor condition. The mast had collapsed and the sail trailed over the side of the vessel, its rigging dragging in the water. As they drew closer, they could see the rudder was destroyed. The shutters below deck flapped open and shut with the gentle rocking of the swell. It was a wonder the vessel was even afloat.

Katanning glanced at Kalgan despairingly. A nod of understanding was all he got in return. Kalgan took control. "Right, men, lower the rigging gently. Feros, we want to pull alongside, we can rub a little timber, no harm done. The rest of you get ropes ready, we will need to pull her in tight as we come alongside.”

Queen of the Seas was deathly quiet as they approached. Not one person was on the top deck of the *Avenger*, and murmurs flowed around the vessel as opinions were swapped. The men threw the ropes, and the *Avenger* was pulled in firmly.

Katanning and Kalgan boarded the *Avenger* with a few men. At least there weren’t any bodies lying about as they walked along the top deck. Ducking under the collapsed sail rigging, the splintered pieces of rudder crunched under their boots.

Kalgan looked at the closed hatch grimly. “Two torches, quick smart, please.”

“Sir.”

Kalgan reached behind him and took the delivered torch. As he descended the ladder, he was hit with the hot, musty smell that wafted over him. Katanning followed him down with the other torch, and slowly they searched the *Avenger*.

Kalgan stumbled. “I have one.” He knelt. “He is …”

“Would you unhand me, you peasant!” The man pushed Kalgan off him and rolled over to get up.

Another man with a forked beard stood. “Who is making all this racket?” There were more groans in the dim light.

A man dressed in black approached through the shadows. “Well, you took your time.”

Katanning shook his head in disbelief. “Man, you have the goodwill kiss of the Gods.”

Jabali straightened his shirt with a cynical grin. “You won’t hold your jealousy against me, will you?”

Another man complained, “Just a little sleep … is this too much to ask?”

Everyone laughed as they began to file back to the ladder, torch bearers lighting the way. Kalgan called ahead. “Be sure all the bladders are ready.”

The men on the *Queen of the Seas* had been waiting with bated breath, listening for any signs of life. When the men began to pour out of the top hatch, a collective roar erupted. *Queen of the Seas* all but shook with the men cheering and jumping for joy.

Jabali wouldn't leave the stricken vessel until all his crew were off. Katanning slapped him on the shoulder. "What should we do with the *Avenger*?"

Jabali looked at the fading sky. "I will drop the anchor right where it is. When the crew has recovered, we can come back for it." He turned to the bow.

Katanning stepped in front of him. "No, sir, you will board *Queen of the Seas*. I will release the anchor."

Jabali turned expectantly to *Queen of the Seas*, his eyes searching for that one person. Her.

29 Reunited

Balzac lit the torches and waited patiently with Admasin on the wharf, watching the *Queen of the Seas* cruise into port. The arrival of Kalgan and Katanning the night before had left Balzac speechless, but now, if they were to return Jabali to them tonight, there would be some very happy people indeed.

Two days ago, one woman had been very quiet on the way home. She had detested him when they set out – the rude man, Jabali, who was completely petrified of the water, yet came alive when he was out on it. He seemed to know what needed to be done and how to achieve it. After they had been set alight with arrows and he himself was hit, *he* asked them to make chase. The thing that she just couldn't get out of her mind was, when they were charging the *Ocean Asset,* the biggest vessel, she'd hunkered down behind the wheel as he had instructed and watched him from under the sail as he stood defiant. The twin-masted vessel looming over them; he'd stood with his cane raised. After the shockwave of the blast, the thick, black smoke of the burnt powder had wafted over the deck. It was the last she saw of the man in black.

People gathered on the wharf as the *Queen of the Seas* docked. Big, broad smiles clearly revealed it had been a successful trip. Kalgan raised his hand to his mouth as he called out, "Balzac, could my men sleep on the beach tonight?"

Balzac waved his arms enthusiastically. "Of course. I will arrange for food and water to be brought out, just as we did last night."

A man hobbled to stand beside Kalgan. "Would it be too much trouble to have my old room back, Balzac?"

"Well, glory be! Jabali!"

Kalgan and Katanning looked at each other, confused. Balzac shook his head. "Yes, yes, it would be my pleasure to have you back in your old room. My, the Gods have shone on us with you, haven't they?"

"One other thing, Balzac."

"Anything, Jabali."

"I seem to have lost my cane. I'm afraid my leg is aching badly."

"And the hat?"

Best he could, Jabali raised his arms. "Why would you ever want to cover a face as beautiful as this?"

Everyone burst into laughter.

After the men swam and washed off, they rested on the shores, swapping stories and, maybe, just a little boasting. Food was brought out, and the men showed gratitude for it.

Jabali swam fully clothed with his men. He undressed only to wring them out, giving them a shake before redressing. He drew a gasp when he saw her. As she brought out food with the servants, her smile captivated his heart more tightly than ever. He flinched when Balzac spoke from behind him.

"Jabali, I have a cane for you. It belonged to my grandfather."

He pulled himself together. "Thank you, Balzac, most kind."

Balzac affectionately adjusted and straightened Jabali's clothes. "You know, Jabali, we, all of us, are very grateful for the sacrifice you made." He stopped flattening out Jabali's shirt, looking him in the eye. "It was one of the bravest things I have ever seen." He smiled. "Maybe a little stupid also, though entirely brave."

Jabali grinned. "We all were that day, Balzac. We were all brave – and a little stupid." He shook his head. "It was a ghastly loss of men. I hope it was for something."

Balzac motioned for Jabali to walk with him. "I agree. I dare say we'll hear in time. I hope we never have that type of event challenge us again."

"Balzac, I would drink to that."

"Ha, another fine idea! The men are all in my office. Come, come on in."

Jabali found himself breathing lightly as he approached the office. His heart pounded. She would be there. He *wanted* her to be there. He *had* to know. His need to talk to her was so strong he burned inside.

Balzac flung open the door. "Everyone, look who I found down the beach."

Cheers echoed around the room. Admasin looked at Jabali, who was leaning on his cane. He'd pulled his long, wavy hair down over the burnt side of his face as he wasn't wearing his hat. Admasin glanced about the room for Lucia. She wasn't there, but she would be soon enough.

Jabali was surprised at the positive attention he received as the men, in turn, came to greet him and shake his hand. He was more comfortable leaning against the rear wall. The drinks flowed, and everyone relaxed.

Admasin, as always, was making plans to rebuild a workshop back in Samos. Balzac really wanted to put it on the island, but Admasin had a fair point when he said he knew the best site in Samos that was now a clear slate, ready for a purpose-built rebuild. A full workshop would destroy the island. "... And besides, it really isn't big enough." Having seen the size of the other vessels, neither Balzac nor Jabali could disagree with that.

"I do have another suggestion, if you would, Balzac?"

Everyone was silent for Jabali. Balzac was instantly intrigued. "Go ahead, Jabali."

"Well, if the rest would like to go back to Samos, to family and friends after all, I, with some of your team, Balzac, would like to stay at the spring and work on new, small vessels."

Admasin broke the ensuing silence. "Jabali, you have more ideas?"

Jabali winked. "A couple, yes."

"Would Yuna and I be welcome for the occasional visit?"

Jabali raised his chin with a smile. "Your room is always yours and, I do feel I may be able to make my way into Samos, occasionally."

Everyone clapped. Admasin quipped he would have to run it by the boss. This idea was only good to Balzac if he could have a share of the venture in Samos and cash in – as a silent partner, of course.

The door opened with a bang, and Lucia walked in. The room instantly hushed. Other than Balzac and her, everyone sensed what was about to happen. It *had* to happen.

She closed the door and faced the room. "I would like to congratulate you. I just want you to know, when we sailed away from you all, I cried for your souls, and I was not alone." She surveyed the overcrowded room. "Yet, here you are, and you saved so many of your men. I cannot begin to understand how you did this." She looked at Kalgan and Katanning. "But what an achievement it was. You are possibly the two most amazing men I have ever met."

Katanning couldn't resist. "Thank you, Lucia, but we couldn't have done it without this man." He backed away, revealing Jabali at the back of the room. Instantly, she tilted her head.

Jabali did his best to smile. "Hello, Alexa." He wanted to walk to her, but his feet felt nailed to the floor.

Everyone stepped aside as she walked towards him. Her mind worked over countless memories, trying to make his contorted face fit. Jabali's heart pounded so hard he thought everyone would hear. Ever so gently, she lifted his hair back. They stared at one another for just a moment, then she slapped him so hard he stumbled on his cane, his cheek instantly stinging.

"You bastard! Is this really you?"

He stood up straight and tried to smile. "Yes, Alexa. It's me, Patch."

This time, she slapped him on the other side of his face, causing him to drop his cane. When he righted himself, he didn't smile. "Right. You've had your shot, now you listen to me!" He flinched at her finger pointing in his face.

"No! You listen to me! I cried for you every night whilst you were living out the back! Go to hell, you gutless bastard!" She paid no notice to the table of crockery and drinks as she stormed past, flinging the office door wide open. The tumblers and plates shattered over the floor as she marched away.

Balzac's jaw dropped. "You are her *Patch*?"

Patch picked up his cane as he limped towards the door. "Don't pull that shit with me, Balzac. You knew every time you brought those vessel plans out to my room. You *knew*."

Admasin watched on as Patch left the office.

The cane made a small tapping sound as Patch shuffled down the alley towards the little cabin. He turned left past the gazebo towards the pool. He approached slowly so he wouldn't startle her. "Simmered down a little?" he said softly.

"Simmered down?! I'll give you …"

Patch smacked his cane down on a low-slung branch, making her flinch and step back. "You will hush your temper before I put you over my knee and cane you like the little girl you are behaving!" Doubt crept over her. This wasn't her Patch either. "I have a story to tell, and you can at least hear me out." He hesitated. "Should I call you Alexa or Lucia? A man just doesn't know."

"My real name is Lucia," she responded in almost a whisper.

"Right, that is the first misunderstanding sorted. I was given the name of Jabali not long after my arrival, but I'm still Patch." He sighed and sat sideways on the branch to relieve his aching leg. "When I got here, I was messed up pretty bad. Then I thought I heard your voice, but the nurse assured me it was Balzac's daughter, Lucia. It wasn't until you were out on the other island and I got a real look at you that I realised it was unmistakably you. I'm sorry, but that is the truth."

Lucia put her hands on her hips defensively. "So, when you realised it was me, why didn't you talk to me?"

He stood up, undoing his shirt to reveal his burned skin. His left chest wasn't the same as the right and the burns clearly went down under his pants.

She looked at his face. "And now, Patch?"

"When we were out on the seas, I was soaked and sitting on the overturned vessel. A man with a forked beard came over and asked if I sat in wet clothes because I was ashamed of my scars? Of course I was, but he told me, 'Never let the unfortunate past dictate the future.'"

"So, what did you do?"

"I undressed and wrung out my clothes. It was much better." She scoffed and he looked at her intensely. "All I know is that to this day, you still haunt my dreams, Alexa."

She tilted her head. He seemed to be at peace with himself somehow. "So, Patch, what do we do now?"

He smiled broadly. "Go and see what Admasin has planned for us?"

Just then, Ordesia came down the branch. He passed Lucia and nudged into Patch. He smiled and began to stroke her. Lucia looked at Patch. "He really seems to like you."

"Yes, when you were all out on the smaller island, I used to come here and talk with him. He really is a great listener, you know."

She looked deeply into his eyes, the windows that held so many of their treasured memories together. Their hands met on Ordesia's back. Patch froze as she looked at his burns, then began to feel the scars. Gently, she rubbed her hand over them. The intense pain he must've endured would have seemed insurmountable. "How does one survive all this?"

"I fell into the salt water, which was a good start, but I was unconscious. Someone pulled me up onto one of the barrels I insisted you carry on the model. A vessel fleeing Samos picked me up and brought me here, where, of course, Kito cared for me greatly."

Lucia reached up and put her hand on his cheek. He held against it, desire burning deep inside. On tiptoes, she reached across to kiss him.

In the dark of the gazebo was a hushed gathering of men. They stood still, listening and watching, but when they saw the two figures at the pool kiss, like naughty children keeping quiet and holding their excitement, they crept back inside, spilling drinks on the way.

On the banks of the river, Baako turned to his five companions. "If you're all ready, we have about a two-day run."

Tzu grinned cheekily. "This place of yours, Baako, it does get a little cooler, doesn't it?"

Baako's deep laugh boomed through the jungle as he turned and led the way.

They made good time along the track, except Tzu, who hadn't been in a jungle before. There was really very little difference to the south of Middle Kingdom but, for Tzu, it was nothing like the frozen north.

"Baako, this jungle of yours is giving me a headache."

Baako slowed a little and handed him his bladder. "Here, my friend, drink this."

"I have drunk along the way."

"Yes, but you're not used to the heat, so you need to drink more than most." Grateful, Tzu drank deeply. "Also, just keep your eyes on the path. By nightfall, you will feel better."

Tzu did indeed feel a little better by nightfall. They spent the night around a small campfire, listening to the jungle. Baako's face ached from smiling so much. He'd only allowed himself to dream of such a day just a few times over all those years.

The next morning, they were up early and on their way. Tzu drank lots, and never said another word about it.

By early afternoon, Baako knew they were getting close, but it was not the welcoming party he'd dreamt of when spears were suddenly thrust out at them. Hao spun, reaching for his sword. It was too late. The group of large, dark, jungle warriors surrounded them. Baako's group was held back by spears, bows and to the bewilderment of the foreigners, some of the warriors held up tubes to their mouths.

Baako held up his hands. "I am the son of Queen Trina and King Mabutu. My name is Baako."

One of the men held a spear close to Baako's face. "No, you lie." The man was as cool as he was tall.

"I have no reason to lie to you. Take me to Chief Kobus, and he will confirm my pledge."

The tall man shook his head. "No. Nobody comes in or out of the Village of the Keepers. This is now law."

"Chief Kobus will be able to vouch for me, though, to do this, he must first see me."

The man stood defiant. "No need to interrupt the chief. Baako died many years ago. The Chief has dealt with many liars of late. You would've passed some of their bodies floating down the river."

A few of Baako's group couldn't help but look at the river that flowed past them. The tension was building, and Hao became concerned with the man's arrogance.

"I should deal with you all right here, just for lying to me," the tall man said.

Tzu could see the muscles in Baako's shoulders knotting up. He stepped forward, creating a nervous shuffle amongst the dark men. "Young man, if I may…" Several spear points were at Tzu's throat instantly.

"And who do you claim you are?"

Keeping as amicable as possible, Tzu tried to explain. "Yes, actually, I am also a King, albeit from a land far away from here."

"I do not care for other lands. You are in my lands!"

"That we may be, though human nature doesn't seem to change that much. I would not like to see *you* floating away down that river either."

The tall man lifted Tzu's chin slowly with the spear point. "Look about. You're outnumbered and out-weaponed. How would you do that, King?"

"I wouldn't have to. You see, if you kill my good friend Baako, your chief will get to know and *he* will kill *you* for me." The tall man drew back, looking about his own men now waiting for him to respond. Tzu continued in low voice. "I learnt long ago, better to be safe than hasty."

The man leaned to the side and, without taking his eyes off Tzu, whispered a message to another man who then ran off into the jungle.

Sometime later, the messenger led three elders down the track to the group. As they arrived, they spread out. The messenger stepped to the side. If there had been an ounce of doubt in the group about Baako's claims, the elders' faces said everything. The elders were not just wise, they also knew Baako before he went missing. One by one, they came forward and took his hands, kissing them on the back. Baako was now older, but he was also unmistakable, at least to everyone but the tall man. He stood to one side, still defiant.

Tzu watched as the spear holders now came forward, overcome with tears of joy as they took Baako by his hands. He was clearly a much loved and respected man of his lands.

Baako faced the tall man. "Do you wish to pay your respects now, my friend?"

"I will ..." was all he got to say as he felt the blow to his abdomen. His lungs whooshed out as Baako scooped the man up over his shoulders and dumped him hard to the earth. He turned to the tribe people before him. "I understand he is too young to know me and was doing his job, but I will not tolerate any man who does not respect the judgment of the elders."

Baako's friends stood with their mouths agape. He was always so respectful, gentle and quiet. If there had been an ounce of doubt about his power here, there wasn't now.

They moved through the jungle to the Village of the Keepers. Hao whispered to Tzu. "If this is the village of a King, I'm not really impressed."

Yaan scoffed. "This is alright. I grew up in a cave."

Hao smirked. "So true, my friend."

A large fire crackled in the centre of the village, and the group gathered around it. It seemed that everyone had come to witness their arrival. As the elders arrived, the people stepped aside. It appeared there was already a meeting underway.

All but two men stood up. They, by contrast, remained seated in the only large, wooden chairs. Baako stood opposite, and his companions spread out on either side of him. Tzu watched, intrigued. The two seated men were dressed in long flowing gowns, woven with feathers. The crowd had similar gowns, only more simplistic. Tzu made a feeble attempt to brush down his ripped, stained tunic and trousers. *What a mixed-up bunch we must look to them. Not the best first impression I have ever given.*

The two men rose together, their surprise revealed in the whites of their eyes, contrasting with their dark faces. The bigger man, Mabutu, began to walk around the fire, his now watering eyes glistening in the firelight. "In the face of the Gods, am I seeing true?"

The anticipation in the air felt larger than the village itself. Mabutu came and stood before Baako, who dropped to one knee and took his father's hands. Baako gently kissed them both on the back then looked up. "King Mabutu, I ask for your forgiveness."

Still clasping hands, Mabutu pulled Baako to his feet. "Baako, you have nothing to be forgiven for. I, too, have not been here to tend my duties." He pulled Baako into a tight embrace, and the village burst into a cheer so loud and instantaneous that the mixed bunch flinched.

The village stamped their bare feet in celebration until Mabutu pushed Baako to arm's length. Silence quickly followed as they waited to hear their King, Mabutu. "We have much to go over, but first ..." He looked at the white faces. "... son, who is it you have brought with you?"

Baako turned, not releasing his father. "This beauty is Tanica. She and her friend Mercanti saved many lives when their city, Samos caught fire."

Tanica frowned a little, noting that Baako didn't mention more of the fire. King Mabutu put out his hand to Tanica. She took it and kissed the back of it, as Baako had asked of them at their last campfire.

"Tanica, is this so? You and your friend saved lives?"

"With help from Mercanti, we did what we could."

The King moved his hand and his attention to Mercanti. "Mercanti, were you not afraid?"

She bent to kiss his hand. "Yes, of course, but it needed to be done. Baako also saved many lives himself."

The King's pride was evident. "Son?"

"As Mercanti said, it needed to be done." Quickly, he moved his attention to Hao. "This man has fought all his life. He has defended not just his country but his beliefs, my King."

Hao stepped forward, his forehead knotted for not having realised just how perceptive Baako had been on their journey. He knelt before the King and kissed his hand as the King enquired, "Hao, may I ask, whom is it you fight?"

"Injustice, King. I thank you for making us welcome in your lands." He stepped back as Baako presented Yaan.

"This man is my equal, in his own land. I give you, Prince Yaan."

Yaan was about to go down onto his knee when the King held him up. "Would you go down onto your knee in your own land, Yaan?"

Yaan lowered himself. "I'm not in my land, King Mabutu. If Baako can go to his knee, then so can I." He kissed Mabutu's hand and stood.

Finally, Baako held out a hand for Tzu to step forward. "And last, but not least, King, this man is also a King in his land."

King Mabutu stood square to Tzu. Though Mabutu was much broader, Tzu was nearly the same height and held as much pride.

They shook wrist to wrist. Still holding Tzu, Mabutu asked, "What, so far from home, brings you to my lands?"

"I believe a cancer has seeped into your lands. It must be stopped and cut from this earth, burned so never to take hold again."

King Mabutu looked at his guests. "Have you all come to our lands to cut this cancer?"

Baako answered before anyone else could. "We have come to face him here before he can return to Middle Kingdom."

Mabutu looked at Kobus with grave concern. "I see."

Hao asked of Kobus. "Am I to believe this is your village?"

"Please forgive me." Mabutu gestured. "Ladies and warriors, this is the chief to Village of the Keepers. I give you all, Chief Kobus."

Hao awkwardly half dipped his head not knowing what else to do. "Chief Kobus, I have much I wish to share with you. Do we have somewhere personal to discuss such matters?"

Kobus stepped back to his seat and addressed the crowd. "People of our village, today we have another remarkable turn of events, so we must be ever more vigilant of our security. Tonight, we must make our new friends and allies welcome with a feast." The villagers cheered before Kobus held up his hands. "But until then, you will give us the privacy for discussion."

Most of the people, whilst singing and dancing, began to move away. Kobus motioned a woman over. "Will you see we have huts made available for our new friends. Towards the village centre, I feel." She smiled and moved away without a word.

Hao shuffled uncomfortably. They were still in the open for all and any to hear. He looked over to Baako, then decided he wouldn't argue on the matter. As they settled, it seemed strange to Tzu to be sitting at a fire when it was so hot.

Mabutu leaned forward in his seat and motioned to Baako. "Son, would you give us all that you know, then Kobus will do the same for you all."

There were so many people Baako wanted to catch up with, even just to walk through the jungle once more a free man, but these were privileges of time, time they didn't have. The Emperor and his guard were already here.

Baako told all he knew and let his companions add their insights as he went, then, as said by the King, Kobus told all he had to tell. Everyone was quiet and respectful until he was finished. The last to be said was that Queen Trina was thought to be in chains in the dungeons of Orion.

Baako's sullen face darkened as he sprang to his feet. "What have we done about this travesty?"

"Baako, son, be calm and be seated."

Baako paced back and forth behind his friends. "This is the Queen to these lands. I ask again, what are you doing about it?!"

"Son, be seated, now."

Baako continued pacing until Yaan stood before him. Baako looked down at Yaan through glassy eyes. Yaan spoke softly. "Baako, I must ask you if you think she would be happy with rash decisions, or your behaviour right now? You know whatever you need, we are here to help."

Baako shook his finger. "You make a brave promise, Yaan but we both know you're all here to save your own lands."

Yaan reached up, placing his hands on either side of Baako's broad shoulders. "Yes, this is true, but we are still your allies, Baako."

"What else could you do?"

"Whatever it takes to right the wrong," assured Yaan.

"This is not your wrong."

"No, Baako but we don't care who claims ownership of the problem, we just care that our friend has one. All you need to do, Baako, is ask."

Hao stood. "King Mabutu, with all the talk we've had, what do you see happening next?"

Mabutu finally drew his eyes from his upset son. "Hao, as you have suggested, two armies will come from the north to join forces with the Emperor's army hiding in this very jungle. The numbers are daunting at best."

Hao lowered his voice. "Baako, as you know, when I talk I like to walk around to think. There is not room for both of us, my friend." Baako muttered as he and Yaan sat back down. Hao began to pace. "King Mabutu, you say the numbers are daunting. Can you give us an idea, exactly what we are up against?"

King Mabutu sat back. "By the time the Pharaoh has joined the Sheik, they will be over a thousand strong. Is this daunting enough for you, Hao?"

Hao continued to pace. "And we anticipate the Emperor has already brought many more before our trip here. I respect Kito for stopping the last shipment arriving, though I fear it will make little difference."

Kobus sat forward. "You know Kito? How?"

The group exchanged glances. Hao had the floor. "Kito has been a large part of our lives for many seasons now. May I ask in what fashion you know of him also?"

Mabutu spoke in response. "It is thought that he is my son."

Baako shot to his feet again. "What?!"

"I am sorry, son. I was hoping to talk with you in person later. It is out now. We think he is the son of Queen Rani and I, making Kito your half-brother."

Baako's face drained of blood as he lowered himself down. "When he told me we were brothers … I just thought he meant, like we are all brothers."

Hao and Yaan swapped disbelieving glances.

For the first time, Tanica spoke. "King Mabutu, does Kito know this himself?"

"Apparently, yes. Kito is not his given name. It was a name given to him in your own lands by one of your own, Tanica." Tanica looked back at the fire. Mabutu saw it. "Tanica, the point of this talk is to have all our stories told without exception, without untruths." Tanica was unmoved. Mabutu lowered his voice. "If we are to fight this cancer in the face of our Gods, we must tell all we know, Tanica. All."

She gazed up at the big man. "I have heard many things of this man you call Kito. I have also seen many things of him."

Yaan urged her. "Do not do this, Tanica."

Mabutu frowned when Tanica eyed Yaan coldly. "You dare to come into their lands and not be truthful, Yaan?"

"This is not about truths, Tanica. It is just your opinion of a man you despise."

"It is still my opinion!" snapped Tanica.

It dawned on Mabutu as he watched the two squabbling. "Yaan, are you the eldest?"

"King Mabutu?"

Mabutu could see it clearer with every moment. "Yes. You and Tanica, you are the eldest?"

"I don't know, Mabutu."

Mabutu paused. "You don't know? Why? Oh …" He sat back. "You are twins, yes?"

Tanica opened her mouth to speak, but Yaan quickly stood in front of her. "Do not disrespect this meeting and do not disrespect their lands, Tanica."

She returned a look of contempt as she ignored him standing over her. "King Mabutu, how many warriors do you have to oppose this monumental gathering of troops?"

Mabutu studied the fire between the young siblings. "Maybe a fifth of that, Tanica."

Her eyes glistened, the tension palpable as she seethed. "Is the sacrifice reasonable, brother?"

Mabutu intervened. "Tanica, if this is not where your heart is, then why did you come?"

There was a long pause before Hao tried to explain. "Tanica and Yaan didn't grow up together. She came here to better know her brother. The rest of us came because Kito asked us to."

Mabutu stroked his chin. "Kito asked you to come to our lands to help us?"

Hao shook his head. "No, I believe Kito asked us to help him to kill the Emperor. We do this because he asked, but we also believe this would be our best standpoint anyway."

"Why here, now? Please explain."

Tzu picked up a stick and poked the fire as Hao explained. "We feel if the Emperor is left unchecked at this juncture, he will stop at nothing to rule the world. That, King Mabutu, would be a dark world indeed."

Kobus leaned forward. "Kito asked you to come, for him?"

Still playing with the red coals, Tzu nodded. "Yes." He looked up at Tanica. "He told me later that if Yaan would come, then so would Tanica and Mercanti. Apparently, they are pivotal." For the first time, Mercanti drew her eyes away from the fire to watch Tzu as he continued. "He said all your people must stay in the jungle, away from the fight. We, just this group, must go out onto the sands to face the coming forces."

Kobus shot forward in his seat. "Never! To win or lose, we must all be there united!"

Hao stood square to the chief. "Chief Kobus, if you come with us to face the Pharaoh and the Sheik, we'll be outflanked by the Emperor's Royal Guard. That is his expectation."

Kobus took a breath to speak, but Mabutu held him back, placing his hand on the chief's arm. "What, Hao, do you intend to do?"

"I understand Chief Kobus is your strongest leader. He must hold your men true."

Mabutu smiled. "And what is your instruction for me, Hao?"

"Kito seemed to think you must be with us."

"Why?"

"You would have to ask Kito that one, King."

Mabutu sat upright in his chair. "And where is this Kito? I have yet to lay eyes on him."

The men looked at one another awkwardly, no one sure how to answer. Yaan and Tanica had sat down. She looked towards Mabutu. "May I ask, King Mabutu, what colour were Queen Rani's eyes?"

Mabutu frowned, then his face softened. "They were the most intoxicating emerald, not unlike your own, Tanica. Why would you ask such a question?"

Yaan nudged her. "Tanica ..."

"Because, King Mabutu, you have dark eyes and he has blue eyes."

"Tanica, this is disrespectful," urged Yaan.

Mabutu was calming in his speech. "Yaan, she was just asking a question. Tanica, my son has eyes of blue, like the clearest ocean or the tropical sky. Why do you not trust him? Please don't hold back, be honest with me. We must know what we are dealing with."

Yaan was silent, though the tension held thick in the air. She was careful with her words. "I watched him spar with Prince Desora, the Emperor's son. He was at the palace as a guest of the Emperor. He stayed in the Royal suite."

Mabutu soaked up the words. Known for his ability to negotiate, he wasn't going to make any assumptions without seeing the bigger picture.

Tanica didn't know Kito like Yaan did; it grated on him when she spoke of him in such negative light. He felt compelled to explain further. "King Mabutu, it is also said that on a later date, Kito broke Prince Desora's nose. An entire village witnessed it."

"I see, and where is the Emperor's son now?"

Hao opened his mouth, then shut it tight, unsure how the King would take the news of what he had done. He stared down at the coals in silence, and Yaan did little more than that, leaving it for Tzu as a witness to speak. "He is dead, King Mabutu."

"Dead! Are you sure, Tzu? We are talking about the son of the Emperor!"

Tzu scoffed. "As sure as I'm sat here. I saw Hao kill him in one of the most heroic sword fights I've ever witnessed."

Hao sighed, rolling his eyes at Tzu.

"What made it so heroic in your opinion, Tzu?" asked Mabutu.

"I led my men on a rampage into the palace. It was a huge battle and both sides lost too many men. We were about to succeed when I saw the Prince there before us. To get a Royal was my biggest objective, so to see him there was truly unbelievable. I was about to stop the fighting to get him alive, but what he did next left me completely perplexed. I had to let it play out."

Everyone listened intently, none more so than Mabutu. "Yes, Tzu. Explain."

"Hao was in front, fighting a losing battle against my men when he suddenly moved away and faced Desora. I couldn't hear what was being said other than they argued over something as they clashed swords. I saw Desora turn and run, but Hao threw a knife that toppled Desora. Hao advanced. They engaged in battle and fought long and hard, clearly Hao the victor."

Mabutu frowned. "Tzu?"

"Yes, Mabutu."

"You said it was a most brave fight. I don't understand?"

"The knife he'd toppled Desora with, he'd pulled it from his own thigh."

Everyone gasped. Kobus looked at Hao. "Hao, you pulled a knife out of your thigh and threw it at your own prince?"

Hao shrugged and looked at Kobus for a lingering moment. "I figured he put it there so it was only right I gave it back."

His dry wit wasn't lost on Tzu, who chuckled at the memory of it playing in his mind. "I stopped the fight and took Hao for questioning. You can imagine my dismay when he passed out whilst talking to me."

Mabutu began to clap. "Well, now I see, Tzu. Hao fought the prince and won, as he himself was bleeding to death."

"Precisely."

"With people like this, we just may have a chance."

"Gods above!" Shooting to her feet, Tanica stamped her foot. "We don't have time for foolhardy stories or for celebrating! As we speak, there's an immeasurable number of soldiers making their way here and they won't stop until they've slaughtered everyone on this damned land! And from here, they will trample all over the entire world. We don't have a chance!" Without a thought, she stormed off the way they'd been led in.

Mercanti dithered between remaining put and running after her. "Please, King Mabutu, Chief Kobus, accept our apologies." She held her hands together and bowed deeply before scurrying away after her friend.

31 Tanica's Struggle

Whether it was from the heat of the fire or the heated discussion, Yaan wiped his sweaty forehead. "Please do accept my deepest …"

King Mabutu held up his hand. "Yaan, Tanica is your twin?"

"Yes, we are full siblings."

The dark King nodded as he amply filled his large chair. "And you didn't grow up together?" He shuffled to get comfortable. "So, how long have you known Tanica?"

"We met just a few seasons before we came here."

Family was everything to Mabutu. His face darkened as if he was expanding even bigger with his growing anger. "Why have you not made contact before now, Yaan?"

"The bottom line is, we never knew about each other. Tanica would have been killed by the Emperor if he'd known about her and at birth I was removed from the Palace altogether."

The King looked perplexed. "So, who was Desora to you?"

"It is thought that Tanica and I are twins. Desora was a third baby born the same day to the same woman, but not the same father."

Mabutu stared intently at Yaan. "I see. Your eyes, Yaan, they are the eyes of Hasuca. And Desora?"

"He was said to be Koe's, through and through."

"I have heard it possible for a woman to give birth to children from two fathers. Here it is considered a blessing, two men to provide for one family." He looked down for a moment. "And your mother, Yaan?"

"Died on the birthing table, Mabutu."

The King sat back. "I'm not surprised, bless the fertile woman."

There was a fuss from behind as Mercanti and Tanica were brought back by five warriors with spears.

Tanica regained her footing as she was pushed forward. "King Mabutu, if you don't remove these men, I will kill them all."

Yaan quickly rushed between her and the warriors, with his hands held out wide to both parties. "Tanica, please don't do this."

The Chief and King Mabutu both stood. Mabutu's large frame could easily cast a shadow over them, but his voice was calm and quiet. "Yaan, how many could she take, do you think?"

"Under the cloak of secrecy, she was trained by the man who trained Prince Hasuca."

"I see. I had the occasion to see him move; it was quite spectacular."

Yaan took a breath. "If she decided to, there would be no one left standing here, including me."

Chief Kobus raised his chin. "I will not have my men …"

Mabutu held up his hand. "Tanica, would you come and stand before me?"

"Why?"

"Because I don't want you killing everyone before we have met the enemy." Tanica blinked. "Tanica, you have nothing to concern yourself with, though you will not disrespect me or my people any further."

Yaan was now sweating profusely. He'd noticed Hao and Tzu both had a heavy stick in their hands, still burning in the fire. Tanica looked at Yaan as she walked around to stand before the King. She could see the disappointment in his eyes. King Mabutu towered over her just as Baako did.

"Tanica, I didn't know you'd only just met your brother, and I can see you don't agree with this journey, but nevertheless, you are here now."

"Only because Kito told him to come." She pointed an accusing finger at Yaan.

"Yet, you are both here, together." She was unmoved. "Your grandfather once had Prince Hasuca put on a show for us." He turned to the fire as he explained. "I had a wager with his father, a dear man of great conviction. I still miss him as an ally and a friend, though on that occasion, I feel he set me up. I put four of my warriors against his son. Hasuca must have only just come into manhood. I, too, was a young man and clearly naive. I thought I had an easy win. Standing in the middle of my men, he appeared almost a child. I nearly called off the match for his own safety, but what I saw that day I will never forget. Standing like a stone, until finally one of my men lunged forward. I barely saw the young prince move but before I knew it, all my men were in the dust groaning whilst Prince Hasuca had hardly raised a sweat. Who trained you, my dear?"

Yaan sat silent, hoping she wouldn't perform with the 'my dear' comment. She gazed up at Mabutu as he waited silently. "I am not your daughter, King Mabutu, my name is Tanica."

Yaan rolled his eyes. *Here we go.*

Tanica's eyes glazed over. "He was a wonderful man, murdered by Koe himself. His name was Xiang, he was a Grand Master."

"If he trained Prince Hasuca, he must've been old."

"He was around the same age as the friend you speak of. They were killed by the same evil hand."

Mabutu lowered his voice. "So, we all have something personal in this, don't we, Tanica?"

She stamped a foot. "But not like this! We have no plan."

Mabutu eased back into his chair. Despite his bulk, today he felt all those years in isolation had made his body soft. "You have come a long way, men. Is there a plan?" Silence. Mabutu played to the leadership in Hao. "Hao, do you have something to offer here?"

"Kobus could take all your men and cover our backs from the Emperor's Royal Guard in the jungle."

"And the rest of us, Hao?" enquired Mabutu.

"We will march out through the elephant grass and set up camp to face them."

"The elephant grass reaches from the Great Dividing Ranges to the sea, Hao. Just where are we to be on this line?"

Hao continued reluctantly. "Kito said we need to go through where your own father …"

Baako's eyes swelled; he watched his father, waiting for his reaction.

Finally, "Hao, I see you are a man of great character. So, are you telling me that only the men and women at this fire are to go and we are to pass through where my father died?"

"Yes. This is the plan I am giving you. With your consent, this is what I will be doing."

"I see, Hao." He gazed over the expectant faces. "You are all going with this plan?" Everyone except Tanica agreed. Mabutu addressed her. "What is it that troubles you? Why is it everyone else has trust in this, but not you?"

"King Mabutu, I mean no disrespect but I have seen this Kito. I have seen him consulting with the Emperor and I have heard the grotesque way the villagers died. Kito was the only one who came out alive. This could only be by design."

Yaan seethed at his sister's insinuation. "Enough! I wasn't there to see the villagers taken in the flood that was sent by the Emperor but I have fought with this man. I know his heart is good! Even the villagers of Middle Kingdom worship him."

Tanica spun on her heel. "He knew the water was coming! How else could he have been the only one to come back out?"

"He wasn't the only one to get back out. He saved one of their own!"

"A small token for those lost, if you ask me! Where was Kito when you were captured in Samos. How did they know about you there, brother?"

"Kito wasn't even there."

"How could you know where Kito was, huh? How did he get off the vessel? Can anyone tell me where he went from a vessel in the middle of the ocean?" She poked her finger in the air at each one of them from the vessel. "He has set you all up for an easy trap at the hands of Koe. We will all perish. Maybe even the trap in the jungle is an easy one. He has enough men."

Yaan's eyes narrowed, and his temper flared. "Kito set up Balzac's vessel to take out hundreds of the Royal Guard along with all their supplies. Our vessel was the only one to make it. This is a huge blow for them!"

"How do you know the other vessels never made it? Besides, they still outnumber us in the jungle, and they are all true warriors."

Kobus reached his limit of patience. "How dare you come here …"

Tzu cut through the anger. "Please, my friends, stop this." Tanica immediately looked down at the fire, aware of the chief's cold stare. Tzu spoke to the King. "I was there in Samos fighting the Royal Guard. I saw the bloodshed of the Royal Guard, setting fires and murdering their own people. These men will follow the Emperor to their own death, too many already have. It is the war no one wanted, in a civilian city. There were guards, as Tanica just said, all well trained and armed. Kito also said that King Mensa is in alliance with Koe."

The chief sat back down. Baako's heart ached for his mother and father. For so many years in captivity, he'd tried to subdue his desire for revenge. "Father, look what Mensa has done to our family. I have heard stories of what he does to his own people, our people. These men must be stopped."

King Mabutu's voice carried an authority that no one was to question. "I have much to consider. I thank you all for your input but these are my lands and, before the Gods that see all, I will be giving the last word. And that word *will* be final. Kito or no Kito, my word is final."

Everyone dipped their heads in agreement. He stood before Tanica, holding her by her shoulders. "My dear girl, who is not my daughter, you have seen much in your short life. You have fire in your belly, a sharp mind and a fierce tongue in your head. You are free to do as you wish in this camp, but you must respect my land, my jungle and my leadership. Tanica, I wish to have you on my side."

She slowly looked up at the King, his size as incomprehensible as Baako's, but ultimately she liked both of them. "I am sorry for my outburst, King. I don't mean to be disrespectful, but I can see you losing all your people. I can see us all dying here. On the vessel, I dreamt of it many times, and now I am here, I see no better."

"Tanica, before I go to rest, do I have your word that you will respect everyone here?"

She stood rigid. "King Mabutu, I only want what is right for your people."

"Tanica."

"Yes. You have my word, King Mabutu."

Mabutu smiled as he let her go. "Now I can rest." He turned to leave the campfire, and the chief rose to leave with him. Tanica looked across at Yaan, who gazed back impassively, then smiled. "Well, out with it, I can see it is burning you."

The chief and Mabutu stopped to hear her answer.

"I will follow you, my brother. I have heard what you did in Samos – twice. You are brave, and stupid, but I will follow you. So, there you have it. I will go with you and do as you say, but in a few days, we are all going to perish."

32 The Temple of the Crystal

High on the mountainside, the Emperor walked out to the breaking day. "Morning to you, Kito."

Kito turned smoothly to face the Emperor. In the morning light, he seemed to be glowing. "Good morning to you also. I believe this is the last time we will do this, Koe."

The Emperor's face lit up. "Yes, I think you are right!" He strode out and peered down over the jungle far below. "It is difficult for me to comprehend that all my life has been for this one day. It would seem even your silly Gods want it to happen."

"Koe?"

"Yes, Kito, they gave me Sha'Doe after all."

"Who gave you a son, Desora, now a Master."

"No, it's much more than that." He turned to face Kito. "For their own protection, I have kept them from everyone, but since you have been so pivotal in getting me here, Kito, I might as well show you." He reached into his saddlebag and slowly brought out a plate made of solid gold. "Kito, with this, along with these gold bracelets I wear, I'll be able to look into the eyes of the Crystal Skulls."

Kito had seen the gold bracelets when they'd sparred together. The plate, however, was a complete surprise. It gleamed in the sunrise as Koe manipulated it around to catch the light. The Emperor watched Kito's face. "Ah yes, you know what it is, don't you, son? It was brought to the palace by my dear Sha'Doe. You see, it was your Gods' will that she brought it from afar directly to me." Kito grew aware of the twin swords on his back humming. The Emperor held the plate forward, tempting Kito as his words slithered off his tongue. "Would you like to touch the plate, son?"

Kito stepped back, his eyes not leaving the shining gold plate. It too seemed to be humming. "No, I feel I'm not pure enough, Koe."

The Emperor threw back his head and roared with laughter into the breaking day. If any of the Masters were still asleep, they weren't now.

***

Kito decided not to have breakfast; instead, he went for a run, instinctively knowing he would need a clear mind for the task ahead.

Once back at camp, Uttah brought out some water. "You didn't join us for breakfast, Kito?"

Kito watched the Masters clearing out the cove. He wondered if it was a waste of time. "As you know, it's easier to meditate on an empty stomach. Today I will need all my concentration."

Uttah grew suspicious. "What exactly will we be doing today?"

"To be honest, Uttah, I do not actually know." Keen to avoid any further questions, Kito excused himself and went to the Emperor's horse. He rubbed it on the nose, and the horse neighed and stepped forward, pushing him back. "Steady, big boy. No need to be pushy about it." It shook its head and nuzzled into his shoulder.

"Would you be so good as to saddle my horse, Kito." It was more a statement than a request.

"No, Koe. I can't get the horse through."

The Emperor stiffened. "Cannot or will not, Kito?"

Kito stood square to the Emperor. "I'm not even sure about the number of men I must take, Koe."

"You must be pleased to lose two of them then, Kito?"

"No."

The Emperor studied Kito for a moment. "Very well, I will leave the horse as I won't be coming back this way, anyway."

Before Kito could ask the question, the Emperor turned back to the cove. "Grand Master, I take it you are ready to leave."

"Of course, sire."

The Emperor slapped his leather gloves in his hand. "Well, let us not waste another moment."

The Masters gathered their saddlebags, and they left the cove to attend to their horses in silence. It seemed that no one felt good about the impending day and what might become of it.

The Emperor was standing by his horse.

"He has neglected to prepare your horse, sire," the Grand Master stated.

"Not at all, Master. Today I have chosen to go on foot." He looked past the Grand Master. "Is Kito not with you?"

"No, and he isn't at the cove either."

The Emperor began to walk on. "Ah, he has gone ahead to prepare. I will wait no longer."

The Grand Master looked at his men; they all looked uneasy. "Is there a problem, Masters?" he asked quietly. They dipped their heads, not daring to respond. The Grand Master's eyes narrowed. "Masters, we must be always open and honest with each other. In me, you can confide."

No one spoke.

The Grand Master stood straight and breathed out to calm his disappointment. "So be it then. I expect you will perform your duties to the very best of your training, as is our oath."

Still no one lifted their head, and the Grand Master turned and quickly walked to catch up with the Emperor.

With his men close behind, the Grand Master trotted along the narrow track for some time. Eventually, they came to the small cove. Kito was on one knee with his hood up and head lowered. The Grand Master shuddered at the cove before him, with its straight walls and flat ceiling; it was all too neat, the corners too perfect. Everything from the floor up was polished, black granite, so shiny it mirrored everything, including the form of Kito, who hardly seemed to be breathing.

Kito could feel the block. *How strong is this woman?* Without losing his preparations, he knew what he had to do.

The eagle soared high in the morning sky, its call floating over the panorama below, seemingly unheard. A cloud swirled by, rocking it in its flight. The cloud swirled, growing as it rumbled. Small flashes of lightning ripped through it. It rolled forwards, as if drawn into the Great Eastern Ranges.

At the cove entrance, a gust of wind whipped up around the Emperor and the Masters. Heavy, dark clouds rolled in towards them, quickly blocking the sun. Lightning tore through, and the Masters covered their faces as it reflected around the mirrored granite. The booming thunder felt as if the entire storm was trying to get into the cove with them. The Masters looked to Kito almost in earnest. He still had his head down, not even a ripple of clothing flapped.

The block was fading, giving Kito the room to move. He could neither hear, nor feel the storm ripping across the entrance, though his concentration held it in tight against the cove, blocking Banji.

He stood with his eyes closed, facing the stone wall, and reached forward. The Masters watched intently as his fingers brushed against the smooth, granite wall. The wall relented. Hands together, he pushed his fingers into the faultless stone. It groaned at his intrusion. He pushed further until the rock accepted his hands. It groaned again as his outstretched arms pulled apart and separated the two walls.

Kito eased forward, and the granite before him faded into a tunnel where the walls became tall and mirrored. The bottom corners were at perfect right angles to the straight walls that led up to an arched ceiling. The rock overhead trembled as he steadily walked forward.

The tunnel began to track downwards as the mountain continued to rumble overhead. The Masters, tentatively holding their twin swords, studied the unnaturally smooth walls as they followed him. The rock was black, yet their trail was lit. The Grand Master caught sight of a dark, sweat patch on the back of Kito's hood and bulging shoulders. He wasn't even sure he'd seen Kito sweat before, and he could only wonder what was going on in his mind.

After a time difficult to measure, Kito stopped, then reached forward. Without touching the stone before him, he began to strain. Even under his grey clothes, they could see his back expanding under the effort. More dark patches appeared over his clothing, yet he touched nothing. The walls tremored as the stone began to shift sideways like sliding doors. Wider the granite spread until Kito's arms were fully stretched and the opening was wider than his reach. The Masters' swords gleamed as the sunlight poured in.

Emperor Koe eagerly stepped out onto the rocky shelf beside Kito. "Son ... you did it! You have me into the Valley of the Crystal ..." His voice trailed off as he paused. He was so taken with the view before him he didn't notice Kito sweating and breathing heavily.

Far below them was a huge circular valley. Small tufts of cloud floated around the top rim. A huge waterfall cascaded down the north wall into the lake below. In its centre sat a small island, covered only in grass. The lake drained into the stream that weaved around through the jungle before them.

The Emperor frowned. "I see no temple, Kito. Have you come the right way?"

Kito was studying the large footprints leading up the path to their position. He knew they were not his, but those of his father. "As you said, I have been here before Koe. Everything you seek is before you." He looked back at the unnatural cave they'd just left. "We may all die here today. It's not too late to return the way we came, Koe."

The Masters gathered around them nervously. The tunnel was open and inviting; they looked eagerly at the Emperor for his command.

"You got us thus far, Kito, now lead us to the Crystal."

Kito led them along the rocky ledge, down into the jungle. They eased through it without a path to follow until they came to the stream with its large, flat stepping-stones. He knew just downstream was where Mabutu had emerged to find the fire he'd left him.

Kito tracked on through the jungle, the sound of the stream now gone. The jungle was so dense they could see neither the lake nor the walls they knew were towering over them.

He slowed to a walk, then stopped at a perfectly smooth, rock path that led in a straight line with no visible end in sight. He stepped onto the path, and the Emperor followed without pause. The Grand Master gripped his sword tensely though he showed no hesitation in front of his men.

For some time, Kito led them along the path until the jungle gave way to the lake. It glistened in the light, though now a column of fog rose as far as anyone could see. Before them, a long, stone bridge stretched high towards the fog, getting thinner as it disappeared up into it.

The Emperor's eyes widened. "Well, come on, son, immortality awaits!"

"This place is not natural, Koe. I recommend we don't go any further."

The Emperor scowled. "Are you refusing to take me there, Kito?"

"No. I just do not see any point in all of us going."

The Masters looked hopefully at the Grand Master. He misunderstood them, stepping forward. "We will not neglect you, Emperor." He glared at Kito coldly. "No one truly serving the Palace would be so insubordinate. Even the suggestion is insulting."

Kito stood impassive as the Emperor sneered. "Kito, we wouldn't want any insubordination here today. So, shall we?" He waved an arm to invite him over the bridge first.

Kito stepped onto the bridge through the cool, damp air and led them silently up into the dense fog. Every blind footstep was taken with the greatest of care and concentration. By its peak, the stone bridge had narrowed until just wide enough for a foot. The descent was as long and arduous as the climb.

Eventually, they reached the bottom and, with just one step, they were out of the fog and onto the island. The fog was so impenetrable at the edge of the island, when they looked back, the bridge was not visible.

Before them soared the Stone Temple of solid rock that reached higher than anyone could see. Not one joint, not one fault, just smooth surfaces with perfectly rounded corners. Numerous stone steps led up to a large patio, surrounded by stone handrails.

The Emperor impatiently waved his hand to the Grand Master. "The Skulls, if you would." The Grand Master came forward with the three backpacks in hand. "Kito, you bring those and accompany me. Grand Master, you will stay here, and if I don't return, you understand what needs to be done?"

The Grand Master fingered the hilt of his sword with a thin smile.

With strides almost as big as his ego, the Emperor ascended the stairs. As Kito followed him, the twin swords began to pulse hot, and the Skulls in the bags pulsed in rhythm.

Kito drew a breath at the massive doors now pinned open. In his dream, he'd gotten out once, though that didn't guarantee anyone would be able to leave today. This time it was different; to the depths of his soul, he knew it.

Koe stepped through the doors, instantly disappearing. The Grand Master stepped forward, chin raised. Kito walked through, and he too vanished from view.

Kito took a moment to orient himself. It was the same huge room without windows, light with no shadows and the same seven corridors leading away, but for one stark difference. In the centre of the room was an enormous, seven-sided Sacred Crystal piercing up through the floor. Like the Stone Temple, the top of the Sacred Crystal could not be seen. It was Rani's Crystal from the cave. He looked about for her despite himself, though he knew she wasn't here, not now.

The Emperor came around from behind it. "This is it, Kito. This is the time!" He walked directly up to Kito, slipping out of his over-gown, revealing the golden plate over his chest. It now seemed to sit there almost perfectly.

Kito frowned. The Emperor's bracelets were pulsing with the chest plate. Dread shrouded Kito's being. It swamped him, carried by the hot blood that coursed through his veins. *Does the Emperor really have protection? Protection of the gold given by Sha'Doe? Maybe Koe will make a mistake and this dreadful moment will not eventuate.*

The Emperor grabbed a bag from him and tentatively removed a Skull. It glowed. Kito heard his name being called deep in the recesses of his mind.

Dropping the bag, the Emperor slowly circled the Sacred Crystal until the Skull throbbed its power. It pulsed so hard they could barely look at it. The Emperor stepped forward, taking a deep breath, and slipped the Skull into it. The Sacred Crystal shone so bright Kito threw up an arm, shielding himself.

The Emperor screamed. The Crystal glowed so intense it was like the sun was before him, then, as suddenly as it glowed, it went dull again. Kito could hear the Emperor breathing hard, hard like he'd just fought the greatest fight of his life. He could feel the swords pulsing on his back so hot he struggled to contain himself. He lowered his arm to see the Emperor walking towards him, stone-faced.

Kito held out another bag, and without hesitation, the Emperor removed the Skull, dropping the bag to the floor. Again, Kito watched in earnest as the Emperor walked around the Crystal looking for the signal. Kito had been so sure the Emperor would be turned to salt or be vaporised, or something. *This one will be too much.*

It dawned on him that the block was still non-existent. He didn't know if the storm he'd summoned that morning was still raging. He couldn't see anything outside the valley. Then it struck him. *She can't see anything inside the valley!*

The Crystal Skull pulsed. The Emperor stepped forward and placed the Skull in the Sacred Crystal. It immediately pulsed hard, and Kito had to cover his ears as it screeched loudly. He pressed his hands hard over his eyes, the impossibly bright light burning from inside his head. He could barely hear the Emperor screaming.

Kito kept his head down until it stopped. When he finally stood up again, the Emperor was coming back for the last bag. Somehow, he looked taller, stronger and younger. The gold chest plate was a perfect fit now. Kito silently called out. *Hasuca, do you bear witness to your brother?'*

The Emperor took the third bag and removed the Crystal Skull. It pulsed, its white eyes flashing as if communicating to the Emperor. He turned and walked directly to the right place and held the Skull to the Crystal. It throbbed, and the Emperor placed the Skull.

Kito immediately put his hands over his ears and, even with his eyes shut tight, it felt he held his face to the burning sun. This time the Emperor screamed so hard Kito could hear him over the Crystal. The noise intensified, and Kito fell onto one knee, his teeth clenched tight with the pain of it. He was sure his ears were bleeding, his eyes crying tears of blood.

Suddenly, it stopped, and silence hung. Kito removed his hands and eased up, searching the room. The Sacred Crystal pulsed with the swords on his back. The Emperor walked towards him, his face cold, and hard as stone yet he glowed gold and pulsed with the Crystal. He smiled at Kito, but there was no warmth with it. "It is time now."

"Time, Emperor?"

Koe laughed hysterically, but there was no echo, like the walls themselves absorbed the sound. "Oh, my Kito. You are so naive. It is time I killed you like I should have the first time you came to the palace ..." The Emperor glared at him through his glowing eyes. "... and lied to me."

"Is that why you sent me to work at the Colonial Dig, Koe?"

"No, fool boy. I had you sent there to see what you would do."

Kito frowned. "What was I meant to do?"

"Leave those worthless peasants and run on back to Hasuca. But no, like the fool boy you are, you stayed and worked." The Emperor took another step towards Kito. "Damn, you worked all day." He rolled his eyes "And then when I let the water go, you just dived right in. Why, Kito? Why did you do that?"

Kito wanted to answer, but his swords pulsed harder. They were so hot on his back he could barely resist pulling them out. "What did you mean, 'It is time now?'"

Koe took another silent step and sneered. "I am no longer Koe, and now we must spar ... to the death. Your ... meagre ... death." He leapt forward, sword suddenly in his hands, slicing down at Kito, who rolled to the side. He pounced to his feet, both swords in his hands, with the Emperor immediately over him.

With every defensive move, Koe rebounded at him, stronger and faster than before. Time passed, neither man letting up one ounce.

Koe neither sweated nor breathed hard. Stone-faced and expressionless, he kept coming at him. This was 'to the death' for one of them. Kito parried and countered his every move, but he saw no other way. He let Koe get in close and did a move he'd never done before. With his two swords, he locked Koe's long sword so they were all but touching foreheads. Using Koe for balance, he drew up his knee and slammed him in the ribs. The air whooshed out of Koe's lungs, a kick to the chest, and he toppled backwards. He rolled twice but could only get to his knees.

He glared up at Kito who stood over him motionless. "Damn you, boy, will you not finish your duties?!"

Kito hesitated. *What is he doing?*

Before Kito could move, the Emperor was on him again, but this time Kito was on the front foot, taking the fight to the Emperor.

The fighting was as intense as it was fast. A whirl of coloured garments diving and tumbling, they fought on. Kito was now wet with sweat, but the Emperor was dry and unmoved by the intense fighting.

Kito saw his opportunity. This time, he kicked out Koe's foot, and as he toppled off balance, Kito lunged forward, driving one sword down beside Koe's neck, past his collarbone, until all that remained was the hilt.

The Emperor screamed out and dropped to his knees. His long sword dropped to the stone floor with a clang. Kito wasted no time. He held up his second sword over the Emperor's other shoulder, looking him in the eyes. "How can one do that to his own brother?"

Koe wheezed. "It doesn't matter *how* one wins, all that matters is one *wins*. Today, fool boy, to win, I must lose."

Kito's mind reeled, confused with Koe's words. All he knew was that he had to finish it. "In the name of my second father, Hasuca, I give you this. Koe, you lose."

Outside, the Masters heard the scream of a dying man, then silence. They remained as unmoving as the fog.

Kito appeared from the Stone Temple, drenched in sweat, with his twin swords hanging down at his sides. They dripped with Royal blood. He glared at the Grand Master as he eased down the stairs. The moment he stepped to the bottom, the Masters lunged forward.

Kito's movement was shockingly fast, even to the Grand Master watching on. As suddenly as it started, it was finished. Kito was covered in blood and not one drop was his own. He sheathed his swords.

The Grand Master sneered. "Ah, the ignorance of youth. Best you be ready to be chopped." Kito pulled the leather strap from behind his back and wrapped the end around his left fist, letting the rest fall to the stone. The Grand Master taunted him. "And what are you going to do with that?"

"I told you when you killed Kinjo."

The smile on the Grand Master's face dropped. Without warning, he leapt forward, but Kito swayed gently to the side, watching the blade whisk past his face. The leather strap was already on its way. It wrapped around the Master's left arm, then Kito snapped it back, tearing off the sleeve before the Grand Master could react.

A thin smile creased the Grand Master's face. "It was a little warm anyway. And I didn't kill Kinjo."

Kito flicked out the strap in his left hand, but this time the Master stepped smoothly to the side, and the strap cracked like a whip. The Master smiled again. "You will need to do better than that, boooy."

Kito shuddered. The word cut him to the core. Suddenly, he was back on Tarrant's vessel, that nameless child that everyone made fun of.

The Grand Master had touched a nerve. "What, cat got your tongue, boooy?"

33 The Gods' Approval

The first rays of a new day shone over the Village of the Keepers. After the clear skies had given a cooler than usual night, a warm morning quickly developed. One by one, they convened at the fire. Everyone sat in their place, and the villagers were happy to serve them. Mercanti wasn't comfortable with it, but Tanica had insisted they do as all the men did. They would all be fighting in the same war in the end. Mercanti simply nodded, not wanting to dwell on it.

It was two days after their arrival when a messenger came to the village. The man trembled with spent nerves and dripped with sweat.

King Mabutu beckoned him. "Come to me. What news do you have for us?" The messenger looked at the strangers gathered by the fire. "Do not concern yourself with them; I have asked for the message, now what is it?"

"My King, they are coming across the desert. There are too many to count."

"How long do we have?"

"Three days, at most."

The King rose to his feet and spoke with strength. "My people, Village of the Keepers, it is time. Messengers, you know what I have instructed. You will leave immediately."

Baako slowly stood. "King Mabutu, I will ask before we leave, what have you instructed the messengers? Is this Kito's plan, or yours?"

Mabutu looked around the fire, everyone on their feet now. "I have given this great thought. Kobus and I have been over it many times. Our tribes will not sit by. They cannot be left out of the fight." Mabutu looked at the concerned faces. "If this is not to your approval, I will think nothing less of you if you leave now. Tanica and Yaan, I would almost *like* to see the two of you leave, either way, I have deep respect for both of you to have come this far." Without further word, he turned to lead the way.

King Mabutu strode away and Baako stepped in with him, Chief Kobus close behind. Feathers adorned the King's gown and head regalia. With his son and rightful heir by his side, they cut an awe-inspiring sight as they took up spears. Holding them firmly, they began thumping butts to the ground as they went through the village. The warriors came forward, dancing with the growing procession passing by, then falling in behind growing the line.

Yaan spoke over the roar of the village on the move. "My dear sister, you are brave, and of the two of us, you are the better warrior. For reasons I do not know, Kito wanted you here even more than I. Will you travel with me?"

Tanica stepped forward and put her right hand over his heart. "My brother, there is something special about you I cannot fathom. If this is to be our legacy, then so be it." Before he could so much as place his hand to hers, she turned and left for Mercanti.

Tzu nudged Hao and smiled. He returned a weak smile, and they all fell into the line.

As they waded through the river, Mercanti pointed. "Tanica, look! … high up on the mountain."

She took some time to focus then saw the strange storm. The sky was clear except for this small, intense storm hard against the mountainside.

As they walked on, Hao leaned forward and placed his hand on her shoulder. "If there was any question as to where Kito is …"

"How could you know *that* has anything to do with Kito?" she snapped.

"It has his name all over it. These are strange times, and he is right in the middle," Hao responded calmly.

"The only thing strange here is your blind love of the blood-thirsty traitor."

Before Hao had the chance to respond, Tzu jabbed him in the ribs. Hao let it be.

Once they'd entered the jungle, they began to trot. The singing grew louder as the warriors knocked their spears onto shields. The sound was formidable, and the jungle reverberated around them. Hao found it quite intoxicating. They didn't know what the songs were about, but they could feel they carried great power. Even the jungle seemed to be opening out for the King's men.

After a while some of the men dropped to the side to eat and drink. Soon enough, other men from the front would drop to the side and so on. Tzu and Hao decided to do the same.

Hao opened the small bag he carried over his shoulder. "Here, they gave me some fruit."

"Yes, me also, Hao. Have you seen such a thing?"

Hao was taking a drink. As he tilted his head back he saw someone looking back at him from high above. Water now trickling down his neck, he leaned to Tzu. "Look," he whispered, pointing high up into the trees, "I have seen something like these with Kito."

Tzu had his hand on his knife when a tall, lean man stopped before them. "It's an ape. You can leave your knife now. They have come to see but they won't interfere, luckily."

Tzu looked slightly concerned. "Luckily, why?"

"Because, my friend, unlike many of us, they are still connected to the land and everything on it. If they wanted us dead, we would be dead. Come, we must keep up." Instantly, the man was a part of the line once more.

Tzu quickly put away his fruit. "This is the strangest place, my friend."

Hao ate the last of his. "Except now I think I'm getting some idea of Kito and his ways. It is beginning to make sense. His lands, his people, are one."

"So are we, Hao, to a degree."

"Yes, but I would argue that compared to these people, we have, to a point, lost our way."

Tzu couldn't argue this. Without further word, they joined in the run. Maybe it was the jungle, maybe the fruit and water or perhaps the singing, but the visitors were amazed at how long they could run for. They were all still going strong at sunset when they stopped to make camp.

That evening, Tzu tried to get reasonably close to King Mabutu as he gave his overnight instruction. It was quick and clean. Tzu walked back to the fire, where Hao was getting comfortable. "Hey Tzu, are you happy with what's going on over there?"

"The King has …"

"No, Tzu, I saw you go over to listen. Are you comfortable with the instruction?"

"Yes, Hao."

"That's all I need. Now I can sleep, I hope you do also." He settled in with a sigh.

"And you also, Hao."

Tzu smiled as Hao put out his first snore for the night. He searched the trees for those eyes that were not human, yet somehow so familiar. They had captivated him, as had the warrior's words.

The next day, they were fed and on the move by sunup. There was little talk, but Hao and Tzu couldn't help but reconsider how they had journeyed and fought in the past. These people seemed so efficient. The drumming of wooden shields had begun immediately, and the jungle was again teeming with life. The apes travelled through the treetops with every bit of speed and agility needed to watch over them. To the visitors, the jungle seemed relatively unchanging. They travelled up over ranges and down through valleys, the streams always good to replenish water bladders.

Late on the second day, they came to a magnificent spot to camp. The locals cajoled the visitors as they stood, almost gaping, at the huge, deep-green lake. In no time at all, there was an abundance of fires going, and following their lead, the visitors made their own.

They were just settling down when a dark man came to their camp. "If you would please, the King has requested your company."

Mercanti looked up. "Just who would the King like to see?"

The dark man's white teeth shone in the firelight. "All of you."

A little perplexed, they followed the man through the huge gathering. Clearly, more tribes had joined today.

The King sat at a large fire, consorting with many chiefs. He stood. "Ah, here we are then. Thank you all for coming." He went on to make the introductions, finally resting his gaze on a woman they hadn't yet noticed.

"This woman, Shay, was a good friend to Chizoba, or *Kito* as you know him, when they were children." He placed a hand on her shoulder as if she were his own. "She, too, wanted the plans of Chizoba to be followed." He looked directly at Tanica. "Tanica, he asked that you and Mercanti go with Shay. Apparently, the three of you are pivotal in this battle."

Mercanti glanced at Tanica; she remained silent. The King encouraged with a gentle smile. "I have known this young woman her entire life. I know her heart, and I know her virtue. I ask that you go with her, though this must be entirely your own choice." Still, Tanica was unmoved. The King prompted. "Do you need time to consider this?"

Tanica shook her head, pointing beyond the King. "Can you tell me what *that* is about? It has been doing that since before we left the Village of the Keepers."

Everyone in the gathering turned to the storm in the far distance, high on the Great Dividing Range. Being so far up the mountains, it may not have been possible to see it, only for the constant lightning highlighting the clouds rolling and tumbling over and over. Immediately, talk began through the tribes.

Shay made her way around the fire. "I have spoken at length about you and Mercanti."

"You have only just arrived, Shay."

"No, Tanica, I have run with the King for some time today to learn about the two of you. Kito asked me to …"

"And where is this amazing man that everyone wishes to follow?"

Shay's beauty radiated as she softly spoke. "He said you didn't respect him; he also said you wouldn't be happy leaving your brother, Yaan."

"Shay, you seem to be a wise and beautiful woman. I think this is why Kito has chosen you to get Mercanti and I away from the others."

Shay raised her hand. "No, no. I'm not trying to separate you."

"Yet you are. Divide and conquer. It is the easiest way to take down any enemy. Even when we hunt, we separate one from the rest."

"But he has shown me how to use the …"

"No, Shay! Look, you seem like a nice woman, but I will not be separated from Yaan. I will be at his side when we walk into this travesty set by the Emperor. *My* Emperor." She glared at the King who, with Baako and Yaan, were the only ones not watching the never-ending storm raging fearlessly on the Great Dividing Range. "King Mabutu, if you have nothing else, I would like to rest. Tomorrow will be our biggest day."

Mabutu, who had bartered with many neighbours and kept the peace in his lands, knew when to let something go. Even with Shay's begging eyes, he dismissed Tanica.

Mercanti took Shay by the hands. "I wish I could've gotten to know you. I think we have much in common, much to share."

Shay could do no more than shake Mercanti's hands as she pulled away to follow Tanica.

That night at the visitor's fire, the feeling was solemn at best. The chatter and gentle laughter at other fires suggested their feelings were not shared.

Yaan went to sit with Tanica. "With the woman Shay, I thought you were very true."

Tanica looked to her only known family. "I wasn't rude again, was I?"

He smirked. "I think direct, and certainly honest." She smiled a little, and he clasped her hands. "Look, I thank you for staying with me on this endeavour. You understand why I'm doing it?"

"Because Kito said so."

"No, Tanica. Hao and Tzu also agree that this will be our last chance to stop the Emperor." Tanica shook her head, but Yaan continued, lowering his voice. "I don't even know what our Emperor is doing any more. He is certainly not a man I can respect, or a man I can follow with faith." He leant forward. "He released the water over his own villagers, burned his own city, and he is here leading those other tribes into this land that is not his and not theirs. Kito said those other tribes aren't even aware his Guard is here; they don't even know his full plan. You saw what happened at the palace. Tanica, can you honestly tell me this is a leader *you* can follow?"

She shook his hands in earnest. "All I'm hearing is Kito this, Kito that. Yaan, he isn't even here. I have grown up a maid, so even if I could get some to follow me into a civil war, I couldn't run the lands. Born a princess, maybe, but brought up a maid. I just wanted to know you. I just wanted to make you proud, my brother. Tomorrow, we are all to surely die."

Yaan held Tanica's face and stared into her deep, emerald eyes. "You forget, my sister, we fought in the palace shoulder to shoulder." He scoffed. "You dumped me on my ass in front of my own people. Remember?"

"I'm sorry for that."

He shook his head. "No, I deserved it. I hated it, but I deserved it." They chuckled together. "I watched how you handled yourself with the King, I also respect that."

"But you opposed me."

"It could be said you got a little, shall we say, passionate about it all, but the fact is, the King heard you."

"I don't care about the King. I don't even care for our Emperor. I just want you to know me and me to know you."

Now forehead to forehead, Yaan whispered, "And me also, my sister. Me also." There was a long silence. He pulled back so he could look into her eyes. "I hope the Gods approve of our actions tomorrow, so we are together in our next lives, my beloved sister."

They held each other for the longest time.

34 Demi-God

High in the Great Dividing Range, at the Valley of the Crystal, Kito faced the Grand Master Daiwa.

"What, cat got your tongue, boooy?"

Kito faltered and blinked once too often. The Grand Master swayed forward, sending his sword out in a smooth arc. Kito barely moved his hand as the cut straps fell away.

"That's it, boooy. This is why *I* am the only Grand Master here." The sword swept out again. Kito barely swayed away as it swept past his throat. He saw his blood blotch over the blade. The Master jeered, flicking the sword. Blood splattered over Kito's face, the dark droplets soaking into his grey gown.

The Master laughed again. Kito was taken aback by the speed of the man. The Master swept forward again; it was all Kito could do to move out of the way, but the Master was a move ahead, tripping him. Kito threw his weight forward, cartwheeling to his feet but the Master was already there, slamming the butt of his sword up under Kito's armpit sending him tumbling to the earth. Kito rolled to the side as the Master's sword slammed down onto the cobbles. He jumped swiftly to his feet, but the Master was quicker, kicking him in the jaw. Kito's head snapped back. He flipped back, trying to gain room to get his balance as the Master's sword swept down on Kito's face, and he felt the sting of a cut cheek, an elbow to the throat and a kick behind the knee.

He was at a loss for what to do next when the sun exploded behind his eyes. He held up an arm to cover his face. He tried to pre-empt the Master's next move, but all he saw was blinding, white light. Wind and dust swirled around him. Over the immense roar, he could barely stay on his knees as he was pelted with flying debris. Over the whirring wind was the sound of the Emperor's laughter far overhead. There was no stopping him now. Dropping his arm, Kito looked at the cut strap on the ground. The Master stood with his mouth gaping open to the sky. The laughing Emperor was a ball of light, speeding up towards the deep-blue sky.

Kito sprinted and dived for the strap, rolling to his feet as he turned to face the Master, who was right on his heels. He turned with a closed fist, and the Master ran right into it, his nose exploding blood over his face. He toppled to the ground, then quickly sprung onto his feet again, egging Kito on. "Lucky shot, boooy. Your last shot."

He cartwheeled to the side and came down low, sweeping his sword at Kito's legs. As the sword swept through at nothing, the Master looked up at Kito in mid-jump, his knees tightly up at his chest and saw the first strap sweeping down around his wrist. Kito's foot followed close behind, kicking the Master's hand and sending his sword skittering across the dirt. The second strap wrapped tightly around the Master's throat. Kito pulled him in and exerted a kick to the chest as the strap swept back out.

Instinctively, the Master pulled his knife in his left hand and drove it where Kito should have been. He wasn't there. A strap tore down his back, completely tearing off his garment. The Master spun, sweeping out with his knife, striking nothing. Kito stood just out of reach, still like a rock.

The Master sneered. "What's wrong, booo …"

The two straps swung in opposite directions and slapped across the Master's face, pealing at his skin. Kito was now a blur of movements. The Master felt the strikes he couldn't see. He heard his knife clatter across the stonework some distance away as he was pulled to one knee, then the other.

The Master's head pounded as he dizzily tried to focus on Kito standing before him. The last thing he felt was a strap bound around his throat, the other around his head and one foot against his chest. When Kito drew the straps back out, it spun the Master's head.

Death was instant.

Leather straps wrapped around his fists, dripping in blood, Kito stood over the lifeless body. In memory of Kinjo, Kito had fulfilled his promise to Daiwa. He felt the swords throb on his back. Dropping the straps, he stepped over the Grand Master and looked at the Stone Temple.

He stopped cold in his steps. The three bodies of the Masters were no longer there. Slowly, he turned back to the Grand Master. He and the straps were also gone. He marched up the stairs of the Temple and through the doors and gazed at the Sacred Crystal. It looked different and emitted a bright light pulsing like his swords, no *with* his swords. It now hovered over a huge chasm between it and the stone floor. If anyone were to have another Skull, they would no longer be able to reach the Crystal to place it in.

Kito walked to the edge and looked down the Sacred Crystal into the abyss. His chest heaved as he walked around it in disbelief. At no point could he get even close to reaching the Skulls. He wanted to remove them; he wanted to know if this would destroy the Emperor.

The swords now pulsed so hard, Kito thought they would burn his back. He began to walk away from the crystal, then, in a fit of anger, he spun about. Snatching both swords out, he sprinted at the Sacred Crystal. His scream echoed through the Temple as, with swords raised like long knives, he took a flying leap into the air, throwing himself at it. His focus was on the Skull as its eyes burned angrily at him. He thrust the two swords deep into it like death blows. It appeared to show two scars, but the eyes burned at him ever brighter and angrier. It screamed its protest as Kito slid down the Sacred Crystal, yelling like a warrior. Down, ever faster, he slid with the swords deep in it. The handles burned like white-hot coals in his fists. The hotter they became, the tighter he held. The Sacred Crystal screamed, and Kito screamed back, sliding downward at great speed.

He slammed down hard onto a stone floor

Retrieving his swords, he stepped back, wiping his sodden hair from his face. His chest heaved as he looked around, bewildered. *I know this place. I have seen this light before.* He spun around. She looked at him in disbelief, horror and shame. He stood before the most precious person in his life. His cheek trickled blood, his neck bled, and he was soaked with sweat. Still with blood-red swords in his fists, he fell to one knee. "Rani," he whispered.

Rani's dress was as black as the abyss. "Chizoba! What have you *done?*"

***

In the Stone Temple, the Emperor had felt every inch of Kito's swords as he drew them back out. He fell to one side as Kito turned and walked to the door. The Emperor watched Kito step out into the light, then he saw another light, *his* light. At first, it beat not unlike his own heart. As his heartbeat grew weaker, the light grew in strength, getting brighter, more intense with every throb. With every drop of crimson blood that trickled out onto the temple floor, the light grew brighter.

When the Emperor died, Koe the Demi-God rose from his corpse. Twisting and turning, he looked up as he became lighter and higher. He could hear his name being called. *Koe, Koe, Koe.* It was the Sacred Crystal calling him. The light of the Crystal glowed more intensely as it drew him in. He didn't resist. He could feel the gold burning into him. The immense power of the Sacred Crystal drew him in ever so slowly. Only with the chest shield and bracelets for protection could he control the power as it surged through him. He held his arms out wide, laughing hysterically. First his fingers began to break into particles, drifting into the Crystal, then his hands and his arms went to the light. Bit by bit, he was pouring into the Sacred Crystal.

Power like he'd never known surged through him. There was now no limit to his possibilities. He flew upwards through the ceiling and into the sky. Down below, the Grand Master was fighting Kito. He didn't care who would win. He could squash them both like insects right now, yet he realised they didn't matter. He laughed uncontrollably as he sped upwards – upwards to rule the Gods. He wanted to find dear, adoring Father so he could show him what a real man should have done.

He felt no restrictions. He felt no time. He felt totally in power, *his* power. He was Hannu Koe, a Demi-God.

35 Hasuca's Resistance

As Koe sped up into the heavens, he looked over the earth. "Demi-God at last! I have achieved what no other mortal could. I am the only one, the Chosen One!" He tumbled and rolled, screaming deliriously at the heavens.

The ball of light sped through the sky over Audun. As he passed over the desert, it swirled up behind him, a whirling mass of sand gathering at great speed.

Koe was learning a world without limits.

He saw Ezra's army and slowed, aligned himself with the sun so he could come in close and look over them.

They were a mighty sight. Hundreds of soldiers, all armed, with at least half on camels or elephants, crossed the desert. Koe knew he had many hundreds of his own army in the jungle. When the jungle people would come out to oppose the sand dwellers, his army would be there to squash the leftovers. He celebrated uncontrollably, waving his fists like victory was already his.

"My perfect plan, timed and executed to the letter!"

Without warning, a lightning bolt blindsided him, sending him tumbling down into the sand. The entire dunes trembled like the thunder had come to the earth, whipping up the sand and turning day into night. The sand blew over the armies, making the elephants and camels scatter in panic. In the chaos, riders were thrown to their deaths and the marching warlords were trampled underfoot. Their steel armour, designed to defend their bodies, were now contorted out of shape, crushing those same bodies in grotesque, unnatural forms.

Howling through the sky, two balls of light locked together over the armies, flaring up into the Ranges.

***

Down below, Ezra turned in horror. "What in the Gods was that?"

Trina's chains rattled as she shuffled up beside him. "What have you done? What have you unleashed onto this world?"

Ezra's eyes widened as he realised. "He always rambled on about it … I thought it was only legend."

Aitan's face contorted with anger as he grabbed Trina by the throat and pushed her down to the hot sands. "You brought this on us like you brought the man in grey. I know you are responsible for this. What evil is it?"

Trina looked coldly into his eyes as she gasped out, "You fool boy." She shook her chains in his face. "Does this look like I am in control? Does it!?"

Aitan turned to his commander as more screams from injured men carried on the hot, desert winds. "Will you get your damn men under control! If you can't release them from their armour, then release them of their misery!"

King Mensa, who had gone back to Ezra to avoid being caught between the commotion, grabbed Trina by the hair and dragged her to her feet. She could only wonder why, with all the unnatural violence and death that was going on around them, was he now laughing.

***

High in the sky, Koe wrestled with the other light. At first, he was confused, but then it dawned on him. He released the other and laughed. "Oh, you are so full of surprises, my dear brother. What are you doing, Hasuca?"

"Clearly, Koe, I am here to oppose you."

"Yes, though you never won over me before and you will not now!" Koe sped at Hasuca, but he swayed, throwing Koe to the side. Koe was ready for the move and counter-moved, throwing

Hasuca equally as hard.

***

Ezra craned his neck to the sky, watching the two balls of light tumbling erratically. Lightning versus lightning, the air was electric as the sky darkened, cooling the desert air. His skin prickled with fear and hope. He turned to move forward, then Trina caught his eye.

She shook her head. "What damned evil have you brought upon these people, Ezra?"

His hatred instantly inflamed. "This proves the legend to be true and real. I *can* get Rani back! I *will* take Rani home where she should never have left!"

"The legend …"

"I will crush your jungle like it did my daughter! I will swap your life for hers!" Standing over Trina, he shook with fury. "I will not stop until she is home with her mother, where she belongs. I will not stop until my daughter is back!"

Trina stood defiant, for she knew Rani could not be raised from the dead. This would mean war. A war her homelands were not prepared for. Like all wars, it would be a war that could have no good ending for anyone. With a firm shove, Mensa moved Trina on her way.

Ezra stormed away to lead his army. He could see the clouds of sand raised by the Sheik and his army not far away. Soon, they would join forces to face off against Zimbali.

Trina watched as the men regrouped. The elephants and camels were returned to order as whips cracked in the air. She looked at the countless corpses, crushed under hooves and feet. Men walked amongst the dead and, with bloodied swords, made sure any in pain weren't anymore.

The two bolts of lightning sped across the darkening sky as the clouds came lower and heavier. They ripped back and forth, sometimes rolling and binding together, sometimes clashing into

388

one another.

Ezra's and the Sheik's two armies slowly moved forward. Eventually, they met at the top of a long sand dune.

The Sheik marched forward and grabbed Ezra's shoulders. "What is this about, Ezra? Are the Gods against us?"

"The Gods are with us, Kohji." Ezra pointed to the blackened sky. "That is Koe! He *is* the legend of the Sacred Skulls!"

The Sheik leaned closer, lowering his voice. "I thought one had to be worthy?"

"All I care about is that he is on our side. Now he is waiting for us to crush Zimbali!"

Kohji desperately shook Ezra. "Zimbali did not *kill* your daughter, Ezra. If the Gods do not approve of this …"

Ezra's eyes flared, and he grabbed fistfuls of Kohji's garments. "If Koe is on our side, he can give me back my little girl!" Kohji broke Ezra's hold with a defiant shove, and Ezra stepped back and pointed to the thundering clouds. "Do you want to answer to *that*?"

Kohji looked up just as the two lightning bolts locked together, tumbling into the Great Dividing Range. Boulders cascaded down the mountains as the lightning bounced off and rushed back up into the clouds.

Ezra prodded Kohji. "See. He is growing impatient. We must keep moving!"

Kohji hesitated, conflicted. *Am I about to be a part of the biggest movement on earth, or am I just sending my loyal men to their unnecessary deaths?* Whatever the answer was, he was responsible. He looked at Trina. She had the look of despair as King Mensa dragged her along by her chains, laughing.

Ezra waved his army forward, then stood to the front of the Sheik's army. "March forward! Join with us this day and destroy Zimbali!"

The immense army began to move together. As it thundered forward, the dead and dying were left behind. High above, the vultures circled.

Hasuca threw Koe to the side. "You were my brother. I could never hurt you."

"Then why do you engage with me now?"

"Because you are no longer my brother. There is so much more than us at stake here, Koe. Never would I have thought you capable of this."

Koe pounded forward into Hasuca with all his might, but Hasuca swiftly threw Koe into the Ranges.

For every move Koe made, Hasuca counter-moved him twice as hard. Koe could no longer catch him out.

36 A Son's Betrayal

The drumming began from King Mabutu's fire. It was the signal to gather in the huge basin where they had stopped the night before. Tzu looked around the lake, surprised to see so many people there. There must have been many hundreds of men, so many that the outer crowds were obscured from his view. He was doubtful that they would hear the King's speech.

Baako stood at his father's side as the King began. "To all my lands, I thank you for your participation. My scouts tell me that for a full day now, the Gods have swept over the sands. The Gods are not happy with the invading armies. Many have already died. We will march out onto the sands and face this unwanted rival. We, people of Zimbali, will not sit by and allow this ungodly cancer to seep into our lands. This is our time to stand! And stand proud before them we will! March before them, we will! Engage with them, we will! Because we are the people of the jungle and this is OUR WILL!"

He thrust up a spear, proud and defiant. The people heard his call as it thundered over the lake, and the deafening drumming on their wooden shields was their united reply.

Tzu leant over to Hao and Yaan. "Not the most encouraging pre-battle talk I ever heard, but that drumming is powerful in any man's mind."

Yaan shouted over the rumbling shields. "If I saw these men coming my way … well, let's just say I'm pleased to be on this side."

Hao slapped his companions on the backs. "Well, let's go kick some ass!"

Everyone began to walk towards Audun. Without a word, the visitors stayed close to the King.

Singing and chanting, they ran through the elephant grass before breaking out on the dunes of Audun. King Mabutu walked to a focal point, looking down over a shallow but never-ending valley of sand that ran left and right as far as the eye could see. It took quite some time for the rest of the warriors to spread out along the dune on either side of the King. Stood with their spears, short bows and long shields, it was a formidable sight.

They watched the sand rising in the distance. As the invading army drew closer, the tribes began to sing and tap their shields. The sound would be heard for great distances over the desert.

Then silence fell as two bolts of lightning streaked across the sky. They went high up in the air, spinning and tumbling around each other before they struck down into the desert sands in the distance.

King Mabutu called to his people, his deep voice carrying over the hot sands. "You saw it! Even the Gods do not tolerate these hostile, aggressive acts against these lands and everyone who inhabits them!"

Collectively, the warriors thrust their spears into the air and began to knock them against their shields. The deafening sound thundered out.

The bolts of lightning shot up into the air, circling around and colliding into each other. Hao frowned. *This is not natural and nothing good will come of it.* The bolts streaked in the dense, black clouds rolling across the sky, ever lower. All eyes then fell to the horizon. The sand was once again rising. And again, the opposing army came.

Steadily, the dune opposite them filled with elephants. Armoured riders sat behind their heads and, from either side of the elephants, baskets carried men armed with crossbows and long bows. Camels carried riders, who sat between the humps, and men in baskets. The warriors of two large nations filled in the gaps between. The numbers simply dwarfed them.

King Mabutu's eyes narrowed at Sheik Kohji and the Pharaoh Ezra directly across the valley. Slowly, Ezra and Kohji's two armies stood before them. They were four times as many deep and three times as long, stretched across the dune where they stood.

Though men stood in front of Trina, she could make out Mabutu and Baako across the valley. Tears streaked down through the dust and grime on her face. They were so near, yet she was no closer to Mabutu and her homelands. She wept, shaking her head at this war of misguided men.

This was her new, worst day.

Vultures circled high above as if in readiness to pick at the bones of fallen men and an eagle screeched out over the now silent desert.

King Mabutu took a breath, his deep voice carrying across the sand rift as he called out. "We, your people and mine, have lived for countless generations in peace. If you needed something you asked and we happily gave. Now you stand before us armed to kill."

"You murdered Rani!" Ezra yelled back. "Do you call that neighbourly? Did any of us ask for this?"

"I loved your daughter and mourned her loss. I still do, Ezra. So do my people. We did not ask for her death, and we do not ask for this."

Ezra held his staff forward, his lean frame shaking with anger and hatred. "You *did* kill her! She was the princess of my lands. It is personal, and I will say if someone is to pay: YOU and your people will pay! Here! TODAY!"

"Did the Gods not just give you a warning, Ezra? Do you think today they turn a blind eye to your actions? No. They see all, and the casualties you've already suffered will be a fraction of what they will do if you don't come down into the centre and discuss this like we always could."

King Mabutu stepped forward showing good faith, encouraging the Pharaoh and the Sheik to do the same, then his blood ran cold as Mensa dragged Trina for him to see.

The Sheik stepped forward and Ezra swung his staff down into the back of her knees. She cried out and collapsed onto the sand.

Horrified at the chains and her bloodied face, Mabutu stumbled back as his entire world fell away from under him. Mensa stood square for everyone to see him in his power. Mabutu held out his arms. "In the name of our Gods, son! *What* are you doing?"

Almost ignoring his father, Mensa pointed his staff at Mabutu's confused warriors. "Mabutu is not your King! He has not been your King for a long time! I, Mensa, have united all these lands. As you can see, these leaders trust ME! King of Zimbali! Do not waste your time or your lives following this old has-been!"

Mabutu shook his head in desperation. "Son, that woman gave you LIFE! The Emperor …"

"The Emperor is a part of this unity. It is only you and you alone that stands in the way of this great move for my lands. Step aside, old man. Be gone like the desert breeze."

Ezra dragged Trina to her feet by a fistful of her hair. It was not heard what Ezra said to him, but Mensa smiled as he grabbed Trina by her chains and dragged her down into the valley.

Mabutu was about to go forward when a hand grabbed his arm. He turned to the stern, cold determination of Baako. "No, my King. This is to be sorted by the brothers." As he marched away, he called back, "There is many a thing to be sorted by these two brothers."

Mensa taunted Baako as he descended the dune into the valley. "Oh, my goodness me, look at you, Baako! Yes, I did make a mistake leaving you alive. Now you give me the perfect chance to rectify this." He sneered at Trina. "Yes, and you will be next, then all these people. The fools that they are will see who is most powerful. *I* am King of Zimbali!"

Nothing but the call of a vulture could be heard on the desert morning, through the distant rumble of the clouds. No one had noticed it growing darker. All eyes were on this one sight, these two powerful brothers.

Trina was again knocked to her knees. Baako walked slightly away from her, and Mensa laughed. "That is very cute, you actually think this is going to save her, you fool br …" Before he finished, he hit out with his staff, catching Baako off guard and hitting him under the ribs. He dropped down in pain, but at the same time, he caught the staff and, swinging his left forearm down, he smashed it in two. Quickly to his feet with half of the broken staff, the two men walked around, eyeing one another off.

"All those years you thought you were King, now you are to see the Gods put you where you …"

Mensa lunged forward, jabbing the broken staff at Baako. Baako swung his half down on Mensa's hand, who cried out and released the staff. As Mensa reeled, Baako swung his staff over his head and down onto Mensa's back.

King Mabutu's army cheered.

Aitan nudged his father. "Let me make them pay. I could just shoot them both right now."

Ezra shook his head. "Yes, son, but not yet. Mensa has the talk. I want to see just how good the man is."

Baako stepped back to let Mensa to his feet. "Come on, my brother, you have wanted this since we were children. I remember you once even tried to drown me, and you would have, but for the King." He pointed up the dune. "That King, the real King!"

Mensa never responded as he stood up straight. He lunged forward, throwing a punch at Baako. It landed heavily, but Baako gave two thumps straight back. On it went, neither taking a break, each punch thumping out the sickening blows. Mensa once again went down to the sand, and Baako again let him drag himself up with clenched fists.

Aitan nudged his father. "Now, let me go."

"No. Whether Mensa wins or not, we have Trina *and* both men down in the valley. King Mabutu can stand right where he is and watch the last of his family perish under my righteous fist!"

Getting up, Mensa spat blood and sneered at Baako. Baako pummelled his fist into Mensa's chest as Mensa turned slightly, deflecting the punch. He bent down, then threw a handful of sand into Baako's face. Eyes blinded, Baako staggered back, and Mensa lunged forward and gave him a full knee to the groin. Baako bellowed out, doubling over as he did.

Trina cried out, "Baako!" but she could do nothing as Mensa went to take up both pieces of the broken staff.

Ezra began to laugh. "Not the most admirable fight, but as they say, history is written by the victors. And today, we are going to be victorious!"

Mensa raised both pieces of the staff in clenched fists and, with all his might, he slammed them down into Baako's neck. The blood sprayed out and hissed as it soaked into the hot sand. Slumped over in the sand, Baako was to be with his Gods.

Trina's scream pierced the ears of everyone gathered there.

A murmur swept through the people of Zimbali. Ezra spun around to his trumpet blower and dropped his arm. The valley filled with trumpeting horns. King Mabutu ran towards Trina. All he could see in his despair was his first love, his Queen love, sobbing, confused and broken.

No one told Mabutu's warriors to charge, but, seeing their King rush forward, they just did.

Ezra watched as Mabutu ran at Mensa with a spear. It ploughed through his sternum as Mabutu drove it down, shouldering Mensa to the sand beside his own brother. Mabutu just got to Trina as the first arrows came down. He tried to shelter her, but it was futile. The sky rained with arrows. Ezra waved for the next onslaught and the elephant riders began their charge down the dune just as the jungle warriors crossed the bottom.

***

In the dark skies high above, Koe tried repeatedly to better Hasuca, but his efforts were futile. Needing to throw Hasuca off balance, he pointed down. "Look below you, Hasuca, now you see some of my power. Look! Those men don't stand a chance. My team *always* wins in the end."

"Yet you are losing, Koe. You are so tied up in your own ego, you've missed some important aspects you should have considered."

Koe threw back his head and his laugh boomed like thunder. "My dear brother, you are so naïve. You still refuse to see my winning side."

***

Tanica and Mercanti rushed forward with crossbows ready to cover Tzu, Hao and Yaan. Bolts protruding from their chests, the elephant riders couldn't know what hit them as they tumbled from their rides.

The three men were unstoppable as they headed directly towards Ezra and his entourage of Royals. Emotionless, Tanica took aim. Every shot had to count. Both women knew this.

Mercanti looked at Yaan at the front. Never had she noticed how he moved; it was familiar to her but, concentrating on her task, she could not think further on it. With Tzu and Hao either side, they left a trail of slaughter in their wake. Ever so close now, they neared the crest of the dune where Ezra and his counsel of men stood laughing, watching the jungle people of Zimbali being overwhelmed.

Kohji looked down to their left. "Aitan, look!"

Aitan, bursting to be a part of the destruction with his sword in hand, pulled his father back. Ezra turned to Aitan, confused, then saw why. Quickly, he turned to his captain.

Tanica was low on arrows and about to pull her short swords when something to her right caught her eye. Her eyes widened in horror, and she dropped her bow. There, pouring through the elephant grass behind them, were the Emperor's Guard. She was too late. The Guards had burst through the jungle, getting *down* on their knees and pointing raised bows.

Pulling her swords, she screamed at the Guard. Mercanti quickly rose to go with her. Tanica only managed two paces before a multitude of arrows landed so hard she staggered in her tracks. Mercanti tried to grab her, but she too fell to the ground. Tanica looked at Mercanti and the many arrows protruding from her. Her eyes welled as she rasped. "I am so sorry."

Mercanti almost smiled. "My princess, I have no regrets, I love you."

The princess looked up as the Royal Guard marched forward with swords to dispatch of them both. Mercanti's last thought was how strange it was that they were there to kill their own princess.

Ezra looked down the dune to the three men. They were some of the last, murdering their way up to his vantage point. For a fleeting moment, Ezra wondered what was driving these three? They looked nothing alike, yet fought like brothers. *How have they been the only ones to not be stopped?*

Yaan caught sight of Aitan and was almost in striking range when the arrows pierced him, knocking him from his feet. Stunned, his body went numb and would no longer respond to his wishes. He looked about for his devoted men. Tzu was on the sand with a man standing over him, pulling a dripping sword from his dead body. Hao had too many arrows protruding from him to count, yet to everyone's disbelief, he stood up. Strangely, no one stepped forward to finish him off; they all just looked at the man as he stood there defying death. Yaan heard Ezra call out, and a dozen arrows followed, slamming into Hao. He fell backwards, dead before he hit the sand.

Yaan's eyes glazed over. The fighting was finished, other than the odd cry from a finishing cut; there were no more left standing.

***

Hasuca smiled at Koe. "Yes. But you still haven't recognised the damage you're doing to your very own."

Koe stopped and thought. *Desora is in Middle Kingdom. Hasuca is playing games with me.* "You fool man, did you really think I would fall for that?"

Hasuca sat mid-air with his legs crossed, arms up opposing sleeves. "My dear brother, you were the smart one, but your ego, Koe, it has misled you. If only you could have controlled it, I think you really would've been a better leader than I. Look, Koe, look to the woman at the edge of the elephant grass. You remember her mother, don't you? Remember those beautiful, big green eyes. She really was something special. As are her *three* children."

Koe's jaw slackened as he swooped down to the two women lying together, their bodies full of arrows. Tanica was slumped out on the sand, her big green eyes open. Looking at the woman was like looking into Sha'Doe's own eyes.

"NO! This cannot be!" He spun back up to Hasuca. "How can this be?"

Hasuca nodded. "Yet there she is, now dead by your own hand. Look over there on the other side. He is the incredibly gallant and ever-brave Yaan. Born on the same day. Listen, Koe, listen to what he has to say."

Koe could not resist; he had to sweep in closer to hear.

***

Aitan walked down the dune with his sword drawn. "Now *that* is what we call a good outcome. The feeble opposition slashed from history and our leadership endorsed to any fool that believed they were too great to follow."

A soldier called out. "Sir, this one still breathes."

"Well, dispatch him, man."

"Sir, he said he wants to speak to you."

Aitan had begun to walk away. "What makes him think I would bother with him?"

"He says he is a prince, like yourself."

"Ha, you must be jesting me. Now *this* I must hear." He walked back down the dune to stand over the man who should've been dead several times over. "Yes? I don't recognise you." Then Aitan saw the eyes, the eyes of Prince Hasuca. "Might you be Desora by chance? Now that would be funny."

Yaan smiled weakly. "No. My name is Yaan. When you see Emperor Koe next, could you tell him the palace is now owned by the Northern people of Magnar and also, that Prince Desora is dead."

Aitan blinked back the news. His mind reeled at who the Demi God, now roaring about overhead, would hold responsible for this revelation. "Desora is dead? Does the Emperor know?"

Blood trickled from the corner of Yaan's mouth. "See the man behind me, with the hat? He killed Desora."

Aitan was impervious. "So how could *you* possibly be a prince?"

Yaan, his body letting him down, waved two fingers for Aitan to be closer. "On the other side are two women, one will have big green eyes. She, Desora and I are the children of Princess Sha'Doe. Desora is Koe's. I and my beloved, brave Tanica over there, are the descendants of Prince Hasuca. You have just murdered the last of his entire family. I'm not sure he will thank you for that." Yaan's breathing was ragged. "May our Gods forgive us all," he whispered.

The soldier looked at Aitan's stony face. "I am sorry, sir. He is gone."

Aitan sheathed his sword as Yaan's dying words rolled over in his head. "It will be your mission to find the woman he speaks of. There were two women shooting from the edge of the elephant grass, just behind where King Mabutu was. If her eyes are as he says, she should not be hard to identify. Have her brought to me, with this one. I need to know if there has been any truth at all here today."

A blood-curdling cry boomed from the heavens. The electric bolt of lightning that surged through the clouds caused the soldiers to hold up their arms to shield their faces. Aitan swore as he ran looking for Ezra. He topped the sand dune to see his father waving his arms and yelling instructions over the raucous thunder. "Father! Father, it is of no use!"

Ezra shouted back. "Son! What do you mean?"

Aitan frantically pointed to the sky. "That is not the Gods. It is Koe! It seems we've just killed two of Hasuca's children, and I think he has just found out Desora is dead!"

Ezra's face paled with realisation.

Kohji stared at Ezra equally stricken. "Dear Gods, what have you done, Ezra? Your hatred and ego have led us to do this!"

The valley of undulating sands was now scattered with dead men. Panicked in the lightning storm, the camels and elephants, mostly without riders, chaotically trampled over everyone and anything.

Out of the rumbling clouds, a lightning bolt surged down and struck the sand dune, ripping along it with deadly power. The men screamed in fear and pain. Koe would not stop until all life was obliterated.

37 Bending Time

Kito sprinted back through the tunnel to the outskirts of the Great Dividing Range. Nothing was natural about the dark clouds that loomed, or the lightning coursing back and forth. *I know who that is.*

The block was completely gone so Kito sat down and cleared his mind. He slipped effortlessly from his body, and he rose upwards. In dismay, he watched the disaster of catastrophic proportions. *What has gone wrong?* He searched the skies until he could feel Hasuca. *Master Hasuca, I know you are here. I must speak with you.* With a gentle chuckle, Hasuca was before him. Kito bowed reverently as always. The chimp walked to Hasuca and placed its hand on his shoulder.

"*I have told you there are no Masters up here.*"

Kito looked forlorn. "*What has happened down there?*"

"*Well, everyone is dying, Kito. Koe is killing the last of them as we speak.*"

"*Yet you sit here. What am I missing?*"

"*I'm afraid you have missed just about everything, young man.*"

"*What, how?*"

"*What was the advice you gave Koe on the vessel, about how to be there to carry out your own instructions?*"

"*I can't be everywhere!*"

"*True. But you have gone back in time, checking different things. Have you not, Kito?*"

Kito struggled to concentrate. He knew what it meant every time the thunder below them rumbled. Koe would take no prisoners. He could feel the death of every soul, cutting his own soul like fine blades. He pulled his attention back to Hasuca. *"Could you not just tell me what to do, Father? Tell me what I must do."*

"No."

Frustration rose in Kito but he did his best to suppress it. *"Can I stop him?"*

"Does it matter, this time?"

Kito held out his hands. *"He won't stop just here in these ..."* Hasuca smiled. Kito lifted his chin. *"At least, not in this ..."* He paused. *"... present time."*

"Now you have it, son. Time."

Kito gazed down at the massive storm below, then back to Hasuca. *"Please forgive me."* Before Hasuca could answer, Kito was gone.

Hasuca laughed, shaking his head. The chimp stood behind him, jumping and waving its arms. *"Still in a hurry, fool boy, when 'time' is his very asset."*

***

Kito returned to his mortal body and wrestled back in. He opened his eyes to the storm abating below. Koe was nearly finished, only searching for that one more life to extinguish, trying desperately to quench his anger and his grief. No amount of lives sacrificed could do that, but Koe would not stop until every single heartbeat had stopped.

Kito turned to the cove, which was made of perfect stone; it was open, and inviting. He took a deep breath and headed back in.

Once through to the Valley of the Stone Temple, Kito began to run down through the jungle. He set a good pace. Seeing some fruit, he called for some salmon to build his endurance. *If I am to get this absolutely right, I must be completely prepared.*

He ate the salmon raw and quenched his thirst from the stream then began his final run to the Temple, sprinting up the bridge without hesitation. He knew his destination: his *destiny* was at the other end.

Walking across the patio to the doors, Kito breathed easily, wiping his damp brow. He drew back his hood and calmly walked through the doors. He pulled Rani's crown off his left arm and sat cross-legged in front of the Sacred Crystal.

***

The dark clouds still swirled over Audun but, as the storm calmed, they came to a stop. For a brief moment, the clouds hung motionless as if suspended by invisible threads, then they began to drift backwards, faster and faster.

***

Kito led Koe through the mist, followed by Grand Master Daiwa and his three remaining Masters. Eventually, they stepped off the bridge onto the island. Impenetrable mist surrounded the edge of it though the island itself was clear. Looking up, they could see clear, blue sky. The temple stood before them, the numerous stone steps leading up to the grand entrance.

The Emperor stepped forward. "Let us wait no more."

Kito walked forward with him. At the top of the stairs, Koe hesitated before the huge doors, smiling broadly. He watched as Kito calmly walked to the side and took off his tunic, folding it neatly, he placed it on the wall. Koe looked at the leather sheathes strapped to Kito's back. "My grandfather made those swords, son. When he made their sheathes, he was apparently ridiculed as no one could fit the harness, it was far too large for anyone. He simply shrugged it off and put them away. Son, they fit you like a glove."

Kito said nothing as he walked out and stood between the Temple doors and Koe.

"Kito, is there something you want to say? I really don't have the time you know, my destiny awaits."

Kito remained unmoving. He stood in the centre of the doors, square to the Emperor. "I am afraid this will be the end for you, Koe."

"What foolery is this, boy?" he whispered with uncertainty.

"No tricks, no time wasted. You … cannot go any further."

The Emperor slowly held out his arm with the bag containing the Crystal Skulls. Uttah ran up the stairs to take them but before the Emperor released the bag, he cautioned, "See you are careful not to damage them. I will be back shortly."

Uttah had trained his entire life to serve the Palace but when he looked at Kito standing firmly before the Emperor, shirtless with the two swords strapped to his back, he was relieved not to be facing down Kito himself.

They had seen Kito and the Emperor spar before but this time was different. This would be real, and to the death. Uttah placed the sack at the bottom of the stairs and stood back with the others. They looked up to the terrace at both men standing still for the longest time. The Emperor unsheathed his sword; still Kito did not move. For reasons they didn't understand, Kito was already sweating. His muscled chest slowly heaved long breaths.

No one saw who moved first but with a clash of steel the match began.

The two men battled, swaying this way and that, using the walls to springboard off, or a roll to deflect a slashing blade. They fought at a pace that no one could endure forever. The Masters could barely see what was happening, other than neither hesitated nor abated. The black steel flashed in the sunlight, Kito's twin swords against the Emperor's long, curved two-handed sword. Koe was known for being deadly even with only one hand and was said to be undefeatable with two. Story had it neither Hasuca nor the Grand Master Xiang could better Koe with the sword.

Suddenly, the two men stood still, facing each other. Small beads of sweat speckled Kito's brow and his chest rose steadily with the heavy breaths. The Emperor by contrast was breathing hard. He glared at Kito. "You are fast alright, but you are short on moves. In finishing you, I will show you some more."

"I know your every move and more, Koe."

The two men stalked around one another.

"Oh, and how could you know my every move?"

"Because I was taught by your own brother, Hasuca." The Emperor's eyes darkened as hatred shadowed his face. Kito's eyes by contrast, seemed an even more iridescent blue. He flashed a smile. "Though the entire Middle Kingdom always knew Hasuca was better than you."

The swords clashed again, the two men fighting on. Now even the Grand Master doubted his own ability against either of these men.

Kito stepped back as the Emperor doubled over holding his ribs, his face contorted. Recovering quickly, he stood up straight and leaned his head, first left then right, stretching his neck with a click. "Not bad for a boy but I have more to show yet."

He lunged forward but immediately staggered back in horror. Directly against the Emperor's head was the handle of one of Kito's swords, rendering Koe's left arm useless. He swiped his long sword about in his right hand. "Now you only have one of those silly swords." He egged Kito on. "Come, come to me, my little apprentice."

Kito didn't move. The Emperor screamed, his long sword raised to strike. Kito's rapid response sent the Emperor's long sword rattling on the stone. The Emperor staggered then stopped, facing the Masters. Kito's second sword was embedded in Koe's other shoulder. His face, framed by Kito's swords, was a picture of shock and disbelief as it turned deathly white.

Kito grabbed Koe by the hair and pulled him onto his knees. "This is the training of your brother. He was always better than you; he just had more respect for his *only* brother. Tanica also had training from Master Xiang and although still young, she is better than I."

Koe's eyes rolled back as he struggled to focus. "Who … is Tanica?"

"She was born the same day as Desora. She grew up at the palace."

"The same day as Desora? To whom?"

"Sha'Doe gave her life also."

"Nonsense," he rasped.

Kito sensed the Masters were hastily pulling their crossbows behind his back. He only had a few moments. "Koe, remember going into the classroom one day, you stood over a very young woman and questioned her sums? That was Tanica."

Koe's body trembled. "*She* was Sha'Doe's daughter?"

"She avoided your eye contact because she has the same big, green eyes but yes, she grew up a maid, right under your nose. You know of the man with the eyes seen in Samos? They are full brother and sister of the same womb, of the same father." Kito watched as Koe remembered that day. "Yes, Koe, on the day of his birth, you dropped him in a bucket and threw him through the window. Remember the following spring ... no one could find the bucket? He is now a fine young man. Your Captain Chenghou also failed to kill him. He will be there to see me fend off your army that is, right now, crossing Audun."

"How do you know this to be true?"

"It matters not what one wants to be true, the truth just is." Behind Kito the Masters loaded the bows. "Koe, Banji did tell you Hao killed Desora, didn't she?"

Blood dripped from Koe's fingers. He slumped back on his heels, his body rendered useless. "Desora is ... no, no, he cannot ... he is my legacy!" He was now incapable of movement, yet the fury of the news was clearly visible.

"No, your *legacy*, Koe, is that you lost the palace to the Barbarians. *That* is what Emperor Hannu Koe will be remembered for."

For the first time, possibly ever, raw emotions etched Koe's face.

In Kito's minds' eye he saw a bow raised. A finger to a trigger, a bolt released. Two more quickly followed that. He swayed to the side. The last thing the Emperor saw was the Master down on one knee pulling the trigger. The Imperial bolt, complete with steel tip and the finest feathers laid back with maximum velocity, whistled through the air. It pierced his forehead, his head snapped back and he toppled over. The other two arrows, without target, disappeared into the Temple.

The Grand Master, filled with rage, swiped his sword and, with one slice, beheaded Master Uttah. Presumably, he had fired the kill shot.

The Temple shook violently, rumbling the ground beneath their feet. Kito covered his ears when the Sacred Crystal's scream pierced the air. As it glowed brightly, the entire Temple glowed with it. The two arrows flew out of the Temple, striking the two Masters holding crossbows. Instantly dead, they lay on the stone alongside Master Uttah.

The Grand Master watched Kito calmly descend the stairs. He swept his bloodied sword from side to side, moving his weight from one foot to the other like a slow dance. Kito kept his eye on the Master as he slowly drew out the leather reins from behind his back and began to wrap it around his left fist.

The Grand Master laughed. "You are a naive boy. With swords you may have had half a chance, but with that …" He lunged forward but Kito ducked as the long sword whisked over his head. He spun then stood still, waiting. The Master lunged again but Kito dived over him. The Master's head jerked back; his sword scattered across the stone. He grabbed at the straps around his throat but with Kito's knee in his back holding them tight, he was stuck. In two moves, he was overcome. As the straps ripped away, burning his throat, he stumbled sideways holding his neck. He gasped for air, searching frantically for his sword. He reached for it but the straps lashed at his arms, tearing away his clothing. Kito breathed deeply with the sweat glistening on his bare body. The Master struggled to talk. "How? How can you do this? It isn't possible."

"I was trained from just a boy in the jungle by no less than Prince Hasuca. Today, I do not carry the burden of ego. I do not carry the burden of arrogance."

"You are pure?"

"No. Though I am working on it. Hasuca taught me to carry as little as I can. I still have far to go."

The Master shook his head. "No. I don't think you do."

"Your biggest mistake was who you backed. It was an easy one to make with your choices at the time, but your ego wouldn't let you undo that mistake when you realised it to be so. You have carried it for years. For years you have *known*. When we arrived here, even I waited to see if you would stop the Emperor."

The Master lowered himself to his knees. "Finish this."

Kito picked up the Master's long sword and gave the misguided Grand Master his rightful death. His headless corpse slumped to the side.

Kito dropped the long sword to the stone. He turned around to see all the dead were now gone.

He returned inside the Temple. The Sacred Crystal gently glowed. He walked around to the back and there was his own form, complete with tunic, sitting cross-legged with feet up on knees and his hood raised. His head was lowered so it just touched the Sacred Crystal and Rani's crown was still in both hands. He smiled as he went to it and eased back into his mortal body.

His secondary plan to stop Koe was not required.

Complete again, Kito went outside to fetch the saddlebag. The Skulls pulsed gently as he picked them up. He ascended the stairs to the chest plate and bracelets. Everything else that was once Koe was gone. He took it all into the Temple. Standing inside the doors, he looked at the Sacred Crystal. The chest plate and bracelets pulsed in his hand, keeping rhythm with the swords in the saddlebag. He looked down at them, unsure what he should do next.

Kito's mind now raced over his conversations with Koe, Rani and Hasuca but he could think of nothing to give guidance, here and now. As he searched for answers, Rani appeared by the Sacred Crystal. Kito immediately went to one knee. "Mother. I had no idea you could be here."

Rani seemed to glide as she came to him. "Chizoba, please stand before me." He did and Rani reached up to wipe the sweat from his brow. "You have worked hard."

"They were the best …"

Rani shook her head, silencing Kito immediately. "No, Chizoba. Everyone who has stood before me in the cave below, has had a story of you, my son."

Kito shuffled nervously. "Mother, once again I don't have much time."

"On the contrary Chizoba, I see you can *control* time. It is most impressive."

Kito grimaced. "Could you call me Kito?"

Rani's laughter filled the cavernous room. "Certainly not."

"You told me you could see nothing out of the cave?"

"Though clearly, Chizoba. I am not in the cave anymore," she graced her hand about the Temple, "It seems I have been given more space."

"How is this? I mean, how did you get to be in here?"

Rani shook her head with a smile. "Chizoba, the cave is directly below this Temple. This Crystal and the one you saw when visiting, is one and the same."

"But how is it you are up here, now?"

"You sound disappointed." Kito shook his head so vigorously Rani giggled. "Take it easy, son, it was only a jest. I don't actually know. I think when the Emperor brought the Skulls here, it awoke the Sacred Crystal to a new level, the next thing I knew, I could move up here. Now I am here I'm seeing many things, though only relevant to the Skulls." She motioned to the doors. "Come, walk with me. Show me what is outside."

Kito walked with his mother. The Skulls and gold throbbed as he left them behind.

"This is going to be a treat for you," he said gently. "So, you can tell me what to do then? What is right?" Rani laughed again. Kito liked the sound of it.

She took him by the arm as they stepped out into the sunlight. "No, Chizoba. I will not." She looked to the grass and the lake beyond, "Oh my, I do believe this *is* a treat."

They talked about where, in relation to Zimbali, the valley was, though Kito also knew his work was far from done. He knew the Emperor was dead but the armies still marched to destinies not of their own doing.

"Mother, I must leave now. I have much to do yet."

"Chizoba?"

"Talking with you now has cleared my head; I know what must be done."

"No more bloodshed, son?"

"I will be working hard to avoid it."

"Yet you make no promise, Chizoba."

"I can promise to return." Kito looked about. "I like your new home. I feel it is more suited for a princess."

Rani's laugh was full and unrestrained.

***

High above, the eagle floated majestically on the light breeze. The trees bent gently then settled motionless, not a rustle of a leaf or a bend of a branch. The outstretched wings of the eagle stalled momentarily then flapped once more but this time, the eagle flew backwards. Backwards over the Great Dividing Ranges, backwards towards Zimbali.

King Mabutu, Chief Kobus and all the visitors were sat around the fire at the Village of the Keepers.

Tanica stood defiant. "Where was Kito when you were captured in Samos? How did they know about you there, brother?"

"Kito wasn't even there."

"How could you know where Kito was, hey? Where did he go from the vessel? Can anyone tell me how he got off the vessel in the middle of the ocean?"

"Well, Tanica, I am here now." A deep voice resonated behind her.

The King shot to his feet looking at the guards with a questioning face. They were just as surprised as any. Kito pulled back his hood as he approached the King. Kneeling before King Mabutu, he took his hands and kissed them both.

"Stand before me … Kito."

Kito did so, his eyes fixed on the King's. He towered over Tanica and she stepped back a little flushed. There was something in the way she moved that caught Tzu's attention. He watched her body language carefully then smiled. *Well, I never saw that one coming,* he scoffed inwardly.

The King waved for everyone to sit. Stepping to the side facing Tanica, Kito dipped his head. "I understand why you think the way you do. I also want you to know, I respect your opinion. Please accept my apologies for your bad feelings." He dipped his head again and moved on before she could answer. He paid his respects to everyone else. "Please accept my apologies for being late. These are important times." He then knelt before Baako and kissed both his hands.

Baako pulled Kito to his feet. "You kiss the hands of your own brother, Chizoba?"

"I show the respect to my older prince, second for the Kingdom." Before Baako could respond, Kito went to Kobus and touched his forehead to the back of the chief's hands.

Baako looked at the concerned frown on his father's forehead. Mabutu didn't know what to make of this man that was his son but wasn't. Even by name, Kito wasn't his son, yet when he looked into his eyes, it was undeniably him. Somewhere deep inside, it was Chizoba.

King Mabutu cleared his throat. "Chizoba, almost everyone seems to trust your point of view on this. Can you fill in some gaps for us?"

Kito nodded. *Anything to avoid answering Tanica's questions about me getting off the vessel.* "In two days, we will get a message that an army, the size of which we've never seen the likes, is getting close. We will leave immediately. Two days travel. At our second camp by the green lake, we will have the favour of Shay with us. She is imperative to this, as is Chief Kobus and his leadership of your warriors." He looked into his father's eyes. "We can win this, but I can only see it working this one way."

Kobus sat forward. "That is not much to go on, Chizoba."

"It is all I have to offer you."

"You want your father, brother and these friends of yours, to stand off a million soldiers?"

"Tanica is right to doubt me. She is also right to say I have sparred with Desora in the palace, but she doesn't know how many times I have tried to sway the Emperor from this. I tried to sway the Emperor because in the eyes of the Gods, it is not right. In the eyes of the soldiers crossing the desert, it is not right. I see no other way than to have faith. Have faith in your people, have faith in your jungle and have faith in your Gods."

Kito's words hung in the silent air only broken by the gentle crackle of the fire. There was little anyone could say to that. Even

Tanica had been silenced.

***

As Kito had said, the message came in two days. They were ready and on the track into the jungle in just moments.

From time to time, Kito ran with Tanica and Mercanti, always his hood up. The women got used to having him around, though Tanica couldn't fathom why he ran with them.

On the second night they made camp on the shore of a huge, green lake. Once the visitors were settled around the fire, food was offered but not much was consumed, even Tzu ate light.

Kito stood up. "Friends, tomorrow we will meet our purpose. Could you all please join me at the King's fire?"

Hao sat up. "What, now, Kito?"

Kito grinned. "Yes I'm afraid so, Hao. It is important for us all."

With groans, everyone was up on their feet. Mercanti tugged on Tanica's sleeve. "Do you think he means us?" she whispered.

Kito called from the front. "Yes, Mercanti. Could you and Tanica please walk with me? This will concern you both directly."

Tanica scowled but Mercanti giggled as they made their way forward, Kito winding his way through the crowds of people around countless fires.

At the King's fire, Kito waited for him to stop talking before addressing him. "King Mabutu, this will be our last chance to talk, if you would like to?"

The King sat still for a moment. "Well yes, Chizoba, we were just talking about you, I was about to send a messenger but you have saved us the trouble."

"And the time, King."

The King waited as Kito made a point of sitting the two women between himself and the King. Mabutu gazed around the gathering. "Visitors, I thank you very much for travelling to be here. Tanica and Mercanti, it has been as challenging as it has been a pleasure to have the two of you in our company, though I do have a special request." Anticipation hung over the King's fire before he continued. "Tanica, I cannot tell you how important this is to the entire mission." Mabutu looked over the gathering. "Where is Shay?"

A woman on the other side of the fire stood up. Tanica thought she was rather tall and gangly, Mercanti saw right away she was totally beautiful. "My King, I am here."

"Tanica, Mercanti, will you please spend some time with this lady at dawn. She will find you at your camp."

Tanica's posture immediately stiffened. "What is this about, please?"

The King took his time to answer. "As I have stated, Tanica, what this woman has for you is of the upmost importance. She will see you in the morning."

"My King, may I speak?"

Mabutu turned to Shay. "Yes, Shay?"

Shay looked at Tanica. "I know why you have come here. I know a little of your past with Yaan. I think you are as brave for what you did in Samos, as you are to have come all this way for your brother. If it pleases my King, I will speak with you tonight?"

The King frowned. "Why would you wish to do that?"

"If it pleases the King, I think if I were Tanica, I wouldn't want to find out my fate on the day. I would rather know, to at least feel prepared. I think they both have the right."

Mabutu was watching Tanica as Shay spoke. "Very astute, Shay. Would this please you more, Tanica?"

"It would please me a little, King Mabutu."

Shay made her way around the fire. Kito stood, grabbing Tanica by the elbow. Once they were clear of the greater crowd, she snatched it away. "You will not handle me like one of your harlots!"

"And you should watch your tone with the King. You may have lost your respect for the Emperor but King Mabutu is not the Emperor and this is not Middle Kingdom."

She pointed her finger into Kito's grey hood. "*You* don't get to lecture me! You hear me?"

Shay was just catching up. "Tanica, I think the entire camp just heard you."

Mercanti followed. "Yes, Tanica. Come on, let's just calm down for a bit."

Tanica scoffed and began to walk away then spun back to face Kito and stamped her foot. "Tomorrow we are all going to die. All I wanted was to be with my brother, now you want to take that away too." She trembled with anger as Mercanti tried to comfort her.

Kito walked with Shay to give the two women a little space. "Shay, you are as beautiful as ever; you are positively glowing. I must also say, the way you spoke with Tanica, very wise."

She slapped him on the chest. "You always were the silver tongue." She reached up and pulled back his hood. "Now you may be seen as human, and I know you are human, Kito, you just try so hard not to be."

"I do not!"

She prodded him. "Yes, you do and you know it."

Tanica watched them over Mercanti's shoulder. She frowned, confused at her own response to Shay and Kito laughing and joking. She stepped back from Mercanti. "Whatever happens, know I love you for this."

Mercanti squeezed her hand. "It's alright, Tanica, it's alright." Hand in hand they walked to join Kito and Shay.

Tanica asked, somewhat sarcastically, "The two of you, may I ask what your amazing plan is?"

Kito escorted the three women back to the fire; it was just the four of them as he had hoped. "Tanica, do you remember the time you were training blindfolded with Grand Master Xiang? He accused you of cheating when you used the rat to see with?"

Tanica's lungs seemed to lose all air as her mouth dropped open. "How could you possibly know about that?"

"Please, Tanica, we don't have an awful lot of time. Can you remember exactly the time I refer to?"

She'd heard all the stories about Kito, but there was no way he could have known. She took a calming breath. "Yes, I remember."

"Good. This is the skill we need you to use tomorrow, but it will not be with Yaan. I think you already know this, don't you?" His blue eyes cut her to the core as he continued. "You understand that I believe you are the only one that could achieve this?"

She tilted her head. "No, I'm sure you exaggerate."

"No, Tanica. It is a family trait, just like the Royal family is the only one that can make the black steel. Hasuca was very strong with the talent, which is where you and Yaan got it from, though he has no training. For now, you are the only one. I know this. I have searched far and wide for these skills."

Mercanti softly cleared her throat. "Kito, may I ask?"

"Anything, Mercanti."

"What does this have to do with me? Why am *I* here?"

Kito reached out and put a hand on hers. "Without you and Shay, Tanica cannot do what must be done either. I have brought the three of you together for this one, specific, task."

Mercanti looked at Tanica confused and concerned. Tanica tried to clear her head and refocus. "You didn't want Yaan – you wanted me all along," she whispered.

Kito smiled. "Yaan is a very important part of the group. Never underestimate the power of a well-rounded group. Sometimes if you take or add just one person within the group, you change the dynamics and it won't work. Yaan has a very strong place in this group."

Shay leant forward. "Chief Kobus has told of some of the stories of what that group has done in Samos. Kito, how do you fit into the group?"

"I am not a part of the group myself. I'm afraid, I don't seem to fit anywhere. I was hoping for a better result here." He looked down. "It seems that if you've been gone for long enough, you can't fit back in." He shrugged his shoulders.

Shay reached out and put her hand on his arm and whispered, "Dear Chizoba, what did they do to you?"

Mercanti spoke quietly. "I heard that name before, Kito. How is this?"

Kito batted the air with his hand. "I have a name in Middle Kingdom and another here." He smirked. "It's most confusing."

They laughed together. Even Tanica smiled a little, keeping her eye on Shay. Kito offered to walk Shay back to her own camp. She gleefully took up the offer, putting her arm through his as they walked away into the night.

As expected, Tanica was not to sleep that night.

***

Not long before daybreak, Shay and Kito returned to the fire. Tanica and Mercanti were already up.

Kito stoked the fire. "Shay, you will be able to find the Sacred Tree, won't you?"

Shay sighed, rolling her eyes. "Must we go over this again? I was there yesterday. We will be there and ready before you break out of the elephant grass."

"Good, see that you are." Kito studied Tanica and Mercanti. "I hope the two of you slept well, you will all need your energy to help us today."

Tanica refrained from spitting into his hood. "And where will you be, Kito?"

He looked directly at her with his piercing blue eyes. "*I*, Tanica, will be putting myself right in the middle of those arguing fools."

She found herself disliking him even more. "Good, Kito, see that you do."

Kito rose smoothly, whispering quietly as he walked away, "Good luck today, ladies." His grey clothing melded with the morning mist swirling off the lake. It was difficult to know where he had gone.

418

"What was that about?" questioned Mercanti.

Tanica gathered up her water bottle and food bag. "He just gives me the shivers." She suddenly realised what she had said. "Oh, the Gods, do forgive me, Shay, I'm not usually this awful."

Mercanti scoffed. "Yes, she is." Tanica gave her a cold look as Mercanti poked out her tongue.

Shay frowned, shaking her head. "Are the two of you ready?"

Tanica stood. "Shay, the two of you grew up together?"

"Yes. It was Chizoba I grew up with. I just don't know about this Kito, as he is now. Come on, Tanica, we can walk and talk." Mercanti approached and Shay smiled at the beautiful woman. "Are you ready, Mercanti?"

"Yes, I think I'm as ready as I will ever be."

As they strolled through the camp, Shay talked of how Baako and Chizoba had gone missing, then Rani and Mabutu had also disappeared and in a little time after, Mensa was running all of Zimbali. It was a brief, dark history of their lands. Shay thought it right for them to know. Soon enough, they were jogging single file along a jungle track and it wasn't long before Shay slowed to a walk.

***

Chief Kobus shook wrist to wrist with the King. "May the Gods be with you."

"You have been ever loyal and honest with me. You are the best a King could ever want." King Mabutu released Kobus, his large strides defined with purpose as he walked away.

Another chief leaned in close and whispered to Kobus. "Was that the kiss of death for him, or us?"

Kobus slapped his comrade on the back. "Come on, my friend, we must prepare."

***

Mercanti craned her neck, still unable to see the top branches of the ancient Sacred Tree that stood before them. Its gnarled trunk, far wider than anything in the surrounding jungle, had sunken its roots deep and widespread into the earth beneath them. For centuries it had borne witness to the inhabitants that had come and gone. As it would today too.

"Wow, how old is this?" she gasped.

Shay shrugged. "Kito said it's over a millennium old but I don't actually know where he got that from." There was a rustling through the jungle and Tanica abruptly spun on her heel, her knife in hand. Shay grabbed her arm. "Easy, girl, they are here for us."

The ground vibrated beneath their feet as hundreds of jungle warriors appeared through the dense foliage. Bare-chested with paint smeared across their faces, they circled the enormous tree. It was with relief that Tanica and Mercanti saw Chief Kobus among them, though his eyes seemed glazed over and unfocused.

Shay began to ascend the broad branches, each knot on its trunk providing ample foothold. "Come on, we don't have much time."

The three climbed up into the broken crown. Mercanti gazed around in wonder. "How did you find this place?"

"Kito brought me here. Please, sit with me."

As Shay sat down she removed a bag from her shoulder and pulled out a large candle, predominately red with slithers of orange and yellow through it.

Mercanti held out her hands for it. "Shay, I have never seen such a candle; ours are just white."

Shay pulled out a flint. "Mercanti, when you are ready, could you hand it to Tanica. It is important that you both handle it." She put her bag aside and rose as Mercanti watched her go to the edge of the tree and look down.

Mercanti passed on the candle and eased herself up to stand beside her. "What are they doing?" she whispered.

Tanica quickly went to see, still holding the candle, and peered down below. "What in the name?"

Below them, the jungle warriors sat with legs crossed and arms over the shoulders of the man either side of them. They formed a solid ring of men facing the tree. This ring of warriors was circled by another ring and another. As far as they could see through the jungle clearing were warriors.

Shay turned back. "Come. They have begun for us."

Back at the centre of the tree, Shay lit the candle and placed it in the centre. She reached out her arms. Following the lead of the men below, Tanica and Mercanti joined with Shay, each resting their arm across the shoulder of the other. She gave them a little smile. "Other than what Kito told me last night, I know very little about you."

Tanica held her tongue. This wasn't the place for jealous comments.

"Last night, Kito instructed Chief Kobus and I to do what is happening below. I will give you one demonstration of what he has taught me, then we must do our task."

Mercanti giggled nervously, but Tanica sat emotionless, staring at Shay.

Shay focused on the flame and breathed out long and hard. "Alright, girls, we can do this. Just watch the flame please, watch the candle. That's all, just watch the candle ..." Her words drifted off, eyes closed, her full lips parted slightly. "Watch the candle ..."

The candle burned steadily as a low humming drifted up from the warriors encircled below.

The men had their heads back and swayed from side to side as they hummed. Mercanti squeezed Tanica's shoulder. She looked back, shaking her head briskly. Mercanti frowned and watched the candle again. With a sigh Tanica looked at the candlelight competing with the morning light. It flickered without any wind then swayed slowly from side to side.

They watched as it slowly grew, growing brighter and stronger. Their hands began to tingle as the flame swayed and grew, turning in spirals as it reached higher. The tingling spread up their arms as the rhythm of humming from below grew louder, more purposeful. Neither woman could move their eyes. Even if they had wanted to, their eyes held, transfixed, to the growing flame.

Their entire bodies began to tingle and the ever-larger flame swayed gently with the humming of the jungle, intoxicating. Tears began to trickle down Tanica's face. Confused, she couldn't remember the last time she had shed a tear. She allowed her head to fall back and saw hundreds upon hundreds of butterflies above her, swarming in a spiral as they descended closer to the Sacred Tree. She squeezed Mercanti's shoulder tightly.

The sky blackened from the sheer number of butterflies as they descended on mass. Tanica thought they would be burned by the candle's large flame as they settled, covering their arms, legs and eventually their entire bodies. The weight was tiring though neither woman wanted them to leave. Still holding shoulders, Mercanti watched the butterflies fluttering their wings. All the wonderful colours of nature were represented, even the most translucent, clear wings flapped delicately around them and the candle flame.

Then, as quickly as they had appeared, they began to spiral back up. Mercanti watched with disappointment as the butterflies swirled around them for the last time then disappeared through the upper branches. They dissipated back into the jungle like they'd never been there.

Shay opened her eyes. Mercanti put her hand over her mouth as she whispered, "Never, ever have I seen … Shay, you did this for us?"

***

King Mabutu walked out onto a sand spur. Ahead of him, a wide, shallow valley ran from the Great Dividing Range to the ocean. Baako, followed by Hao, Yaan and Tzu were behind him.

"Where is Chizoba … anyone?" The men looked about, then shrugged. The King swore, shaking his head. "Entire nations are resting on this one day. All of Zimbali have put their trust in him, and he's late for his own plan." He grizzled some more, then heard a small commotion behind him. He frowned at the sight of his men shouldering a large, wooden chair. "What is *that* for?"

422

The men looked at one another a little bewildered as a few more men came forward with a shade-canopy. The King thrust his fists onto his hips. "What is this about … anyone?" The men hesitated, awkwardly wondering whether to continue forward or make a hasty retreat.

Kito emerged from the crowd. "Every good King needs his throne; some shade in this hot sun won't go amiss either. We can't have our King getting burned now, can we?" A nervous chuckle went through the men close enough to hear it. "It is here now, King Mabutu, so please, seat yourself."

It was a cool-looking King that glared at Kito, then sat down with a grunt. Kito placed a water-jacket beside the throne, straightened the King's gown and stood back to see that the setting was good. He then nodded to the men, and they left. Now it was just King Mabutu, Baako and the visitors.

The day was clear; not a single cloud floated through the blue sky. The sands were growing hot already as the sun beamed overhead. In the distance, dusty plumes of sand rose from the desert, though it seemed that the procession was getting somewhat slower. Vultures circled overhead.

Kito leaned to Baako. "Not a good sign for them, is it? I hope they aren't struggling with this heat." Seeing the smirk on Kito's face, Baako raised an eyebrow.

Sometime later, an eagle screeched on the hot currents well above. Kito smiled. *I know who that is.*

Watching the procession lining the dune opposite them, the King shuffled about in his seat and groaned, trying to get comfortable. It was an army far greater than they could ever imagine – elephants, camels and armed men on foot. This was what an army a million strong looked like.

From the moment the first men began to arrive, Kito had stood motionless with his head down. At one point, the King resisted the urge to shake him, just to appease himself that Kito wasn't actually asleep standing up.

As the army gathered along the opposing dune, a shirtless Mensa appeared amongst them.

Mabutu went to stand, but Baako quickly put a hand on his shoulder. "No, my King, this is my duty to the throne."

Kito slowly lifted his head. "No, Baako, you are next in line to the throne. This is my duty first."

***

Still transfixed from what she had witnessed, Mercanti awaited Shay's response.

She shook her head. "No, *we* did it." She looked at Tanica. "But now with the help of the men below, we must do so much more."

Tanica pulled her hand back. "How much more, Shay?"

"The men are down there to build the vibration for us to perform on, Tanica. It is our job to intervene the Royal Guard from your homelands. Do you understand this?"

"Will we have to slaughter them?"

Shay reached out. "No, no, Tanica. Our job is to put a barrier before them, that's all … hopefully."

Mercanti dipped her head, concerned. "Hopefully? What exactly does *that* mean, Shay?"

"I have no control over how they will react to our barrier. Providing they stop, or even retreat, not one drop of blood should be shed."

Tanica's eyes narrowed. "And if they advance?"

"I am sorry, but they cannot win."

Tanica put her hand back on Shay's shoulder. "The Royal Guard has no right to be here; let us just hope they stop, for their own good." She shook Mercanti's shoulder. "You alright, sister?"

Mercanti took a deep breath. "You are right, Tanica. Let's do this."

There was something in the look Mercanti gave Tanica that left Shay questioning. She shook off the thought; this wasn't the time. "Do you both trust me?"

"Well, it's a bit late for that, isn't it?" Mercanti responded.

Anger flashed over Shay's face. "No, Mercanti. You must get yourself into a comfortable and peaceful state of mind. We must be fully united."

Tanica intervened. "I'm alright, Shay. Mercanti, I think I'm getting this. You do trust *me*, don't you?"

Mercanti nodded, turning to Shay. "I will follow you with your every move. I'm good."

"Whatever happens, we must stay strong. Whatever happens." Shay let out a heavy sigh. "We will only get this one chance. We must be as one, or all will be lost."

She looked down at the candlelight, barely seen in the growing daylight. The tingling began to grow with the swaying flame. This time, they were surprised at how fast and how strong it grew. The hum of the tribesmen grew louder as the flame intensified and the tingling sensation increased throughout their bodies.

Images began to flash before them. Too fast, too blurry at first, but as the tingling washed through their young, strong bodies, the visions grew slower and clearer. There were many animals that Mercanti and Tanica had never seen before, though somehow they knew them and their power. In their visions, they approached the lion with his big mane, exemplifying his dominance. It growled like it was looking at the three women. It tilted its head and roared, then backed down with its front paws outstretched on the jungle floor. Shay spoke with him, and he roared again.

Another roar came from the dark jungle. The women only saw the eyes as the black panther trotted forward. Shay spoke as she bowed down before it. Repeatedly, they approached animals of all kinds. Shay talked with the baboons and chimps, and they shrieked their understanding.

Tanica and Mercanti watched on, their eyes widening as they approached the great ape. It stood upright on the branch, walking to them. It looked into each of their eyes without a word being said, its hot breath wafting on their faces. When Shay finally spoke, it looked directly at her and sat, listening to extended instructions. It was only then that the two women truly understood. The ape seemed to consider what she'd said, then stood tall, baring its teeth. Shay did the same, then he turned and left.

Shay smiled at the girls and looked up. Tanica and Mercanti were nervous as they drifted up higher through the canopy, but they had assured Shay they would stay true to her. Focused on rising, they glided up over the jungle. It was wondrous.

The eagle soared so high with the three women gliding on its wings. It cried out over the hot desert. Below them, a seemingly impenetrable army faced nothing but one small, shade-canopy placed over a large, wooden chair. They watched as the man dressed in grey with his hood up walked down into the valley before the army. Then a dark, shirtless man approached from the army to face him. He was heavier set, and the man in grey seemed unprepared, too casual somehow.

The fight was hard, fast and to the death. In shock at the violence of it, the women had to go back.

***

Ezra walked to the front with Kohji and Aitan just behind. He saw the shade-sail and pointed disbelievingly. "Is that …?"

Aitan took a breath. "I believe it is, Father."

"The cheek of it! He comes to a war with nothing more than a seat and shade-canopy!"

Swear they might have, but every one of them would have almost given their thrones right now to have shade, a seat and a water bladder. Ezra turned as Mensa pushed through, dragging Trina by her chain.

"Alright, let's get this done so I can go back to my kingdom."

Ezra raised an eyebrow. "Mensa, I don't wish to be accused of stating the obvious, but your father has no army here. Could you enlighten me?"

Mensa paused, peering across the valley. "He hasn't brought an army because he is a fool. They have probably already been wiped out by Koe's Royal Guard."

Ezra very much doubted that. "Very well, Mensa. Be a good fellow and leave Trina with me. Go see what your father thinks he is doing, would you."

Mensa scoffed, dropped the chains and headed down the dune. Watching the huge man go, Ezra mumbled to himself. "By the time this is done, boy, you won't have a home."

Trina was on her knees beside him, resting her chains on the hot desert sand. "You scum. You cannot win this!"

Sarcastically, Ezra pointed across the valley. "Would you have a look! It is futile. We will wipe your people from history. I'm not even sure I needed to be here to see it done properly!"

Aitan tapped his father on the shoulder. "Look, now they are fighting among themselves! Now that should make it even bett …" He tilted his head with confusion. "Is that … Kito?"

Ezra shaded his eyes from the beating sun to get a clearer view.

"Murderous bastard," Aitan muttered. "Mensa should be just the man to sort him out for good."

Trina sat up, her bottom lip trembling. This was her new, worst day.

***

Leaving the eagle, the three women drifted back down into the jungle, settling back on the Sacred Tree. Sitting around the candle, they had images of countless Royal Guards making their way through the jungle.

Mercanti began to concern herself. *What if they come towards the Sacred Tree? The jungle warriors will be sitting with their backs to them. It will be a slaughter.*

Shay came to her thoughts. *Think not about the men, think about the animals. The animals we have seen are key.*

Mercanti refocused.

The women watched from under the tree's canopy as the Royal Guard swept through the jungle. These men were silent, organised, prepared and disciplined. Even in the jungle heat, they made great progress. Concerned, the women could only look on as they came ever closer to the Sacred Tree and made their way up onto a flat, semi-cleared area.

Suddenly, they were faced with something they had never trained for: wild animals of all kinds. Stunned, the Royal Guard stood in front of countless animals, then on cue, all the big cats roared together, sending echoes throughout the jungle. The entire Guard dropped their equipment for a hurried retreat. They fled, shouting to their Gods. The women were about to laugh, but the ape stood up, wielding a club and began to smash it onto a huge, hollow tree.

The sound reverberated far and wide.

***

Kito stood in the centre of the valley, his arms up opposing sleeves and his hooded head down. Mensa smirked at the fact that Kito had not heard him coming. He marched straight in.

From under the shade-canopy, King Mabutu sat forward. "Dear Gods, what is he doing?"

Baako held his hands on his head. "Kito, no, no, NO!"

Arriving within reach, Mensa swung as hard as he could. Kito swayed to the side, kicking out and catching Mensa behind the shoulders, sending him tumbling face-first into the sand. Armour rattled as an assembly of soldiers readied themselves.

Kito lifted his head, preparing himself; he would only get one cheap shot with this wharf bully. Mensa recovered quickly to stand over him. "I beat you on the vessel, and everyone here will see me beat you now!"

"That's a lot of beating, Mensa."

Mensa leapt forward, throwing a jab. Kito took the hit then stepped to the side as repeatedly, Mensa came back, giving Kito a thumping. Kito took it all and bounced back, always stepping back to the side, making Mensa follow him around. Mensa began to sweat.

***

King Mabutu sat upright in his seat. "What is the boy doing? How much of that can a man take?"

***

On the other dune, Aitan pumped his fists in the air as if he was doing the fighting. "Smash him, Mensa. Crush him." Ezra was no less with his encouragement. Kohji stood still, whilst tears washed their way down Trina's dirty face.

***

Kito threw a punch that made everyone flinch. A groan washed over the soldiers in unison. Sweat now flowed freely down Mensa's face and into his eyes. Still the punches were thrown both ways. Kito was careful with Mensa; he was a wharf fighter who carried a mean reputation. They were known for their tricks, and this man certainly knew how to land his punches. Finally, Mensa was beaten with the heat. Kito gave him several sharp jabs to the ribs, then one good one to the jaw as the big man toppled.

Kito stepped back.

***

Across the dune, Baako cried out. "No, Kito! He will pick up sand!"

Mabutu slipped forward in his seat. "What would make you say that?"

"I don't know, I just think …"

***

429

Mensa slowly stood up. He let Kito get in close before he threw a fistful of sand into Kito's face. Kito reeled back. A million-strong protest washed down the valley at the dishonourable tactic. Kito dropped quickly to one knee with his hands held out wide. Silence. Mensa charged in with a savage kick, but Kito grabbed the leg as he came up, swaying to the side, catching Mensa off balance. He slammed his fist down into Mensa's ribs, and his lungs bellowed out as he doubled over.

***

Mystified by Kito's abilities, Aitan's arms fell to his side. "How did he do that?"

No one answered.

***

Mensa stumbled around, trying not to let a blinded Kito know where he was. He was almost behind Kito when he came back in, swinging hard. Kito dropped as he spun around with clenched fists and drove them back up, spreading Mensa's arms. He dealt several heavy blows into Mensa's torso. His ribs snapped like dried twigs. Without pause, Kito stepped forward and drove the palm of his hand into Mensa's chest. To those close enough to see, it really seemed Kito's hand went through Mensa's chest. Mensa cried out as he fell backwards onto the sand. Sweating profusely, he squirmed in pain, trying to hold his torso as he coughed out blood. It splattered over his chest and trickled down his neck. Never had he known defeat. His shattered chest might have been hurting, but his arrogance didn't know where to hide.

Still with his eyes shut, Kito stood over Mensa. He reached behind his back and pulled out a knife from beneath his clothing. It was perfectly designed, encrusted with jewels and boasting an impeccable finish. "Mensa, do you remember this?"

Mensa squirmed about on the sand. "What are you on about?"

"Look, Mensa, the knife, you do know it. Have a good look now."

Mensa's eyes widened, giving himself away. "No, Kito! Where did you get that?"

"Yes, I knew you would remember it."

Mensa began to squirm again. "I didn't do it. I didn't do it, I promise you!"

"I know, Mensa. You had the poor fisherman, Acron, do it for you. He is now in a tar pit. Funny how that works sometimes, isn't it, Mensa?" Kito leant over and put his knee on Mensa, pinning his arm over his broken chest. "Not unlike how he dumped Queen Rani's body in the river at the Village of the Keepers, only to have my friends in Middle Kingdom find her. Without the Gods' intervention, Mensa, what do you think the odds are of that?" Using his left hand, Kito pulled back Mensa's eyelids, holding his eyes open.

The white of Mensa's eyes bulged. "What are you doing? Get off me, you … get off me!"

Kito raised his mother's knife. "May the desert sand drink down your blood like the summer rains. As the Gods are my witness and in the name of Queen Rani, I give you this."

The knife glinted as Kito raised it high, then drove it down. Mensa's body contorted, shook for a few moments, then fell still.

***

King Mabutu slumped back into his throne. "Dear Gods, forgive my son," he whispered.

Baako still clasped his hands around his head. "How many will die for that?"

***

Queen Trina screamed out her anger. Despite all he'd done, Mensa was still her son. Ezra turned to her. "Now you know my loss! Now you know the pain which drives me!"

She looked into his bitter face. "I am way too strong to put all these men to death for my own grief. It is not the pain that drives a fool, it is the bitterness!"

431

Kohji was stood behind her. "Tell me, Ezra, where is this marvellous Emperor, the Emperor of Legend?" He shook his head as Ezra looked about. "No, Ezra, this is all wrong. You and me, we have lost our way."

Aitan pulled on Ezra's sleeve. "Father, look! What *is* he doing?"

Down in the valley, a blind Kito stood alone. He slowly waved the bloodied knife from left to right, then stopped, pointing it directly at Ezra. With a hefty grunt, Kito threw the knife high into the sun. Ezra quickly signalled, the trumpets blew as the soldiers raised their armour and began to charge.

Just then, Aitan shoved his father back. "Look out!" He held a guarded arm across Ezra's chest. They looked down at the knife stuck in the sand just before them. The jewels sparkled in the morning sun. Ezra knew it immediately to be the one he'd had made for Rani, given to her to celebrate her coming into womanhood.

He shouted to stop all the soldiers, but it was too late, none would hear his shouting over the roar of the charge. Ezra tried so hard. "STOP! STOP NOW!! The Gods forgive me, what have I done?"

***

The ape repeatedly smashed the enormous club onto the tree. He made a call for all to hear, and they did. The animals began to move swiftly through the jungle. The springbok alongside the big cats, the primates swinging through the jungle tops. The women, in spirit, had to fly quickly to follow the charge.

Breaking out from the jungle, they charged through the elephant grass. The women swept over the grass to see Kito standing over the dead man, with a million-strong army storming down the dune towards him. They caught their breath as Kito remained unmoving.

Again, the animals sounded their protest. It echoed over the hot desert with menace and power.

The charging army clamoured to an abrupt halt. At the bottom edge of the valley, they looked on in disbelief. This was nothing natural, yet they were seeing it before them. The animals roared, and with the clinking of armour and shuffling of feet, the army began to back away. The great ape looked up at the three women and showed his teeth. All three women bared their teeth in return.

The lions' roars broke the desert's silence. An elephant trumpeted. Animal after animal sounded until the soldiers had completely stopped their advance. Barely at the bottom of the dune, they faltered, looking up at the opposing dune. It was lined with everything from the long-horned antelope to the big cats, to the elephants. The great apes stood with long, heavy clubs. Anacondas stood up twenty feet tall and hissed as the hooded King cobras spat.

Kito stood in the middle of the valley. "Ezra! Ezra, you will come to me, or these animals will go to you. The choice is yours!"

The huge army of soldiers shuffled as they waited for Ezra to respond. He stepped forward, but Aitan moved before him. "No, Father. *I* must face this murderous man."

Trina looked up from the sand. "You couple of fools. Look at you both standing behind your army, stroking your egos, pumping your bitterness while neither of you has the testicles to face that one man. Have you never looked into his eyes? Both of you fools go. Go down there now!"

The two men looked at one another, bewildered. Kohji spoke. "Ezra, this nonsense has gone unchecked long enough. Koe is not even here. Stop this stupid war before we all go down in history as the fools we are. Here and now, Ezra, stop this."

Ezra glared at Kohji coldly, but Kohji was unmoved. Clenching the bloodied knife, Ezra headed down the dune, Aitan beside him.

Trina felt a hand under her arm. "If you stand, Queen Trina, I can better remove your chains."

Trina struggled to her feet. "You were never really a part of this, were you?"

Kohji waved for one of Ezra's men to come forward. "You will remove her chains. I know you have the key."

The man shook his head. "No, sir. Not unless the Pharaoh has …"

A long, curved broad sword was swiftly at the man's throat. "Then give *me* the damn keys." As Kohji undid Trina's locks, he spoke quietly. "I take full responsibility for my own actions, Queen Trina. I have no need to hide behind anyone for my mistakes."

She looked at the man she'd known most of her life. "For this, I am grateful, my friend," she said as the last chain fell away.

He humbly offered his hand. "Do you need help?"

"To walk over this blessed valley? Never."

***

Yaan snatched up a water bladder and sprinted off down the dune. Baako pointed. "King, look!" Making her way slowly down the dune from the other side was Trina. He stepped forward. "I will go for her."

"No, son, the King has got this one." Mabutu walked down the dune into the hot valley, disbelieving his own eyes. As they neared each other, he went down onto one knee before her and reached up for her outstretched hands. "My dear Trina, how could you ever forgive me?"

She took his hands tenderly. "Forgiveness is for a known mistake. You didn't know I was alive, so there is nothing to forgive."

Mabutu shook his head. "But I did know you were alive. Everyone told me I was wrong, so eventually, I let you go."

"I, too, knew you weren't dead, but couldn't know where you were. Let us not worry over this. We have much work to repair our lands." Mabutu nodded knowingly. Dehydrated, sun beaten and exhausted, Trina's knees finally gave way. He swept up her weary frame and gently carried her up the hill.

Under the shade-canopy, Baako looked at Trina with alarm.

"Will she survive, Father?"

Trina lifted her head from Mabutu's shoulder. "Oh, don't be so dramatic, son. I'm back to pester your life for some time yet. Come, give your mother a kiss."

Mabutu gently placed her down, Baako immediately embracing her. "This is the day we always talked about, Mother."

"Indeed, it is, son. Indeed, it is."

When Baako was finished hugging his mother, he sat her on the throne and stepped back. Mabutu interrupted his doting son. "Baako, I need you to run an errand for the nation."

Baako frowned. "King?"

"Go over to Kohji, tell him if his people drop all their weapons and armour where they stand, they are welcome to camp as guests of our nation to recoup before they head home."

Baako raised his brows. "King, considering their intention here, do you think this is wise?"

Trina urged him on. "I can't speak for the Pharaoh and his prince, but it would be a great gesture for Kohji and his men. You will see when you go and speak with him, Baako, you'll see."

***

Kito stood his ground, his arms up his sleeves again . He could hear the army stationed in the valley before him. He had to resist the urge to not smile at their predicament. The occasional lion roared, then a cheetah would answer, and so on. Each time, armour rattled as the front men tried to shuffle backwards up the sand dune.

He sensed the two men coming his way. As they neared, they slowed. Kito bowed deeply, then stood to his full height. "I do not want any more bloodshed. Come closer."

"What? Had enough for one day, Kito?" snapped Aitan.

"Aitan, you brought Queen Trina up from the basement as I asked. I see she is now safe. I thank you."

The two men kept their distance from Kito. Ezra sneered at Kito standing with his eyes shut, sand still stuck in his long eyelashes. "I keep any cards I need to win, boy. That is how the game of nations is won and lost."

Kito frowned with a smirk. "Dare I ask, Pharaoh Ezra, how has that worked out for you today?"

There was a moment's silence before Ezra responded. "Kito, where did you get the knife? Honestly."

Kito turned his head slightly. "Who is coming down the dune to my left, Aitan?"

"I don't know, other than he is one of your brave warriors."

"Really, Aitan. Have you seen him before?"

"No. Never. I don't even think he is of your lands."

"Then how do you know he is a brave warrior?"

Aitan shrugged. "I don't, other than the way he moves, I suppose."

The man on foot slowed. Kito spoke over his shoulder. "Yaan, you're right on time."

"I have brought water for your eyes, Kito."

"Yes, I thank you." He held out a hand to welcome Yaan into the small group that stood in the centre of the valley. "Yaan, I would like to introduce you to Pharaoh Ezra of Orion and his son, Prince Aitan." He then addressed Pharaoh Ezra. "Yaan is one of my best friends. The fact that he has saved my life on more than one occasion is beside the point."

Aitan immediately looked at Yaan. It was hard to believe anyone could save one like Kito.

"Yaan also has another claim to your life here today, Pharaoh Ezra." Ezra and Aitan glanced at each other. "Yaan is the one who found the knife."

Ezra's jaw tightened. "Yaan, do you know what this is to me and my family?"

"No, Pharaoh. I have no idea."

"Just how did you come to have it?"

"I found it. How it came to be in a dried-up riverbed in Middle Kingdom is beyond me. I am sorry I don't have more for you,

Pharaoh."

"In a dry riverbed! You expect me to believe this nonsense?"

Kito held up a hand, and Aitan and Ezra immediately leaned back. "Pharaoh Ezra, have you ever been to the Village of the Keepers?"

"Yes, once."

"The river that goes into the Mother mountain comes out in the Middle Kingdom."

Ezra's shoulders slumped. "Are you to tell me she went into the river?"

"Yaan said her knife was found with her body. I believe Mensa had her murdered and dumped in the river." Again, Kito held up his hand for Ezra to settle. "I killed Mensa with her knife, because he was responsible. After he got rid of Trina, Rani arrived. The man who did the job was thrown into the tar pits by a friend of yours – Banji."

Ezra almost stumbled at the news; this was worse than he could have imagined. "What have I done? The Gods, what have I done?"

"There is more." Ezra was positively ashen as Kito continued. "I think if you come quietly, you will be welcome at the King's fire tonight. It's time to release the past and its pain, so to move forward and heal, Pharaoh Ezra."

Dark rings of puffy skin cradled Ezra's eyes. "Who are you to invite us to the King's table? You are setting us up; they will gut us all!"

Kito dipped his head. "It's your call, Pharaoh, but if Sheik Kohji is willing to make peace, aren't you?" Ezra spun to see Kohji shaking hands with Mabutu in the shade tent. Kito continued. "His men are removing all their armour and weapons, then going to the lake for a swim. They will stay and rest the night. Under the same agreement, you are also welcome, Pharaoh."

"Father, I think it's time," urged Aitan.

Kito stepped back and bowed.

Ezra slowly shook his head. "But who are you, Kito?"

Kito straightened up and raised his arm for Yaan to put his shoulder under it and guide his way. "Shall we all go to the shade tent, Pharaoh Ezra? I'm sure Baako would be pleased to talk with you."

As they began walking to the shade, Kito whispered to Yaan. "Have you heard from the girls yet?"

"No, but I haven't gone back to the camp, either."

"Why ever not?"

"Because, I had to stay to save your ass. Again." He gave Kito a gentle shove as they joked.

Once at the shade tent, Kito knelt and turned his head up to Yaan. "Like old times, isn't it?"

Yaan sighed. "Come on then, you know what to do." He laughed as he tipped water over Kito's sand-crusted face.

As Kito had assured, Baako welcomed the other two men, as only one with such integrity could do. Discussions were made as Yaan flushed Kito's eyes. By the time he was good to open them, he saw Aitan returning from disseminating the commands to their relieved army.

Baako was watching Aitan return when it dawned on him. "Ezra, you do know who Kito is, don't you?"

Aitan stood beside Ezra, watching Kito dry his eyes. Kito blinked several times, removing the last of the grit, then knelt before Ezra. As he pulled back his hood, he took both of Ezra's hands and looked up.

Ezra drew a breath as he stared into Kito's eyes, and his own. "Oh no, no, this cannot be …" he whispered in anguish.

Kito shook the man's hands. "Can you ever forgive what I have done on your lands, Grandfather?"

Aitan stumbled back, as would have Ezra but for Kito holding both his hands.

Yaan's mouth dropped open. "You are a prince in Orion, too?"

Kito was focused on Ezra. "Grandfather, I need your forgiveness."

Ezra fell to his knees. "Rani still lives … in you! My dear boy, my dear grandson, how could you ask this old fool to forgive you? No, you cannot ask for what is not needed."

"I was never proud of what I did in your lands, but it was a plan with reason. The Emperor is now dead."

"What! When?"

"Just know it has been done. I think we should be joining with the others."

Aitan stepped forward. "Kito, I would really like to know about the Emperor. Last time I saw him, he seemed to think he was going to be immortal."

"I don't think anyone is ready for immortality," Kito responded flatly. He thought about how Koe had behaved the moment he was immortal and how disastrously that had turned out. He shook off the thought. "I don't wish to be rude, but I do need to check that our friends are well and fine. Could we?"

***

Mercanti had thoroughly loved what they had done, but it was certainly tiring. It was also apparent that the men in the jungle were somehow supporting them. *Shay, have we finished?*

Shay surveyed the scene below. It was done. She led them back to the Sacred Tree, and they settled around the candle. *No, I have one more thing to go over. It will not take long but I feel we need to see the past.*

The women held on for a sudden wild ride as colours spread through their minds' eye then gently cleared again. They were floating over a river, and a small canoe bobbed in the water below them. Two men were dunking a small child in and out of the water, held by one leg.

Then they were at the wharf, and they saw a big, black man. Mensa was instantly recognised as he put the boy in a sack.

Shay's tears flowed freely; she knew the boy to be Chizoba. She watched as Mensa took him onto the largest vessel at the wharf then kicked the sack down the stairs. The boy rolled out in front of another huge, black man. He was shackled by a steel collar and a heavy chain attached to the floor. The big man looked over the boy. Shay caught her breath, and the man looked up from the boy as if he'd heard her. Just for a time, it seemed Baako was staring into their eyes. They had been seen. Baako had seen them.

39 Banji's Witchcraft

Deep in the dark hull of Koe's vessel, Banji shook with anger. The brazier glowed white hot as she stalked around it. "No, you bastard child! You cannot do this!" She rubbed her belly. "My Godchild will have his Demi-God father! I will ruin you, Kito, if it's the last thing I do, you and all your do-gooder friends."

Her eyes danced like the flames over the brazier coals as she paced, her hands going from rubbing her belly to raised talons over her head. "I have underestimated you, young man. You have had help I feel."

She reached into her pouch, drawing out bones in her scrawny hands, and rattled them in her palms, still pacing around the fire. "I see you have mastered time, as have your little disciples. Well let me show you a trick or two, boy. Let old Banji show you and your wenches how to play for keeps." Her cackling rose higher than the bats as they flew around the vessel hull.

Holding the bones in her two fists, she moved around crowing and screeching. The bats followed in the circle around the brazier. She thrust the bones at the fire and instantly, red-orange flames leaped up, reaching high through the ceiling. She began to rise and sweep around the flames, higher and faster. The bats rose with her then began to change into crows, thousands of crows, lifting Banji with them.

They were no longer in the vessel.

The men on the top deck were overwhelmed with the crows. Confused, they screamed, running for cover. Banji's screeches melded with the beating wings of more crows than they could count. In their panic some of the guards fell into the river, others in desperation, simply dove in.

Banji's shrilled laughter was barely audible through the chaos.

Higher the flock rose, into the blue sky. They travelled quickly east, making the colours of the world blend. A kaleidoscope of visions rushed by as time bent and warped backwards.

Then Banji saw what she was looking for. The vessels. *"Ah, there you are my little fleet. Now, what do we have going on here?"* One vessel had broken its run further north of the rest. Another little vessel was just turning towards the remaining four. *"Ah yesss,"* she hissed. *"The brave little Kito followers, though this will not be your day, I feel."*

Two guns pointed forward of the vessel. *"Futile. Let me show you some real power."* She watched as the little vessel quickly made ground on the bigger fleet. *"Shame, you really are the most loyal followers to take on these big vessels with that. Hmmm, silly little people, you really should keep your top deck clean. Maybe I could be of assistance."* Now excited, she let out a piercing shrill.

***

The little vessel was moving faster than ever now, riding down the swells. Most of the men had never been on a vessel like this before; they looked about nervously. Feros and Ushma had both done time as slaves before finding work with Balzac and enjoyed the ride. Their howls and hoots gave the other men confidence that it was perfectly normal. The truth was, they were just happy to be top deck and not pulling ores with collars of steel.

But the good mood was quickly broken with one call. "There! More vessels over there!" Everyone looked with great anticipation. Admasin and Balzac walked slowly to the starboard side of the vessel. Lucia swapped sides of the wheel to get a clearer look, awestruck by the size of the sails. They were huge. She shook her head.

Just then another call went out. "What is that?" He didn't have to shout; his call was riddled with fear as he pointed in the opposite direction. Hurriedly, they all moved back to the port side, Balzac taking a firm hold of the side. As the colour drained from his face as he mumbled, "What, in the Gods, is that?"

Admasin stood beside him. "I have heard of them, though never did I think for a moment they were real."

The entire vessel of men stared at the black tornado twisting down from the sky, strangely, its top was only a small, black cloud. As they watched, it grew and reached down all the way to the water. It touched the ocean, sending plumes of spray high into the air. The spout grew until it was a massive, black, spinning spout of dense water.

"What is it?" Balzac's voice was barely audible.

Lucia swallowed hard. "It's called a waterspout and *it*, Father, is coming this way."

Admasin hurried his crew to order. "MEN! We will turn downwind. Man the blocks, starboard side turn."

Lucia was quick to the wheel but almost outdone by the men on the blocks. Admasin went beside her, holding the deck rails and, white knuckled, Balzac clenched the side tighter than ever.

The vessel leaned hard. It was the tightest turn they had ever achieved. Balzac looked at the water rushing along the side of the deck. It was pouring in through the railing, churning about then sucking back out. He glanced at Lucia, who was watching the sails and the lack of freeboard.

Lucia looked over her shoulder at the waterspout. *Did it just change direction with us?*

Admasin made another calm call. "Pull those blocks, men. Those sails will need to be tight. Everyone, now!" The men sweated and groaned under the strain of their efforts.

***

Banji laughed. *"Oh, you delightful little try-hards, can you not see it is futile? No one can outperform Banji's power. Poor little mortals, they do go to such lengths to live."*

***

Lucia looked over her shoulder. *It is gaining on us.* "Admasin, look!"

Admasin's face knotted with confusion. "Wasn't it going …?"

"Yes, but it isn't now."

He turned back. "Man the blocks, turning port. Quarter turn, port."

The men changed tack as Lucia moved the vessel under the sails. Again, white-water churned through the side railing. The little vessel barely lost speed.

Admasin stood proud. The men might be afraid, but he couldn't fault their efforts. He didn't even have to ask for that last inch of rope to get the sheeting tight. *If the sheets go any tighter, they will tear to bits.*

They could now hear the thundering, twisting mass. Balzac stepped in beside them. "Is it just me or ..?"

Lucia shook her head. "No, it really has changed its direction … twice."

Admasin mopped his brow. "Vessels get caught in storms, storms do not chase down vessels." He turned back to the men. "Men, turning port, eighth turn, port."

Lucia followed his instruction with no one missing a beat. It would slow them, running so tight across the wind, but Admasin had to see if this thing was going to cross the wind also. The sails were stretched dangerously tight. They could hear the power of this thing thundering on as it changed direction with them, towards them.

***

Banji was on the edge of the dark cloud above. She stamped her feet gleefully. *"This is so much fun. Look at them, trying ever so gallantly."* She screeched with the thundering storm twisting and tearing her dress.

***

Lucia stepped back, almost releasing the wheel.

"Lucia, what is it, my dear?"

She shivered. "Can you feel it, Admasin? I can hear it sometimes."

"Lucia?"

"It is alive, I tell you."

Admasin stared at the spout. Clearly, it was running them down. They had changed direction three times, and so had it. He feigned a modicum of control. "Balzac, would you man the guns?"

"What?"

Admasin turned square to the man. "Will you, immediately, man the guns."

Balzac's jaw fell slack. He pointed a weak arm. "We cannot …"

"I will, Admasin." It was Jabali on the lower deck. "It is now running us down crosswind. Storms don't travel crosswind. If nothing else, we will knock a few damn holes in this thing!"

Relief flittered over Admasin's face. "Quite so, Patch, on your way then."

Patch faltered. *So, he does know who I am, but by the Gods, Alexa would kill me now if she knew.* Not wanting to see the expression on Lucia's face, the man dressed in black didn't wait a moment longer. He hobbled for the hatch as quickly as he could.

The colour had drained from Lucia. "P-Patch ..?" she stammered.

"Man the sails, men! If this thing is to run us down, then, as the man has just said, we will knock a few holes in it! Downwind turn! Turnabout we go, starboard!" ordered Admasin.

Lucia grabbed the wheel. This would be a big turn, but she wouldn't let Admasin evade her question. "*Patch*, Admasin? What are you saying?"

He looked sheepishly. "I am sorry, my dear. I have not known long. I thought I would let the two of you sort it out yourselves."

Tears welled up, and her hands trembled with the grief of losing him the first time. "You knew?" She still worked the wheel whilst looking at the sails.

"Please don't be too hard on me, my dear. I simply thought we had more time. Besides, you did talk with him on the beach, and I thought you would have gotten the picture when Balzac showed us the amended plans. Did you really not recognise his hand on that brilliant work?"

Lucia shot Balzac a cutting glare. "Did you know, Father? Did you hold out on me, knowing this was my man? Did you!?"

Balzac kept his eyes on the extraordinary amount of whitewater washing over the deck yet again.

***

Banji's laughter grew richer than ever. *"Oh, now they squabble amongst themselves and at a time like this! This is positively the best day ever. I really must get out more often!"* Her shrill pierced the little vessel as it turned about. *"Ha, another futile change of direction. So where are we off to now, my little mortals?"*

***

Balzac stammered. "My dear, please forgive me. I did like the idea of you thinking I had done the plans but, no, I honestly didn't know who he was, until now."

Before Lucia could say another word, he hurried down the stairs, then stopped and turned, holding his hands up to her. "I know why you didn't tell me about Karlec. That was wrong, my dear, it was too much for you to carry, but I understand. Never has a father been as proud as I am of you." He didn't wait for an answer.

Admasin avoided looking at Lucia as she wiped her face. The dark waterspout loomed ahead of them. With full sails, they pushed forward.

Admasin gripped the other side of the wheel. "Mind the sails, men. Dead ahead. Be sure to get every ounce out of them."

Just then, the man in black came back to the top deck, stopping for a moment to look up at the spout, the thundering noise now

446

deafening. Admasin was about to call his name when Patch turned towards the stairs. Without hesitation, he walked directly to Lucia. "Balzac said I need to report to you, Lucia?"

Lucia tried to see through his eyelets. "Could you take off your hat?"

Patch shook his head.

"Take off the damn HAT!"

He slowly removed it, gazing at her. In a sudden movement that no one saw coming, including her, she slapped his face so hard he almost fell off his cane. Patch stumbled back. Lucia was quick to follow, as if she were going to do it again. "YOU KNEW?"

Patch waved his cane between them. "Just sit back one moment woman! You weren't exactly going by the truth all these years were you, Alexa … or is it *Lucia*? I thought it was you, but Kito gave your name as Lucia, and then you were gone!"

"You saw me on the island!"

Patch was momentarily at a loss, then in one violent movement, he tore his shirt completely off, exposing his burnt face, slumped shoulder, warped arm and lost muscle. "Who, in their right mind could love THIS!?"

***

Banji was beside herself watching the little vessel gallantly sailing right into its own demise. It was so delicious that she even stopped moving forward just to extend their pain. Watching Lucia and Patch fighting on deck was just priceless.

Suddenly, the little vessel thundered! Banji flinched with pain. *"What was that?"* Parts of the dark cloud fell away, turning into crows and then bats. They were now dead bats. They tumbled down, falling into the abyss.

"NO, MY BATS!"

***

Admasin held firm on the wheel as the men peered up at the strange waterspout. It roared so loudly that the two shots fired were barely noticed.

Lucia held Patch by his face. "But don't you see, it wasn't just your body I loved. Patch, why could you not trust me?"

He leant forward so their heads were touching. "And you should have told me about Uncle Karlec. I would have loved you just the same, maybe more."

Balzac's guns fired again, and the storm screamed out its pain. The waterspout began to fail, raining down hard. The men gestured to the spout, unable to contain the profanities that erupted from their mouths.

Admasin looked to his favourite young couple, who were hugging closely. He smiled through the rain as he turned back to the spout. They were just about under it now, just as Balzac's men fired their last shots.

***

Banji looked on in horror as more of her precious birds turned into dead bats falling away. In a fit of fury, she released all the water, returning her remaining crows. She squawked as the little vessel was instantly crushed to splinters as she darted through the air laughing deliriously.

"You dared to take on Banji. Burn in hell, mortals. May you all pay for each and every one of my lost friends." She shrieked some more as she watched the four remaining vessels of the fleet moving forward. *"You could do better than that. Even the little piss pot was quicker."* She gave them favourable winds to push them on. *"But you don't interest me. It's Kito I want!"*

The dark, swirling crows that remained carried Banji as she moved forward, searching over the big, blue ocean. Finally, she saw the sail in the distance. *"Now there you hide. Why are you doing so well?"* She swept down silently alongside the vessel. *"Ah, how sweet,"* she said, watching Baako talking with the captain.

***

Baako pointed to the side of the sailcloth. "If you see one of the sides flapping, then an adjustment needs to be made. If it flaps gently, then it probably doesn't have enough weight over it from the breeze. If it flaps hard, then you need to let off some pressure."

The captain agreed. "Yes, I see. Just how do you know this, with a new vessel and all?"

Baako shrugged. "We are doing very well for time, aren't we?"

"Oh yes. Without doubt, Baako. We are doing much better now."

***

Banji searched high and low. *"Where could that beastly boy be? Has he slipped my talons just as I'm sharpening them?"* She rose above the vessel, looking landward. *"Now I feel you, boy. I see you ..."*

Banji rose even higher. Her crows swarmed around her as the colours of time began to blend. Faster she sped as she watched time warp again, this time to the war.

***

Three women climbed up into a tree over a thousand years old. Mercanti looked about. "How did you find this place?"

"Kito brought me here. Come on, sit with me." As Shay sat down, she removed a bag from her shoulder and slowly pulled out the biggest candle Tanica had ever seen.

Mercanti held out her hands for it. "Shay, I have never seen such a candle. Ours are just white." Tanica nodded as she admired the thing.

Shay pulled out a flint. "Mercanti, when you are ready, could you hand it to Tanica? It's important that you both handle it."

***

Banji clasped her scrawny hands together. *"Oh, you dear little mortals, so cute. It's almost a shame for what's coming ..."* She shrugged. "... or not."

The butterflies came, and she watched as Shay carefully led the women through the meditation. *"Pure amateurs. So serious and controlled."* She chuckled. *"Not long now, girls and, you will get to be one of those butterflies yourselves. I will send you to your Gods. This is going to be as blissful as the pathetic, little vessel."* She swiped her hand and froze the women in place, and the Emperor's guard crept forward through the jungle.

Banji flew over the jungle towards Audun. There he was – Kito – standing over Mensa's dead body in front of the million strong army. *"Ah, Kito, there you are, right where I need you. This is to be easier than I thought!"* She flew back over the jungle in a big arc, arms spread as wide as her smile. *"Oh, this is going to be Banji's day. The Gods won't know what to do with so many of their precious little mortals flooding their way!"* She swept back through the jungle and past the Sacred Tree.

***

Many hundreds of the Emperor's Guard had arrived safely on the vessels and were now silently making their way through the jungle. The Guard silently spread out around the warriors who encircled the Sacred Tree and were humming in unison. The men looked to the captain. In the jungle, not everyone was going to see him drop the flag, but once some went in, all went in. They eagerly searched for the huge Sacred Tree in the centre. Their trophy for those first in was in the treetop.

The flag dropped, and it was a blood bath.

Neither ready nor prepared, the warriors were slaughtered where they sat, most still with their heads down meditating for the three women, who Banji released back into time.

The meditation was shattered with the women thrust back immediately. Flustered, Shay tried to stand but stumbled and fell. Tanica leaned to the side and vomited several times. Mercanti held her palms to her temples, screaming with pain.

***

Banji had watched intently as the army came across the meditating warriors. It had been as easy as she'd assumed and had told Koe to inform the Captain of the Guard, *It will be like picking flowers from the spring meadow.* She looked down as the lust-hungry men slaughtered their way to the Sacred Tree. Droplets of spittle sprayed from her mouth as she gleefully watched the first man crest the crown into the Sacred Tree.

***

Tanica spat the last of her vomit in the face of the first guard, and with the two black, short swords, she cut away his greedy grin. Swords flew fast as she slashed her way around, and bodies tumbled down, knocking unsuspecting guards to the jungle floor with them. She moved with intense speed. No Royal Guard had either her training or talent. Mercanti did her best with her single, short sword. Shay could do no more than kick the first heads coming up.

***

Banji's eyes widened as she drew a breath. *"Who is this woman? Where has she sprung from?"* She moved in closer to look into her eyes. The speed and the way Tanica moved intrigued her. She had seen this somewhere. She waved her hand, and Tanica slowed to a halt as Banji moved in, being careful not to touch any of the blood splashing off the swords.

She peered into Tanica's big, green eyes. *"Where, oh where have I seen those before, my dear?"* Suddenly, she drew back, catching her breath.

Banji's mind reeled back two decades. Intrigued, she watched the vision from the past.

***

451

A small vessel with two hulls carried just a young couple and their toddler. On the banks of the River Samos, they dragged themselves up onto land.

Wearing strange bracelets on both arms, the man gallantly looked out for his family. He built a fire in a small, disused Temple, taking shelter from the storm blowing overhead. Over the next few days, they walked to the city of Samos. Once there, they waited for nightfall before creeping in, searching for supplies to fix their vessel.

Unknown to them, Banji had her own plan coming into play. Just on daybreak, as the couple were about to leave the city, they were jumped by the Royal Guard. The tall woman was well-trained and quick to kick the Guard to the ground. The man, a hero it would seem, stayed fighting the Guard to give her time to escape.

The tall woman hid the toddler under some patchwork blankets on a wharf. She fled back to her husband, but it was all too late. As she rounded the corner, she saw him on his knees, arms pulled back wide. He was arguing with the captain. The tall woman ran forward. "NO!" she screamed, but the captain drove his knife to the hilt in the man's chest.

***

Banji snickered.

***

The Guard immediately turned on the woman, clearly distraught for her husband. With an arm outstretched, she tried to get to him as his body was dropped to the cobbles, crimson blood flowing freely over them.

The guard quickly seized her. The captain walked boldly forward, then slowly wiped his short sword on her clothing. Defiant, she spat into his grinning face.

***

With the wave of her arm, Banji froze the scene. She moved in closer to the woman wearing a golden headband, and fascinated, she stared into her big, green eyes. Banji backed away. *"Well, I never!*

I had missed this one completely."

***

The captain slapped the tall woman hard. "Load her into the lockup carriage. Remove all the gold and take it with her for the Emperor!"

***

"So that is the infamous Sha'Doe." Banji slowly glided upwards. *"I know how the rest of this has to play out."*

She moved time forward again to the Sacred Tree, looked at Tanica, frozen in time, with her same green eyes shining. *"A shame really."* She wiggled her fingers and the scene ran backwards to when Tanica first stood. She let it play once more. Tanica's movements were not of this world. Not a guard would get her, not a chance. Realisation swept through her tingling body.

"Oh my. Only Hasuca moves like that, my little dear!" She gasped again. *"Hasuca had Sha'Doe' when Koe did!"* She clapped her hands in glee. *"Oh, this is golden! This is the best day ever!"*

***

Shay's scream pierced the jungle. Three men were pulling her down onto the old tree, greedy hands tearing at her clothing. Tanica spun to see Mercanti slashing them down, but now most of the trees had no one guarding it, and the men swarmed up. Two arrows slammed into Tanica's chest, then another to her back. She didn't even look down at the arrows as she leapt forward with the two swords held like knives. It was the last thing she was to do for her friends, stabbing downwards, killing both Shay and Mercanti instantly.

Tanica was numb to the swords driving into her. She whispered an apology to the Gods as she herself was lost to this world.

***

Banji cackled as she flew upwards. *"It's almost a tragedy really. Still, Koe couldn't have her alive either way."* She drew up higher then glided out over the jungle towards the elephant grass, chuckling at the scene below her.

***

Aitan nudged his father. "Look, now they're fighting among themselves! Now that should make it even bett ..." He tilted his head with confusion. "Is that ... Kito?"

Ezra shaded his eyes from the beating sun. "Murderous bastard. Mensa should be just the man to sort him out for good."

Trina's bottom lip trembled as she sat up on her knees, staring at the shade canopy. She could see her King watching what was unravelling. He would save her. She didn't care for the armies. She didn't care for the talk of the Royal Guard coming either. This was Mabutu. He always had a plan. He always knew what to do.

Trina's sun-beaten face creased as she listened to the fierce fighting in the jungle. She didn't know what made her say it, but she turned to Ezra. "It might be the tiger that takes you, or it might be the lion, but know this, you have not behaved right in the eyes of the Gods." Somehow in that moment, Ezra looked older, more ragged. She watched him as he gazed at the opposing ridge, concern stricken on his face, then he smirked. "My dear Trina, this is just not your day."

She saw the Royal Guard break through the elephant grass and gasped. "Oh no! No, no, no…"

Ezra stepped forward. To the rear of the tent were three men he didn't recognise. They were different in every way. Fighting alongside King Mabutu and Baako, the men fought with skill and pace, never missing, almost cutting a wedge further forward, through the Royal Guard.

As gallant and skilled as the men may have been, the numbers were simply overwhelming. It was only a matter of time before they were surrounded and cut down. The little shade canopy was torn down and soaked blood-red.

Trina screamed out her rage at the disaster before her. This was her new worst day.

40 Entombed

Banji shrieked as she glided over the desert, death and destruction sprawling out below. Just one more body to account for, and she could go back and get Koe. Laughing deliriously and almost overwhelmed with delight, she descended towards Mensa's body. Her laugh began to choke as she searched. *"Where is he? Kito must be here, he must be. No!"*

She sped up, driving herself on towards the Great Dividing Range. Ever faster, with her eyes on just that one place. *"I should've known he would run away to there."*

So focused on the cave entrance way up on the Great Ranges, she didn't notice the dark cloud rolling up behind her. As it drew close to her, the flock of crows trailing behind began to turn white. Laden with ice, their wings ceased to beat. The crows turned back into bats, their bodies silently falling from the sky. Thin, frozen wings shattered the instant they touched the hot sand. The desert drank down the ice, erasing them from history and from any future.

Banji frantically searched for the cave entrance. *"There!"*

A grey, hooded figure sat at the entrance to the cave of perfect stone. He was in the lotus position, looking out to the desert where the battle had taken place so far below.

Banji felt a chill and looked down at her toes. *"ICE?"* She swirled around. *"Where are my birds, my beloved bats?"* The cold mist caressed her body, and the ice expanded up her legs, covering her black gown. She spun back to Kito. *"What have you done?"*

Kito's eyes opened. He rose smoothly and stepped forward just short of the clifftop. *"Why do you question me, Banji? If you compare this little spectacle against all your interference in Middle Kingdom, I have done very little."*

Her hands went directly to her abdomen. *"Kito no, I am pregnant."* Her demeanour suddenly changed. *"You wouldn't hurt this unborn child, would you?"*

"In order for that to be a baby, Banji, you would need to be human."

Banji's face turned dark like the storm. She struggled to move as the cold enveloped her. *"How dare you!"*

Kito held up a hand. *"Careful now, Banji, ice that cold is very brittle. I would hate for you to lose a foot or something."*

"You bastard …"

Again Kito raised his hand. *"Now, Banji, it's ill for me to lecture an older woman like yourself on etiquette, but I must point out, you are possibly closer to the Gods than you have ever been."*

She shuddered despite the rage that boiled within her. More wisps of icy cloud swathed her as she floated before him. *"Oh, come now, Kito. You and I, we have never really been enemies."*

Kito slowly came forward, his toes at the cliff edge. *"And we aren't now. Tell me, Banji, as I don't understand, you could've borne a child to any Royal over all these lands. Instead, you played this elaborate game just to get Koe's seed, yet he probably would have been the easiest from the beginning."*

Banji's face contorted. *"Fool boy, can't you see?! Koe is the only one who could've given me the seed for what I want."*

"Yes, sadly, I see this, but you could have simply gone to him and received it."

"Never would I have been one of his filthy concubines. It was beneath me."

"That, too, you could've worked around."

"Nonsense, he was too arrogant!"

"It was simply a game to you, wasn't it?" Kito extended his arm to the jungle below. *"All this, nation against nation, Kings pitted against Kings, Pharaohs and Sheiks, it was all just an elaborate game."*

"I have taken seed from all the leaders for generations, boy. That was

easy. Even your pappy came to me on more than one occasion!"

Kito pondered the bigger picture. "So, it really was only Koe? Only Koe was dark enough to impregnate you?"

"When I got him to kill his own father, I knew he was the one."

"That was also your doing? Koe was just the puppet?"

"Oh, Kito. You can be quite delicious and naive. I tried your grandfather and your father, but it was Koe who finally did the deed. That's when I was sure he was the one. He had the backbone."

"You are a sorceress of the darkest kind, Banji. Could you not just take a child and ..."

"No fool boy! It had to be mine and his!"

"Then I shall put you down together. You cannot say better than that, my dark witch." Kito turned and began to walk along the narrow track. Instantly, Banji's dark cloud followed him. There seemed to be nothing she could do about it. From her waist down, she was entombed in ice, frozen, brittle and powerless. Her eyes widened. *"Where are you going? Release me this instant!"*

Kito ignored the trapped woman's rantings.

The black storm cloud carried Banji up through the skies and over the mountain ranges. Kito now had his shirt tied to his waist. His body glistened with the effort of the climb.

Banji saw a mountain peak, far in the distance. *"No, you can't leave me out here! I will burn you for this, Kito! You hear me, boy? I will burn you to a crisp and scatter your ashes."* Her spat threats fell on deaf ears. Waist deep in her own black cloud, she continued to float along behind Kito. For possibly the first time, she was not in control of a single element of her entire being.

The highest, snow-covered peak shone brightly in the sunlight, but this wasn't Banji's destination. Kito took a wide berth around to the back of the peak. Hidden from the sun and shrouded in darkness, volcanic rock jutted out through just a thin veil of snow. The smell of sulphur hung heavy on the air, released in large belching coughs from the pools of bubbling mud below.

Kito eased her into an overhang. *"This will keep the snow off your head, but be careful, Banji, it's a frozen ledge and could break away at any time. Eventually it will, maybe tomorrow, maybe in a millennium."*

Banji screamed. A small amount of snow crumbled from above her head. *"Kito, you can't! I am with child!"* She rubbed her swollen belly again as if Kito hadn't noticed it.

"No Banji. The seed is without a soul yet. You, on the other hand, will be frozen in time, never to age."

She spat at him. Her saliva instantly froze into a small pebble that landed at his feet. *"You coward! You don't even have what it takes to kill me!"*

"I still have on me the blood of my own brother. This is not about the killing, Banji."

Her wide eyes darted wildly as she looked about her dark tomb. *"This is it?"*

"This is the side of the mountain where you will never see the sun again. I have removed your satchel, so your spells are now incomplete and irrelevant, Banji."

The rock cracked, and before her an ice wall rose to the ceiling. The ice melded to the rock, locking her into the frozen tomb. She struggled in horror, but it was futile, frozen from the waist down and cocooned behind a wall of impenetrable ice. *"Bastard boy! How? You can't leave me like this!"*

"I can and I will. Now, my father is waiting for me, so ..."

"He is dead," she hissed. *"I have killed them all!"*

"If only you had gone to the temple and reversed the death of Koe first, then the two of you might have stopped me. But I knew you would come to the desert. You couldn't wait to see all the death and destruction. Things are now back to when you first left Koe's vessel. Even Admasin and his crew are safely home at Devil's Pass with Balzac. So now I will leave you with this." Kito began to walk away.

"This? What's this?" Blood coursed through her icy veins. How she hated this boy, so calm and detached. It was enough to drive

her to the edge of insanity.

He turned back and flashed a smile. *"This, Banji, is the choice we all have in life. If only you had chosen another. This is just one choice, you could have had."*

Banji looked at the small puffy cloud before her as Kito said one last thing. *"First, you see another choice you could have taken, then you will see me cutting down Koe, your failure in this choice. It's on a cycle. You will sit in the dark and watch it over and over until your frozen roof falls in. Enjoy."*

The puffy cloud slowly parted before her to reveal an image. Banji instantly recognised the palace.

***

The sun was shining on a beautiful spring morning. A young man, Hannu Koe, walked out with his hands behind his back. "Ah there you are, my tyrant." A little boy came running from the garden.

Banji smiled at the sweet boy.

Koe swept him up and twirled him around. The boy protested. With a chuckle, Koe put him down.

"Grand Master Papa, come see what Grandfather is doing!"

"Oh, very well. But what's with all the excitement, son?"

The boy pulled on Koe's hand as they made their way over to his grandfather. Once there, the boy released his father and put his hands together, as did the two men. They all bowed.

"Morning, Father. What amazing feats have you on this day?" asked Koe as the older gentleman gently laughed. The top of his tanned head shone in the morning light. Long, grey hair hung from the side of his head and down over his shoulders with his moustache reaching to his chest. His eyes, one yellow, one blue, sparkled with mischief. "Nothing, other than the usual garden pruning."

The boy put his hands to his hips. "No, Grandfather. That's not fair now, is it?"

The elder man held the back of his hand to his forehead. "Oh, you mean the other thing?" The grandfather turned and continued pruning. Without warning, hundreds of butterflies appeared. The boy knew to hold out his arms and keep very still. His eyes gleamed as he smiled in wonder.

Banji looked on in distaste and faked a yawn. *"The butterfly thing, always the butterfly thing."*

As the butterflies began to move away, the young boy watched them rise into the morning sky. Koe looked to his father. "Any word of my brother?" The Elder paused, inspecting some of the spring buds. "No word yet, but you know the winter is harsher up there."

"Yes, though I wish he would stay here for the winter. It's just safer."

"Oh, leave him alone. There is beauty up in the North, you know. I have seen some of the most spectacular countryside when hunting as Tzu Hsi's guest."

Koe smiled coyly. "I'm just not convinced he is enjoying the countryside, if you …"

The father pointed his pruners at Koe. "Yes, I think even the young apprentice got that one, thank you, Koe."

Koe wasn't watching him. "Father, there is a carriage coming."

"It's spring. I expect many carriages, Koe."

"No, Father, this one has bars and an escort."

The Elder looked up. "Oh."

"I will go and see." Koe turned back. "Son, stay with Grandfather."

The boy scrunched his face and put his fists back to his hips.

"Oh, Grand Master …" The grandfather had returned to his pruning. "… do as your father bids. He knows best, and you should respect that in him."

Banji rolled her eyes again.

Koe reached the bottom of the palace garden just as the men dismounted. Several men ran to the back of the carriage and unlocked the door. A man got out. He was tall, fit and well-tanned. Koe eyed the chains. Then a woman clambered out, carrying a bundle in her arms. The blanket fell, revealing the head of a toddler. The woman struggled with the chains. Her man took the toddler so she could get down, then handed the toddler back. They stood proud.

Koe looked at the captain. "Who are they and what have they done?"

The captain bowed slightly. "They are not of this land, sire."

"Even my son could see that, but why are they in chains?"

The captain looked flummoxed. He glanced about his men for support, but their eyes were transfixed to the ground.

Banji laughed. *"This is silly and they are stupid."*

Koe sighed. "Have they at least been patted down?"

"Oh yes, sire, and again this morning, just being careful."

The woman spat at the feet of the captain, her big green eyes dazzling in the morning sun.

Banji saw her eyes and gasped. *"No. This is Kito's trickery. It must be."*

The captain reached for his sword, but Koe held up his hand to the captain and stepped before the male prisoner. "Do you understand my words?"

The captain spoke from behind. "No, sire. Not one word."

The captive man spoke with strength. "Yes, Prince Koe. We know of you, your father and the Emperor Hasuca."

Koe smiled. "I see. Why have you come here, to our lands?"

"It was our hope to come and learn your ways in life, as we are neighbours, of sorts. I feel we have made a grave mistake."

Koe pondered the statement. "The day is not over yet. Can you assure me you mean no harm to our lands and everything on them?"

"Yes, Prince Koe, I can assure you. Look at us, we came with no weapons. We are a family wishing to learn."

Prince Koe looked at the captain. "Remove all their chains and ..."

"Sire, I feel ..."

In one smooth, swift action, Koe swiped off the captain's hat and ripped his tunic over his head, leaving it inside out on his back, locking his arms back. Koe didn't take his eyes off the captain. "Guards, you will take this man, remove his Captain's clothing and weapons. He is to bathe and eat with you, then be escorted to see me in the morning, wearing a private's uniform."

There was a flurry of activity. The chains were removed from the captives, and the captain was ushered away, leaving some guards behind with the prince and the couple.

Satisfied, Koe brushed down his silks. "I'm sorry you've not had the best start to your new life. I will see to it that you are washed, fed and kept safe here overnight. If you would like, we could start to get to know each other over breakfast."

The couple dipped their heads.

"You know my name. May I ask yours?"

The tall man stood proud. "I would be Shaikarn, this is my wife, Sha'Doe. Our little boy here is Izan."

Prince Koe smiled. "Maybe in the morning I could …"

"There you are, Koe. I have been searching everywhere for you."

Banji put a finger in her mouth and bit down hard, then began to rock back and forth with tears of rage running down her face. *"No, no."* Shaking with pain, she looked on.

Koe turned around and welcomed the pregnant woman. "Shaikarn, Sha'Doe, this is my wife, Banji. As you can see, she is pregnant with our second child."

For the first time, there was a glimmer of a smile from both foreigners. Sha'Doe looked at Banji's rounding belly. "How long to go, Princess?"

Banji was still rocking as she put her hands to her head and squeezed it tightly. *"NO NO NO! Stop it, stop it now!"* She screamed out the words, though her prison cave heard not a sound from behind her wall of ice.

This was one vision Banji couldn't block. Even with her eyes shut tight, the vision would repeat and repeat for an eternity.

41 Differences Buried

The evening on the edge of the desert was warm and clear. A multitude of fires burned around the lake, and, without the reminder of uniforms, people intermingled without judgment. A gentle breeze blew into camp, and with it came Kito.

At the King's huge table, not far from the lake's edge, King Mabutu saw him. "Ah, Chizoba, we have missed you. It's quite rude this disappearing and reappearing without word. Where have you been?"

Kito glanced at the expectant faces. If he was a little hot from the day, Tanica's face soon cooled him. "I am sorry, my King, just a little something to take care of. I do not expect to be leaving again for some time now."

The King couldn't keep a straight face. "Hmf, see that you don't; people here rely on you now." He pushed back his chair and studied his youngest son a little longer, then stepped up onto the crudely made, heavy timber table. "People of the Lands!" His deep voice carried well over the lake. "There are many uncertain stories circulating. This is unhealthy. Even I can't stop the tall fishing and hunting tales I hear from time to time." A genuine chuckle echoed off into the distance. "The other stories we hope to extinguish tonight."

Mabutu prompted Baako to stand. Tzu and Hao frowned at one another, then eased back from the table. With these two bulking men stood on it, who was to know.

Mabutu and Baako stood proudly side by side. Mabutu turned back to his audience that stood tightly together as far as the eye could see.

"As you saw, in a fair fight, Mensa has been sent to face his Makers and face them he will. However, as you can also see, we are rejoicing in the return of Baako!"

Everyone cheered loudly, some for the loss of Mensa, but they all respected Baako. Anyone from any land who knew him knew his heart to be the best. Mabutu held up his big arms and waited for silence. As the crowd settled, he looked for Yaan at the table. He leaned over with his charming smile. "Would you and Tanica come to my side?"

Yaan stood. Tanica's mouth dropped open in resistance, but before a word came out, Yaan turned to her. "My dear sister, today everything has changed. You will never be a maid again. You will stand at my side and you will support the throne of Middle Kingdom, the throne that is *ours,* Tanica."

He put out a hand for her. Closing her mouth, she slowly took it. Yaan squeezed it. "You don't have to speak if you don't wish to, but you will now always support me in this new journey of ours. Ready?"

Tanica shook her head and shrugged. "No, but let's do this anyway."

"That's my sister." He led her around to Mabutu's seat.

Murmurs and whispers rumbled quietly through the crowd, confused at the special recognition these two young people were getting.

The two stood at Mabutu's side. He took a breath to speak. "Today, I got word that Emperor Koe of the Middle Kingdom has also been sent to meet his Makers! He will be having a difficult time with that one, I would think." A murmur came from the crowd. "Only a few days ago, I was privileged to meet several new people. These brave few individuals came all the way to our lands to challenge their own Emperor, to stop his plan and his painful onslaught. Now I will introduce the first two."

He held his arm for Tanica to take. She stood somewhat nervously in her tight leather trousers and tunic. Mabutu motioned a hand as he introduced her. "I give you, Princess Tanica of Middle Kingdom!"

Tanica stood in awe as the crowd cheered wildly. A few wolf whistles sounded, and Baako stepped forward. He pointed at the crowd, pointed at his own eyes and then back to them with a straight face. Gentle laughter rippled out.

Mabutu held up his strong arms again for quiet. "This next man is, to me, rather extraordinary for his age. From Middle Kingdom, I give you, Emperor Yaan!"

Again, the crowd roared. Yaan acknowledged their cheers, but this wasn't just about him. These were soldiers who were exhausted, ready for a war they never wanted, and today, without loss of their lives, it was all over. The tension was released, almost.

Emperor Yaan raised his arms, commanding his audience. "You can all see I am but a pup, yet here we are, and I am the Emperor. I do hope to get some help from my sister..." The men began to hoot again. "... who apparently holds more of a following than I."

More chuckles and laughter followed.

Mabutu looked with surprise at Baako, who simply nodded. Silence fell, and Yaan continued. "But with her help and the help of some of my friends, Baako, Tzu and Hao, I know that we can once more get back to ..." He looked at Tzu. "... being, as one people!" The crowd roared, hooted and shouted wildly, and Yaan had to yell over them to get them to settle.

"We must all learn to respect the differences in one another, learn to use those same differences to help one another to be a better people." Yaan had to again call above the excitement. "I promise, from Middle Kingdom, you will never in my time see another army come to your lands."

The crowd, in unison, thumped their feet heavily into the dirt. Yaan was now shouting.

"My Royal Guard will go home, burn their uniforms and, still under the employment of this throne, rebuild our own lands!" He stepped forward with his hands raised high and open to the crowd, who jumped and shouted at his words.

Mabutu leant over to Baako and shouted. "Who is this fellow?"

Baako smiled cheekily. "Why, Father, he is my friend. Taught him everything he knows!" They laughed, and continued to clap.

The crowd soaked in Yaan's words, then he waved as he backed up to stand beside Tanica. She stared at him blank-faced. Yaan frowned. "What?"

She began to shake her head. "You are not my brother."

He smiled and winked. "I heard what you did today, Tanica."

"What do you think I did today?"

"You and your new sisters held back three armies. *Three!*"

Mabutu couldn't stop the excitement, and he was pleased for it, though he needed to say more. He called for silence, and the crowd settled quickly. "I had better watch this young man. I may wake one day to find him leading my own people." A good deal of chuckling resounded from his people. "I can't say how much I agree with him, but I have more surprises to go yet. May I have Kito up here … please."

Kito smoothly mounted the table. Mabutu put his hand on Kito's shoulder. "You could not imagine my confusion when I learnt this young man was indeed my son to our Queen Rani – Chizoba!"

Many had seen and the rest had heard how Kito had killed his own half-brother, even after Mensa had put sand in his eyes. Most knew how long Chizoba had been missing; to see him return was beyond belief.

"Though my fortune didn't stop there!" continued Mabutu. With a wide smile, he welcomed Trina onto the table. "Here, before your very own eyes, is Queen Trina!"

Everyone immediately went down to one knee. A breathtaking hush fell over the excited crowd, well over a million men were silent. It was all Trina could do to stand tall before her people as they gave a mumbled prayer of thanks to the Gods for delivering one of their beloved queens back to them.

Mabutu waved up Ezra, Kohji and Aitan.

The men looked at one another, confused. Kohji whispered to Ezra. "What's he planning, a lion feeding?"

They had little choice but to move up onto the makeshift stage. Everyone shuffled to make room. Kohji was the only one who could look at Trina.

Mabutu's deep voice carried over the hushed crowd. "I must take this opportunity to thank my good friend and neighbours for looking after our lost Queen." It was an untruth at best, but they understood Mabutu was trying to leave the dark past for a brighter future. "I must finish these talks so we can celebrate a new future, but I must mention two more extraordinary men. One is King to a land far away, and the other his good friend. They both came all the way here to stop Emperor Koe. I give you King Tzu and Hao!"

The two men were stunned to be mentioned when there wasn't even a war. Hao awkwardly pulled down his silly hat a little more despite the warmth, and they both stood and acknowledged the crowd.

Tzu could only ponder what he would find when he returned to his homeland. Hao wondered where his home was to be.

42 The Young Emperor

It was a happy journey on the way back to Batavia. Strangely, everyone ate vegetarian. Along the way, different chiefs bid their good wishes to the king, his queen, and the two princes then divided off with their men, returning to their villages.

Mabutu talked to Baako about going to the wharf to take control and restore calm and prosperity, then to return to Batavia to plan their future for Zimbali. On the walk, Tanica had stayed clear of Kito, who'd primarily walked just behind the king, queen and his half-brother, Baako.

They were not far from Batavia now. "My King."

Mabutu stopped. "Yes, Chizoba, what is it?"

"I have people who have saved my life, some more than once. May I be relieved so to thank each of them?"

"Must you do this now, Chizoba?"

"My King, you and the Queen have much to repair here. I am of little use."

The King stepped before Kito. "You are a prince to this land. Do you wish to neglect those responsibilities, Chizoba?"

"I am also a prince to Orion's lands, and Grandfather would like me to be there with Sofira."

Everyone had gathered and listened intently to how Mabutu would react. He studied his son, who had grown into this strong, intriguing man. His voice was calm. "Are you bargaining with me for your time, Chizoba?"

"No, I'm merely pointing out that many people are calling on me. Today I would like to help Tanica and Mercanti, King Tzu, Hao and the Emperor Yaan to get safely back to their homes. They have all saved lives here, including mine."

The king lifted his chin. "I see, Chizoba. Can they not go back the way they came?"

"I'm afraid that vessel may have left, King."

Mabutu looked to his first wife, Trina. Her nod was subtle and reluctant. He pondered Kito. "I see you are your own man, Chizoba." Although aging, Mabutu was a formidable man in anyone's mind. He put out his arm, and they shook, wrist to wrist. Mabutu placed his hand on Kito's shoulder. "I don't know how you do the things you do, but as your father and King Mabutu of Zimbali, I am in your debt. Please return soon. We have much work to do, son."

Before Kito could respond, Mabutu pulled him into a strong hug and whispered in his ear. "The coconuts, son. Sorry, the old man missed that one." The two men quietly laughed together. It was a strange story they had, as father and son, though everyone could see it was to be a long and strong relationship, born of the worst circumstances, to endure to the best place.

Once done, Kito went to Baako. "You risked your all for me when you didn't even know who I was. I am forever in your debt."

Baako shook his head. "No, Kito, three angels came with you and let me know that you were special."

Kito blinked in surprise. "You knew all along, Baako?"

"No, Kito, though I knew you were to change everything somehow. Not all boys come with three beautiful angels."

Baako glanced at the three women standing nearby. He already knew Shay, and Tanica's big green eyes were burned in his memory. He'd recognised her the moment he saw her top deck in the sunlight. He smiled at Kito. "You had to work it out for yourself, but then I didn't count on you being taken away. I assumed after you'd saved it, you were to stay on the *Shiraz*. Chizoba, I am sorry, but sometimes life doesn't go as one intends. Do not forget, I had no idea that we were family either."

Kito was silent for some time, then said, "You are right, my brother. You are right."

Next, he moved on to Queen Trina. "You had much bearing on my life with Hasuca. I thank you for those years, my Queen." He bent over and kissed both her hands.

He was unprepared when Trina pulled him into a tender hug and whispered in his ear. "I didn't understand my own life for all those years. Now I see the purpose, it was worth it. That time with you and Hasuca has left me looking to you truly as one of my own, Kito."

The depth of her feelings warmed Kito. He'd been without the love of a mother for most of his young life and was almost without words. "Thank you … Mamma." He released the woman who'd been so influential to him and turned to Shay.

Through her tears, Shay asked, "You sure you have to go, Chizoba?"

"Yes, I must leave. I have far to go to make my apologies and thanks. Many people made this possible, and you, Shay …" He cradled her face in his big hands. "… you are as brave as you are beautiful. A very rare gem. I thank you for looking over us." He pulled her close and kissed her on both cheeks. "Farewell, for now."

"When, Chizoba?" she whispered. "When will you return?"

"If I make no promises, I can break no promises."

He backed up and then bowed to everyone individually. Not wanting a long goodbye, he turned to look for his group of friends. He didn't have to look far. They bore witness to his farewells. "If you are ready, I feel I must at least escort you home."

Tanica had her arms folded. *You won't do it for me, like you did her.*

Kito addressed Yaan. "I mean no offence, but the Royal Guard all know we were with the enemy. Now we must walk in and tell them *you* are their Emperor."

Yaan looked at his companions. "Won't be an easy sell, Kito.

You don't think we should go to the wharf at Begonia and catch a vessel there?"

"No, I think if we can win the camp over, they will go back and talk to everyone else."

Yaan questioned Tzu. "You have led more than any of us. What do you think?"

"I think it would be easier to win over a thousand guards here than a whole nation back in Middle Kingdom."

Yaan nodded. "Very well, Kito, but what do we have to prove I am who I say I am?"

Kito snorted. "When the Emperor wanted you dead, what was it that would have given you away?"

Tanica nudged Yaan. "Now that is ironic. The very thing that gave you away for your bounty is the very thing that will support your true identity."

Kito led the group towards the Royal Guard's camp. The jungle air was hot and musty, but with so many things burning their minds, no one noticed.

Once there, it was as Kito said it would be, a hard sell maybe, but Yaan's eyes were undeniable. Some of the older captains had known Hasuca personally. Once they'd looked at Yaan and given their approval, it really was just a formality. It was decided that some of the captains, with a few hundred of their men and all of Yaan's team, would go back on the first vessels.

The following morning, two vessels – the *Titan* that they'd come on and the *Ocean Conqueror* that former Emperor, Koe, had used – were loaded with supplies and all the men they could hold. Yaan insisted that all the armour would be stacked and left behind as each man was awarded his ride back to the homelands, allowing more men per trip. He told the Royal Guard that the vessels would come back for the armour after everyone was home safe. Deep down, Yaan thought they might smelter the armour for carriages and hinges.

Kito stood at the rudder deck and spoke to all the remaining men lining the banks. "The King and Queen both know you are here. You have seen what the jungle can do when it turns on you. Treat the lands with respect while you wait, and you will be safe, my friends." He bowed, and the entire Royal Guard bowed back.

The river carried the vessels swiftly out to Port Begonia. The ocean was suspiciously favourable, both in swells and breeze. It really didn't seem to take long before they were pulling into Devil's Pass to pay Balzac.

Yaan, Hao and Tzu disembarked to greet Balzac, who had his usual bodyguards in tow. "Morning, gentlemen. On our way to Samos, are we?" Balzac queried.

Yaan dipped his head, then stepped forward to shake wrists. "Indeed, we are, Balzac, though I feel we may have a problem that requires your assistance."

Balzac raised his eyebrows. "Very well then, out with it."

"Emperor Koe has been killed. Until I get back to sort things out, Middle Kingdom doesn't have a true currency."

Balzac had heard all the excuses in the world — one man even claimed that he had the taxes ready, but demons had stolen them — this, however, was the last thing he'd imagined hearing. "Just when was Emperor Koe dispatched?"

"Only a few days before we left Zimbali."

"I see. And *who* was the brave fool to face off the Emperor?"

Yaan realised the depth of his story. "Actually, it was a very good friend of mine. His name is Kito."

Balzac squinted as if trying to read Yaan's face. "And where is Kito now?"

Yaan went to motion towards the vessel when a calm voice beat him to it. "I am here, my old friend." Kito was walking down the plank onto the wharf.

"KITO!" Balzac nearly sent Hao and Yaan into the bay as he pushed between them. "Kito, you've come back to see us!" He didn't wait for the formal introductions but grabbed Kito in a huge bear hug. He stepped back and grabbed him by the elbow. "You have to stay; you must stay, Kito." They marched back down the wharf past Yaan and his friends with barely a look.

Kito slipped out a quiet whisper as he passed by. "Get Tanica and Mercanti also, please."

Balzac marched him on. "You see, Kito, you really did make the difference to our people. Oh, they are going to be pleased to see you. You are staying now, aren't you? Yes, yes, you will stay."

Balzac happily rambled on as he walked Kito up the alley and round the back to the gazebo. Kalgan, Admasin and Yuna, with Lucia and Patch, sat together.

Patch leapt to his feet. "Well, they are treating us today. Kito, my brother!" He hobbled forward to greet Kito. "My goodness, Kito, have we got a story for you!"

By the time Kito's friends had gathered behind him, all the customary greetings had been made. Letting everyone settle down, Kito cleared his throat. "People of Middle Kingdom, I bring news of your Emperor." He gazed about at the expectant faces. "I'm afraid Emperor Koe has perished in Zimbali."

Admasin was the first to respond. "Kito, where does this leave Middle Kingdom? I mean, is Desora to lead us now?"

Yaan watched his people carefully. Every grimace and every smile was noted.

"No, I'm afraid he was also dispatched ... by one of our own."

Admasin relaxed. "I would like to shake his hand." Yuna frowned, slapping him across the chest.

Kito turned to show his friends. "It's funny you say that. My good friend Hao, could you come forward?"

Hao hesitated, though he knew it would all have to be put down into history. That was how it worked. He stepped forward, and Kito put a hand on his shoulder. "This man is Hao; he served on Magnar Wall for some time. In the battle to protect the people of the palace, he was attacked from behind by Desora. He then went on to defend himself and, as you can see, he won."

Next came Yaan. He stood on the other side of Kito, facing the small gathering. Kito pointed. "Look into his eyes, my friends. Tell me, what do you see?" The people did as he bid, frowning at his request.

Admasin's chair screeched across the floor as he abruptly stood. "Glory be! Can the stories be true?" Yuna tugged on Admasin's shirt, gently prompting him to sit. He didn't listen. "Yaan, where did you grow up?"

"In caves with my family – Maki and Sen Ya San. They were very good to me and I hope when I get home that they are still keeping well."

By now, Admasin was directly in front of Yaan. "This family that raised you … wasn't yours?"

"No, Admasin, they were not."

Admasin was beaming when he stepped back. "But they saved you, this Maki and San from the palace?"

"Yes."

Admasin was positively overcome with excitement. "Balzac, do you know who this is?"

Balzac shrugged. "Enlighten me, Admasin."

Admasin fell into a full bow. "Balzac and friends, I give you Prince Yaan, the son of Prince Hasuca and rightful Emperor of Middle Kingdom!"

The reaction was immediate and overwhelming to Yaan as everyone bowed before him. He knew how this needed to be handled and cleared his throat. "There is a little more to your stories than previously told. I would like to introduce my full sister …"

After the surprised group settled a little, Tanica was bombarded with possibly more questions about her than Yaan. It seemed they'd heard of the legend about Maki, San and the missing bucket, but no one knew about the maid, the warrior, the princess.

They all stayed the night. Stories were swapped both ways, and Tzu was also made welcome; Yaan and Hao would have had it no other way. One of them sat by him all night, although it wasn't long before Tzu was at ease in the group.

***

The following morning, they prepared for their return to Samos. They sailed the inland sea, then manned the oars for the last leg upriver. The vessels were quiet with anticipation as they docked.

Leaving the wharf, they walked the familiar streets back to the salt well, where there was a hive of activity. This time, it was the Barbarians and local men rebuilding the houses together. The only blade carried now was the wood-saw. The clattering and sawing hushed as the procession of legends walked the streets of Samos.

Tzu surveyed his own men working on the rebuilds. They appeared to be happy and relaxed with what they were doing, right up until they saw *the Hat*. The hat of the legend re-aggravated deep scars. Tzu turned to Hao. "You know, Hao, now that this is all said and done, maybe you could lose that thing on your head. You would even look a little tidier, I think."

Hao grinned. "When you are as handsome as me, it doesn't matter what you wear, Tzu."

This was not the answer Tzu was hoping for. "I can see it would be a handy thing up north in the winter and all, but down here, Hao?"

Hao sensed something in Tzu's voice. He watched him closely. "Why, after all this time and after all we have been through, is it an issue now?"

Tzu was eager to avoid any ill feelings when they'd just returned to Samos. He lied with a broad grin, slapping Hao on the back. "No Hao, it's of no issue to me." But it was going to be a time of tension between the people for a while yet.

On the first night back in Samos, there were more stories to be told. Yaan had made a point to sit like everyone else, but Kito's plan was true and right. By morning, he had grown accustomed to groups of city folk coming to stare into his eyes. In the breaking light, they would whisper, "Just look into his eyes, what colours are they?"

He took it all in his stride, but his mind was focused on only one person, one woman. He looked and looked but couldn't see her, or the red scarf.

The men stayed together for a few days, but Yaan noticed Kito was growing restless. "Where is it you would like to go now, my brother?"

"I have many friends at Kadra village that I would like to see."

"It just so happens it is on my way, Kito. May we join you?"

Kito looked inquisitively. "You aren't going to the palace?"

"No, it's not ours, Kito."

Tzu was approaching Yaan from behind.

Kito nodded. "Yes, Yaan, but it was once."

"I have much to work out, Kito. What I do next with the people of my lands *and* the people of the North is critical." He spoke with passion. "We absolutely *must* get this right."

"*We*, Yaan?" Kito questioned.

"Where is Tzu?"

"I am here, Yaan."

Yaan turned around and welcomed Tzu into the semicircle. "Tzu, you must agree, what we do next is imperative to the lands."

Tzu nodded, expressionless. "Yours or mine, Yaan?"

Yaan slapped his thigh so hard Kito and Tzu both flinched. "Damn you, Tzu Hsi. Both!"

Tzu held up his hands. "Alright, Yaan, you need to relax or you're just not going to make the distance as a leader."

"Yes. Though you get my drift?"

"I do, Yaan. I get it."

Kito smirked at the two men. "Yaan, would you like to leave in the morning?"

"We have plenty of daylight to make a start now."

"May we leave in the morning, Yaan?"

Yaan shrugged. Insisting with Kito was futile. "Well, in the morning then. Is there something on your mind, Kito?"

"Yes, could you help me? It shouldn't take long."

Yaan frowned. "Every time you ask for help, we end up in deep trouble … and then I have to save you."

Tzu laughed aloud. "This is true, Yaan, but does life not get better with each time?"

Yaan slung an arm over Tzu's shoulder. "You know, Tzu, you have a valid point."

With the mood lightened, this was as good a time as any. "Tzu, in the morning, Kito and I are leaving for a nearby village. They are very good friends. I would really like you to come along with us." Yaan immediately felt Tzu tense up. He eased back to stand square on to Tzu but left him to think over his answer.

Eventually, he responded. "In these lands, I am clearly a Barbarian, Yaan. You may have accepted me, but many will not." Yaan listened quietly as Tzu took a breath and continued. "What about my people here?"

"I have spoken with Norinko and Porteous about the palace," Yaan gently replied.

"So did I. Porteous told me that most of my people are now at the palace. Your people and mine are not going near each other. They're both going out to hunt, but they return to their own places." He looked around, then back to Yaan. Finally, he asked, "Just what is it you want from me?"

"I want to take you to the villages where I have either family or friends. If you are with me, then they will be like a safe house for you."

"What is the point, man?"

"I want them all to get to know you, Tzu. I want you to tell the story of your grandfather, Tzu Hsi and the Emperor. Together, we might change the small world to believing that although we are different, we can live together. We are but one people."

Tzu scrunched his face. "You used that line before. Where did you get it?"

"From a very brave and wise man. Will you trust me?"

"No. It's all very nice having these men working together while both parties have strong leadership, but we are not the same, Yaan. We will never be the same."

Yaan looked down, visibly disappointed yet resigned. "Alright, Tzu, alright."

Kito nudged him. "Yaan, now that you are free, may I have your time, please?"

Yaan raised his head to see Tzu walking away. "You know, I really thought he would've done this."

Kito squeezed his arm as they began their walk through the city. "I know, Yaan. I see your plan and I feel it is a good one."

"But?"

"He is much older than you, and he has served many battles on the Wall."

"That damn wall, Kito. I respect each person who gave so much. It was too much for any good leader to ask of his people. Damn wall. I might just tear it down with my own two hands. Sick of it! I just hate it."

Kito raised his brows. "I would be leaving the Wall just as it is, Yaan. You are wise to acknowledge the grief that all those families have suffered, but you must also respect that, like me, if you have not served *real* time on the Wall, you couldn't know how it changes a man. There is no substitute for what I am saying." Kito noticed a few people gathered at a corner, watching Yaan approach. "Yaan, I think you should lift your head and acknowledge them."

Yaan looked up to see what Kito was on about. Stopping, he smiled and gave a curt wave. "Hello," he said almost too cheerfully. Once again, the older folk looked into his eyes, then pulled the younger ones onto one knee, whispering frantically, "Bow deep, this is the *real* Emperor." Yaan shuffled uncomfortably.

"Best you get used to it, brother." Kito slapped Yaan on the back, and they moved on.

"Kito, I have something burning I need to discuss with you."

"Anything, Yaan."

"I am not sure about you and my sister. May I ask your intentions towards her?"

"I think she would like to cut me to pieces, and I would like to keep my life."

Yaan stopped walking. "No, really."

Kito slipped his hands up opposing sleeves, his young face ever placid. "I think you have your father's talent, Yaan. You have not tapped into it yet, but you will. Tanica, however, is something special and very powerful. She has no idea yet what she can do."

"Well, if you think she is good ..."

Kito shook his head. "No, Yaan."

Yaan drew back. "With training, might she be as good as you?"

"No, Yaan. She is far stronger, far better than I." Before Yaan could speak again, Kito turned about. "Oh, here, down this alley, Yaan."

As they walked down, Yaan's head swam with Kito's predictions. *He is never wrong.* Yaan looked up, then turned about. He knew this place, he felt.

Kito knocked on a door. Yaan had stayed back, frowning at what Kito could possibly be up to now. The door opened to a neatly dressed woman wearing her favourite red scarf.

Kito bowed politely. "I know you have no idea who I am, but I think you remember this man?" He stood back so she could see Yaan. Kito felt the change in her immediately.

Yaan was staring at her as if she were the only woman in the world. "Hello," he stammered. "I have not had time to go to the markets, so ..." He finished with an awkward smile.

Majito fell into a bow. "My Emperor, it is my pleasure to have you in my presence."

Yaan almost backed up a step. He looked at Kito with deep furrows in his brow. Kito interjected. "Majito, I feel we may draw unnecessary attention out here. Could we step inside?"

Majito never lifted her head to Yaan. "Yes, of course." She walked backwards a few steps, still with her head down and went inside.

Yaan stood frozen to the spot. Was this how he wanted to live for the rest of his life? Kito waved to get his attention. Yaan could feel the blood draining from his head as Kito closed the door behind them with a click. "Majito, we have neglected to have morning tea."

Yaan stood with his back to a broken window now boarded up, making the room quite dark. An oil lantern burned on the table.

"Yes, it would be my honour to bake, if it pleases the Emperor?"

Kito didn't wait for Yaan to answer. "No, just some tea would be fine, thank you, Majito."

Yaan took a breath and blurted out, "It is great to see you again. I was worried about how you would fare; the city was quite the mess as we left."

"Indeed, it was. Many lost too much, sire."

Yaan's posture slumped a little. "You have already heard of my title. May I ask when you heard?"

Majito placed the tea on the table. She was quite meticulous about the placement of what cutlery she had. Yaan suddenly realised there was only tea for two. She stepped back from the table. "Please forgive the lack of my house, I live but a humble existence."

Yaan found that his feet were unable to move. Kito, by contrast, took his seat. "Yaan, would you please sit with me?"

Yaan shook his head. "I will not." He looked at what was possibly the most beautiful woman he had ever encountered. "Majito, I will not be seated until you are."

"As you wish, sire." She stepped forward and sat, albeit with her head still down.

Kito poured Yaan's drink, then his own. Yaan eased into his seat and looked at Majito. "You didn't answer my question. When did you hear about my title?"

"When you were gone, sire. The rumours about Desora and the palace were circulating. The Barbarians in the city seemed to support that rumour, then the others that swept the city, I think within hours of your return."

"And the later rumour for you personally, Majito?"

"I went to the markets near the salt well. I saw how the people were acknowledging you. As the people came and went, I could hear it was indeed all true."

Yaan nodded keenly. "I was looking for you, Majito. I had hoped you would come to see me."

"It has been my pleasure to have known you, my Emperor."

The comment struck Yaan like a wooden mallet. His world spun until he could see he was now completely separated from her. "I see." He looked glumly at Kito, who sat passively. It began to dawn on him what the visit was about. "Majito, how do you see the future of this great nation?"

"I know our Emperor will do what is right."

Yaan leapt from his chair, sending it scuttling across the floor. "Stop the politically correct bear-shit! I want a damn answer!"

Kito sipped his tea. Majito hadn't flinched until Yaan swore. He walked around and leaned on the table, staring her down, willing her to peer up at him. "Answer the question."

Her hands were still, and she sounded calm. "I think the Barbarians are genuinely helping us to rebuild our city. A city broken by our last Emperor. They have given no trouble."

"Yes, I see this already. So, what should a *good* leader do next?"

"Change the image of the people, our people's image concerning the Barbarians."

The furrows on Yaan's brow softened as he stood. "And how does one change that?"

"First, he must disassociate the past from the present."

"Yes, yes. Then what?"

"Spread the word, but also ..." She hesitated.

Yaan leant back on the table. "Please do continue, Majito."

"When I was a little girl, I would listen to my uncles and father talk of where the true borders of our nation's north actually were."

Yaan stood up straight and glanced at Kito still sipping his tea. "I have heard Hao and Bolli speak of the same thing. Could it be that my predecessors used the war to steal land?"

Kito gazed at Yaan but said nothing. Yaan watched Majito, her head down again, looking at the table. It hurt. He felt sad, angry and disappointed. She was showing correct etiquette, though somehow he had naïvely thought she would throw open her arms to his greeting, if such a beauty was even still single. Either way, none of this was to be.

He downed his tea. "Kito, if you are ready?"

Kito was already halfway out of his seat. He faced Majito, who also stood. They bowed deeply to one another. He turned to Yaan. "I will be outside, brother."

Yaan nodded knowingly. As Kito stepped out, he closed the door with a bump. Yaan looked dejected. "So, this is it then? This is how you are to greet me?"

She bowed deeply, then stood, not lifting her head. "My family was always very insistent on appropriate etiquette. I do hope I have made no mistakes."

"Well, Majito, I thank you for taking me in when the city would have had me burned to a crisp." He looked at the sparsely set table. "Also, I thank you for your tea and your honesty. I wish you the very best, Majito, the very best in life."

The front door was left swinging wide open as Yaan marched out.

Majito held her hands over her mouth as she eased weakly to the floor. He couldn't hear her crying as she listened to his footsteps striding down the alley.

Yaan stomped ahead of Kito most of the way back to the salt well. Suddenly, Kito was stopped abruptly as Yaan spun, holding a fist to Kito's face. "WHY? Why, when you knew what was going to happen, did you take me there?"

Kito remained still, his hood up, as Yaan walked in small circles, strong emotions coursing through him. He trembled as he waved his finger in Kito's face. "She saw me but never came forward to speak. You took me to her, for what? To see my heart broken, Kito? I know, Kito … I know you knew how I felt about her." He walked in another small circle. "I know you knew how I felt. I have seen some beautiful women in my short time, my friend but *never* have I known a woman like her, not even close."

Kito said nothing.

"Damn you, man! Would you not give me the silent treatment now?"

"You do seem to be swearing an awful lot these days."

Yaan stepped back, his eyes still watery, though he began to laugh. He folded his arms. "You are my brother, and you know I love you as such, but man, this is hard to swallow."

"Though you *do* know what that was about."

"Oh, is that so, Kito?"

"You have too many emotions flowing. Just let it be, brother. Just let it be, and all will be clear in time."

Yaan scoffed. "Well, thanks for that one."

"There is another lesson here also."

"Really? Oh, do tell."

"You will also hurt for your sister, Yaan."

Yaan's forehead knotted. "Tell me she is in no danger!"

Kito shook his head gently. "She is in no danger whatsoever, but you will both hurt for a time. Just for a time." He began to walk on.

Yaan marched up beside him. "Kito, you must warn me. How can I help?"

"Be patient, be understanding."

"Yes, but what can I do?"

"Nothing, Yaan. This is the lesson, remember?"

"That's it?"

"Yes." He continued to walk with easy strides. Yaan didn't push him any further. There was no point.

Soon enough, they arrived back at their impromptu camp. Once Yaan's raw emotions had settled, he asked Norinko and Kai if they could continue their work in the city. Kai bowed politely, waiting for Norinko to answer. "It will take all winter just to get everyone housed properly, sire. It would please me if you would allow us to continue this task."

Yaan smiled grimly.

Later that day, they all gathered by the salt well. Yaan had asked Tzu to be present for the meeting, on the grounds that his men were also there. "Tzu, what would you like your men to do? You can take them back to your homelands or stay for the winter? We will be more than happy to host your men through winter."

Tzu pursed his lips. "Your supplies have burned. How will you manage to feed the numbers?"

"I spoke with Kohji, Ezra and Mabutu. They all said they could send a little food on a regular basis. I make no promises about the volume, but hopefully some supplies are already on the way."

"Already you impress me. I will put it to my men, those who wish to go back to loved ones can, but those who would like to stay, as goodwill to our new relationship, Yaan, can also stay for the winter. But know now, in spring, I will be calling all my men back to our homelands. We will be needing to plant our crops the moment the ground has thawed."

Yaan, remembering his own life at the caves, knew it was hard enough to the south; he could only wonder about being so far north. "Tzu, there are good grounds just south of the palace. I understand it to be very fertile. I will send Assets to message neighbouring villages that it is my will for it to be left for the palace."

"I have no option but to trust you, Yaan. Do not let me down." There was power in the older man's voice. "Yaan, what are we to do with the Wall, and the palace for that matter?"

"Could you release the rest of my people on your return?"

"Yes, I can do this."

"Will I be welcome to visit the palace whenever I wish?"

"For what purpose?"

"Every good alliance needs true and strong communication, Tzu."

"An alliance, Yaan. For what?"

Yaan shrugged. "We have only one land. The Gods didn't put in any borders. Your people are from the north and mine from the south, but maybe we can blur where that line is. Maybe those blurred lands can be what binds us as one people under the Gods' sky."

"You speak with wisdom. You and your people will always be welcome at my table." Tzu eyed Yaan for a moment. "Yaan, you didn't answer my question about the Wall?"

Yaan shook his head as if to shake away the very thought of it. "I thought it was an ugly thing, but now I think it is just a wall of stone, mason and earth. Can it stay for now?"

Tzu brushed his shaggy, red hair back. "You must realise it offends our people because of what it represents."

"I can see this, but can it stay for now? I just feel there may be something better for it, after our raw emotion has ebbed."

"If you think so, Yaan – for now, it will be.

"I have taken advice on this matter, I'm just not sure yet. I thank your patience and trust, Tzu." Yaan bowed and left.

Porteous leaned in close to Tzu. "Do you think we can really trust him?"

"I hope so. Nations are living on it."

"Have you the Sacred Skull then, Tzu?"

"Kito has put it in the valley with the rest."

"So, we don't have this, either? I'm not comfortable. We seem to be moving very quickly onto unknown grounds. I just don't know if we should be letting our guard down so much."

"He just bowed to me, my Shaman."

"That doesn't mean the trust you speak of is written in stone."

"Nothing of people of this earth is written in stone, Porteous." Tzu turned to face his friend, the Shaman. "Sometimes we must trust for the sake of trust itself. What makes or breaks that bond is how you behave to have others respect that bond."

The Shaman carefully watched Yaan walking away. Tzu slapped him twice on the back and moved on himself. Porteous dropped his fake smile. "I don't like this. Not one bit."

A well-built Barbarian stood just a few paces back from Porteous. The scar diagonally down his face revealed he was a fighting man. "I would like to remove that hat whilst still on the head." He flicked his chin up in Hao's direction, now talking with Yaan. "I will offer that for nothing, Porteous."

"Our day will come." Porteous prodded Dren. "Be patient, my friend, we *will* have the hat."

***

Tzu was sitting on the edge of the stone well, eating fruit, when Tanica approached him.

"Tzu."

"Tanica, what can I help you with?"

Tanica smiled nervously and Tzu frowned but waited. "The night we met …"

He held up a hand for her to stop, but Tanica shook her head. "No, Tzu, I need to say this." Tzu lifted his chin, keeping silent. "That night, Yaan was right, I am young, but now I know you for who you are. I now know how wrong I was, and I'm sorry. I was rude and disrespectful."

Tzu chewed slowly, then swallowed. "You served in the palace?"

"Yes, though only as a maid."

"They say it's hard to be any more than the environment you grow up in. I see you're already outgrowing that environment." He took a bite of his apple. "You remember what you thought of

486

Kito?”

Tanica stiffened. “Yes.”

“Now it’s all done and we’re here safely, what do you think of him at this point?” Tzu watched the young woman as she chose her words carefully.

“I was wrong … about his secret ties to the throne.”

Tzu smiled at her honesty. “You are strong, Tanica. Don’t be too hard on yourself, and Yaan was right, you still have plenty of time.”

She relaxed a little. “Well, I just wanted to say sorry. You deserve much respect, I understand this now.” She took a deep bow and held it for just a moment before leaving.

Tzu continued to eat his fruit, her words echoing in his mind. Her last line kept coming back. ‘You deserve much respect, I see this now.’ Then, with a chill, it dawned on him.

***

That evening, the entire group sat around the fire. Talk was rife, full of boasting and fun.

Hao sat at Kito’s side. “Brother, may I ask what is wrong with Yaan?”

“He has much on his mind.”

Hao snickered. “He is the Emperor, I suppose, and he has no training for it.”

“That might be his biggest asset, Hao. Also, not entirely true either.”

“I don’t follow.”

“He has grown up and lived like any man of Middle Kingdom. He has seen the workings of a real village and the expectations from those people of their Emperor. He has not been sheltered from real life; he’s had neither concubines nor opium. These will, I feel, along with who he surrounds himself with, make him the better Emperor.”

Yaan was sitting on his own, though Tanica sat not far away.

Hao turned back to Kito. "Well, I feel you might just be right. One thing I know for sure, Kito …"

"Yes, Hao?"

"You're right about his friends, they are the best there is." He grinned broadly, and the two men laughed openly together. On hearing them, Tanica wondered why Kito's deep laugh affected her so. She pursed her lips with distaste.

The next morning, as had now become routine, everyone ate together, sitting shoulder to shoulder in a circle. No beginning, no end.

No sooner had they finished breakfast, six horses were brought over. Yaan took his by the reins from Kai. "You have miscounted, my friend," he said, leaping up into the saddle.

Kai shook his head. "No, Emperor. I think not."

Tanica and Mercanti leapt onto theirs followed by Hao and Kito. Then Yaan saw Tzu speaking with Porteous, who was offering his arm towards the horsemen. Yaan waited patiently, watching Tzu shaking his head about whatever they were discussing. Eventually, they parted, and Tzu walked forward and sprang onto the horse beside a confused Yaan. "Tzu, do you have something to talk about?"

Tzu looked briefly at Tanica. "Boy, do we have some things to talk about."

"Well, this *is* the best start then." Yaan looked down at Porteous. "I will be taking Tzu only to villages I know he is safe in, then I will ride with him and expect to be at the palace by the first frosts, before the snow." He turned to Norinko. "When Porteous and his men are ready, send them with a guide and several men clear on translation, for safe passage to the palace."

Yaan's horse pranced about, eager to be on its way. He looked back at Porteous as the horse began to move off. "We are going the long way. You could stay here for some time and still be at the palace to greet me and Tzu on our arrival."

Porteous gave a thin smile. "This is most kind, sire."

Yaan lowered his voice. "Not at all, Shaman." He looked at all the men working together. "All this work has been most kind and not gone unnoticed." He waved to the men and kicked his horse to lead the way.

Well-wishers lined the streets to see them off. The riders all felt a little silly sitting up on their horses with everyone waving to them.

They'd only gone a few blocks when Yaan saw the red scarf. His jaw clenched as he stopped his horse. He gazed down at her head as she stayed bowed. "Look to your Emperor, Miss Majito."

Slowly, she looked up.

"Just remember, young woman, I am just a man trying to bring peace to a land he doesn't know. Just a man." He trotted on without looking back.

***

Once out of the city, they broke into a strong canter. Hao sensed early on that Yaan was eager to reach the first stop, and they did make it to Kadra by nightfall.

Yaan slipped from the saddle and walked his horse through the gates, leading them to the well to water the horses. He walked clear of the horses. "Hello, does anyone live here?"

Nothing.

Concern gathered on Yaan's face. He turned to Hao, looking troubled.

"I'm sure they are fine, Yaan. How would they not …"

Just then a door on the second level opened, and Luhou walked out and leaned over the railings. "Look who it is. Come on then, we've prepared dinner and await your company."

Yaan beamed with relief, and the laughter and jesting began. Hao stopped Yaan. "You and Tzu go ahead, I will tend your horses."

"I can tend my own horse, thank you," objected Tzu.

"I know this, Tzu, but the talks you and Yaan are about to embark on up there are far more important. If these are the days that we are to lay our foundations on then tending your own horse won't help. It would be my privilege, Tzu."

"I am neither your commander nor your Emperor. Why would you serve me?"

"If we are to have peace, King Tzu, you are then as important as our own Emperor." Tzu had no more arguments. Hao grinned, taking the reins.

Luhou watched Hao taking the horses to the stables, then saw someone who made her heart skip a beat. It took her back with unprepared emotion. She looked at the beautiful face which seemed to glow when she looked up at Mercanti. Their eyes locked.

Emperor Yaan made the introductions, being very careful to introduce Tzu as the Northern King. The word Barbarian would never be spoken. Yaan led the talks with the elders – Manchu and Kale. Tzu was welcomed and encouraged to relay his every thought. The elders sat back, trying to understand Yaan's big plans.

Hao was in the stables tending the horses. A horse nudged him from behind as he continued grooming. "Back off, you never even did any work today." It nudged him again. Hao laughed as he finished the horse he was grooming then turned about. His face dropped with disbelief. "Yunma?"

"Yes, it is, Hao." Hao turned and dipped his head for Luhou. She reciprocated and then stepped forward. "He just trotted into our village one day. We knew who he was so …"

"Thank you, Luhou." Hao's eyes narrowed. "You're not upstairs; the plan's not for you?"

Luhou smiled mildly as she patted the big horse. "Before Yaan left with some of our villagers, I asked him to reconsider taking ..."

"Kai, who is now twice the man he was."

"But the other three died for nothing."

Hao interrupted before she'd finished. "I, Luhou, have killed many men. Too many men; good men; family men, I'm sure. I know your village also lost many to the Tark family. Though painful, you must let it go. Just let it be."

He stroked his horse. "The risk Yaan took in Samos before we went to Zimbali was second to none. What he is trying to do with Tzu now is also very dangerous, for them both. But if they succeed, our children and their children for many generations, just might live in peace. That's what this man is trying to do, Luhou. This is the Yaan you and I know. He has already achieved amazing things; just give him some space, and your support. Your three died in a city undecided on its leader. The demise made up the minds of thousands who witnessed their wrongful deaths. Their sacrifice will be spoken about for generations, Luhou."

They stroked the horse in silence, both with their own problems consuming their minds.

***

Yaan, Tzu and Hao went fishing every morning. Tzu was fascinated; never had he seen such a spectacle. It was a good-sized clinker they took, and there were plenty of villagers offering to row the legends. Soon enough, Tzu was trying this rowing thing himself. It was a laughable sight enjoyed by all. In time, he could row straight, almost. Tanica and Mercanti enjoyed taking long walks then soaking in the hot baths every day. Luhou was keen to join them as much as she could.

Kito kept to himself, though every man wanted to sit with him and talk about what had happened in Zimbali. He told of the bravery of Tanica, Mercanti and the woman named Shay, for they held back the entire Royal Guard. Kito said he wasn't there at the time and so couldn't say exactly how this was done. He spoke of Yaan, Hao and Tzu standing before the sand warriors. Though greatly outnumbered, they stared them down and returned to tell the tale. He also told it as he saw it in Samos. Tzu and Hao, fighting side by side, were said to be impossible to defeat. According to Kito, they alone divided the Royal Guard and so crippled them. Yaan had shown no weakness when he saved Janing, though it was at the sacrifice of others who bravely gave everything.

As Kito told his stories of extreme bravery, everyone was captivated. Perhaps it was because the stories came from the legendary Kito himself, or perhaps it was because the stories were told in raw truth. By day, however, Kito left on foot every morning and returned by evening with a catch. Everyone was always amazed – a huge wild boar – a deer. There were rumours that he was seen sitting at the edge of the jungle with a large panther. Kito never spoke on the matter, though one boar skin was ruined with huge claw marks. Kito would skin the good ones and cure the skin as a gift to the village.

On this evening, Kito gave Manchu a prized deer skin. Manchu turned it over, inspecting it closely. "But it has no hole, Kito. How did you kill such a beast?"

"Every hunter has his secrets," Kito said as, smiling broadly, he looked about the room. "I thank the people of this village for making me welcome. I know to you all I look a little strange, but you have always looked out for me as one of your own. I am forever grateful." He bowed to the room.

Tzu wasn't surprised when the entire room, on cue, stood and bowed back to Kito. Tanica watched and frowned, her jaw locked tight.

Yaan made his thanks to the village for making them all welcome after arriving unannounced. He also made a point of thanking all the people who went to Zimbali to wage into the war that could have crushed nations. He made a special point of thanking King Tzu for, on more than one occasion, saving his own life.

Tzu was caught off guard when Yaan bowed to him, then the entire room, slowly but steadily stood and followed their Emperor's lead, bowing to the Northern King. Yaan would not stand from his bow, until everyone had joined him.

***

As promised, at first light the following morning, Yaan's group was saddled and ready for their next journey. All but one.

Tanica grabbed Mercanti by the arm. "What do you mean, you won't be going any further? I can't go with all these men on my own!"

"But you *can,* Tanica. Each one of them would give his life for yours. You must be there as Yaan will need you."

"No, he doesn't!" Tanica urged. Luhou came and stood beside Mercanti. They held hands and smiled at Tanica, who leaned back. "Oh, I see … I um, never realised that." She now understood it would be selfish to ask Mercanti to leave. "Mercanti, I want you to be happy, you know this, but I just don't know if I can manage without you. We are like sisters now."

Mercanti tenderly wiped away Tanica's tears. "And we always will be, Tanica, but we must also live our own lives. You don't even know where you are to end up, but I do know Yaan will need you and you will need Yaan. I have no place in your world that's now not mine. I'm not a maid, not a warrior and no princess. At best, I'm a hunter."

Tanica had nothing left to say. Mercanti hugged her tightly and whispered, "This may be the only family that I get to have, please release me to live it."

Tanica nodded reluctantly as they pulled back to arms' reach. She placed her hands on Mercanti's shoulders. "I owe you my life. Never have you failed me. Whatever happens north of here, never will I forget your name. Please never forget mine." She gave her a final squeeze, then swung into her saddle, looking at Luhou. "She is the best of people. Take the best of care with her. Love her deeply." And with that, she trotted her horse out through the gates.

All the horses had set off, except Kito, who stood quietly talking with a few young village men. He made his polite goodbyes and, some paces behind, followed the departing horses.

43 The Talent

There was a sense of homecoming as they travelled through the jungle. The damp, humid air carried with it the sounds of life teeming all around them. Tzu smiled as Yaan would sometimes hum a tune; he was taken with the beauty of the place and these southern lands. The group stopped only to refresh their horses or take a little food and water.

They guided the horses through some fig trees, the horses stopping intermittently to eat their fallen bounty. When they reached the green pool, Hao and Yaan remembered the great leap off the clifftop, which was a miracle that anyone, including the horses, had survived. Being early afternoon, everyone was keen for a swim to clean off and freshen up. In keeping with modesty and respect, no one completely undressed today – there was, after all, a princess in their company. Unfamiliar with swimming, Tzu was never far from the shore.

They made camp under the fig trees. Yaan began the story of how Bolli had almost lost his hat down the river and how he risked drowning to retrieve it. Hao slipped away quietly, leaving Yaan with his most amazing way of telling a great story. He would rather go on a hunt. Seeing him gone and everyone else settled, Tanica slipped away to relieve herself.

On her way back, she was admiring the rainforest with its hum of the bees and birdsong ringing from the treetops; she was startled when Kito spoke.

"Hello, Tanica."

"Kito, were you following me?" She looked defensive.

"No, Tanica, though I am guilty of coming to intercept you on your return."

"And you have," she grimaced.

"We have a small problem a few days ahead. I need your help if you would." She folded her arms. "Tanica, you, with Mercanti and Shay, did an amazing thing in Zimbali. I need your help to do something similar here."

Tanica's arms fell open. "That was Shay! I don't even know how she did it."

"No, Tanica, we have already spoken on this." She shook her head vigorously, though Kito gently continued. "Yaan has the same talent. Have you not noticed just how apt he is in his new role? This is no accident."

Tanica glared at him. "No, he is just a natural-born leader."

"He is that also, but tell me this, Tanica, when the rats in Samos came and ate just one man and left again, who was responsible for that?"

"Who told you about that?"

"No one. He called me and I witnessed it."

Her eyes flared as she stepped forward, pointing an angry finger. "You bastard! He called you for your help, and you watched him being tormented? Damn you and your arrogance!" She sprang forward so quickly that it almost startled Kito. He swayed to the side but she got him with a foot as she went by. They both rolled in the long grass, then back to their feet. Kito readied himself to meet her next onslaught and she parried him each time. Neither drew their weapons.

The tussle continued for quite some time as Tanica released her pent-up anger upon him. She went at him again but he was one step ahead and she landed in the grass, purposely winded. He pulled her arms tight across her chest, pinning her there for a moment. Then he released her, springing back and she stumbled onto one knee. Her hair stuck to her face and sweat stung her eyes, her chest heaving she looked up at Kito. His hood had been down when he'd first approached her, but now it was up. Other than that, he looked the same.

She cried out in frustration. "How is it you don't even sweat? It's not normal, Kito."

"Your father showed me this trick, and many more. If you would allow me, I could teach you."

"Hasuca was ..."

Kito's broad chest expanded. "Please don't, Tanica. There is much I can show you about your father, but until you understand better, you should not misrespect the dead."

Tanica frowned. "Misrespect. That's not even a word."

He shrugged. "I don't care. You understood its meaning didn't you?"

"Yes, well, not entirely, no."

"If you disrespect someone, it is intentional. If you misrespect someone, you didn't mean to, but the fact remains, you still have."

"Where did you get it?"

"From a friend. Now, I need to freshen up." He pointed to a calm spot on the river well down from the camp and rapids.

She pulled the hair away from her face and smacked away the hand that Kito offered her. "I am not an invalid."

Trying not to laugh, Kito turned towards the river. She followed with her head down, deep in thought about how he'd moved.

Fully clothed, Kito cut the surface of the water with barely a ripple. He turned upstream and began to swim against the current. Tanica waded waist-deep in the warm water. Seeing the logic in this, she followed his lead. Side by side, though with a wide gap between them, they swam together.

Kito knew she wouldn't stop swimming until he did. He didn't wish to drown today, so made his way to the shore. He took off his shirt and pants to ring them out. After flapping them in the warm air, he redressed. He lay down on the shore with his hands under his head, gazing up at the changing colours of the afternoon sky.

Eventually, Tanica waded out. "If I ring out my clothes, you won't look, will you, Kito?"

"There are a few old fig trees behind me. You can go over there if you wish."

"Though I could hide under a rock and you have the talent to see, don't you?"

"I will not look, Tanica."

"See that you don't."

Kito grinned. "Or you'd whip my ass, Tanica?"

Tanica scowled and shook her wet hair over him, then left him laughing. When she returned, she sat cross-legged not far from him and pulled a few long-stemmed flowers from the riverbank. "So, you think Yaan and I have some magical talent, do you?"

Kito propped himself up on one arm and gazed at the river babbling its way down over the boulders. "No, I *know* both of you have your father's talent – it is not magic."

She scoffed as she plaited the four stems. "So, how do you think you're to unlock all this for me?"

He looked into her big green eyes. "It is no throwing of the bones, Tanica. It will take a lot of work and all your patience, and …"

She'd never noticed his incredible blue eyes before. *How could I have missed those?* "Yes, Kito?"

"You will have to trust me."

"Is this a big deal?"

"For you, yes."

"Why?"

"Because in your heart, you think I'm a traitor. This is almost as bad as what my grandfather called me."

Embarrassed at his observations of her, she moved on. "What did your grandfather call you?"

"To him, I was just a murderous monster."

She stopped plaiting the flowers. "Ouch."

"He wasn't wrong. It was what I was set up to do at the time."

"And?"

"Long story. You do understand the talent, don't you?"

"I worked with the best of the best in the palace. I mean, those men risked their very lives helping me, but I could never get to that next level …" She smiled, rolling her eyes. "… as you just saw."

"I just saw great moves, amazing technique, but no talent whatsoever."

She grimaced. "Why?"

This was by far the most open he'd ever seen her. *Nothing like a good old-fashioned whipping to sort things out.* "It's no one's fault. It's a man's world, and I'm surprised you got the level of teaching that you did. Did they know *who* your father was?"

"Master Xiang did, but he came to an untimely death. His successor probably not. No."

Kito sat up properly. "Tanica, would you trust me with this?"

She paused momentarily. "Do I have a choice?"

"Well, of course you do. Say yes or say no. This is the last time I will ever bring it up with you."

"Really, Kito?"

"It's called respecting one's decision. Yes."

She fiddled with the plait that was nearly at the end. Kito looked at it. It was a barrel of plaited flower stems with the flowers at the top. Never had he seen this before. Not commenting, he lay back down and looked skyward again. She sounded annoyed. "What are you doing?"

"Watching the evening sky changing colours. It can be quite beautiful."

She sighed lightly. "What is it you want help with today?"

Kito didn't sit up. "It may be getting a little late in the day now. You have heard about the Colonial canal dig?"

"The one where the Emperor let the water go a day early?"

"The one and the same. I want to put the water back where it belongs. Not yet, but soon."

"You just said it might be a little late today?"

"Yes I did. I wanted to take you for a look first, then, when the time is right, we could do the job. If you like?"

Her eyes lit up. "Like a test run?"

"If this doesn't offend you, yes."

Her head tilted. "I am a little hard to get along with, aren't I?"

Kito sat up, facing her, and crossed his legs. "If I were to answer that honestly, I may find myself on the verge of a beating." He warmed at how her face lit up when she allowed herself to laugh.

She shook her head. "You have a wonderful way with words, Kito." She now looked serious. "Is there still time or not?"

Kito's eyes twinkled. He checked around, then held out his large hand. "You know this does come with some danger attached?"

She grimaced as she tentatively put her small hand in his. "Explain."

"When you leave your mortal soul, you run the danger of your body being interfered with. If it dies, it will leave you stranded in the void." Her eyes narrowed. Kito shook her hand gently to keep her focused on him and the now. "Also, if you meld with an animal and it is killed, you risk dying with it." He scoffed at his own naivety. "I learnt that one the hard way." He watched Tanica, her face becoming stricken. "Do you still wish to join me?"

"I did all that travelling with Shay and *now* you tell me this?"

"Think back to how you felt about me on the vessel, or even in the Village of the Keepers. Could we have had this discussion then, Tanica?"

She sat blank-faced.

"Exactly. But this is now, and I am again asking for your help."

"How do you know when your mortal body is safe? We could …"

Kito smiled, lowering his head for a long moment, leaving Tanica wondering where he'd just gone. Her hand tingled in his. For a moment, Kito's eyes were unfocused. "The rest of the men are sitting around the fire talking about grand plans for their lands and Hao is on his way back, knowing it's growing dark.",

"You did *not* just see all that!"

"Hao will have a pheasant and two rabbits. Tzu has never seen pheasant before so will make short work of the rabbits. And Yaan will work the pheasant. We are running short on time if you want to do this, Tanica."

To her right now, he seemed to glow. "Let's do this." She reached out her other hand and put it in his giant palm. He held it with a gentle thumb.

"Slow your breathing. Long, deep breaths. Ease your mind …"

Her body tingled, and she smiled at the memory of it. Suddenly, Kito was gently pulling her upwards. She looked down at Kito holding her hands, then peered up as they went through the tree canopy. It was the most exhilarating experience of her life, again.

She felt safe as Kito released one hand so they could travel side by side.

He led them faster just above the canopy. She could see clearly that they were following a ravine. Knowing their direction, she could feel her own power driving her quickly forward. They travelled a short time then began to slow. Tanica saw the problem. She looked across at Kito as he spoke in her mind: *When the time is right, we will use the animals to cut his menacing dam wall and let the waters flow as the Gods intended.* It was all Tanica could do to nod and smile.

They travelled slowly over the huge clay wall, looking at it from all angles. Long clumps of grasses and small bushes had taken hold, making it even stronger and harder to breach. She understood the task now. Collapse the canal wall back into the stream. Kito motioned to go back along the dry stream once more. She didn't want to go. She didn't want to go back to her mortal body ever again but she also knew Kito wouldn't let this happen. *But if I learnt …*

They cruised all the way back down the ravine. At one point, Kito slowed, gazing down at the dry riverbed. His face was solemn and tinged with sadness, then once again, they were on their way.

She felt euphoric from the experience.

Kito saw the excitement on her face. *You good for some more?*

Give me more. I need more!

He sped ahead over the jungle canopy. She felt him hold her hand a little tighter, then suddenly the canopy was gone and they were high over the green pool. They dove straight down into the water. Tanica became concerned as Kito pulled her ever deeper then she realised he was showing her the capacity of their talent. He turned upwards, and they shot up out of the pool. Soaring high in the sky, Kito stopped, and they looked over the Gods' beauty under the setting sun. Taking a moment, they soaked it all in, then gently cruised back down and over the beach. Tanica almost burst out laughing as she saw Yaan and Tzu staring blankly at the pool.

They eased back into their bodies, Tanica breathing deeply. She lifted her head and shook Kito's hands vigorously. "You *must* teach me the talent. I must do this!"

"Shh, not everyone understands, even less approves. This needs to be kept quiet."

She scrunched her face. "Why? Is this not approved by the Gods, Kito?"

"I feel maybe a little closer to them myself but remember what you said to King Mabutu about me leaving the vessel in the middle of the ocean without a trace? People are the ones you need to defend yourself against, Tanica. People. Providing we respect the talent, the Gods are just fine."

She looked at the grass and pulled back out of his hands. He smiled and lay back down, clay banks on his mind. Not knowing what to say further, she excused herself and headed back to the campfire.

The fire was now flickering in the evening light. No one was there. Tanica became concerned that she'd shirked her responsibility to the group. She looked about frantically, her heart racing when she heard Kito's voice. *Slowly, deeper, slower. Think about them, search them …* She could feel her skin prickle as Kito's talent helped her. She gasped when she had a vision of Yaan and Tzu sitting together not far away. The tingles stopped.

Her blood rose when she reached there and saw Yaan plucking the pheasant and Tzu skinning two rabbits. In her distant thoughts, she heard Kito laughing. She stamped her foot and slumped down, watching the men.

***

They'd trekked for three more days when they came to a clearing in the jungle above a dry riverbed. Hao glanced at Kito knowingly. Yaan spoke quietly. "There is a good place for a camp, further up on this side of the river."

"Yes, I will see you there," Kito quietly replied.

Tzu wondered at the solemn men but never questioned; they quietly moved on without word. Tanica recognised the place. It was where they'd slowed on the way back from the canal. She watched as Kito slipped from his saddle and spoke to the horse gently. He wrapped the reins around the pommel and the horse continued on, quietly following the other men. She was about to tell him, then realised. She stood, immobile, as Kito walked down onto the riverbed. He slipped his hand into his left sleeve and pulled out a small crown. Her eyes swelled as it sparkled brightly in the scattered light of the jungle. He turned his head to one side. *Could you leave me, please.*

A chill ran up her spine. Quickly, she turned her horse and cantered off, though she couldn't help but look back just once as she went.

Kito looked at the stack of rocks on the opposing wall. Hood up, he lowered his head with a big sigh.

"Hello, Chizoba."

Startled, Kito spun on his heel. There she was! He dropped to one knee. "Mother, I ... how?"

Rani's dress glowed a warm orange, and her entire being seemed to sparkle. "Stand before me, my son. You know you do not bow to me."

Kito stubbornly refused. "Hasuca and Xiang say the same, but I like to bow to them as I will kneel for you. It is my respect for you."

She walked forward, her arms outstretched to him, though she knew here, she couldn't touch him. "Chizoba, my son, as proud as I already was of you, never did I think one of my own would do all that."

"I think I was lucky with the people who took me in. Baako, Hasuca and Trina were all so very good to me, their influence on me true and right."

Her laughter was almost offensive. He frowned. Her gown fluttered but he couldn't remove his eyes from hers. "No, son. You were sent on a journey to meet with all those people because you are *that* man. This … this was all how it was meant to be. You told Mensa the same thing as you avenged my death in the desert. The Emperor drained the river and your friends found this very place dried up, and it delivered you the very thing that helped you do what you have done."

Her eyes flickered, warming her smile. "You are that person." She laughed again. "You even alluded to it in the cave on our first meeting. I think you said, 'whatever this is, I'm right in the middle.'" She chuckled again.

Kito had so many questions that he could hardly think where to start. "How do you know what I said to Mensa?"

"Hasuca has been to visit me in the valley."

Kito's eyes shone with excitement. "You have spoken?"

The jungle echoed her laugh. "Son, I think that man is even prouder than I. He spoke only well of you."

"You have some freedom in the valley; I'm pleased for you, Mother." He searched for his next words.

Rani's dress flickered and darkened. "What bothers you, my son?"

"I am conflicted, Mother."

"By what nation is home, and where are you to be?"

"Yes. Mabutu is clearly my father, and Baako my brother. I think Grandfather and Aitan would both like to take me home and put me on a podium as a monument to you, but Hao, Yaan and Tzu are also my brothers, and I remember nothing but Middle Kingdom as my home."

Rani recognised he had not mentioned the beautiful and talented Tanica. Inwardly, she laughed. "Popularity is your problem now, Chizoba?"

Kito looked to the ground, confused. When he looked up again, the bottom of her dress was departing as butterflies.

"Son, you have your whole life ahead. Just enjoy each day and don't fret for what you can't control." The butterflies were dissipating up into the jungle as the last of her words hung in the warm air. "Until next time, my son."

Kito could all but taste her words and, with the last butterfly to bat its fragile wings and leave, so did she.

***

It was quite late when Kito trotted back to the camp and dismounted. Everyone was leaning back with full bellies. Yaan sat forward when he saw Kito approaching.

Hao quickly pulled some meat they'd set aside and put the tea back on. "Hey, brother, you alright, my friend?"

Kito lowered himself to the jungle floor just in front of his saddle, looking at Tzu. "Thank you for tending my horse."

Tzu's mouth dropped open slightly, holding out a hand, questioning. Yaan smiled knowingly. Kito quietly took his food from Hao. "Thank you." He ate in silence. There was little talk until finally Kito looked up. "Hao, Yaan, I know what you did down there for a perfect stranger. She is ever grateful, as am I ever grateful." Without further word, he pulled up his hood and lay with his head on his saddle.

Hao, now with his trusty horse, lay with his head on its neck. Tzu grunted as he did every night. Never had he seen such a thing – this Hao and his horse.

***

They rode for several more days until they came to a clear field, a large oak right in the middle. Kito trotted up beside Yaan. "Would you mind if we stopped here for the night?"

"Kito?"

"Yaan, if you would."

Yaan studied Kito momentarily. "Very well, but we have a long way to go and can't do this every other day."

Kito smiled, thinking of Yaan's uncle, Koe. "Just this once, Emperor."

Yaan rolled his eyes. "Only because I like you, my brother."

As always and bursting with enthusiasm, Hao was gone hunting in moments. Tzu nudged Yaan. "Does he not like us or something?"

Yaan burst out laughing. "I know, Tzu, I know. Though you must admit, he gets a result every single time."

"That he does. He is one canny hunter."

Kito approached Tanica as she pulled her saddle down. "Tanica, when you are finished there, can you join me?" He hadn't spoken to her in days, in fact, he'd not spoken to anyone really.

"You want me to drop everything at your beckoning?"

"I said … when you've finished what you're doing. If it's too much, we can simply do what the men did when they came down this way eons ago."

She placed the saddle over a log and put her hands on her hips. "Which is what, Kito?"

"They disrobed completely and swam their horses across, dragging a raft with their dry clothes on it."

She squinted. "Would you like this option, Kito?"

"Yaan is just over there – you may ask him if you wish. As I said, it's entirely your call."

"Argh, sometimes you are insufferable."

He did his best not to smile as he walked around behind the tree. There, they would not be noticed from the fire, but being so close would also have some benefit. Tanica saw the safety in his choice of location. Readying herself, she sat down opposite him.

Kito crossed his legs, and Tanica took his outstretched hands and lowered her head. Their breathing quickly matched and slowed. The immense power Kito had in his talent was both intimidating and reassuring. She loved the tingling feeling washing over her, from her palms resting in his, to the very soles of her feet. With a gentle tug, Kito pulled her free of her body.

He purposely led her to look down on Tzu and Yaan, chatting as they built up the fire, then they sped up and over the canopy. Kito looked at Tanica; her smile was as wide as it was captivating. *She really is loving the talent, completely unafraid.*

They slowed at the canal ahead. Large numbers of animals lined the banks, unable to migrate south over this man-made barrier for the impending winter. Concerned, she looked at Kito. He pointed. There were already hundreds of holes in the embankment. He motioned down to the jungle's edge. A herd of elephants began trumpeting as they moved forward, rocking against the trees. The trees swayed and pushed back, but they offered no resistance to the elephant.

One by one, the elephants carried the huge fallen trees over their impressive tusks. Walking up the clay embankment to the canal, Tanica watched in fascination as the elephants tossed the trees into the canal, then turned towards all the holes and began to trumpet loudly, stamping their feet, making the entire embankment shudder.

Kito nudged her as hundreds of rabbits emerged from the holes and fled back to the jungle. Slowly, the water banked up against the piles of trees, turning muddy as it swirled and rose, then the rabbit holes began to take in water. The elephants worked slowly and constantly, and as the tree dam built higher and wider, so did the water level. The elephants made low grunting, groaning noises as they worked. Tanica knew the animal kingdom had its own communication, but now somehow, she could feel it, without words, understand it.

Eventually, the elephants stopped and watched the embankment darken as the water level rose, putting more and more pressure on the wall.

The wall began to wane: small tuffs began sliding away, giving way to bigger pieces that broke and cascaded down. Quickly, the entire wall collapsed. Water thundered down, violently turning into thick, heavy mud, smashing everything in its way, cascading over rocks. The Colonial river was drained from both sides, sucking down the tree dam with it. It would be a ghastly mess for a few days then it would clean itself and return into the old river it once was.

Like a winter's blast, it washed over Tanica. She remembered the story of Kito, diving into the muddy flood to save an old woman. Now, seeing the power of this dam giving way, she felt ashamed. Gazing up at him, watching his plan come to reality, she realised how arrogant and naïve she had been.

Slowly, they rose and drifted over the diminishing wall as the torrent gained momentum, quickly eating it down to the bedrock. Kito turned them back to the elephants that now stood side by side along what was, again, the riverbank. He gave thanks. They raised their trunks and trumpeted together. Thrilled, Tanica squeezed his hand tightly. Laughing together, they made their way back.

Tanica was enjoying the journey when she felt Kito tense. She looked down at their mortal forms sitting in the grass. Tzu was crouched down by their side. Kito held up a hand and she paused, confused, then her blood ran cold when he slipped his hand from hers. She was suspended there as Kito slowly descended. When he was just opposite Tzu, he lunged forward at him. She didn't see exactly what he did but there was a bright flash and Tzu leaped back, tripping over himself as he scarpered to the fire, glancing back over his shoulder.

Tzu hurriedly sat at the fire. Yaan saw his drawn face. "Tzu, whatever happened to you? You're as white as a ghost."

"Shut up, Yaan. Just shut up!"

Kito beckoned Tanica, and she steadily descended to him. Retaking his hands, they slipped back into their bodies again.

He slowly lifted his head. "Are you good?" he asked with a wink.

She beamed, wide-eyed. "This is amazing! You must teach me everything."

"You are strong, Tanica. I feel it will not be long, and you will be taking your clothes with you."

Her mouth dropped open. "What?"

Kito smirked. "You haven't noticed?"

Instinctively, she put her arm across her chest. "You are jesting me. You are a tease, aren't you?"

"It took me some time to learn that. Quite some time."

Tanica stood up with a look of disgust. She spat to the ground between them, then stormed off to the fire. Kito lay back in the grass, gazing up at the sky. His smile was wide and enduring.

***

Two days later, they arrived at the bottom of the embankment. Hao turned in his saddle. "Any wild leaps of grandeur planned today, Yaan?"

"Oh, everyone's the comedian, aren't they? Today, Hao, your horse may falter."

Hao laughed as he leaned down and slapped his horse on the neck. "This beauty chose me, may I never let him down."

Tzu stared at Hao, though the burning question could not be asked. At least, not yet.

They trekked up the embankment and peered over at the dry, barren canal bed.

"What the …?" exclaimed Hao.

Kito glanced at Tanica; she'd barely looked at him since they did the work. Tzu turned to Hao. "So, what were you on about?"

"Well, it's hard to explain, now. Last time we were here, we leapt into … all of this is hard to explain."

Yaan gazed at Kito. "You wouldn't know about this change, would you, Kito?" Yaan's face dropped in horror. "Kito, did you move the bones?"

Kito kicked his horse down one of the tracks that the animals had already begun to etch into the bank. "Mother said they were just bones, nothing to be excited about."

Watching Yaan sit back in his saddle, Hao caught onto their cryptic conversation. Without further word, Kito made his way to the bottom of the embankment and crossed the dry riverbed.

44 Hao's Home

In Tarim Caves, Tammirie was stirring the night's food, Jeng close by. She was idly talking with Sen Ya San when she noticed Maki looking at her. She frowned. "Father, what is it? You look …" She tilted her head inquisitively. "… actually, I don't know this look."

San wiped her hands on her apron. "Maki, is everything alright outside?"

"I think you'd better come out and see for yourself."

Tammirie checked that Jeng was not far away and, pleased she was safe, she continued with dinner.

"Tammirie, you too."

Confused, she put down her wooden spoon as another woman stepped in. "Go on, girl, be off with you."

Sen looked worried as she held out a hand for Tammirie and they quickly stepped outside into the afternoon sun. They stood with their hearts in their mouths. Sen released Tammirie. "Yaan? Son, is this really you?"

Yaan jumped from his saddle, grinning broadly, and gathered his mother up in his arms. "I have missed you, old girl."

San responded with a choked sob in return.

Tammirie rejoiced for her mother and father. They sure did love their son, and so they should. Then he spoke. Her heart skipped a beat then almost stopped. She would know this voice anywhere. In total disbelief, she slowly turned to the most amazing man she'd ever encountered. "Hao?"

"It's me, my angel."

She sprung into his arms, almost knocking him from his feet. Their dead hero was back from the dead before their very eyes!

How had even *he* managed this one? Tammirie whispered, "What of the Emperor?"

"He's dead, as is the prince."

"Now you will never leave again. Do you hear me? Never!"

"Yes, Tammirie. This is my thought also." Finally, he pried her off and reached for his shoulder bag. The entire village watched, intrigued, as he pulled out a smaller, leather bag and went down to one knee. Slowly, he pulled the drawstrings open.

Tammirie waited with her breath held so long she thought she might pass out.

Hao pulled out a leather cord. An intricate bone carving dangled on the end with a loop at the top where the leather cord went through. Two separate bones intertwined around each other without touching. The bones widened, until at the bottom, they came together in a loop to join as one. Cradled in the bottom was a small emerald. The people could only wonder how the carver got it in without breaking the bone.

"I have no money to have it set, but if you would have me, I would ..." She sprang into his arms. Holding her small waist, he grinned. "I will take this as a yes."

The villagers cheered loudly, then quickly settled as Hao turned to Jeng. From the same pouch, he pulled out a small seashell, smooth as ice and shining with beautiful colours in the fading light. "Jeng, would you accept me into ..." Jeng snatched the shell as she jumped to hug him. He laughed loudly. "Must be a family trait!"

Maki called in his best voice. "Tonight, we must celebrate our good fortunes!"

Standing back from the group, Tzu had observed the joyous welcome Yaan and Hao had received. His eyebrows raised when he first heard Maki's high-pitched voice. Tanica noticed and remembered back to when she'd also first heard him, wondering the same. Kito leaned between them and said quietly, "This is the man who stole the baby Yaan from the ranting Emperor and the burning palace to bring him here in the middle of winter. I know you won't be too quick to judge."

Tzu nodded; the pieces were coming together.

Two boys came running over. "May we take your horses, please?"

Tanica looked at Tzu. "Suits me." She smiled at the boys as she handed over the reins. "Lucky it is not winter, hey?"

"Yes, I'm getting a little chilly myself." Tzu rubbed his hands together, then noticed the hot vapours coming from the stream.

Tanica shrugged. "I don't really know. I've not actually been here before either."

Maki came scurrying back through the last of the group. "My dear, Tanica, what are you doing standing out here?" He didn't slow his approach as he pulled her into a hug. His chin up on her shoulder, he did his best to drag her down to him. "My dear girl, you need to know, *every night*, mother and I have prayed for your wellbeing."

Tanica was speechless. She'd had great friends in the palace but never like this, and this was Yaan's family. She pulled back, looking into his face. "Maki, from the bottom of my heart, I thank you both. I really do." She had to bend over a little so he could touch his head to hers. Struggling with his emotions, Maki held her there a while longer. Tzu wondered if he should go for a walk, then Tanica stood straight. "Father, next to Yaan, I have here the most important man to possibly ever grace your caves."

Maki stood back to face the new man, knowing immediately he was of the north. Tanica was shocked to see something wash over Maki. Tzu stood unemotional. She spoke before it could go horribly wrong. "Maki, my second father, I have the honour to introduce you to Tzu Hsi, the Northern King." She turned back to Tzu. "As Kito eluded, this is the man who fathered Yaan from the day he was born."

Tzu put out his arm and waited. Maki was unmoving for some time, then finally his face softened into a welcoming smile, and they shook like men. "I think you and that crazy son of mine might have some truly amazing stories to share."

Tzu scoffed. "Don't be letting the imagination of the younger generation lead you astray. Hao and I will see you right."

Maki's high-pitched laughter was infectious.

Tanica watched them heading inside, chatting. "Yaan, you just might do this, you crazy man. You just might," she whispered to no one in particular, then a voice from behind responded.

"And what of you, Tanica? What is it you want?"

Without turning around, she shook her head. "I just don't know, Kito. I really don't know."

Kito walked around to face her. "May I suggest?"

She raised a single eyebrow. "Do I keep my clothes on?"

"Maybe." His eyes twinkled with mischief. "Maybe not."

She laughed so loud she had to put a hand to her mouth.

***

King Tzu and Hao were in the stables grooming the horses. They acknowledged Kito warmly when he walked in. After the habitual heckling subsided, Tzu looked more seriously at Kito. "Yaan and I will be leaving in a few days, Kito. It would be my pleasure to have you along with us."

"That is most kind, brother, but I wish to get back to the jungle where I grew up. I have some personal work to achieve. If the snows are not to block my way on foot, I need to leave tomorrow."

"Tomorrow?" Hao exclaimed. "Kito, these people would gladly give you a horse. I will give you mine if you wish." Tzu glanced at Hao. That was a big offer.

Kito smirked. "I would not like to come between you and that horse, Hao. Sometimes I think not even Tammirie could come between you and that horse."

Tzu chuckled. He'd wondered the same thing. He put out his hand to Kito and they shook, wrist to wrist. "Kito, on our return home, I had bad dreams of dying on the sand exactly as Tanica had prophesised, but here we are and not a drop was spilled. I don't know how you did what was done, but please don't be a stranger to us northerners. Some of my people have already seen you, but the rest all know of you."

"It is gracious of you to speak so well of me when all along you went to another land you didn't know, to fight for a people you'd never seen, and oppose a delusional man with three armies. Never will I forget your spirit. It is very strong." Kito turned to Hao and the two men bowed. "Hao, the legend. The man who came back from the dead to risk his life many times over to save another. Always will I remember you."

Hao was lost for words as Yaan strode in with Tanica. Yaan's smile slipped away as he looked about the room. "Kito, this feels like a … I don't like the feel of this."

Kito bowed deeply to him. Yaan, now almost panicked, held out an open hand, shaking his head. "No, no. I'm not bowing, Kito."

"You ought not bow to me. You are the Emperor, and I'm a peasant not of this land."

Yaan struggled with his emotions. Accepting the inevitable, he mumbled, "You always did have your own journey." He grabbed Kito into an embrace. "Promise me you will visit us in the caves from time to time?"

"If you truly need me, just say my name, Yaan," Kito whispered back. Abruptly, Yaan stepped back, struggling with Kito's words. Kito continued. "We'll be going to Hasuca's haven." He didn't get to finish as the reality of what he'd said soaked in.

Yaan grabbed his sister by the hand and dragged her outside. "Tanica, may your brother ask, what is it you are intending?"

"I need … no, I *want* to know about Father, the real Hasuca. Kito is the one person who can give me this." She looked serious now. "What do you know about the talent, Yaan?"

Yaan drew back. "Now *that* is a big question. Let me ask you this, sister, what do *you* know about the redirection of the canal?"

"Kito took me with him. I saw him do that."

Yaan shook with anger. "So now you're going to leave me with all this? You want everything. The talent." He waved his arm helplessly. "The talent …" Pain and fear caressed his young face.

She brushed the back of her hand against his cheek. "Yaan, you are very special. In the last few months, you've moved mountains. I am but a fraction of that; now even Mercanti has left me."

Yaan's face darkened as he stood over her. "So that means you can just walk away, too! Mercanti was great value for us, but she doesn't have *our* blood running through her veins."

Tanica stepped back as his anger flared further.

"But you do, Tanica! You are one and the same as I, yet you get to leave for your own needs." He paced as he vented his despair. "So, I have no needs? It's all about the lands, everyone putting together their own pieces, their own agenda and their expectations of me! I'm just one man, now standing on his own." He scowled at his headstrong sister. "Go then! Go do your own agenda. I'll cover the expectations of these broken lands."

Tanica's eyes welled over. She opened her mouth twice, but nothing came out. Yaan flicked a dismissive hand as he turned away. She barely heard his last words. "Just be gone. Be gone, girl."

She didn't know which way to turn, whether to chase him or walk out into the night. She stood still, her feet anchored to the ground. Never had she felt such pain. *Is this what a family brings onto itself?* She gazed upwards as if seeking the answer.

Footsteps sounded behind her. Kito stood impassively with his hands at his sides as she turned squarely to him. Her face darkened, and she took a full swing at his face. He swayed, letting her angry fist whisk by. She then landed a few heavy punches into his abdomen. Even still, he didn't move a muscle as she pummelled him. Eventually, she lost strength, unable to speak properly for crying. He slowly drew her into his chest. The only thing he thought he heard her say as she sobbed was, "This is all you. You did this."

***

The next morning, after a poor sleep, Yaan went directly to the horses. They were all still there. He marched outside and looked about. It was barely breaking dawn. He knew there would be no sign of them. He gazed at the horizon. "Please, my brother, be very careful with her."

A small stump of sawn wood drew his attention. He frowned, puzzled. He turned away to go back inside when the strangest of things caught his eye. He slowly turned back to the length of wood that stood on its end. On its top was a goblet. Not any goblet, but a small, black goblet. He could only just make out its form in the early light. He approached cautiously, like it was a venomous snake. Slowly, he crouched down and picked it up. He turned it in his hand. It was perfect. He knew it immediately to be Royal. The morning was crisp, but holding the goblet made his blood run hot. He looked carefully in the poor light at the Royal symbol then read the inscription.

To my first child, may you learn the way of peace.

Yaan scoffed, looking to the breaking morning. "What more could I possibly do?" He shuddered as he read the second inscription.

To gain the remarkable, you must first release the great.

He looked again to the horizon.

✳✳✳

Far away, Tanica and Kito ran side by side. She threw her crossbow without looking; he snatched it out of the crisp, morning air. Not missing a stride, Tanica removed her fur overcoat and tied it around her waist. Kito lobbed the crossbow back. Nothing but the crunch of frozen grass underfoot could be heard as the two young bodies pushed themselves northward.

45 The Reunion

A fire crackled as Tanica poked it with a stick, pondering the last few weeks. Kito had taken them near enough to the palace so she could see it once more. For her, it was now an empty shell. She knew why Kito had done it, and was grateful.

Every morning, they would do their stretches and then spar. She'd come to love this time with Kito. He challenged her in every way and was so different to anyone else she'd ever sparred with. Grand Master Xiang was exceptional, obviously, but Kito even moved differently.

They would run for most of the day before making camp near a river or spring, then once the fire was going, they'd sit holding hands and meditate. He always made sure they checked their mortal souls were safe before he would take her out, then they would fly forward to find their next camp. This was her favourite time. The talent, the power, but most of all, the freedom. She was travelling fully dressed now, but still checked every time they went, and every time Kito scoffed.

Despite all of this, guilt still gripped her.

Kito dived into the warm waters of Turtle Pool. As he descended, all his favourite water-dwellers were there. He reached the sandy bottom, sat and closed his eyes, focusing on his heartbeat. This morning, he aimed to impress.

Movement brought Tanica's attention back to the fire and her surroundings. Carrying the strangest thing she'd ever seen, Kito emerged from the water with that captivating smile, taking long strides up the beach carrying his bounty.

"This is why your father loved this place. I think you will also."

Tanica thought on the comment for a moment. "What was he like? I mean, not as a prince but as a person."

Kito had hoped this day would come. "We can search him out, if you feel up to it?"

She gasped. "You can do that. I mean, *we* can do that?"

"Yes."

"You still talk with him?"

"Yes, on occasion." He placed his freshwater cray on the beach and sat at the small fire opposite her. He would need to watch his every comment on this fragile subject. "If I need guidance, I try to find him. Sometimes it seems he finds me. Either way, I am grateful when we connect."

She lowered her voice, revealing her vulnerability. "Has he ever asked about … me?"

"Every time, now he knows I've been in your presence, as has the Grand Master."

Her eyes lit up. "You have spoken with the Grand Master Xiang?"

"Be careful with this, Tanica. I don't choose them. It is only if they wish that they choose me. I can only try." He sat placid, breathing deeply, fully aware that this was the first time she'd even been open to the idea. He patiently left her in her own thoughts.

"I think it is time I saw the truth."

He gently reached out and took her by her hands. "You're trembling."

She wriggled a little. "I'm a bit nervous."

"This is no different to any other day on our journey here."

"That's not what I'm nervous about."

He smiled warmly and lowered his head. Their heartbeats slowed in unison as they controlled their breathing, then gently slipped their skins. As they spiralled up above the deep, green pool, Kito felt a tug on his hand. He looked to his left. *You alright?*

What if he doesn't show?

Then we'll return and try another day, that's all.

His quiet manner gave her confidence, and she rose with him, looking up ever higher. An eagle glided along on its broad wings. He hesitated. *This is different.*

She heard him. *Kito. What's wrong?*

He watched as the eagle's wings flexed on the rising warm air. *Nothing. Come on, we have far to go.*

They drifted much higher than he'd taken her before. Tanica rubbed her eyes as a cloud wafted over and enveloped them. She was sure they were still travelling, though she couldn't tell. Tentatively she watched Kito. His eyes were shut but his eyelids twitched as they rolled beneath them, searching, then through the cool mist, she heard a chimp cooing.

Kito squeezed her hand then released it. *'Hello Hasuca. It's a privilege to be in your company once again.'*

Tanica slipped in behind Kito, staying close. Sneaking peeks, she could just make out the two forms in the thick mist. It was only as they approached that she realised it wasn't as she had first thought. The taller form was a chimp standing with its hand on the shorter form, Prince Hasuca, her father. He sat cross-legged, and Tanica was certain she saw his face light up as she moved out from behind Kito.

'Ah Kito, my son. What gift have you brought here for me today?'

Kito moved aside and sat down. This was not about him. Hasuca's jaw trembled as he stood. *'You are your mother's daughter, dear Tanica. Please forgive my manner. This is a surprise I didn't see coming.'*

A multitude of strong emotions, including guilt, raced through her. They stared, face to face, unable to touch, then Tanica finally harnessed her words. *'Could you tell me about how she died?'*

Hasuca willed Tanica to sit. They talked at length about Sha'Doe and her bravery at the palace, her unwavering courage and her traumatic death. She reacted with surprise when Hasuca's eyes glistened with sorrow as he spoke about her with all the respect of two young lovers. She listened. The smallest window about her own mother opened just a tantalising bit.

'Is she why you left the palace, Hasuca?'

His head stooped. *'No, my dear, I left the palace because I was getting the most horrendous visions preceded by terrible headaches. Every time I slipped into a coma, I would dream of a nation divided by its short-sighted brothers locked in a bloody war. Then the Barbarians came down from the north in search of what didn't belong to the palace, to the brothers.'*

Tanica knew this to be true. *'The Crystal Skull. How could you be sure this was how it was to be?'*

Hasuca smiled at the candid question. *'At the end of the day, one cannot know really, not at that time. But I do now.'*

'Really, how so?'

'I know because I also had an opposing dream. It was like I was shown a choice. Only one could be followed. The second dream was of a little boy crossing an ocean. That little boy was my destiny, the Chosen One. I watched him work his gifts even when he didn't know them himself.'

'But you were the next in line. The throne should have been yours.'

Hasuca shrugged. *'I had spent my entire life training to be the next on the throne. I wanted to be on throne; I wanted to make my father and my people proud of me but sometimes life doesn't go how we think it should. Sometimes it throws us something we're not prepared for, Tanica but, I also understand it will never give us anything we cannot handle, always pushing us to our limits then letting us settle to take a breath.'*

'Hasuca, the people of this land are being pushed all around. Many lives have been lost, the lives of town folk, workers of the land. They're not warmongers like us, they're croppers and fishermen. They will not see another level.'

Kito wanted to reach out and touch Tanica, to give her a little shake to remind her of her place, to take a breath and show more respect. Hasuca, however, could only admire her raw honesty. *'You are right, Tanica. It pains me also to see this but it seems that the human spirit needs the worst in times, to bring out the best of them. These are to be* some of those times.' His tongue had slipped, and he immediately saw his mistake.

'So, we haven't seen the last of these times, Hasuca?'

'Tanica, it is not for me to say.'

'No, you could tell us and we could help stop it.'

'I don't see all from here. I did not see you coming here, right now.'

'No, you said it already, you at least have an idea about what is coming. As we celebrate the evil Koe gone, it is still not over! What more is to come?' She stood abruptly and stamped her foot. The cushioned cloud puffed up around her. Kito quickly reached out his hand and she swiped it away, glaring at her impassive father.

Another voice carried through on the mist. 'Have I failed to teach you better manners than this, young lady?' The form of Grand Master Xiang emerged. He was the man as in his prime, wearing his full combat suit, complete with twin, black swords on his hip, a fearsome sight for any to behold. Tanica was the only one to bow, but when she stood, Xiang looked at her coldly. 'What is this about, Tanica?'

'Prince Hasuca ...'

'There are no prince's up here, nor do we bow to anyone. We are all but equal people waiting to see where we are to return to and best learn our next lessons. No one is more than the other. My question was not about what anyone had said; it was regarding your lack of respect, Tanica. What was it about?'

She'd lost all her anger in Xiang's presence and stood motionless.

Kito spoke to her gently. 'May I offer my view?'

Staring absently into the mist below her, she leaned ever so slightly and nodded. Her move didn't go unnoticed by Hasuca.

Kito smiled. 'Xiang, nice of you to come to see us. I believe Tanica is not at fault here; I am. I have brought her too far, too early. I thought it would be nice for her to meet and know her father. For my own selfish reasons, I was premature. Please, both of you, accept my apologies.'

Her anger flared as Kito offered apologies she didn't agree with. She stayed silent as Xiang astutely saw her plight. *Tanica, is there something more you wish to add?'*

'No, though I must take this opportunity to thank you for the training at the palace. It was done at great risk.'

'It was my pleasure, Tanica. I had trained three generations of the Royal family. Never have I known the talent so strong in anyone.'

Tanica watched Hasuca swelling with pride. Confusion washed over the anger. She didn't understand why it was quickly consuming her.

Xiang watched Kito closely. To Xiang, Kito was impressive; he also showed respect with his hood down and a kind eye. Kito moved the conversation. *'You didn't go on the hunting trip after all, Xiang?'*

'I had intended to Kito, only other people had their own plans for me.'

'It was a bad blow for the Emperor just the same. He didn't count on that.'

'I don't understand, Kito.'

Kito motioned to Tanica. *'When I told Tanica you graced my presence sometimes, she was delighted and called you a Legend. Even now you've passed over you have affected lives, Xiang. When the Emperor had you dispatched, it shocked the nation. The way he dispatched you deepened that shock.'*

'I see it's the actions of Hasuca that are brave, completely unselfish and without ego.'

Kito almost cut Xiang off before he'd finished. *'I agree, though I wasn't comparing. You lived different lives for different reasons. Your death was the second time the people of Middle Kingdom had truly questioned the intentions of their leader. Both occasions carried a great deal of weight.'*

Xiang smiled. Kito was a clever player. All Xiang had to do now was ask the question. *'And what was the first time?'*

Tanica glared at the three men. *'Don't you dare play me like this! How dare you!'* Before anyone could reciprocate, she leaned into the mist and dived down. They all snatched out in reflex, but she was too quick. The clouds swirled and she was immediately gone.

'*Go, son, go quick,*' Hasuca said sadly.

Another swirl of mist, and he was gone also.

'*She will be alright, my friend.*'

Hasuca shook his head. '*She is not in control of her emotions, we both know how that can end, Xiang.*'

'*But she has Kito. You were always right about the boy.*'

'*Though I'm not sure his intentions to my girl are as pure as he might have us think.*'

'*Remember how Sha' Doe made you feel just to be in the same room with her, Hasuca? Don't you think she felt the same with you?*'

'*You think Kito makes her feel the same way?*'

'*You couldn't feel it? There was enough power in the air between them to start a small cyclone.*'

Hasuca couldn't help but smirk at the analogy. He had seen how Tanica had leaned towards Kito when under pressure. '*As always my friend, I feel you are right.*'

Xiang raised his eyebrows. '*Although I must say, rather him than I.*'

Hasuca threw him a look of contempt. '*I beg your pardon, Xiang?*'

With a wry grin, Xiang added, '*She has a lot of spirit, my friend. A lot.*'

'*Nah,*" Hasuca batted the air with his hand, "*You're just getting old.*'

***

Kito could just make out the streak that he knew was her, spiralling down. She had no idea how dangerous this was. Even worse, he could feel she didn't care. *Tanica, breathe, girl, breathe.*

I can't believe after all we've been through, you tried to do that!

I made a mistake. I should never have put you in that position. He felt a shift in her. *Breathe, Tanica. Breathe deeply.*

She levelled out. *Where am I?*

If you wait there, I will find us a way back.

Back, Kito?

To Turtle Pool, Tanica. I need to eat, and you need to get back to safety. She curved around, almost stopping. Kito eased down, not getting too close. *Xiang is right about you. Your talent is exceptional.*

Can we just go back now?

He led the way back slowly, giving her time to think things over. There was a lot to take in. Tanica was behind him as he swooped over the jungle canopy, then eased down over the pool. As he neared the almost burnt-out fire, he turned to her. They needed to hold hands as they slipped back into their bodies. She had no choice but to take his hands.

The moment he released her into her mortal form he sat upright, stretching his back. Tanica snatched her hands away, and leapt to her feet. He took a breath and sat passively as she began pacing up and down the beach, ranting.

"You set me up! That was so not fair. You never told me anything. You told me nothing!" Kito let her march around, releasing some of her energy. Finally, she stopped some distance away. "Well, what are you to lecture me on?"

Kito threw a few twigs onto the embers. "Remember the night you and Mercanti cleared the bridge out of Samos? You killed three …"

"Yes, I know, Kito. The question is, how do *you* know about that?"

Kito gently blew onto the fire, and a few sparks crackled. He ignored her narrowed eyes and stiffening posture.

She couldn't help her questioning voice. "Did you and Mercanti talk about me?"

"If I had a question about you, I would ask you." She frowned at his broad white smile. "Besides, Mercanti is totally loyal to you, but you already know that, Tanica."

He was right. *Bastard.*

"That night when you and Mercanti were walking up out of the city, she talked to you about Prince Hasuca; about what her father and uncle had discussed about him. Have you thought much on her words from that night?" Tanica glared at him. He leaned forward and blew on the fire again. It crackled some more and a small flame burst into life. He knew he was being read. He placed a few more sticks onto the embers, building it back to a glowing fire.

"That was you, wasn't it, Kito? Up on the ridge."

"Yes, Tanica, and on the rooftops. I got too close trying to read you, just as you are reading me now. I was very impressed with the two of you that night. You almost cut me with your sword, you know." He leaned down and breathed yet more life into the fire.

"How much have you watched? I mean …"

Kito gazed up, smiling. "No, Tanica. I have told you, I would never take advantage like that."

"What, never ever?"

He rose to his feet, placing a little more wood on the fire. "I need to catch some fresh breakfast. We can talk more later."

She paused. She hadn't noticed. "Where is that cray-thing you had?"

"A black panther wanted it more than us, apparently."

She moved a little closer. "Are you telling me a cat came and took dinner whilst we were sitting there?"

He took off his tunic, carefully folding it before he dropped it on the pebble beach. "Yes." Tanica cautiously glanced into the jungle beyond. He chuckled. "She is well gone now."

"She?"

"She has a family and was grateful for the easy meal. Now I need to get another."

Tanica softened a little, looking almost coy. "Could you take me with you?"

He smiled at her as he removed his trousers and folded them too. "I would like a little time to myself, Tanica. Would you mind caring for the fire?"

"Oh, well of course, Kito … umm, good luck then."

"Luck has nothing to do with it, it's pure skill." He laughed aloud as he walked down the beach.

She watched him wading out into the water, stopping waist deep. Shame washed over her. She'd never noticed the scars that criss-crossed his back! *How could I have missed all of those?* He slipped under the water without so much as a ripple. Composing herself, she went and sat by the fire. It turned out she also needed a little time. She picked up a stick and began to play with the coals, feeling bad for her behaviour that day. *Xiang was right to question me, to put me in my place.* She thought about what Mercanti had said about Hasuca that night leaving Samos. She missed Mercanti. Maybe Kito would take her for a return visit, back to the strange village of stone.

Kito was gone a long time.

Tanica just couldn't remove the feeling that the prince, her father, had deserted the people. In Middle Kingdom's darkest hour, he'd just walked away. No, she felt justified to be angry with him. Maybe he could take the high ground before, but he was no longer the prince. He needed to take responsibility for his actions. All those years, he'd simply camped in the jungle, safely out of sight.

Kito still hadn't returned.

She frowned, checking over the pool. Yes, she would tell Kito how she felt, although, Kito looked up to Hasuca like his own father, so would he be blind to it all? No, she would be silent.

She gazed over the pool. *Maybe he came up behind one of those big rocks? He must have.* She thought about the scars on his back: how many painful stories he must have to share.

The pool rippled as Kito emerged, his hair spreading down over his broad shoulders. His chest heaved in the fresh air and his golden body glistened in the sun. With his huge smile and carrying his new catch, he walked up and bent over, letting his hair drip over her. She squealed. As he put his bounty down on the pebble beach, she reached up and put her hand onto his broad chest. He froze.

She was as lost in those brilliant blues as he was in her big green eyes.

She reached up and kissed him passionately.

Later at Devil's Fork, all of Balzac's family, along with Yuna and Admasin, gathered at the rear of his place, enjoying another fantastic lunch. As everyone tucked in, Balzac was making yet another speech.

"As always, my friends, and never have I had so many, it is our pleasure to entertain you unruly lot." More chuckling. "I know that Katanning and Kalgan should only be days away from completing their last voyage to Zimbali, retrieving the last of the Emperor's Guard. I have to say, those two boys have been tireless in their endeavours to return the men back to their families and rightful place."

He paused, thinking of the two men and their crews. "Today, however, we really do have an announcement of grand proportions. Lucia and Patch, would you come here, please?"

Lucia rolled her eyes, embarrassed. Patch held her hand as they walked forward.

Balzac held out his big arms. "Ladies and …" His jaw dropped open, cutting his words off mid-sentence.

One by one, the small gathering turned around, following his gaze. Their eyes couldn't deceive them. Heading towards them, glittering in gold, was a large group of men. The one to the front was tall, heavily built and very fit. He was the only one wearing a massive head mask made of gold. It formed the head of a cobra snake, its emerald eyes sparking in the sun. The mask framed the sides of the handsome man's face, with long ivory fangs sweeping down either side. Over his ears was the bottom jaw, with two more fangs up each of his cheeks.

Balzac searched frantically for his guard. Nothing.

The man walked directly towards Balzac and lifted his mask. Patch flinched. Lucia looked at him; she could see something in his expression, but couldn't read it. The man took his time gazing over everyone. No one dared move; they were mesmerised by this band of men in gold. They carried it well, surrounding the gazebo and its inhabitants.

The stranger placed his mask under his arm. He spoke with a heavy accent but clearly had a good understanding of their language. "At this point, we mean no harm, at least, not to any of you." He looked around as if admiring the view.

Balzac tried to speak calmly. "My name is Balzac, and this is my island. It has been in our family for generations. What is it you would be seeking from us?"

"I am Lord Hazaar. We are from the lands you never visit. You are not yet capable."

"Yes, Hazaar. I see," though Balzac didn't. "What is it you are intending to get from us?"

An armed man spoke in their own language. The leader nodded and answered.

Patch hobbled forward with his cane. "No! These people are not armed; they never are. They have lived in peace for all their generations Balzac speaks of. Please, state your business. If we can help, we will. That is how we do things on the islands."

He stood as straight as he could, showing no fear. Until this point, he had no idea he'd just spoken in their language. Lucia and their friends gazed at him with their mouths gaping.

Hazaar stepped forward, his voice raspy with intent. "And who are you?"

Suddenly confused, Patch lost his confidence. "They call me Patch. My name is Patch."

Hazaar looked disdainful. "Patch? Is this even a name?"

"I have asked that same question."

"Your delivery is rusty to say the least, Patch, yet you know my language?"

"Would you mind, with respect to this humble family, speaking in their language?" Patch managed to hold Hazaar's intent gaze.

"No. How long have you lived with these people?"

"My whole life, Hazaar."

"Clearly not."

Patch looked skyward to settle his nerves. He had no idea what he was doing. "Well, let's just say, I don't remember being anywhere else."

"No, Patch. We will not say, because you speak my language. When did you come here?"

Patch tried to avoid looking at any of his friends right now. "That much is true. I have no memory of my homelands, or how I came here though I do have dreams of drowning." He smiled nervously. "I was found on the wharf in the city of Samos." He waved his cane in a general direction. "Samos is …"

"I know where Samos is, Patch. Carry on."

"I was found on the wharf there, raised by a family as one of their own."

Hazaar squinted. "Is this true, Patch?"

Patch nodded, trying not to lean too hard on his cane. "Every last word of it."

"How old are you?"

Patch shrugged.

"Exactly, Patch!"

Several people flinched. Balzac stepped forward. "I have …"

"Silence!" roared Hazaar.

Patch stepped towards Hazaar, waving his cane in front of Balzac. "It's alright, Hazaar. These are peaceful, respectful people. They have no idea what we're discussing."

Refocusing on Patch, Hazaar calmed a little. "He is completely unarmed?"

"Not even a fishing knife."

"Hmm. So, you care for them?"

"What is it that you have come so far for, Lord Hazaar?"

Hazaar turned away, and two men came forward. They weren't young, though very fit. Patch couldn't tell them apart.

"These two men tracked our princess to the Palace of Middle Kingdom. She sent them back to us so we could know her fate."

Patch stared at Hazaar, wondering where this was leading. "Patch, my cousin, your real name is Izan." He wobbled on his cane as Hazaar placed his hand across his chest, speaking in the language of Middle Kingdom for everyone to understand.

"Twenty-two years ago, a princess came this way on a stolen Royal Yacht. She had a toddler and was said to have come through Devil's Fork in a storm. Badly battered, they were lucky to have lived. They went directly to your city of Samos. The bastard man she left with had stolen our Royal Jewels, sacred to our lands. He was murdered in Samos. For the safety of the child, she hid him just before she was taken by your Royal Guard. She was taken to your Emperor where she died giving birth."

Hazaar had everyone's attention and so continued. "She was my aunt and your mother, Izan. Her name was Sha'Doe."

About the Author

Gregory Thomas grew up on a dairy farm in the north of New Zealand, where his early desire to write grew despite the challenges of dyslexia. In the early 2000s, Gregory moved to Australia, and several years ago, he decided to channel his creative imagination into writing, resulting in his first fantasy novel series, *The Sacred Skulls*.

Gregory now resides in Perth with his wife. He balances his time between working in the mines of northern Western Australia and writing in his free time, continuously crafting ideas for new worlds and stories for his readers.